THE SPECTACULAR SWORDSMAN

THE SPECTACULAR SWORDSMAN

THE FORGOTTEN SWORD

· NICOLÒ MAZZA ·

To my parents,

for raising me to believe that anything is possible.

PROLOGUE

13 years ago...

Miss Eleanor, the Western Town librarian, recognized the rhythm of the horse's hooves before she even saw it coming. She'd been dwelling in her back room when ever so slightly, a light gallop could be heard. She had exited into the main library, noticing some customers looking in wonder outside, as a large hazel horse thundered up to the library. Eleanor hurried outside as a man in a simple tunic, cape, and a sheathed sword on his belt leaped off his horse and raced towards her, holding a scroll in his hand.

"Maximus!" she exclaimed. "What in the name of Lyzix is going on? Are you alright? Is Marlton okay? What about Kornus?"

The man was gasping, however that did not stop him from answering her.

"No. Not...okay. Urgent...from Mayor...Kornus." Maximus handed over the scroll.

Eleanor ignored the gaping townsfolk as she unfurled the scroll, her hands shaking. What had happened? She didn't want to press Maximus, as the man was still wheezing, however she felt bile rising in her throat and she began to read the scroll.

Eleanor,

There's not much time. You need to know this. The enemy has struck. We are being invaded by King Chada, a king from the south, leading his Titan army. I don't know what he's up to, but I have many reports of children being stolen away by the Titans. Infants, no more than a year old. I don't know what he is doing with them, but it can't be good. It makes no sense.

I must get this letter to you before Chada takes the town. I know you were looking into his attacks, so I trust and hope you know more about this than me. And thank you for sending Maximus. He is a good man. You choose your friends well. I'm sure he will get this to you.

Be safe until I see you again,

Mayor Kornus

Eleanor stared, shocked. Marlton, attacked? And by King Chada?

She looked at Maximus. "Is everyone alright? Did Kornus get away?"

Her friend seemed to have gained some of his breath back. "No," he said sadly, "he told me to deliver this to you at all costs. Right when I left the town, his tower burst into flames. The Titans had been throwing torches and flaming arrows at it. And he was inside."

Eleanor felt a tear slide down her cheek. How? She would never see him again. One of her dearest friends: gone.

She looked at Maximus, who seemed completely sick. "Here, come inside. I'll grab you some water."

They two entered the library, and Eleanor quickly reached for some water that was sitting on her desk in the back room. However, as she handed him the glass, a scroll that she had been examining earlier caught her eye.

And Eleanor suddenly wobbled and was only just caught by Maximus as a horrible realization entered her head.

"Hey, careful," Maximus said. "Maybe you need this water more than I do."

Eleanor ignored him, picked up the scroll, and stared at it, eyes wide.

"Is everything okay?"

Once again, she ignored her friend, and instead she traced her finger along the scroll, which was in fact a map of the continent, Lyzix. Little dots marked different kingdoms and towns. However, seven gold stars were placed on the map across the continent, marking very specific kingdoms and towns. Eleanor had plotted them herself. Six of them were crossed out with large X's. These six locations with the X's had been attacked in the past year.

And Marlton was the seventh, untouched town. Except now it was no longer untouched.

Perhaps Chada was after something much bigger than she had previously thought. Could it be possible? No.

But there was so much evidence…

Eventually she couldn't deny it.

Chada was after the Spectacular Swordsman.

CHAPTER I

AT THIRTEEN YEARS old, Drake Philosopher had been train-ing for six years as a swordsman, with Sahara Cortez. One of the greatest teachers on the continent, Sahara wanted him to stay safe, healthy, and become a very skilled fighter. But over the last six months, Sahara had been pushing Drake harder than ever to perfect his skills. He kept him training until the late hours, day in and day out, limiting his visits to friends and even his time outside in the kingdom. Drake sometimes felt more like a prisoner than an apprentice. And he didn't understand why.

Tonight, Sahara was finishing up a sword move with Drake. It was the tuck and slash, and in Drake's opinion, his master was being especially harsh.

"Drake, this isn't good enough. You should have mas-tered it by now. You must pick up the speed. Only if you're swift and thorough with your moves will your enemies be stopped," Sahara explained.

Drake nodded. He faced a tower of three boxes that Sahara had set up, and then returned to his ready position.

"Remember, you must crouch first." Sahara began to

show him, getting down in a squat. "Then, you slash, and jump up in the air, using your momentum to land back on your feet." Sahara went through the moves. "Now, try it once slowly like I did, and then faster. It will take a few times."

"Okay." Drake sighed. Sahara was like a father to him. Drake had lived and trained with him since he was four years old. Maybe that was why his lessons and demonstrations were at times so bothersome, because he'd heard them countless times in the weapon-equipped training room. Sahara always explained things in such detail; much more than Drake thought was necessary.

But his master was good to him and cared for him. And the feeling was mutual. So, Drake suppressed his emotions and listened. He went through the moves slowly a few times and then readied himself to do it at battle-like speed, as Sahara called it.

"So, remember, you want—"

"I got it," Drake snapped.

Sahara stepped back, crossed his arms and narrowed his eyes "Fine. Go on, then. I'd watch your overconfidence, though. Never a good thing to have in battle."

Drake went into his move. He crouched, waited a second and then swung, but the momentum carried him forward as he jumped. His sword completely missed the boxes. Instead, he crashed into them, knocking them all to the ground.

Sahara brought his hands to his face and shook his head. "I can tell you're tired. We'll try this again tomorrow. Why don't you get some sleep?"

"Thank you," Drake said as his master helped him up.

The two walked out of the training room towards the bedrooms. Some books on swordsmanship lay open on a small table in the hallway. A few candles flickered, lighting the paintings of famous Lyzix battles that hung on the wall. There was even a portrait of Sahara in dueling position, sword at the ready. It had been painted by one of Sahara's good friends. He had died many years ago, and Drake didn't remember him well.

"Can I meet Jerome tomorrow before our lesson?" Drake asked. It had been a long time since he had seen his friend.

"No," Sahara said simply. Drake was shocked. What did his master mean, no? "I want you to stay here. I've decided to put you on lockdown for the next few weeks."

"Why?" Drake asked. "I need to go outside. See my friends. Breathe fresh air."

"It's for your own good."

"Of course," Drake mumbled angrily. "Everything is for my own good, according to you. But—"

"What did you say?" Sahara stopped in his tracks.

Drake paused. Should he go on? Yes, he should. He had been thinking about it long enough. "You say everything is for my own good. For this great future that lies ahead, if I do everything you say. Is it just to inspire me—what am I destined for, Sahara? I don't see anything special. I'm just a teenager who needs more swordsmanship training."

"Enough!" Sahara exclaimed. "Go to bed. I'll not hear any more of this."

Drake tossed his sword aside with a clang and stormed into his room. Sahara had always told him he was great, but never told him why. And that was what Drake wanted to know—he always valued the concept of reasoning: Why? He had never known his parents and didn't know if he had any living relatives. He didn't even know where he came from before Sahara had taken him in.

If he was just a normal orphaned swordsman, then how truly great was he?

Drake was fed up with his master's restrictions. Tomorrow, he would sneak out to meet Jerome anyway. His friend had probably had a hard day in the blacksmith shop, too. He would understand.

Drake grabbed his covers and pulled them closer, trying to ward away the chill of sadness and loneliness. But yet as his eyes slowly closed, and he began to relax, he still felt a small knot in his stomach. It wasn't working.

Then, he fell asleep.

*

The sun was coming close to rising above the horizon when Drake snuck across the room, fully dressed and ready to go. He opened his door slowly and crept down the stairs. He didn't need his master catching him and going ballistic. Sahara usually woke up early, but today was unusual. Drake could hear his master snoring in his bed, sound asleep.

At the bottom of the stairs, Drake noticed a lamp still shining inside his master's study. On the desk sat a small book, with a simple, wooden framed quill lying on top of it. Drake knew he needed to hurry before Sahara woke, but… there was something about the way the notebook had been left there, the lamp still lit. Did his master write a journal and if so…what would he say about Drake?

Drake knew it was wrong—very wrong; but he looked at the latest entry anyway.

I can't train him. It's too hard. He needs to learn patience and how to accept help. Why did I even talk to Eleanor about this? I need to sleep. I should never have agreed to train him.

Drake felt a rush of shock and anger pump through his veins. How could Sahara write this? What did it mean? Was Sahara going to pass him on to another master? And who was Eleanor, anyways? Would she become his new master?

Drake, quickly realizing he didn't want his master to catch him, hurried from the study, snuck out the front door, and stepped into the cobblestone lane.

Even this early in the morning the streets were busy. Carts wheeled by, merchants called out their wares and people went about their daily business. Drake loved the bustle of the town and his worries began to ease as he walked towards the square. He and Jerome always met there. There was a market and often a theater set up in the center. On festival days and holidays, there were merchant stands, music, and games. As he reached the top of the street, he could see the treetops of the nearby forest that led northwest and out to the center of Lyzix.

The Kingdom of Wendil was an amazing sight. The area around it was wonderous too, and even though he had only travelled further afield once, when he was seven, he remembered much of it. Past the forest westward was the Western Town, and another kingdom, the Seaside Kingdom, lay beyond, situated right next to the large bay that fed into the ocean. There were even more kingdoms and towns to the west and south as well that he'd never seen. One day, perhaps, he would. One day. For now, he would cling to that memory when he was seven for as long as he could.

When Drake reached the square, he spotted Jerome waiting for him at the fountain. They ran towards each other and exchanged a friendly hug.

"How's it going, buddy?" Drake asked.

"Pretty good, thanks! Burned my apron against the forge last Tuesday. I was mad because it was my best one, but at least it wasn't my arm," Jerome replied. "You don't look so good. How is training going?"

"Meh," Drake replied.

"Two months ago, you said it was terrible, two weeks ago you said it was great, and now you're saying meh." His friend looked concerned. "What's up?"

Drake shrugged. "Sahara and I had a disagreement last night. He told me I needed to stay inside the house. Said it was for my own good."

"Then why are you here?" Jerome asked.

"I snuck away," Drake replied.

"Don't you think he'll be—"

"Nah, it's fine. I don't want to bother you with my problems. Shall we spar?"

Jerome hesitated, as if wanting to talk more about the issue with Sahara and Drake. He opened his mouth for a moment, then closed it and nodded. "Sure," he said finally. "Check out these new blades. Dulled of course. Hammered them out myself last night."

He handed Drake a blade. They walked off to the side,

away from the bustling crowd, and began their usual sparring contest.

As the day progressed, they walked around the city, daring each other to flirt with the girls they met until, bored, they chased and tackled each other back around the square. They were about to visit a famous storyteller, which they frequently did, when Drake saw a kid being harassed by—Drake growled to himself—Logan and his two bullies.

Drake had had a few run-ins with Logan before. And they weren't pleasant. He was a hothead who had no respect for anyone. Drake pointed to the child. "We should help him."

"Why? We don't even know him…" Jerome said, but Drake was already on his way over.

"Hey, let him go!" Drake hadn't even been listening to Jerome. His friend could stay back, but Drake was going to help the young lad.

"Ah, Philosopher," Logan said. "Did you bring your shy blacksmith friend to help you this time?"

"Yes, but does it matter?" Drake asked. "Let go of the kid."

"Make me." Logan smirked and began to approach Drake. "I think it's time I actually see what your friend can do. Or is he just some useless, little—"

He didn't finish his sentence. Jerome rushed in and punched Logan right in the mouth, then spinning and kicking him in the stomach, knocking him to the ground. Drake's best friend wasn't a fighter, but he was extremely strong from all the work in the forge. So, a punch or kick from him would definitely do damage. Especially if it was provoked.

Logan lay on the pavement, limp, with blood gushing from his nose. He had been knocked out. In the blink of an eye, Logan's two friends grabbed him under the armpits and then dragged him away.

"Ummm…thanks," the kid said in awe, staring at Drake and Jerome.

When the two friends didn't reply, the boy nodded slightly and ran away. Drake had been too busy soaking in his victory, or rather, Jerome's, to respond.

"Thanks," Drake said.

"No problem," Jerome said. "Now, let's do something fun. I prefer not to spend the rest of today saving kids from bullies."

Drake nodded. "Okay. What else do you want to do?"

Drake didn't hear a response. Instead, tremors shook the earth beneath his feet. He fell to the ground. Windows in nearby shops and houses cracked and shattered. A merchant stand selling clay accessories collapsed, kicking up dust and rubble. People peered out their damaged windows with worried looks on their faces.

"What was that?" Jerome struggled to his feet and swept the dust off his pants.

"No idea." As Drake replied, an even louder explosion shook the city. People hurried from their houses to see what was going on.

"What's happening?" Jerome cried.

"I don't know, but it doesn't sound good." Drake glanced in the direction of the gates and heard yells and shrieks of pain. Three arrows whizzed by him. A platoon of Wendil's guards raced towards the gates.

Drake had heard of ambushes in nearby towns, cities,

and kingdoms, but he'd never expected anything to happen to Wendil.

Yet here it was:

An attack!

"Go back to your house. Find your master. We'll meet back here and decide what to do," Jerome ordered.

"You're telling me to find him after what I told you about last night? Are you—"

"He's like a father to you, isn't he? Don't let one argument cloud your judgment, Drake!"

"Ok, ok," Drake grumbled, "I'll go. See you soon."

Drake raced back to Sahara's house. Like Jerome had said, Sahara was the only person he had. He scrambled through the door and began searching the house.

"Sahara?" He called, his voice becoming more frantic as the sounds of battle got louder.

"Sahara!?"

No answer.

Drake ran through the house, searching all the rooms. His heart began pounding faster. Yes, he'd had arguments with Sahara, but they were practically family. Drake then checked his master's bedroom last. He wasn't there, either.

Sahara wasn't in the house.

Drake almost kicked himself. Sahara was probably fuming, and worried. If the tremors had hit and he'd realized Drake wasn't home, he was probably out in the kingdom looking for him.

He needed to find his master, fast.

In a panic, Drake grabbed all the valuable items, including gold, silver, and copper as quickly as he could and packed them into a pouch. If they were going to be driven out of Wendil, they'd need money. His only hope now was to find Sahara on the streets.

As Drake ran back to the square, he noticed more and more enemies in strange black uniforms invading the city, scattering frightened civilians everywhere. When Drake entered the square, Jerome was waiting while others look around at the commotion. Not as many enemies were in the square yet. "Do you know where your master is?" Drake asked.

"No," Jerome replied. "Do you?"

"No. We must find them," Drake replied, but even as he spoke a volley of flaming arrows fell into the square from somewhere to the west. They fled to the shelter of a shop awning and watched in horror as everyone scattered. Carts crashed into buildings, and fires began to break out all around. Another explosion rocked the city. Drake and Jerome were picked up with the force of the impact and thrown through a shop window.

Drake screamed in pain as he landed on the ground, glass sinking into his skin. Jerome stood up and pulled Drake to his feet. The two leaned on each other in shock.

"You okay?" Jerome asked.

"I think so. You?" Drake only had a few scratches and cuts.

"For now," Jerome replied. "We need to get out of here."

Suddenly, the building began to collapse. The two teens sprinted to the door. Jerome escaped into the street, but Drake tripped and tumbled to the floor, rolling across the ground as sparks singed his skin. A wooden beam crashed on top of him, making his back burst in pain.

He twisted as he fell, but only managed to turn as the beam settled onto his chest, pinning him to the ground.

"Drake!" Drake could tell from the panic on Jerome's face that he didn't know what to do. Neither did Drake. His lungs felt like they were going to collapse. He began to squirm, but that only caused the beam to press down further on his chest. He struggled to breathe, and as the seconds passed, less and less air moved through his lungs. His vision blurred. He felt his head spin. And then another explosion rocked the kingdom. Jerome staggered back, and the beam, which loosened, allowed Drake to escape from its crushing weight. He sucked in a lungful of air and retched a few times before rising to his feet.

"Come on." Drake said, drawing his sword, "We need to find them."

Jerome nodded, and they began to run through the streets. Drake noticed the city had descended further into chaos. However, he realized that now figures dressed in black clothes hurried through the streets, combing and attacking anyone in sight. He grimaced as he saw a family being separated. The father tried to fight but was knocked out in seconds. A boy about his age was taken away, and as the mother ran after them, yelling, one of the figures struck her with the flat of his sword, rendering her unconscious too.

Drake, feeling anger, readied himself for battle.

"Are you crazy?" Jerome said, understanding his intentions. "We can't fight! We need to run."

As Drake tried to charge at another six enemies, different from the first, he felt Jerome's strong arms grab him, restraining him. However, Drake whipped his arms around, and with a loud sigh, Jerome let go of Drake, who then sprinted off. His best friend quickly followed. He felt confident in his abilities and made a strike at the man's legs.

However, the figure blocked it with extreme agility, and Drake felt extremely incompetent as the flat of a sword smashed into his cheek sending him sprawling to the ground. Drake then found himself surrounded by the five other attackers. As they closed in on Drake, he jumped to his feet. He was sure he would be killed, but then he remembered Sahara's lesson the previous night: the tuck and slash. He'd show Sahara just how trainable he really was.

Drake faced the first attacker crouched down and slashed at the attacker's legs. The attacker collapsed to the ground. Drake smiled to himself briefly before swinging his sword backwards, slashing another attacker. He spun in a circle, effortlessly parrying and slicing two more. He kicked one with his boot, and then leapt up in the air, performing the tuck and slash on the final man.

He'd just defeated five men in a matter of seconds. They weren't dead, but they were definitely injured, and that was enough for now. Drake glanced over and saw Jerome knocking out the last man. Drake nodded to his friend but didn't have time to speak. More arrows shot by them. He and Jerome began to run, Jerome still seemingly shellshocked at Drake's achievement.

When they had a moment, his friend said, "Man, that was amazing!"

"Thanks," Drake replied. As he ran, however, his eye caught a strange flash of gold. He turned towards it for a moment, and when squinting, he realized it was a figure on a roof in the distance. And the flash of gold he had seen was a crown.

A crown?

An arrow flew by, disrupting Drake's vision, but the

figure and crown remained, unwavering. Suddenly, Drake felt a blinding burst of sunlight hit his eyes, and Jerome pulled him around a nearby corner.

Who was that? Crowns only established someone as king, and Drake doubted that he imagined a king on the roof.

But was it possible?

Maybe he should tell Jerome?

Yes. Yes, he probably should.

"Hey, Jerome, did you see—"

"So, how are we going to get out of here?" Jerome interrupted, not hearing a word, and Drake decided to drop it. His best friend would probably think he was crazy anyway. "And how are we going to find our masters? Because we need to escape the kingdom soon."

"Sahara told me about old gate that's near the castle," Drake said, "Not as popular as one of the main gates. It may not be guarded. Let's try to get out there."

Drake and Jerome adjusted their course, running towards the towering castle. However, as they turned a corner, an attacker suddenly sliced Drake across the arm. Drake collapsed on the ground and struck Jerome as well. His friend fell into a door of an abandoned store, knocking it off of its hinges and tumbling out of sight.

What just happened? Drake was lost and in a daze. He looked up to see his assailant about to grab his arm when a whirling mass of man and sword came through and cut the attacker down. It was Sahara at the head of a squad of Wendil's guards, and behind them, more guards flooded the streets, firing volleys of arrows and hacking away with swords and spears.

"You disobeyed me!" Sahara shouted. "I told you to stay in! You need to stay safe! This is exactly what I didn't want!"

"The Kingdom was attacked. How could anybody have known—"

"Quiet! You must leave! Run to the forest. Past that you'll find the Western Town. Find Miss Eleanor, and then you'll have a clear path. Please, Drake. If you are ever going to listen to me, now is the time! You'll see me again. You will, Drake. Just trust me."

"But—"

"No buts," Sahara ordered.

Before Drake could protest further, Sahara was gone. Drake yelled after him, but Sahara didn't turn back. How could he have let his master go, after his outburst the previous night?

He was the worst apprentice ever.

Jerome scrambled back up the steps, "What's going on?" Then, he saw Drake's arm and the blood running down from the slash.

"We have to leave," Drake said, as much as he hated to say it.

"Can you even move that arm?" Jerome asked.

"More or less," Drake replied. "Come on!"

The duo ran through the streets until they reached the shadow of the towering castle. There were bodies everywhere, rubble littered the streets and smoke rose from the windows of burning shops and houses. Drake saw the baker yelling for his lost daughter, and the tailor, searching through the rubble for something. He also saw the librarian, running with her husband, towards the main gate, trying to escape.

Drake couldn't deny it. Wendil was crumbling. In one morning, his entire world was gone. He looked up towards the blinding sun and suddenly caught sight of the figure on the roof again. It was much closer. It could be a hallucination, but his stomach churned, and he felt dread creeping into him.

"We need to go. Come on, Jerome!" he screamed.

Drake didn't look back as he and Jerome cut through what appeared to be an apothecary shop, though because rubble was littered everywhere, he wasn't entirely sure. The two sprinted out of a hole in the back wall, as one arrow soared by him, and another skinned his cheek, drawing slight blood.

For a split-second Drake didn't believe they were going to make it. Then he spotted the gate, and the two friends sprinted for it, racing into the outskirts of the kingdom.

Drake turned around for one last look at Wendil. He saw fires and smoke, the last of Wendil's citizens being plundered, and one of the castle towers collapsing to the ground. They had lost. And Sahara? Drake had no idea where his master was.

He should have stayed. He could have helped. He'd failed, and maybe Drake slowed his pace too, for suddenly Jerome was yelling, "Come on. Let's keep going."

As they continued toward the forest, Drake started to feel terrible pain in his back, and his arm felt as limp as a noodle. He stopped and slumped against a nearby tree, gasping for breath, and felt hot blood seeping down his cheek from the arrow. His vision blurred as Jerome knelt down beside him.

Drake groaned and then passed out.

Chapter II

Jerome looked up at the sun, which was slowly dipping past the horizon, and gasped for breath. It had been hours, and he didn't think he could walk any further. Drake was still unconscious, and he weighed a ton. Yes, Jerome was a blacksmith's apprentice and his arms had muscles some men would envy, but right now he was exhausted.

He then used both of his hands, pushing Drake up his shoulder towards his neck, as he was slung over him like a sack of grain. How was he ever going to get Drake all the way to the Western Town? It was hopeless. He needed to stop somewhere in the forest, but how safe was it? The attackers were probably still in the area, and would eventually spread out past the kingdom.

And who were they, anyway?

Wendil did not have any direct enemies as far as he knew. After all, King Noxy was a wonderful king—Wendil had not faced threats in multiple decades. This attack was a complete surprise. And he had not seen any sign, crest, or insignia on the attacker's black clothes. No clues as to what kingdom or town they came from.

Jerome set Drake down, slumped against a tree, and buried his face in his hands. When he finally looked up, he saw a glint of grey. He sat up. On looking closer, he realized it was the start of a very overgrown, hidden path.

"That's strange," Jerome said, as if Drake could hear him. He didn't know of any ruins or civilization out in the forest. He picked Drake back up, and after stumbling for a moment, he regained his footing and decided to follow it.

Who knew? There could be someone at the end of the path who could help them. Drake especially needed help, that was for sure.

However, Jerome hesitated. There could also be someone down there who could do harm, be against them—there could even be the mysterious attackers there.

Then he looked at Drake, with the gash in his arm, the cut on his cheek, scratches and wounds everywhere, and he immediately made up his mind. They didn't have a choice. Jerome had to take a chance and hope for the best.

So, Jerome stumbled down the path with Drake slumped over his shoulders. After a few minutes the path disappeared into the nearby foliage. Jerome felt Drake sliding off of him but didn't even try to move him. He had nowhere else to go. His friend was injured. His kingdom had been taken over. And he was lost in a forest. What was he going to do?

"Could I help you by chance?" a voice asked.

Jerome whirled around, only to topple backwards because the weight of Drake's body had shifted. He collapsed to the ground, barely avoiding landing on top of Drake, and he looked up to see a kindly woman.

"Who are you?" His first thought was that the attackers

could have sent her. She could be an enemy. His hand went to his belt where his hammer sat, and hovered there, ready to take immediate action.

The woman ignored his cautionary actions. "My name is Amanda. And I mean you no harm. In fact, I believe I can help you."

"What are you doing out here?" Perhaps she was a refugee from Wendil and had run from the attack. Though Jerome didn't recognize her, it was his best explanation so far.

"I live here," Amanda replied. Jerome frowned. He'd never heard of anyone living in the forest. "I'm an apothecary. I used to live in the city, of course—"

"Then why did you move?" Jerome asked.

"I was forced to. Expelled. Banished," Amanda face saddened, and Jerome refrained from asking questions as it seemed to be a sensitive topic for her. "But enough of that. All the herbs I needed were out here. It worked out fairly well. What brings you here?"

Suddenly, a moan escaped Drake's lips, and Jerome nervously looked at Amanda as she frowned.

He had no choice but to trust her. They were out of other options.

"The kingdom has just been attacked," Jerome said

"What? Who attacked? Did…did we hold them off?" Amanda asked, and Jerome shook his head sadly.

Amanda's face fell, and a tear dropped from her eye. "What happened?"

Jerome shrugged. "No idea. It was all so quick. People dressed in black clothes. Only able to see their eyes."

"Hmm. I'm afraid I can't help you with their identity,"

Amanda said. "But I can help your friend. If I get him to my hut, and I finish picking these molo weeds, I can treat him. Molo weeds are one of the most powerful healing plants in Lyzix. They should fix him up in no time. We must hurry though. Let's take no chances."

"Thank you," Jerome said as she led him to her hut.

It was a simple home, made mostly of wood and stone, overgrown with moss. As Amanda opened the door, Jerome saw that the inside was equally simple, but he was puzzled by a row of simple beds in the hallway. The beds were framed with wood and the mattresses filled with straw and other cushioning.

"Why are these here?" he asked.

"Oh, they're for the people I treat. If they seek me out and need healing, I help them," Amanda replied.

"That's, uh…very nice of you." Jerome set down Drake on a nearby bed, and Amanda went into her kitchen to retrieve some food for Jerome.

"Wait here while I finish gathering the molo weeds," she said as she walked out the door and back into the forest.

Jerome sat for a while, staring at the wall thoughtfully while he ate. His life had changed in an instant. Only yesterday he'd been happily working in the blacksmith shop, yet now he was a refugee running into an unknown forest with his kingdom in a shamble behind him. Where was his master? Was he dead? Did he escape? Jerome sighed. Life had been so wonderful. He had learned many things, and his master had said he only had to work two more years before he could get his own master's permit and go out on his own. Only two more years…and then this.

Jerome looked at his best friend unconscious on the

crude wooden bed. Jerome had never been one for fighting, even though he was as strong as a bull. And there was Drake, not even half as strong as Jerome, but fierce as they came. The two weren't at all alike, yet they'd been the firmest of friends for years.

The clopping of horse hooves and voices outside interrupted his thoughts. He frowned. Horses? He peered out the window with a sickening feeling—were the attackers already looking for refugees? Jerome readied his hammer, ran to the door, threw it open, and was about to swing his weapon when he recognized who was standing in front of him.

"King Noxy?" Jerome immediately sank to one knee. It was the King of the Kingdom of Wendil! He had survived!

King Noxy seemed just as surprised, "Is it Jerome? Master Pental's blacksmith apprentice?"

"Yes!" Jerome replied, thrilled that the king recognized him. King Noxy was known for trying to visit and speak to all his subjects in the town. He wanted his subjects to feel on an equal level to him. He was a wonderful king.

"Why are you out here? What is this place?" King Noxy asked gesturing for Jerome to rise to his feet.

Amanda appeared behind the king and answered for him. "It's my hut."

King Noxy turned, and his smile slowly slipped from his face. "Oh. Hello Amanda."

To Jerome's surprise, Amanda completely ignored the greeting. "His friend was injured running from the attack on your Kingdom. Drake Philosopher, I believe."

"I see," King Noxy said. "Is he all right?"

"I'll treat him."

King Noxy twitched nervously and let out a long breath. "Amanda, please, can we let this go? Are you really still angry that I expelled you from Wendil?"

"Wait, you banished her from the town?" Jerome asked. For some reason, it hadn't occurred to him that King Noxy had been the king who'd sent Amanda away.

"You must understand, Jerome, many of the people were in favor of the idea. The story is complicated. Many felt her healing jobs were half-hearted and those she disliked were not treated well by her," he glanced at Amanda and she scowled back at him. "I would have requested her to stay, but a good king listens to his people. And besides, I—"

The king suddenly grimaced, and his hand moved to a deep cut on his leg.

"Dear me, that wound looks serious," Amanda said. "Off your horse. Let me treat it."

King Noxy slid off his steed. "I thought you were just about to yell at me."

"I never refuse to help the injured. Besides, the people of Wendil would probably be even more upset with me if I let that wound get any worse."

King Noxy cracked a smile as Jerome and Amanda helped him inside. "Does that mean you can forgive me, after all this time?"

"I'm still deciding," Amanda said, but Jerome noticed a quick smile flit across her face as they laid King Noxy down on a bed.

"Take these," Amanda gave the king a clump of molo weed. "Eat them now. I better not see you up and walking around. There needs to be time for the molo weed to set in."

"Yes, miss," King Noxy said with a grin, and he

swallowed the clump in one gulp. Amanda left to treated Drake, while Jerome decided to stay and talk to Noxy and keep him company. The king already seemed to be doing a bit better from the treatment, his wound a little less of a violent color.

The two explained how they escaped and talked about other things. Then, Jerome broached the topic of what to do next.

"Drake's master, Sahara, told us to go to the Western Town. He said to find someone named Miss Eleanor, and things would be clearer," Jerome said. He didn't understand what Sahara had meant, but Drake's master was a trustworthy and honorable man.

Noxy frowned. "I see. Well, then, you shouldn't go alone. I'll come with you. I need to gather help from nearby towns and kingdoms to retake Wendil. But first we will head to the Western Town. Perhaps Amanda wants to come as well. A healer will be useful."

Amanda then entered. "You should be able to walk soon, Noxy. The wound won't begin to truly heal for a bit longer, but a little exercise couldn't hurt. Before you leave, though, I heard my name. What is it you mentioned?"

King Noxy stood up. "I'm going to escort these boys to the Western Town, and thought it would be a good idea if you came along with us."

Amanda looked at him for a moment, hesitantly.

"Come on, Amanda. We could use someone like you. And perhaps we'll be able to get more bonding time, considering you've been out here all this time…"

"No thanks to you," she replied, but Jerome could sense a little banter in her tone. "Fine. I shall come. We should leave soon after Drake awakens, though. Don't want to give those attackers more time to react, whoever they are."

"Wonderful. I'll be outside," King Noxy said, and as Amanda walked off in the small cooking area of her hut, the King exited the door. Meanwhile, Jerome leaned back in his chair. He'd had a long day. He closed his eyes, and before he knew it, he was fast asleep.

*

Drake stirred and sat up groggily. He felt better. Much better.

A blurry form leaned over him. "It's me, Jerome. You're safe."

Drake then realized he was on a nice, comfy bed, in a small hut. Jerome must have found them shelter. "Where are we? What happened? Are Sahara and Master Pental with us?"

Maybe it had been a dream. Maybe their masters had come with them, or better yet, the attack hadn't happened at all.

Jerome shook his head sadly. "No, we're on our own." Drake's hope dropped to the ground. Their masters were really gone, and Drake had no idea how they would find them.

Jerome recounted the story of how he arrived at Amanda's hut, and Drake began to remember the events of the attack, but when he got to the part where King Noxy arrived, Drake immediately jumped up.

"The King? Where?" The king was a frequent visitor at Sahara's house. Sometimes he would practice swordsmanship with Drake's instructor. Other times they would talk, but always behind closed doors. And occasionally, Drake and Sahara would be summoned into the castle at Wendil itself. Because of this, Drake knew the castle's layout well.

Maybe King Noxy would know more about Sahara's mysterious message.

"Can I see him?" Drake asked excitedly.

"He's outside with Amanda. They'll be back soon." Jerome continued with his story. "Then, I decided to ask them if they wanted to come and—"

"You asked them to come?" Drake asked.

"Yeah. I thought they could be helpful. Why, is something wrong?"

It was like his master was standing right in front of him, speaking through Jerome. Sahara had always taught him lessons about gratitude and teamwork, but…that might have been the one thing that Sahara hadn't taught him well. Or Drake just hadn't taken it to heart.

But Drake didn't see the value in it. And so, he was not going to change his ways anytime soon.

"No, nothing," Drake lied.

Amanda and King Noxy walked in moments later. Drake jumped from his bed and sank to one knee. "Your Highness! I am so glad you are well."

"Drake Philosopher! The student of Sahara Cortez. How nice it is to see you, awake and lively. And please, just call me King Noxy. No formalities. After all, we're not in a formal setting. Nor a normal one."

Drake was still in awe. "I can't believe you survived. I'm so happy to see you!"

King Noxy chuckled, but it wasn't as lighthearted as he'd seen before. "As am I. However, we have no time to waste," he lowered his voice. "It is good you are awake. I am afraid we are being watched. I'm convinced I saw something moving in the bushes just a few minutes ago. Anyway, Amanda has the horses. We must be on our way."

The three exited, and without speaking, quickly mounted their horses. As they began their trek, Drake felt the cold biting at him more than usual, and when he glanced behind him at the overgrowth and bushes, he swore he saw a pair of eyes staring back at him.

*

A figure moved quickly through the forest with an almost frantic sense of urgency. If he didn't report back to his master soon, he would be a goner. And the man near the hut had almost seen him. He couldn't be so careless next time, unless he wanted to be executed.

Suddenly, a little further away, he heard the crunching of leaves. Mondoor, his name was, crept closer and saw four figures leaping on to horses. They were moving quickly, and Mondoor knew that the man was worried about something. He looked closer, wondering who they were and where they were going, when one of the boys turned directly towards him, staring. The figure froze, and after a moment or so, the boy turned away as the horses cantered off into the forest.

"You saw them, didn't you?" a man next to him asked. He was dressed in the same black outfit, and the two had been tracking the small caravan ever since they'd left Wendil. There was also a third among them, who was trailing back and would be catching up soon.

"Yes. But where are they headed?"

"The Western Town," his comrade replied, and the figure felt a jolt of excitement. They knew their prey's next move. Now they just needed to notify the king.

"Well, we must return. Tell Your Majesty," Mondoor said.

"Yes," his comrade gestured towards the group. "You continue to follow—take our third scout with you—see if they reveal any more of their plans."

Mondoor nodded, and without a second glance, as he was so consumed with excitement, he moved slowly after the group, through the underbrush expecting his third comrade to be showing up soon.

His king wasn't a man who gave high praise, but Mondoor knew how much this meant to him.

And so, in Mondoor's mind, this discovery guaranteed him high praise.

Very high praise.

CHAPTER III

THE SUN WAS just starting to set when Drake, Jerome, Amanda, and the king left the forest. In front of them a plain of golden grass and rocks spread out to the horizon. Small groups of trees added intermittent pockets of shade, and a miniature forest was positioned off to the left. The group's horses rode at a slight gallop, as King Noxy stated that the plain provided no protection, and that he wanted to get out of the open and into the Western Town as soon as possible.

"The Western Town is at the end of this plain," King Noxy said, breaking the silence.

"You've been here before?" Drake couldn't even imagine what it must be like to be king, and he was eager to learn from Noxy.

"Oh, I've done many voyages. Missions of all sorts," King Noxy said. "Diplomatic issues. Peace treaties. And my own travels prior to becoming a king."

They entered a small grove of trees, so as to get into cover. The group rode their horses through the grove cautiously, keeping a lookout for any strange signs. Drake led, and he felt himself breathing a little harder than necessary, and blood rushing through his ears.

They were near the end of the grove when suddenly, there was a loud rustle, and something black dropped from above. A blur of metal flew toward Drake. Before he could even think, he had drawn his sword and deflected the strike, leaping off his horse. As he landed on the ground, he recognized the pure black uniform of their attacker. It was one of the invaders of Wendil.

With a rush of anger, Drake spun, threw a right swing, then a left swing, and then stabbed directly in front of him. There was a squelch, and to Drake's shock, he realized he had pierced the attacker right in the abdomen. Life drained from the attack's eyes as he crumpled back. Drake stared at him, horrified.

He had just killed a man. How could he have done such a thing? Drake trembled, his sword ringing slightly. His legs felt unstable, and he almost couldn't stand upright.

"My goodness!" King Noxy exclaimed as he came up behind Drake. Drake heard Amanda and Jerome yelp with fright. "What in the name of Lyzix happened here?"

"I—" Drake didn't know what to say, and King Noxy grabbed him to stop him from tipping over. His swordsmanship training had always been sparring and practice. Never had he even thought of killing someone.

And yet he just had.

"Drake, we'll talk about this later," Noxy said, "For now, we must go. There might be more. We have no time to waste."

And so as quick as he could, Drake leaped back on his

horse and the group galloped off, his horrific deed still at the forefront of his mind.

*

"There it is!" Drake felt a rush of excitement flow through him. Despite the occurrence with the mysterious attacker, he was elated that they had finally arrived at the town!

At first, the town looked pretty basic. But as they drew closer, Drake could see ballistae

and soldiers on the walls. Soon, the group was close enough that they were in view of the guards on the walls.

"Lower the gates!" a man, who Drake assumed was the head gatekeeper, yelled. "Send out an inspection party."

The gates opened as they approached, and four guards came forth with their weapons drawn. Drake felt his stomach sink.

"What's your business here?" One of them asked.

"We've come for sanctuary." King Noxy said. "We lived in the Kingdom of Wendil, and it was attacked yesterday."

The guard nodded. "So we've heard. We're providing some sanctuary for refugees. We've had other reports of this. Glad you can give us more credibility to the claim. Come in."

The gate creaked as it was lifted off the ground. The guards went back to their posts as the group walked into the town. It was only when the gate closed behind them, that for the first time since the attack, Drake felt safe.

Almost safe.

Almost.

"Well, my friends, we need somewhere to stay, and

I wasn't able to take any money, just my horse," King Noxy said.

"I brought some, but I don't think it'll be enough to pay for shelter." Drake said, looking in his pouch.

"In that case we will just have to find a nice little alleyway to stay the night," King Noxy said. "We must lay low."

The town was sizable, though not regal like the Kingdom of Wendil. There were people bustling along the streets, buying things from merchant stands, but no one was leaving the town. Maybe the attack had scared them into staying inside the walls. Or it was also possible they were on a lockdown for the time being.

It took an hour to find an alleyway sufficiently tucked away and empty of people. It wasn't pretty, but it was the best they could do. They settled down for the night, as the sun was just beginning to set.

Drake dropped his sack down and slumped down on the wet, dirty cobblestone path. And suddenly, he felt his mind going to the dead Titan's face. And those lifeless eyes. Drake began to shiver, and it wasn't at all from the cold. How? How could he have just killed so mercilessly? How—

King Noxy then abruptly had a hand on Drake's shoulder and was steering him away from Jerome and Amanda, who were in deep conversation.

"I have been meaning to talk to you, regarding the attack earlier," King Noxy looked at Drake with a concerned expression. "Listen, Drake, I understand your guilt. We must avoid bloodshed where we can, but sometimes, the fight comes to you. And when it does, you must remember, it is either them or you. I doubt he would be feeling any remorse if the roles were reversed."

Drake nodded, remembering the gruesome squelch and his horror. "But what if this keeps happening, and soon I feel no guilt? I don't want to become a psychopath—"

"You won't," King Noxy promised, putting a hand on Drake's shoulder.

"How do you know?"

Noxy smiled. "Because you care, Drake. You care about life—you value it. Taking it away from someone will always cause you to feel remorse. And I don't know if this coping mechanism will help, but I imagine them going to a better place after death, some sort of sanctuary where there isn't war. An afterlife, if you will. It may not be accurate, though we can hope it is, for their sake and for ours. Even so, it has helped me over many years, and maybe it will help you."

Drake looked at him. He wasn't happy to know that there could possibly be a lot of guilt in the future, but he appreciated King Noxy's wise words.

"Thanks," Drake said, and he walked back to where his pouch lay on the ground. He sat down, glanced up at the night sky, and thought about King Noxy's words. Maybe they were going to a better place. It was possible, and the thought did help Drake a little bit. He would probably use that for his future battles. Because as much as he would like to believe there were no more battles ahead of him… his current situation said otherwise.

Drake reached for his pouch, but his hand touched nothing but air. He turned to look. Sure enough, his pouch was gone. Then, he heard feet scuffling above him. Two figures were holding his sack, up on the rooftops.

"What in the actual—"

Drake was cut off by King Noxy. "I see them," he

shouted. They all leapt to their feet, to see the thieves disappearing over the rooftops.

Drake and Jerome climbed up after them, the two friends scaling the stone and vaulting themselves onto the roof, while King Noxy and Amanda pursued them along the street. But the thieves were far more experienced than Jerome and Drake. They ran easily on the rickety tiles and sloping roofs while the boys slowly lost ground. No matter how hard Drake tried, he always slipped on the loose and unstable footing of the tiles. Jerome almost plummeted off the roof at one point, and only Drake's quick reactions stopped him from suffering a severe injury.

After that, King Noxy began shouting instructions. "When they reach the corner up ahead, they'll have to jump. You must follow them."

Drake and Jerome both nodded, but Drake felt queasy as the thieves came closer to the corner and then leaped. He'd never done this before. Could he make the jump? Before Drake could even think about it any further, he and Jerome followed, Drake's hair blowing around as he tucked his knees into his chest, thrust out his legs and landed solidly on the ground. King Noxy and Amanda had already blocked the thieves' escape while the boys ran up behind them to box them in. The thieves tried to dodge the two friends, but Jerome and Drake knocked each one to the floor.

"Stop," cried one of the thieves. "Don't hurt us."

Up close, Drake could see the thief was a girl. She was probably the same age as Drake, with light skin, long, wavy chocolate-auburn hair and sparkling light-blue eyes. She was pleading for help. The thieves were obviously very poor.

They didn't look like the people who attacked Wendil and Drake decided that they were not in league with them either. They were just simple thieves in rough and ragged clothes.

"Spare us. We mean you no harm," the other thief said. He had jet-black hair and the girl's same blue eyes. "We can return the pouch. We're just trying to get by—"

"We understand," King Noxy said. Drake was taken aback by the extreme composure in his voice. "Now, who are you?"

"Isabella," the girl said quietly. She looked at both Jerome and Drake with curiosity, making Drake look away.

"And I'm Leo," the other said.

"I see." King Noxy considered this for a moment. "You two look very—"

"Siblings," Leo said simply.

"Ah," the king said. "Well, that makes sense."

Isabella was now looking curiously at something glinting on King Noxy's belt, partly concealed by his cloak. King Noxy tried to hide the crown, but it was too late.

"Are you a king?" she asked, her blue eyes widening.

He smiled kindly. "Indeed I am. Now, before any more is said, I would like to ask you two something."

Leo frowned, "What?"

"Young scruffs like you have dreams and wishes, am I right?" Drake could sense the king was up to something but wasn't sure what.

"I don't want to be living like this," Leo replied, "if that's what you mean."

Isabella nodded.

"What would you do if someone approached you with an opportunity for a new life?"

"I would take it, no question. And I'd honor any terms or agreements," Isabella said quickly. Noxy beamed.

Leo narrowed his eyes, "What are you up to?"

"I think you know exactly what I am up to," King Noxy said.

Drake thought he could guess exactly what the king was about to say: Noxy wanted to recruit them. He opened his mouth to protest; he wanted to help the thieves, but like this? There were other ways. But it was already too late. King Noxy was already making the offer.

"We have…a bit of a situation." The king lowered his voice. "If you aren't aware, the Kingdom of Wendil was attacked. We're refugees and are working to regain some support, and eventually, the kingdom that we lost. However, right now we don't have enough money for food, water, or shelter. You two could help us with that. In exchange, as I implied earlier, I could give you a better life."

"I guess. But what does a better life mean?" Leo replied suspiciously.

"A better life?" King Noxy did not seem perturbed. In fact, he seemed amused. "Well, how about you come live in my castle after everything is done? Special treatment from the king. How does that sound?"

Isabella and Leo looked at each other again, and then back at King Noxy, hesitating for a moment.

"Okay," Isabella said finally. "Thank you very much."

King Noxy beamed. Drake heard how grateful she was, but he still felt a small lurch in his stomach. He was annoyed at King Noxy. More people were being added to the group. It went against all of Drake's instincts. You couldn't keep relying on other people for help. He didn't know why he felt this. He just did.

"Come on Drake." King Noxy interrupted Drake's thoughts, insisting they all shook hands. He was smiling at Isabella and Leo the whole time. "Well, you two, I think it's time you help us with what you promised."

"Yes," Leo said, with a newfound mischievous grin as he led them away from the street, towards a nearby tavern. Drake could tell the thief's mood had improved significantly.

"Let's go steal us some food."

*

A few days passed. It felt strange camping out in the town like street beggars, but King Noxy insisted that he remain in disguise. He didn't want to attract any unwanted attention. Leo and Isabella did a fantastic job of stealing. Sometimes they brought the rest of the group along, giving them tips on how to be stealthy, like always breathing through your nose so you were not heard, and staying close to buildings to blend into the shadows.

In all truth, Drake felt guilty about stealing food from the people of the Western Town, but he kept telling himself it was for a good cause. They had to retake Wendil, and they needed energy to do that. Lots of it. Besides, they weren't taking an excessive number of supplies. It would be fine.

However, their situation wasn't the fault of the towns-folk. It was the attackers and that mysterious figure, whoever he was. Drake hadn't mentioned it to anyone else, yet. Jerome didn't seem to have noticed him, but Drake couldn't help thinking he was somehow important.

Drake and Jerome had gotten to know both Isabella and

Leo much better, and Drake was definitely beginning to like the two of them—so similar and different at the same time. They, like Drake, were orphans, but only as of late, when their mother abandoned them after their father—a sea merchant—was killed in the far southern coast of Lyzix. Drake had already assessed that Leo did not take many things seriously, and acted like a comedian despite the hardship in his life. Isabella had a better grasp on reality—and she was also very kind and generous to the group in general.

King Noxy became Drake's "master" so that he could complete the lessons that Sahara hadn't finished. He was a strict teacher and made Drake spar or discuss tactics most of the day.

Sahara.

Drake's mind unconsciously traveled to his lost master. Where was he? During the cold nights, when Drake was unable to sleep, he wondered if his master was alive. No. He must be dead. But Drake would avenge him. He vowed to do it.

He needed to.

Sahara was like his father.

But there was something else that had been bothering Drake ever since he came to the Western Town. Sahara's words echoed in his head: *Run to the forest! Past that you'll find the Western Town. Find Miss Eleanor, and then you'll have a clear path*. Nothing had become clearer. The king was in hiding, they had no plans for what to do next, and now they had two thieves on their side. If anything, the future was becoming less clear by the minute.

Drake couldn't stop thinking about this, not even during his daily training sessions with the king on a piece of wasteland at the far edge of town. Not even now, when King Noxy was swinging at his legs with a wooden sword, practicing some sparring moves they had covered the day prior. Drake was so absorbed in his thoughts that King Noxy sliced his pant leg right open and Drake tumbled to the floor.

"Drake, my friend!" King Noxy exclaimed. "You seem a bit distracted, shall I say."

"Sahara told me that if I came here things would be clearer. He said that I needed to talk to someone named Eleanor?"

King Noxy frowned. "I don't know what to say, Drake. I don't know what your master was talking about, and I am not aware of any Eleanor living here. I am surprised that he may have kept something from me."

"Well, Sahara always had his ways." Drake shrugged. "Like when you two used to talk behind closed doors all the time."

"That was more my doing, Drake. And trust me, it was nothing about you. All related to Wendil," King Noxy said. "But you are right…he did have his ways. Look, why don't I give you a break? Walk around town. Clear your mind. I am sorry I can't help you with this, but when you're ready, come back and we'll finish up the lesson, okay?"

"Okay," Drake replied. "Thank you." King Noxy nodded.

Drake walked down the cobblestone path toward town. As he turned the corner, he realized that even though King Noxy didn't know any Eleanor here, the locals probably did.

Except he stopped. He couldn't do it. It was too painful for him. He missed Sahara terribly. Even more so, Drake felt his subconscious constantly pushing fear at him whenever he thought of this Eleanor and her answers. What would she tell him? Probably something that would ruin his life.

Wait.

Sahara was rough sometimes, but he cared for Drake. He wouldn't let something like this be light or destructive towards his apprentice. Sahara would want it to be beneficial. And if Sahara believed it to be beneficial, then Drake would have to trust him.

Now, a bit less reluctant, but still trying to keep his nerves at bay, he began to walk briskly. There should be plenty of people at the center of town who would know of an Eleanor who lived here. He would start there.

Drake observed the town as he walked. He saw the guards patrolling the walls. He glanced at people walking by, entering stores and trading with merchants. He looked into the tailor's shop, and the apothecary. Inside, women were grabbing various herbs and tending to injured people lying in beds.

As he walked on, he entered the main square. It had a large fountain in the middle and there were many stands erected near it where people sold food, accessories, and even weapons. In one corner there was a blacksmith forge. Two boys were working inside wearing aprons as they hammered red hot bars of metal. Finally, as he looked up, he saw a large tower to one side of the square. He guessed it was the mayor's tower—Lyzixian towns usually had superb living spaces for their mayors.

He walked up to the nearest stand and approached a woman behind the counter who was selling jewelry.

"Can I interest you in something for a young lady

friend, my lad? We have some very nice quality jewels here," she said with a smile.

Though Drake had to agree with her on the quality, now was not the time to become distracted. He felt his nerves creeping up, but then pushed them down quickly. "No, thank you. But by chance do you know if a woman named Eleanor lives here?"

"Hmm. Well, I am not a resident, but I believe there is an Eleanor who runs the library."

Drake felt his pulse quicken. "Where's that?"

"Over there," the woman pointed across the square and down a side road, where a tall, rickety old building sat. It looked as if it would collapse with the touch of a finger. Drake quickly thanked the woman and practically sprinted towards it. He entered, and inside the library, an aged woman sat at a small desk near the entrance. She looked up with a kind smile on her face. But when she saw him her eyes seemed to widen in shock. "What can I do for you, young man?"

"Are you Miss Eleanor, the librarian?"

"Indeed, I am," she replied.

"And you know Sahara Cortez?"

This time the surprise was evident on her face. "Yes— why?" Her eyes widened. "Are you—"

"Drake Philosopher, yes." Drake took a deep breath, hesitated, and then spoke. "Sahara said that 'things' would be clearer if I found you. I think we have much to discuss."

Chapter IV

"I can't believe you came here," Eleanor suddenly seemed flustered. They were inside the library, sitting near her front desk. "I knew you would eventually. I just—where is Sahara?"

She looked so concerned and worried, that Drake suddenly had to fight back tears. All of his pent-up feelings dissolved into sadness. "Wendil was attacked," he said at last. Eleanor gasped. Drake's voice broke as he continued. "I don't know where Sahara is. The last time I saw him, he was scrambling back into battle. He could even be…"

Drake couldn't finish that sentence. His master had to be alive, he had to be.

Eleanor leaned towards him awkwardly and gave him a reassuring pat on the shoulder. He could see her getting misty-eyed as well. "Drake, I know your master. He is a strong man. He'll be all right."

It didn't help, but he nodded his thanks anyway. Eleanor then leaned closer and whispered in his ear. "He really said to come to me?"

"Yes," Drake replied.

Eleanor then stood up, pulling him with her. She led him through a door at the back of the library into another room lined with bookshelves. She went to a desk, picked up a scroll, which had an insignia of a circle with two swords crossed inside it, and handed it to him.

"If he sent you here, then he really wanted you to know your destiny," she said sadly. "So you should know."

Drake unfurled the scroll and saw what seemed to be a family tree. What could this be about? He felt excited and nervous as he read the title, *The Spectacular Swordsmen Descendant Line.* This was it. He almost couldn't believe it. He was about to discover his destiny that Sahara had mentioned countless times.

He felt Eleanor watching him as his eyes scanned the page. The first man was named Atticus, but no sooner had he read that, his eye was drawn immediately to the bottom of the page. His jaw dropped.

Philosopher, it said. *Lloyd Philosopher.*

And directly below that, his own name:

Drake Philosopher

What?

What was his name doing on a family tree of this Spectacular Swordsmen Line?

*

King Noxy was walking briskly around the town square, looking around frantically. He opened the door of a nearby store, and then sighed, closing it abruptly. "Where could he be? I told him to take a walk. He's been gone for far too long." "Isabella and I have scoured the town. We haven't found a single trace of him," Leo said.

"This is not good. I don't understand why he would just disappear like this. We need to find him, before anyone else does. Leo, get Isabella and look again," King Noxy said.

"Yes sir," Leo replied. The thief had been extremely polite with the king ever since Noxy had offered him rooms in his castle. Noxy didn't know how long that gratitude would last, but he was grateful for it, however temporary it may be.

King Noxy looked up to see thin wisps of smoke rising in the distance. His kingdom was still smoldering. He needed to help his people. He needed to retake Wendil. But that meant recruiting more soldiers across all the neighboring kingdoms.

And he couldn't leave without Drake.

*

Drake was astounded. Why would Eleanor have a piece of paper with his name on it, saying he was part of some Spectacular Swordsmen Line?

She must have made a mistake.

He glanced up at her.

"This is no fluke or silly mistake, Drake. It's true," she said as if she'd read his mind.

He looked at her in awe. "I don't even know what a Spectacular Swordsman is. It sounds terrifying…and amazing at the same time."

"Yes, you are right, it does have that ring to it," Eleanor began. "Anyway, not many know what it is. They are long lost, almost completely gone from Lyzix. But it's believed the Swordsmen existed to defend Lyzix from evil throughout the continent. They could even be called 'Defenders of Lyzix'. Atticus was the last Swordsman and when he disappeared, or perished, much of their art, ways, and history were lost. Since then no other Spectacular Swordsmen have come forward."

"Then how can I be one of them?" Drake asked.

"Because you're a descendant of Atticus. As I said, you are one of the Spectacular Swordsmen's descendants," Eleanor explained.

Clearly, this was a big deal, and even though no one knew exactly what they did, this Spectacular Swordsman legacy was apparently centuries old. Drake had never dreamed that he would be a part of something so huge.

But could it be real? It felt like a dream.

"I don't know what to say," Drake said. "How did you discover all this?"

"It took a long time," Eleanor said, "And much research. But as I stated earlier, I am certain that I'm correct."

Drake was still too shocked to notice the uncertainty in her voice, "You know for sure that you are talking about me?" Drake had always wanted to be a part of something great, but he didn't want it to be given to him and then ripped away just when he thought it was his.

Eleanor nodded. "Yes, Drake, I'm sure. Like I said, I have been searching and searching. This is all very real."

Drake nodded. Now he could soak it in.

Wait.

Eleanor had just said he was a part of some kind of descendant line. Drake didn't want to get his hopes up, but could that mean…

No.

It was impossible.

He couldn't have any living relatives.

Or could he? Drake was going to ask when he saw Eleanor's expression drop, as if she'd already guessed what he was going to say. "I'm sorry, Drake, but your last relatives died over a decade ago. This helped me narrow it down to you. I've had my eye on you from the beginning, due to your lineage, and once Sahara began to train you, your skill shone through."

The two stood silent for a few moments. Drake could not believe this was happening. He was unable to process it all.

Eleanor suddenly frowned. "Oh, Drake, I was so concerned about Sahara and explaining this to you that I didn't ask who attacked Wendil?"

"No idea," Drake said. "There were people dressed in black."

Eleanor cursed. "King Chada and his Titans," she looked at Drake, sadly. "They have been searching for you for the past thirteen years, ever since you were born. This is why I had to hide your lineage, even from you. They've ambushed many other kingdoms where your relatives used to live—that's why so many are now no longer with us."

Drake's heart went stone cold at Eleanor's last sentence. He felt the weight of guilt and shame pressing on his back, like a hot piece of metal. The attack on Wendil wasn't a fluke at all. It was his fault.

He slumped against a nearby bookshelf. He had caused this horrible event to happen. He had caused all of Wendil to lose their homes. He had caused his master's disappearance.

"Drake," Eleanor said. "Drake, listen to me. I know that you believe this attack was your fault, but it wasn't."

"So whose was it?" Drake snapped.

"Chada's," Eleanor replied, calmly. "He chose to attack,

didn't he? He wanted to capture you. It is not you, but Chada who is the enemy of Wendil. And of Lyzix. But this is where you can stop it. With proper training and the right gear, you can end the threat of Chada once and for all."

Drake was intrigued by her words. What could this mean? Was he almost a superhero now? It seemed so silly, yet he now knew that Eleanor spoke the truth. He trusted her, but he was now concerned. Why did Chada want him? Perhaps it was because of a certain power he had, or was it he himself? And did that mean that Lyzix depended on him? He certainly hoped not.

"Oh, right. Since Sahara is…" Eleanor trained off sadly, "did you come alone, or are you with someone else?"

"Yes," Drake said, barely thinking of what he was saying. "A few companions."

"Well, I think it is time I meet them. There's much we have to discuss." Eleanor led Drake out of the back room and into the main library.

"Such as?" Drake asked.

Eleanor sighed. "I still think it is too early, and that you are too young—this is a lot to take on. I believe at least one reason Chada wants you is because you stand in his way," Drake swallowed hard. "That is no easy thing to accept. In addition, this role has been forced upon you. So I need to make sure you're ready to step into it. In order to do that, we are going to have to take a little trip to the center of Lyzix."

"Why?" Drake was confused. There was very little in the center of Lyzix, except a few rolling hills and grasslands. Just scenery, and nothing more.

"Because that is where you will perform the Spectacular Swordsmen trials."

CHAPTER V

"Trials?" Drake didn't like the sound of that.

"Yes, trials."

"What do you mean?" Drake asked.

"Well, my young friend," Eleanor lowered her voice as they left the library. "In my research I've read about Spectacular Swordsmen trials testing the skills of their youth throughout the ages. It isn't enough that you're a descendant—you must also possess the legendary natural skill. The trials test for that." She paused, leaning in to whisper. "And there is something else. I believe the Spectacular Swordsmen were not only defenders of Lyzix but were also guarding something. Something that coincidentally, lies in the center of Lyzix."

As they walked through the square, Drake felt his stomach sink. A test. The trials were tests? How could Drake pass these trials if he couldn't even master some of Sahara's lessons? He remembered his failure with the tuck and slash a few nights prior. He knew this was too good to be true. There had to be a catch. There was always a catch. And here it was.

As for this "thing" in the center of Lyzix, Drake didn't know what to make of that. Was he responsible for something enormous, vital, key to Lyzix perhaps? He didn't know whether he could take on that responsibility yet. He'd only just learned about his lineage.

"Do you know what is in the center of Lyzix?" Drake asked.

"The center of Lyzix has always been a strange and almost magical place. I believe it is something connected to sorcery." Eleanor paused.

"Sorcery!" Drake exclaimed. He barely knew anything about the strange concept, but knew that sorcerers did exist in Lyzix, and there weren't many still around. "I thought it was rare!"

"Yes, sorcery," Eleanor replied. "It is. I know the Spectacular Swordsmen were not interconnected with it, or users of it. But I bet, from the clues, that they guarded something involving sorcery, in the center of Lyzix, that is still there—and I am guessing this is another reason Chada wants you—to obtain what the Spectacular Swordsmen have been defending. This, of course, we cannot allow him do." She took a deep breath. "I plan to do more research later about this, to see if there is any more information about it. Now—"

Drake suddenly heard a voice behind him. "Drake! I have been looking all over for you! Where have you been?" Drake and Eleanor both turned to face King Noxy. Behind him Amanda, Leo, Jerome, and Isabella were running through the crowd, trying to catch up. "I told you to go for a walk—not lose yourself in the town. Where did you…"

King Noxy trailed off as he noticed Eleanor next to Drake. She cheerfully extended her hand.

"Eleanor," she said. "Pleasure to meet you."

"Yes, and you as well." Noxy looked slightly confused.

"King Noxy," Drake said, "this is who Sahara sent me to find."

Eleanor and Noxy both spoke at the same time, Eleanor expressing surprise at meeting the King, Noxy about Sahara's order to Drake.

Amanda, Isabella, Leo, and Jerome joined them, adding to chaos. Jerome slapped Drake on the back, Amanda and Isabella kept asking if he was okay. "Let's head back to the library," Drake said. "We all have a lot to talk about."

*

"So let me get this clear," Leo said slowly, as if he didn't believe what Drake had just told him. They were all in the back room of the library, seated around Eleanor's desk trying to take in the new information. "These Spectacular Swordsmen have been around for centuries, defending Lyzix and this sorcery thing beneath the center of the continent?"

Drake nodded, looking at Eleanor. She said nothing. "Yes. And Atticus was the last one, because after he perished, the art died out."

"And you're related to this Atticus?" Leo asked.

"Yes," Drake said.

"And now this King Chada, the attacker of Wendil, wants you for some reason, probably because of your lineage—and the thing in the center of Lyzix?" Leo asked.

Drake felt shame heating his cheeks—he still felt guilty about the attack on Wendil. "Yes."

King Noxy leaned back, folded his hands in his lap and looked at Eleanor. "And were you planning to tell him this now, or…"

Eleanor sighed. "Sahara and I had never decided exactly when to tell him. To be honest, I was hoping his skills would never be needed. But since Wendil has been attacked, and Sahara sent him here, I've had little choice. It's earlier than I would have liked."

"So what do you propose we do?" Amanda asked.

"Well, I've already discussed some of this with Drake. Traditionally the Spectacular Swordsmen underwent trials to prove he was worthy—"

"So you are planning to do these trials here, and then what?" King Noxy asked.

Eleanor gave a smile. "The trials will not happen here, Your Majesty. They will happen in the center of Lyzix." King Noxy scoffed. Drake felt slightly uncomfortable. He couldn't understand why the king was being so dismissive of Eleanor.

"Why?"

"Because—the Spectacular Swordsmen defend something there. Otherwise, there would be no reason for the trials to be located there." King Noxy didn't reply. Eleanor sighed slightly. "Your Majesty, I assure you—"

"Enough of this!" King Noxy exclaimed. "You expect me to let you whisk him away to this strange adventure that I am just finding out about? I've already lost my Kingdom, and I know Sahara would have told me about something this important—"

"King Noxy!" Drake seethed with frustration. He was a wonderful man, but his protective nature was getting the better of him. "I know this is very sudden, but it's not completely out of the blue. Sahara mentioned my "destiny" to me multiple times. And he told me to come here. In my opinion, to question Eleanor is to question my master!"

Drake could see he had struck a nerve. The king seemed surprised, then he spoke in a much quieter voice. "I am sorry, Drake. You're right. If Sahara ordered you to come here, there must be some truth to this…"

"Thank you," Drake said, "And besides, while I take these trials, you can gather help from the surrounding kingdoms—perhaps the Seaside Kingdom a few days journey from here? And they," he gestured to Amanda, Jerome, Leo, and Isabella, "can help."

"So this is really happening, then?" Jerome asked, sadly. "You're going away?"

"We will return as soon as possible," Eleanor said. "I would give you more time to think about it if not for the current situation with Chada. Drake must be ready, to protect himself, Lyzix, and whatever lies beneath the center in order for us to defeat him. Once he is ready, through the trials, we can focus our attention on Chada, and your fallen city," she looked at Noxy when she said this.

"Let's get ready" Amanda said. "We should leave as soon as possible."

So, the group stood up, and exited the back room. Drake followed Isabella, Leo, Amanda, and Jerome not wanting to see them go. As he left the room, he heard Eleanor asking Noxy to stay. It all seemed too strange, too sudden to be real. But Drake knew he had to believe in it. After all, his master had sent him here. And though they had their disagreements…Drake trusted him like no other.

*

King Noxy remained in the library with Eleanor. She seemed genuinely concerned and empathetic, but King Noxy didn't know what to believe. He had no idea what was true or not. The woman seemed harmless, but that didn't prove anything. And Drake seemed so convinced, but what kid wouldn't have his head turned by the promise of greatness? This "destiny" talk was surely pure madness.

And he still couldn't believe Sahara hadn't mentioned anything about it.

"You are skeptical, Your Majesty," Eleanor must have seen the doubt on his face. "I completely understand. I would be bewildered and suspicious if an old woman told me about the mysterious destiny of a kid for whom I cared. But you must understand, I'm telling the truth."

King Noxy huffed.

"If you don't believe me, please, believe Sahara. I know you two were very close. He thought of you as a friend, a sparring partner, a—dare I say it—brother."

King Noxy grinned, remembering how they used to visit the tavern and drink. How they used to spar whenever possible. They were practically brothers. Only a very good friend of Sahara could know the things Eleanor had said. Maybe she was telling the truth after all.

"But he never said anything…"

"I told him to keep it quiet. For Drake's own good," King Noxy was surprised to see tears rolling down Eleanor's cheeks. "And I know that one thing Sahara would have wanted was for Drake to see his destiny through. The trials are a part of it. And I know you don't want him to go, but he needs to do this with me, alone. I need to reveal what I know about the Spectacular Swordsmen gradually—and he will need time to process and take on the responsibility, alone."

King Noxy nodded. He was beginning to understand.

"I assure you," Eleanor's lip was trembling as she spoke, "that I have Drake's best interests at heart. He is a good boy—a boy who will soon become a man. And I will help him get there. You just need to trust me."

King Noxy looked at Eleanor, the woman who was weeping over Sahara, who was desperate for his trust, who cared about Drake. And then he made up his mind.

He extended his arms and let her sink into a long hug.

Chapter VI

Drake looked at the shiny, new sword strapped to his belt. He, Amanda, and the other three teens had just purchased new weapons at the Western Town's blacksmith shop. Eleanor had thought it would be a good idea to buy more weaponry, as with Chada, there could be an attack any moment.

But Drake couldn't let go of his old sword. Not after Sahara had disappeared. He'd still bought a new one, but now the old one was slung across his back. Jerome hadn't bought anything. He'd insisted on keeping his old hammer, and Drake had a feeling his friend was doing it for the same reason he was keeping the sword Sahara had given him—it held too much emotional value.

Amanda had picked up a simple dagger. Leo had grabbed some arrows, and a bow. He was adept at shooting and wasn't a big fan of close combat. Isabella had purchased a crossbow and a short sword that could also be wielded as a dagger.

They were now headed over to the stables to meet King Noxy and Eleanor. Eleanor was eager to leave as soon as possible. As they rounded the corner, the king waved at them. Ever since he and Eleanor had spoken in the library, he seemed more at ease with this whole idea, and more comfortable trusting Eleanor.

"Ready?" King Noxy asked as they approached.

"Yes," Amanda said. "I think we are all set."

There was an awkward silence, and then Drake stepped forward and hugged Amanda. "We'll return as soon as possible."

She pulled back and looked at him. "Please do. And good luck."

Isabella hugged him quickly. "You'll do great," she whispered in his ear. "I'm certain of it." He smiled as she pulled away. Drake and Leo clasped hands. "She's right. You'll definitely beat those trials," he paused for a moment, "unless I was fighting you, of course. Then, it'd be pretty close."

Drake grinned, shaking his head. "Thanks, Leo."

He returned the smile. "Of course." Drake hadn't known the siblings for long, but he was struck by how much he'd miss them...

Drake then faced Jerome. Suddenly, everything felt a lot more real. He and his best friend hadn't been apart, ever. And now, here they were—unsure about how long it would be until they saw each other again. They hugged each other like brothers. Heck, they'd survived the Wendil attack together. They could survive this too.

"I know you'll make a great swordsman," Jerome whispered. "You've always been one."

"Thanks," Drake said. "Keep them all safe. They'll need someone like you on their way to the Seaside Kingdom."

After the two parted, Drake leaped on his horse. King Noxy was already in the saddle.

"Thank you," Drake said. "For letting me do this."

"I've no doubt, Drake, that you will succeed. You're a great swordsman. Your master taught you well. And even more important, you have listened well. Just, please, be careful."

Drake gave one last nod, and then turned to Eleanor, who was astride her own horse. She had a blanket rolled behind her saddle, and a bag on her back, the same as Drake, but other than that, they had not brought much.

"Ready to go?" she asked.

"I think so," he replied. He still felt like this was a dream. He was still shocked by how much had changed for him in a matter of days. Yet, he knew it was all very real.

And it would only become more shocking from here. In a few days, he would be performing the trials.

For the next few hours they rode mostly in silence. Now that he had some quiet time, Drake was able to mull things over properly. The one thing he had trouble accepting was that Wendil had been attacked simply because he lived in the town. Innocent people had been killed because of his existence. Eleanor had said it was Chada's fault—but he still felt guilty. It was a vicious, almost never-ending cycle.

Drake steered his mind away from these thoughts, however, trying to focus on something else. And his mind landed on Atticus, the last known swordsman, and Drake's distant ancestor. Eleanor hadn't told him much about Atticus. Perhaps there was something that could help him understand more about the Spectacular Swordsmen.

"How long ago did Atticus live?" Drake asked.

Eleanor looked at Drake. "You're busy thinking, and that is a good question. I would say many centuries ago—the legacy did need time to die out, and because there was not much information, Atticus must have lived a long time ago."

"Yeah…" Drake trailed off. He didn't know what else to say. It was almost like they were walking into a dark cave with a small torch that was an inch tall, and about to burn out. However, Drake trusted his master, and he trusted Eleanor—she seemed to know what she was talking about. But there were so many unknowns.

No.

He couldn't doubt this, not yet. Eleanor hadn't given him a clear reason to do so. He was going to see his legacy through, no matter what.

*

They continued for a few more hours until the sun began to set. Just as the sky started to darken, a building appeared ahead. Drake squinted.

"It's the Brass Bee Inn. Let's make the most of it. Tomorrow night, we'll have to camp, unless we push the horses hard."

The inn was crowded and noisy with music, laughter, and the clinking of drinks. In the far corner three people were playing instruments as the crowd shouted for more. Some people were even dancing.

Eleanor and Drake sat at a corner table away from the ruckus, while someone immediately brought them two steaming hot plates of potatoes, roasted vegetables, juicy steaks and crusty bread. Though the food was hot, Drake dug in, and it warmed his insides. He looked at Eleanor who was smiling as she watched him devour his food.

"Good, isn't it? I've been here a few times before, and the food is always delicious."

"Yes, it really is," Drake said, though he hadn't been to any inns except for a couple in Wendil, mainly on his birthdays with Sahara. Tavern food was usually really good. And this was no exception, because as he bit into his steak, he tasted a perfect medium rare.

"Drake," Eleanor said, catching his attention. "Before we go to bed for the night, there is something I do want to explain to you — the innerworkings of the trials."

"What innerworkings are there?" Drake asked, taking a large bite of steak. "I just fight, don't I?"

"It's not that simple. The trials are, in short, conjured by sorcery."

Drake choked on his steak, coughing. Once his throat was clear, he spoke. "What?"

Eleanor smiled. "I will be conjuring your foes."

"You?"

"Me."

"So you…"

"Can use sorcery? Yes, I am trained in those arts," Eleanor said. "I was about to tell you before we left, however when your friends had found us, it then slipped my mind."

Drake wasn't too concerned with her forgetting. He was instead now even more in awe of her. The one thing he knew about sorcerers was that they weren't very common. Otherwise, everything was basically a mystery to him. However, he also did know that most people were in awe of their sorcery, some wanted them to use it for ill intentions, some were even afraid of it. And so, to find himself in the presence of a sorcerer completely caught Drake off guard. There were so many questions he wanted to ask.

"How will you conjure my trials?"

"I will create an illusionary image, one that moves, looks, and feels like a real person. And using my sorcery, I will control this artificial image, causing it to be much more effective than any human could be."

"What are you going to do with it?" Drake asked. He was slightly confused.

"I think the question is what are YOU going to do with it," Eleanor said with a twinkle in her eyes. "And that answer is, you are going to fight it."

Drake stared at her, nonplussed.

"Drake?"

"I…I'm going to fight it?"

"Yes. Once you have successfully completed the trials, you are worthy to become the Spectacular Swordsman."

Drake felt as if he'd been struck in the face. He knew that these trials would be hard, possibly even gruesome, but the last thing he expected was to be fighting a magical illusion…controlled by Eleanor…that somehow had superhuman abilities.

How was he supposed to beat that?

"I know it seems near impossible, Drake," Eleanor said, obviously seeing the fear on his face. "But you must understand, this is when your skill will show itself. Chada is seeking you out. You must be as prepared as possible. These trials will do that."

"And if I fail?"

"Then you are not a Spectacular Swordsman."

Drake wondered if his master had known about the trials. And he wondered if his master would have believed in him.

He hoped so.

They finished their dinner and as the crowd began clapping loudly after an energetic song from the band, they summoned the innkeeper's attention, and he showed them to their room upstairs. He entered the room, and as Eleanor continued to talk to the innkeeper, Drake smiled to himself. Though he was surprised, and caught off guard, and confused, and nervous, and so many other emotions, he couldn't help feeling a bit exhilarated. He was finally a part of something big, something significant.

It was just the trials he had to get through. Then, he would be on the road to victory.

*

The morning after King Noxy had said goodbye to Drake and Eleanor, he sat on his horse, the beast's weight shifting underneath him. The sun was only just over the horizon, but they had been on the road for while already. He'd wanted to get an early start.

King Noxy was still nervous about Drake's trip with Eleanor. The librarian had proven she was trustworthy. He'd even hugged her, for goodness sake, and he hadn't even known her a day, but he still couldn't completely process all this information about the Spectacular Swordsmen Line and the trials.

And that was what made him nervous.

Eleanor seemed like a smart woman. She had thought all this through carefully, it seemed, and had a good plan as to what they should do. But Noxy felt that she could have easily been misled, perhaps even by Chada himself. Noxy knew from many reports of friends, nobles, and other kings that Chada was a slimy, slippery, and ruthless man. Noxy would definitely not put it past him to trick Eleanor into a fools' errand.

Furthermore, King Noxy had never heard of these Spectacular Swordsmen, nor of something magical in the center of Lyzix. It all seemed too timely, too coincidental to be true. Chada could have easily planted this fake idea, and therefore, sent Drake and Eleanor to who-knows-where. And this made King Noxy worry, a lot.

It was all too much for him right now.

Instead, he would turn his attention to another pressing matter: his captured kingdom.

After Chada had attacked, Noxy knew he would need to get help from surrounding kingdoms. There was no other way to mount an assault against Chada. And so, he was planning to travel to the Seaside Kingdom—the closest kingdom near the Western Town and talk with the king there. Hopefully, King Nyle would be accepting—Wendil and the Seaside Kingdom had traded much among each other, and many merchants from Wendil traveled to the coast and took a ship from there to the Seaside Kingdom. So, the two kings were on fairly good terms. They hadn't spoken in a bit, however. And, regarding favors, it was sometimes all about timing. The Seaside Kingdom could be having a crisis too.

At that moment, he was brought into a conversation among the group by Jerome.

"King Noxy, when do you think we'll be able to take back Wendil?"

Jerome was an ambitious and smart young lad. Noxy knew he wouldn't like the answer to his question. "My boy, once we get help, if we get help, we need to train them according to our plan. We'll need to assemble all weapons, mounts, and other materials. We'll need to send out scouts…" King Noxy continued listing preparations for the attack.

Each time he said something else, he saw Jerome's face fall. King Noxy's heart ached too, thinking of how difficult this would be. He couldn't believe Chada had actually taken over Wendil. It would haunt him for a long time to come.

"…and then, we'll need to assemble the army outside of the forest, on the outskirts of Wendil, before we'll attack," The king finished.

"So, how long?" Leo looked at him as if he was crazy.

"Can't say exactly," King Noxy said. "A few weeks, at least."

"A few weeks?!" Isabella blurted.

"But—" Jerome began.

"No buts," King Noxy replied. Couldn't they understand? These things took time. They couldn't be rushed. He hated to disappoint them, but he didn't want to be dishonest.

They began a steady climb in silence. As they continued, King Noxy felt his excitement growing as he saw the peak coming closer and closer. Soon, it was right in front of them. They rose over the top, and everyone gasped.

The view was absolutely stunning.

A small stream trickled down the hill to their left, and

then widened into a river that wove through the countryside below like a crease in a piece of paper. Trees were scattered across the plain. In the distance, towards the right, was a small fishing village on the edge of a lake. To the left, the grass began turning golden, the land flatter and drier.

It was a wonderful sight.

"This amazing plain will eventually lead us to the Seaside Kingdom," King Noxy said. Because he was a king, Noxy had been to many places of Lyzix, and he'd also had many of his subjects travel to the Seaside Kingdom for the trading—he knew the geography of Lyzix. He and the king of the Seaside Kingdom were on good terms too.

"It's one of the biggest ports, right?" Leo asked eagerly.

"Yes," Amanda said. "Most of the goods Wendil imports and exports come through this port."

"Mhmmm," King Noxy said. "Well, we'd better continue. We still have a trek ahead of us. And I'd like to arrive before nightfall, if possible. Once we're inside, we need to organize a meeting with the king. He is the one who will be able to grant us an army."

And so, without another word, the group set off, the horses clopping down the steep hill and into the breathtaking valley below.

Chapter VII

MONDOOR WATCHED THE group from the summit of the hill, hidden behind a large boulder. This was the closest he'd been to them since his companion had tried to attack them and had been quickly slaughtered. He shuddered. It was horrible to witness. His comrade had been young as well.

However, he'd continued to track the group, as the scout who had returned to Chada was bound to come back with a report. And Mondoor did not want to lose the group, as that might mean he may lose his own life.

They were journeying to the Seaside Kingdom.

And he felt very excited, as this would mean that if they could get a message back to Chada in time, perhaps they could mount a small ambush upon Drake and his friend, maybe with a squad of Titans?

Mondoor felt his mouth go dry as, suddenly, he heard galloping. Thinking the group had spotted him and was thundering back up the mountain, he ducked further behind the rock, his heart pounding, blood roaring in his ears.

However, as abruptly as it started, the thundering

stopped. The Titan waited a few moments, and then heard grass rustling. He drew his sword. He wasn't going down without a fight, that was for sure. Perhaps he could even target that boy Chada wanted…

Except it wasn't the group. Instead, Mondoor saw a small figure clothed in black, crawl into view. It was his counterpart who had gone to report to Chada.

"What in the name of Lyzix are you doing?" Mondoor hissed. "I almost had a coronary."

"I didn't want them to see me," his comrade responded. "What was I supposed to do?"

The Titan had many sarcastic responses to that comment, but he was too eager to know what King Chada had ordered. "Well? What is the word from Your Majesty?"

"The king suspects they are heading to the Seaside Kingdom for help. He's sent Lieutenant Ossenna and a squad to stop them. They should be coming up the hill now."

"Wait," Mondoor was getting nervous. The higher-ups in the Titan army always made him anxious—they were brutal. "Does that mean—"

"—Lieutenant Ossenna will be with you? Why, yes, Mondoor, in fact, she is here now."

Mondoor practically jumped down the hill, and he saw Ossenna crouching next to him. It was like she was a ghost—Mondoor had not seen her a second before she had spoken. Her narrowed blue eyes showed between the small, exposed area of the dark black suit. She also had small purple designs on her clothing, marking her rank.

Mondoor and his counterpart lowered their heads. "Lieutenant Ossenna."

"Mmm," she barely acknowledged their greeting. "My

squad is camped on the other side of the hill. I was going to bring them over, but I didn't because I suspected you buffoons would forget to tell me we'd be in plain sight. I decided to be safe."

Mondoor cringed. "I apologize, Lieutenant."

Ossenna stared hard at him. "We must wait until their caravan is out of sight. Then we can continue to trail behind, so we won't be seen."

"But what is the plan?" Mondoor's counterpart asked.

"We need to take them by surprise," Ossenna said, "And we should do it as they are returning home. Which means we'll need to find cover…"

"Should we look for a grove of trees, then?" Mondoor asked.

"Yes," Ossenna replied. "Let's look."

And so, after Ossenna rounded up a few more Titans, the squad set out, looking to discover where their next attack might occur.

*

Eleanor and Drake were on the road once more. The sun was peaking up high in the sky and beating down on their backs. Drake felt the warmth of the rays soaking into him, heard the birds chirping and the bees buzzing. But he couldn't completely relax. His mind was consumed with what was to come.

"Did you get a good night's sleep?" Eleanor asked.

"Yes, thanks. This was my first overnight stay ever at an inn. Definitely a success." Drake paused. He wanted to ask Eleanor something, but had been slightly apprehensive to do so—something he could not explain. Perhaps with the weight of the trials and the swordsman business, he felt overwhelmed. However, today his curiosity had gotten the better of him. So, he asked.

"Why are you researching this in the first place? Why are you so interested in this Spectacular Swordsmen stuff?"

"Ah," Eleanor said. "Well, what do you think?"

"I have no idea—that's why I'm asking. I mean, I don't think you're a part of the blood line yourself. You don't seem to be one who holds grudges, so I don't think you're doing this because you have something against Chada. And I don't know what you'd even gain out of it!"

Eleanor looked at him thoughtfully. "You truly believe that I wouldn't gain anything?"

"Yes," Drake said.

"Absolutely nothing?" She raised an eyebrow.

"Yeah…yes. Nothing." He was a little unsure. The way she kept asking him, it seemed like there was an answer. He almost rolled his eyes. It felt as if the trials had already begun—except these trials tested his mental strength.

"I am doing this because I saw the need to. When King Chada started attacking all these apparently random towns, you would not believe the confusion and chaos it caused. The pattern of the attacks was meaningless—they didn't make any sense. Such dark and desperate times for Lyzix.

"We've been at peace for countless decades. And then Chada stirred up trouble in the south, at his kingdom. He took the military power, many of those who would become Titans. He began his attacks, causing everything to fall apart. So, I began searching everywhere. In historical documents, libraries, and then asking around, if anyone knew why these attacks were happening. I saw Lyzix crumbling, and I knew I needed to do something, and quickly.

"So, to answer your question, Drake, there was a motive, but it wasn't necessarily a personal one. Chada is unhinged and ruthless, and I must stop him."

Drake felt surprised, and proud, that Eleanor could be so selfless. Sahara had made a wonderful friend, he realized.

"That's very noble of you," Drake said.

"Not noble," Eleanor said. "But I thank you for the compliment. True heroism is helping others, Drake, remember that. Selflessness is a quite valuable quality."

Drake nodded. He would try and remember. "So after you started looking…" he trailed off, hoping Eleanor would continue her story. He was interested in learning something more about Chada.

"Well, I stumbled upon a scroll about the Spectacular Swordsmen, explaining how they were almost protectors of Lyzix. Something in my gut told me this was vital information. So I investigated who was descended from the line," Eleanor replied.

"How did you do that?" Drake asked.

"I was able to find a tree that showed all of Atticus's descendants, including you on your father's side. Soon after, I received a report of another attack from a dear friend of mine."

Drake noticed her voice caught when she said 'friend.' But he was too intrigued to think more of it. "In a place called Marlton. And it was then I had my epiphany: Chada was after the remaining Spectacular Swordsman. His attacks were all on kingdoms that housed Spectacular Swordsmen Line descendants. I felt excited and terrified at the same time. Chada is after something so significant that it could change Lyzix forever. I had finally cracked the secret code. And…"

She trailed off, looking ahead. Drake followed her gaze and felt his heart swell with excitement and anxiousness.

The sight ahead was majestic.

It was as if a giant piece of earth had been raised from the ground by a giant hand. He could see the top even out into a plateau. A large waterfall cascaded down one side, and Drake could hear others hidden from view, too. The water ended up down below, in a moat, seemingly circling the whole plateau.

Drake had never been here before, had never known the center of Lyzix looked like this. And now, he was impressed as could be. They were here.

They had reached the location of the trials.

Chapter VIII

As King Noxy rode his horse, he felt his mind worry about King Nyle's verdict. They knew each other, but King Noxy, unfortunately, wasn't so certain about what his decision would be. Humans were subject to so many distractions, and things like that caused betrayals and other scandals. He and Nyle were definitely friends, but the situation Noxy had gotten him in was like no other. Most of the kingdoms attacked by Chada had been abandoned by him soon after.

This, unfortunately, wasn't like the other cases. King Chada was using Wendil as his home base.

And the king had a strong suspicion, now knowing Drake's lineage, that it had to do with the young swordsman.

In the end, all he could do was hope for the best.

More time passed as the group continued in silence. The plain stretched further and further ahead of them, and King Noxy felt like he'd been riding on his horse in place, not getting anywhere, for much of the day.

It was when the sun was setting, and only then that, ahead, he saw a little light.

"That's it, it must be!" Jerome shouted as a large wall

came into view, light sources casting a small glow out onto the plain.

"It sure is!" King Noxy grinned. This was the biggest ray of hope since the attack on Wendil. Here was his way to get back on his feet. He needed men. And hopefully, this was where he was going to get them.

They nudged their horses faster, and soon were riding at a light gallop. The kingdom began to stretch out before them and soon Noxy spied King Nyle's towering castle. It was beautiful, built in stone, with accents of blue on the tops of the towers. Flying from the center was a flag with a large trident on it: the symbol of the Seaside Kingdom.

He remembered once being on the battlements of the castle, during some trade negotiations, and looking down on the kingdom's dock. There was no northern wall to the Seaside Kingdom. Instead it opened onto a large port. Countless ships from all over Lyzix sailed in and out daily. It was a wonderful sight and made the Kingdom a very wealthy one. Noxy, like many others, had to pay Nyle well for the privilege of using the port.

As they drew closer, King Noxy noticed that the gates were open, but there were six guards stationed outside: three on each side. That was strange. They were very well-guarded. Had the news of Wendil's' attack reached here as well?

They all dismounted and walked their horses forward, gripping the reins.

A guard stepped out to meet them. "Travelers, I see."

King Noxy nodded. Since he wanted an audience with the king, there was no reason to hide his identity. "I am King Noxy of Wendil. And I request an urgent meeting with Nyle."

The guard raised an eyebrow. "Indeed. And where is your crown?"

King Noxy reached inside his cloak, pulled out the golden crown and placed it on his head. The guards around widened their eyes and knelt down before him. The guard who had spoken, bowed. "My mistake, Your Majesty. It's just, we've had—"

"King Noxy!"

Noxy looked past the guard to see a cloaked figure walking towards him, arms extended. King Noxy squinted. Was he seeing things? He took two steps past the guard. The figure threw back his hood.

"Cyrus!" Noxy exclaimed. The two men embraced, as the others watched curiously.

"What in the name of Lyzix are you doing here?" Cyrus asked.

"I could ask you the same question, my friend!

"This man has been my closest friend since childhood," King Noxy explained to the group. "And a guard in one of the roughest garrisons in the Harobi Desert for the last twenty years. How did you get out? And when were you going to tell me?"

"It's been so hard to reach you, with the communication and being isolated in the desert," Cyrus said apologetically. "I would've if I could've, but—"

"No issue, I understand completely," King Noxy replied. "But tell me, how did you escape?"

"I got lucky," Cyrus said. "There have been a whole bunch of strange skirmishes happening around the Seaside Kingdom over the past few months. Nothing too significant," he said quickly, when Noxy appeared worried. "But

some of Nyle's guards have been killed. King Nyle was looking for a guerilla warfare expert and my skills caught his
eye. I'm head gatekeeper and the guards' commander, too."

"Cyrus, that's wonderful!" King Noxy was overjoyed to
see his friend after so long.

"Now, what brings you here, my friend?" Cyrus asked

King Noxy looked around, slightly nervous. "Do you
mind if we talk in the gatehouse?"

Inside, Cyrus listened intently as Noxy introduced the
group, and then explained everything that happened to
them since the attack on Wendil. He even told him about
Eleanor and Drake's destiny—he trusted Cyrus completely,
and knew the man would not abuse that information.

Cyrus raised his eyebrows. "Sounds like you've been
through quite a lot. I don't quite know what to say about
this Spectacular Swordsmen business—" Cyrus began.

"Trust me, I didn't either," Noxy muttered.

"However, there is one thing I will say about Chada."

King Noxy perked up. "Go on?"

"I heard about the scandal in his kingdom all those
years ago, when he simply left with the military force. Now,
recently, when I was down in the Harobi Desert, I heard
that he established a stronghold base near his kingdom, on
the coast. Don't know what it does, since he's been really
attacking kingdoms to the north, but I think it's important
for you to know."

"Yes, thank you," King Noxy frowned, making a tough
decision. "I think we should try and focus on Wendil first.
Then, we can deal with his stronghold if need be."

"That sounds fine." Cyrus said. "And in order to take
back Wendil, you'll need to meet with King Nyle. Why

don't you sleep here? Consider it a welcome from me. And the first thing in the morning, I'll make sure to set you up with a meeting with the king."

King Noxy smiled at him, "That sounds wonderful. Thank you."

Cyrus nodded. "Anything for you, my friend."

*

Drake slowly sat up, his back sore from a night on the ground. He was at top of the plateau, which marked the exact center of Lyzix, where he would perform the trials. The sun was just peaking over the horizon, the red, yellow, and orange sunrise colors filling the sky with striking beauty.

The fire that he and Eleanor set the previous night was burning brightly again. New branches at its center slowly turned black and grey from the relentless heat of the flame. Eleanor must have replenished it. And there was some bread and fruit laid out already.

Just then, he saw Eleanor carrying a large bucket and two waterskins that were dripping wet. "I thought that since today is a big day, I would get you some fresh water in the nearby stream over there. It will definitely be better than the old water we packed."

"Thanks," Drake said, taking the waterskin and sipping thirstily. She was right. It tasted delicious, even though it was simply water, and he felt as if his senses were heightened.

Suddenly, he remembered the events that would be taking place later today, and his mood darkened. How was he going to complete these trials? He felt like all the lessons he'd ever learned were just wiped from his mind, and he was destined to fail.

He noticed Eleanor looking thoughtfully at him and glanced away. She cleared her throat and said, "I know you're nervous, Drake, and I wish I could help you with that. The best thing I can offer is some breakfast."

Drake felt sick to his stomach. "I'm not hungry."

"It will be good to get something in your system."

He shook his head again, feeling bile rise in his throat. "But—"

"No buts," Eleanor gave him an apple, a banana, some nuts, and a few pieces of bread. "Now eat this."

Drake bit into a piece of bread. It was dry and tasteless, but the next bite was slightly better. By the time he was on the next piece, it tasted delicious. Maybe he was hungry after all.

He soon devoured the apple, nuts, and banana. Eleanor wore a smug smile as she passed him some dried meat.

After he was done eating, he asked, "So, what now?"

"Well, this morning you can practice your own moves and go through any lessons that Sahara has taught you. But by midday you must be ready. When the sun reaches its peak, we'll begin the trials, okay?

Drake nodded. "Okay."

"There will be a few different levels. If you succeed in them all…"

"Then I'll be worthy to become a Spectacular Swordsman." Drake finished.

"Indeed," Eleanor's eyes twinkled. "And the first in many decades." She paused. "I should let you get to practicing. But remember, Drake, believe in yourself. Remember what Sahara has taught you."

Eleanor walked off towards the western end of the

plateau, leaving Drake to trek to the east a good distance away from the camp, carrying his two swords.

He stood for a moment, looking off towards the rising sun. It was blinding, yet somehow it brought him comfort. Maybe it was the tingle of warmth in his arms, or the stunning array of the colors in the sky. Or, as light sometimes does, it simply gave him hope. Whatever it was, he was going to use it to his advantage.

He started by focusing on the most basic offensive moves. He walked himself through the four main ones: the right slash, which was a horizontal cut to the attacker's right; the left slash; a straight thrust, which aimed for the abdomen, stomach, or lower torso of a person and a downward strike, which was often used as a distraction for another, sneakier strike.

He began to practice, and as he did this, he felt his confidence growing. They were easy moves, but he couldn't help feeling proud of himself. He knew these well. And even the most basic strike in a fight could be the deadliest.

He then turned to defense. Sahara had taught him four core defensive moves, and had taught him that any defensive move, no matter how complicated, was derived from these four protective movements. So, he began with the first: a simple upper parry, on one's right or left side. This was to block an incoming attack towards the upper torso, neck, or head. The lower parry focused on blocking an attack to the lower torso and legs.

The overhead parry blocked downward strikes even projectiles, if the timing was right.

The fourth was a spin and inside parry, on one's right or

left side. It could protect one's core, and the spin ensured you didn't have to bend unnaturally to fight off a counterstrike.

Drake imagined an enemy in front of him and began to run through the defensive strikes. His confidence grew even more as sweat poured down his face. As the sun began to rise higher in the sky, he combined his attacking and defensive moves. This was it. He could defeat any sorcery that Eleanor conjured up, no question about it. He had gotten himself here. Now it was just the trials.

Eventually, he walked over to the camp, grabbed his waterskin and took a sip. The sun was almost at its peak. Satisfaction filled him almost as much as the water. He had planned this perfectly. There was only one more thing he wanted to work on: the tuck and slash. The move he'd failed to master the night before Wendil was attacked. He needed to get it right before the trials. Now was the time.

He set down his water and, grabbing his sword once more, he imagined he was with his master, in the training room, listening to his every word.

Remember, you must crouch first, he had said. *Then, you slash, and jump up in the air, using your momentum to land back on your feet.*

Drake crouched down, and then, as he leaped into the air, he tried to slash. He misjudged the timing, and the swing caused the momentum to pull him too far. He landed face first in the grass. He couldn't give up now, though. He had to keep going. He still had more time.

He stood back up and got into position. He crouched down, and then, with lightning speed, leapt up and slashed at an invisible enemy. He felt exhilaration fill him. He had done it! This was it! He was sure he could defeat anything Eleanor threw at him—

But in his excitement, he'd forgotten that he still had to stick the landing. His feet hitting the ground came as a surprise. His knees buckled, and he lost his grip on his sword as he collapsed to the ground for the second time.

It was okay, he promised himself. This last time he would nail it, for sure.

And then, as he stood up, he tensed as he heard the words that he'd been dreading since waking up. His heart felt like it was going to burst from his chest.

"Drake, it's midday. The trials are waiting for you."

CHAPTER IX

King Noxy walked nervously outside of the looming doors of the Seaside Kingdom's war room. Two enormous tridents, one on each door, towered over him.

"Noxy, relax, it'll be all right." Cyrus's reassuring voice soothed him slightly. Yes, yes, he just had to be honest, and hope for the best.

He glanced at the rest of the group staring, stone faced, at the doors. They were all feeling the same as him. And though he felt slightly guilty about it, it calmed him even more. He wasn't alone.

"When is he going to let us in?" Leo asked impatiently from behind them.

"Leo, watch yourself," King Noxy warned. "He'll let us in when it is time."

The doors swung open and King Noxy felt his entire body tense up. Two guards stood on both sides of him and Cyrus led them inside.

The room was large. In the center was a long table at which a bearded man sat with a golden crown on his head. King Nyle. His arms rested on large, intricate wooden armrests, and the back of the chair shot a few feet higher over his crowned head.

Around the table all the nobles of the kingdom had been gathered to hear his proposal. They all turned to watch as he approached. King Nyle stood, bowed and gestured for him to stand in front of the table.

Noxy's heart skipped a beat as he continued to observe the room. However, there wasn't much more to see. A few chandeliers were spaced evenly over the tables, hanging from the ceilings. Desks were placed around the room. The Seaside Kingdom's crest sat on the walls, and the floor was lined with a gilded blue carpet.

"Greetings, King Noxy. It's been a long time." King Nyle said.

King Noxy jumped slightly. "Yes, oh, yes, it has. How has your evening—I mean afternoon—your morning been?" King Noxy felt like smacking himself. What was he saying? He needed to get a grip! Their future lay in this decision, and the last thing he needed to do was act like a fool.

Nyle raised an eyebrow. "Is everything alright?"

Noxy took a deep breath, considered his answer, and shook his head. Honesty was key here. "No, it's not. And for good reason—this conversation we have right now is going to determine the future of my kingdom."

King Nyle looked at Noxy. "Indeed? Cyrus did not tell me it was this serious. What can we do for you?"

Noxy cleared his throat. "Men. Wendil must be retaken from Chada, and for that, we need soldiers. I want to secure an army first, and then formulate my plan—the attack won't happen right away. After all, if this goes awry, not only will Wendil be in jeopardy, but so will Lyzix."

Nyle looked at Noxy thoughtfully and glanced at his nobles. "Definitely understandable. What do you all think?"

"No," one man said.

"Myer…" Nyle said warningly. King Noxy's jaw almost dropped open. Who was this fool, to be challenging the king's will? Two kings in fact. Wendil was in need. What was the hesitancy?

"Why should we risk our kingdom for Wendil? We could simply stay out of this and remain at peace."

Some of the nobles started muttering and nodding. However, King Noxy wasn't going to back down. They needed this. Wendil needed this. Heck, Lyzix needed it. And that was exactly what he was going to say.

"If we don't stop Chada now, he'll have the Seaside Kingdom very soon. Within months."

"That's impossible!" Myer exclaimed. "He's simply a king. We can protect ourselves from some man in a crown."

"You don't understand," Noxy said. "He won't have just the Seaside Kingdom in months. He'll have Lyzix."

Myer's mouth no longer seemed to work. The nobles hushed their muttering and were staring at Noxy.

"Lyzix is in jeopardy. King Chada's conquered land will only grow from here, along with his strength. We need to stop him now. Otherwise, Lyzix may never be the same. And that, my friend," he looked at Myer, "will include your kingdom."

Now the nobles were looking at Myer, shaking their heads. Myer looked down, away from Noxy, and after a hard look at his outspoken lord, King Nyle looked at Noxy. He smiled.

"I think Lyzix deserves to survive, don't you all?"

Noxy felt hope swell in him. Almost all the nobles were nodding their heads. He felt a grin break out on his face as Nyle said the words he'd been hoping for all along.

"You have our army."

Leo gave a whoop of delight behind him as the group joined each other in a small hug. As the nobles began to file out of the room, Nyle, walked over to shake Noxy's hand.

"Thank you," Noxy said, "You don't know how grateful we are."

"Oh, I think I have a pretty good idea," Nyle replied. "About how many soldiers are you thinking?"

"Whatever you can give," Noxy said. "I know you'll need to keep some, in case you must defend your own kingdom, but we could really use the help."

"Alright. I will keep some of the army. But I can try and give many of my platoons."

"That would be wonderful," Noxy replied.

"Your Majesty?" Cyrus asked. "I was thinking…could I go with Noxy and help him? He's been a friend for so long, and I think it would be wonderful if I could accompany and assist him."

"Cyrus, thank you, but you don't have to—"

"Of course I have to, Noxy," Cyrus said. "You are my best friend."

Noxy sighed. In fact, he really did want Cyrus to come with them. But Nyle needed to be all right with it.

"Go ahead. They need you more than I do right now."

As the group laughed and continued to talk with Nyle, King Noxy looked out a nearby window. He saw birds soaring by, ships slowly sailing out to sea, and what appeared to be very small dots down below walking among the streets.

He remembered Wendil and having a view similar to this every day upon awakening. His sadness was lightened by the smallest sense of hope.

They were one step closer to taking back Wendil.

*

Drake felt himself sweating as he stood with his sword in the middle of the plateau. Eleanor stood off to one side, muttering to herself, probably doing final preparations for the magical apparitions she would conjure.

He took a sip from his waterskin, his mind on high alert. He continued to imagine himself taking part in the trials. In one version, he saw himself completing them, celebrating with Eleanor, and later the group. And in another, he saw his defeated face as Eleanor and the group looked upon him, their disappointed expressions boring into him like knives.

And Drake was now very nervous, realizing that he was going up against something he knew nothing about. Sorcery was foreign to him. Drake hoped the conjurings couldn't actually kill or seriously injure him—if they could, he'd be in much more trouble than he thought.

He shuddered at the idea.

"Okay," Drake hadn't even noticed Eleanor approach. "It's time."

Drake swallowed; his mouth was so dry he could only speak in a rasp. "Could you…tell me a little more about the sorcery, so I know what I am fighting?"

"Trust me Drake, anything I tell you wouldn't help. Later, I will explain sorcery. But for now, let us focus on the trials. I know you'll ace them," Eleanor said. "Remember what Sahara has taught you."

Drake nodded. Sahara, his master. He was facing his fears for Sahara. He needed to make his master proud. Yes, his master would never steer him wrong. He could do this. He just needed to believe.

"Ready?" Eleanor asked.

"Ready," Drake replied firmly, the dryness of his throat gone.

Eleanor waved her hands. "The first trial."

Immediately a wavering image appeared. Drake sucked in a deep breath. How could he be ready for this? It was the towering figure of a knight, clad in metal armor with a large sword at his side.

And the knight wasted no time in attacking. He immediately threw a feint swing right and then attacked left. Drake had no time to feel scared, and barely managed to parry before feeling a shockwave of strength blast through his arms. The knight was slow, but his blows were much, much more powerful.

As Drake fended off the attacks from the large knight, he began to weave in, out, and around him, throwing up parries and defensive blocks. He would have to use the knight's immobility to his advantage. If he could just get in a swing by the knight's lower body…

Drake tried just that, and it was completely unsuccessful. The knight swung his sword in an uppercut arch, smashing against Drake's sword. He not only blocked the strike, but Drake was sent flying off of his feet. His sword clattered to the ground somewhere to the left as he skidded across the dirt of the plateau. The knight strode towards him lifting his sword ready to strike Drake where he lay. Drake looked for his own weapon, and when he spotted it, he completely panicked. It was too far away from him. He'd never be able to grab it in time.

He wouldn't pass this trial.

As the knight raised his sword, Drake braced himself. What would happen? Would he be knocked out? Would the trial simply end? He didn't know for sure, but all he knew was that he had failed and—

Wait.

As the knight's sword began its downward descent, Drake reached over his right shoulder, and grabbed the hilt of his old sword on his back. Drawing it faster than he ever had, he blocked the knight's strike. While the knight recovered from the shock, Drake twisted the sword into a backhand grip, spun, and plunged it into the knight's abdomen.

Immediately, the knight burst into dust. Drake had done it. He'd completed the first trial.

"Impressive," Eleanor said, but Drake could see her face was slightly pale. She seemed relieved. "Remember, Drake, it's as much a mental game as it is a physical one. Keep that confidence growing."

Drake smiled, and then, after he had retrieved his new sword, she waved her hands again. "The second trial."

However, Drake's smile immediately disappeared as he saw what materialized in front of him.

It wavered, just the knight, but as Drake looked closer, he immediately realized it was something he'd never seen before. And after a double take, he realized that he probably didn't want to see it again.

An enormous creature, it had the head of a grey-skinned elephant, yet with protruding tusks that curved—they looked like with one hit, Drake would go reeling off the plateau. In addition to this, the animal had a body of a black bear. The claws on all four paws were very long, and sharp.

Faced with this strange creature, Drake couldn't have been more confused. First a giant, powerful knight, then this?

And then, fire erupted from the creature's mouth, and a very un-elephant like roar shot from it. Drake saw the trunk then aimed at him, and before his could move, he felt a torrent of water strike him, knocking him back. As he skidded across the ground, he saw the creature approaching him.

And now, he was worried. He quickly leapt to his feet and sprinted to his left to avoid another torrent of water. Suddenly, the creature was upon him. Drake frantically dodged a giant claw slash. He swung his sword, but a jerk of the head stopped it, one of the gargantuan tusks sending it spinning away. Drake drew his backup sword, and then retreated back, as a shot of fire scorched the ground where he'd been.

Drake knew he would need to do something, or he would be stuck running around the plateau, on this second trial, fighting whatever this was, until a tusk or claw smashed into him, or he got caught in an unlucky blast of fire.

The creature began to rush him again. Drake stood his ground, waiting patiently. He would need to get under the beast and try to impale its stomach. It would be risky, but it was his best option.

The elephant swung its head, and Drake blocked the tusk. He leapt over it and avoiding a fire blast and a torrent of water from the trunk, he slid under the creature, and with excitement building up in him, plunged his sword into the underside.

The creature, just like the knight, suddenly disappeared into dust. Drake slowly stood up and looked over at Eleanor in shock. He could see the pride in her eyes. She seemed extremely affected by Drake's astonishing skill, and though Drake felt happy he impressed her, the creature was still on his mind.

"What was that?" Drake asked.

"Ah yes, an interesting creature indeed. It is called an Obilor. They haven't been spotted in Lyzix for a long time, but they used to dwell in significant numbers in the Moai Mountains."

"Okay…" Drake had never heard of it. And he surely hoped that they weren't still there. That was one creature he never wanted to see again.

"Very well done. Now, you still have one more. Prepare yourself." Eleanor began to conjure up another being. "The third, and final trial."

Drake faced the now solidified apparition of the swordsman. He wore a garment, with a shortened cloak on his back. He held a sword in a front hand grip with one hand, with another one strapped at his waist belt. And, as Drake met the swordsman's eyes, he saw a soft, light brown color in them.

Drake shivered. This swordsman felt a lot like himself.

His doppelganger, or whatever it was, didn't move. He stood still, in a similar position that Drake held, in fact. Drake felt an uneasy feeling creep along his back, a tingling, and the swordsman then moved towards him, taking a single step. He then stopped again, freezing into position.

And Drake was lost. What should he do? Attack? Stay back?

Drake thought about the training his master had taught him. Did this conjuring resemble him in knowledge, too? No, it couldn't. As far as Drake knew, that was impossible. He should be able to have the advantage on this conjuring.

Maybe this would be easier than Drake thought—

Drake lifted his sword in front of him as he realized the swordsman was suddenly upon him, slashing at him with three fast powerful strokes. Drake retreated a good distance back across the plain, parrying them as he went. Barely able to hold onto his sword, however, he finally managed to block a strike and push hard against it, sending the swordsman stumbling back for a moment.

Yet before he knew it, the swordsman was attacking once more, and Drake was sliding, ducking, and dodging as much as he could to get away. He couldn't keep doing this. He hadn't delivered one offensive swing yet, and he'd only been able to block a few strikes. He was doing a dance to avoid them. This was a trial for swordsmanship, not a trial for dancing.

He needed to observe the swordsman, observe himself. Perhaps if he attacked the swordsman quickly, just as the swordsman was doing to him, he could gain the upper hand.

And so, he tried it. Once the swordsman stepped back for a moment, though Drake was exhausted, he leapt forward, threw a right slash, left slash, thrust, another thrust, spin and slash, and more. The swordsman surprised, began to lose ground.

Drake felt himself start to fill with triumph. He was doing it! It must be a weakness of the swordsman, to respond with quick attacks. And, after another moment, Drake realized that it was a small flaw in himself, too. A flaw, now that he was aware of it, could be covered up. He'd have to try and work on that. But for right now, he had to focus on staying alive.

Unfortunately, the swordsman wasn't as susceptible to it as Drake thought. Blocking a strike, he quickly kicked Drake back, and then once more started his attacks. Drake backed up, but when he looked behind him, he saw the edge of the plateau nearing. He couldn't afford to lose any more ground. He had to stand and fight.

So, Drake stood his ground in the next flurry of attacks, realizing it was a mistake right away. The swordsman threw a high strike, and then snuck in a slash across Drake's leg. Pain exploded in his thigh, and hot blood dripped down it. Drake stumbled back as the swordsman took a swiping stroke, barely missing Drake's chest. The swordsman continued to approach. Drake retreated backwards and looked behind him. His heart dropped.

Now, he was at the edge of the plateau. There was nowhere else to go.

Drake drew his second sword. This was it. It was now or never.

The swordsman took an enormous leap and swung downward. Drake crossed his two swords directly in front of where the strike was headed. There was a loud clang, and the swordsman was thrown off balance. Drake threw aside one sword, and knowing that if he was going to win, he had to throw a fast strike. So, he crouched down, and then immediately bouncing back up, threw a lightning speed-like slash across the off-balance swordsman's neck.

And as the sword connected, the swordsman disappeared into a cloud of dust. Drake, shell-shocked, exhausted, and weak, collapsed to his knees and dropped his sword. It was finally over. He had completed the trials.

He was worthy…

Now worthy to be a Spectacular Swordsman.

CHAPTER X

KING NOXY WAS feeling better than he had in a while.

He and the small caravan left the Seaside Kingdom some hours ago, heading back to the Western Town. And now with the assurance of many platoons, Nyle had also said that he would send them on their way soon after the group left. Despite his worry about Drake and Eleanor's well-being, not to mention his kingdom, he felt momentarily as if the situation were under control. It was manageable. And that was enough for now.

After a bit more time passed, King Noxy rode towards a dense groove of trees. This was an interesting spot, as there were not many pockets of shade on the plain near the Seaside Kingdom. It would be a good place to camp.

"How about we camp for an hour or two up ahead?" Cyrus asked from behind him.

"It's like he read my mind," King Noxy muttered. "Sounds great. Let's do it," he called behind him.

King Noxy's horse pushed through the dense grass at the entrance to the grove. Once the beast was through, the foliage began to thin out, and the dense canopy above blocked most of the light. The floor of the grove had small bushes across it, but not much else.

King Noxy continued on, searching for a good place to set down their belongings. He looked behind, to make sure the group was with him, when he heard a rustle to his right and the grind of metal on metal. He immediately swung his left leg over the horse and sprung off the right stirrup, spinning in the air. When he landed, he felt his stomach tense as he slashed his sword…

Right at an attacking Titan. Behind him, five other Titans stood, their eyes wide, hands frozen on their weapons.

"It's an ambush! Look out!" Noxy yelled as he charged the squad of Titans, hoping there weren't too many. No matter the skill of the fighters, eventually it came down to who had more on their side.

Immediately two Titans turned and sprinted away. However, one was thrown back, a nasty cut across his chest, and the other, Noxy could see, was now engaged in furious combat with Cyrus, who had just entered the battle.

Noxy was now facing three. One of them sprinted towards the king, throwing a clumsy strike. The king ducked the sloppy swing and stabbed one of the other, hesitant fighters. He then slashed to his right at the other Titan, who was able to parry just in time. Noxy, however, was already defending himself from the Titan who had charged him. With a perfectly timed block, he deflected the strike and slashed that Titan in the legs. Then, doing a counter spin, he wacked the flat of his sword blade into the other Titan's face, causing him to fall back and whomp into a nearby tree.

King Noxy then ran to his horse, who had retreated a few steps away from the skirmish. He hoped the rest of the group was safe. Cyrus had now finished two men and was fighting a third, but King Noxy felt more confident in his fighting skills than the others. He could help Cyrus later if needed. He rode back a few paces and saw something that surprised him.

The group was handling itself well. Amanda was fighting two Titans at once, sliding her dagger into sneaky parries and slowly dishing out small injuries on her opponents.

Jerome was wielding his hammer, whacking Titans off to the side as he plowed through them. His enormous strength was no match for the weaker Titans.

Isabella fired a crossbow bolt into a Titan who was running up behind Jerome. She then shot another one high into the leaves of a nearby tree. There was a yell of fright, and a body tumbled from the canopy to the ground, crumpling at the foot of a trunk.

"Noxy, watch out!"

The king whirled around to see a Titan descending from a nearby tree branch, winding his sword back to attack Noxy. Before he'd even begun the forward motion, an arrow lodged into his neck. His grip on the branch went slack, and like the other Titan, he fell, collapsing into a heap at Noxy's feet.

Noxy looked back to where the arrow had come from. Leo stood with his bow at his side and gave him a firm nod. King Noxy felt proud. That had been a great shot. He wondered how the thief had become so good at shooting. Perhaps it had been luck? There was no time for such considerations now. King Noxy scanned the trees for more Titans. There were around twenty to twenty-five in all, both dead and alive. King Noxy guessed that there weren't too many more, unless reinforcements were arriving.

King Noxy turned his horse to fetch Cyrus but faced two Titans instead. One was a woman with a purple stripe to one side of her black suit. Noxy was facing the leader of this operation, in addition to a likely trusted guard. He slid off his horse, oblivious to the clashes and sounds of battle in the background. He readied his sword and had barely done so when the male Titan advanced on him.

King Noxy threw up a parry and then tried to counterattack with a spin and slash, however this Titan was much more skilled. He blocked Noxy's strike with ease and attacked inward immediately. King Noxy leaped back and deflected the strike to his right.

Suddenly, he heard a slight whistle of the air, and dropped to the ground as he felt the female Titan's blade swipe over his head. He rolled to the side immediately afterward, hearing the thump of the sword on the grass as he stood up.

As the Titans attacked again, King Noxy knew this would be the toughest battle he'd fought in a long time.

Noxy blocked the man's high strike, and then attacked the female. He spun to his right after she blocked and threw a backwards strike at the male. As their swords clashed, he ducked a swing from the woman, and kicked her stomach, sending her flying back.

He immediately turned to the male Titan, and began to drive him back, swing after swing. The man tried to block the blows, but King Noxy continued to pound his sword down on him until he had him against a tree trunk. The Titan ducked Noxy's final strike, propelled himself off the tree trunk, brought his sword in a downward slash and cut into King Noxy's back.

Noxy cried out in pain as hot blood slowly ran down his skin. He turned to see the Titan looking triumphantly at him. The woman, now recovered from Noxy's kick, joined them.

The king felt drained, tired. He hadn't fought this hard in a long time. The Titan raised his sword. King Noxy felt exhausted as he tried to haul his sword up. This was it. He was outnumbered and wounded. And then he saw the Titan's eyes dart to the king's left side. He immediately realized what the Titan was going to do. King Noxy threw his sword to the left, parrying the spin and slash, the move with which the Titan had planned to finish him off. Noxy then side kicked him in the stomach and slashed his sword across the man's leg.

The Titan fell to the ground, gasping in pain. The woman, obviously shocked, leaped towards her injured comrade, hoisted his body, and fled back to the rest of the Titans.

King Noxy tried to run after her, but his back burst into pain. He couldn't let any of the Titans spread word of their whereabouts to Chada. "Stop her!" he yelled. He could only hope for another member of the group to assist. Cyrus was too far away. Isabella was focused on a Titan who had come at her—she was fighting him with her sword and was winning.

But Leo heard his cry. The thief looked towards the fleeing Titans, raised his bow, nocked an arrow, drew, and fired, just as the woman dragged her comrade to the shelter of some trees. Leo's arrow lodged itself in one of the thick, wooden trunks.

Suddenly, at the disappearance of their leader, many

of the Titans began disappearing. Isabella, pouncing on a Titan nearest to her, sliced his arm and then kicked him back, where he fell to the ground and crawled away. Cyrus ran to where the group was gathered, his sword ready, but their opponents had all fled.

They had fought the Titans off. The ambush was over.

For a while, no one spoke. Then, King Noxy cried out in pain as his back spasmed.

"Oh dear!" Amanda ran over to help. "Don't say a word." She rummaged through her sack, pulled out molo weed, and set it aside. Then, she began to clean his wound with some water and a cloth.

"Thank you, Amanda."

"Well, I'm not going to sit here and let you die of blood loss, am I?"

"No, I suppose not," King Noxy said. They were silent for a bit more. Then, Leo spoke. "So, that was some fight, huh?"

"Yes," Cyrus said. He looked at King Noxy. "Did any get away?"

King Noxy felt his heart sink at the reminder. "Yes. A decent amount, in addition to the commander of the entire squad and one of her guards. They were very skilled fighters. Her companion was the one who gave me this wound."

"In that case, Chada will know where we are soon," Cyrus said. "We should leave while we still can."

Chapter XI

"So, Drake. I think we've talked about many other things enough. I owe you an explanation," Eleanor said.

The two were in the final few hours of their journey. There was a slight rain, and though their vision was somewhat obscured, they knew the Western Town was a short distance away, and their individual time together was coming to an end.

"About what?" Drake asked.

"About sorcery." Eleanor's eyes twinkled, and Drake suddenly sat up straighter, paying attention. "Like I said, I promised you I would explain it—it's always good to know about, as Chada could bring sorcery into the fight at any time. And, considering the job of the swordsman involving the center of Lyzix, it's good for you to know as well.

"Sorcery was discovered a long, long time ago. People were able to channel power from their surroundings and use it as energy. This was its earliest form. And as it progressed, people learned how to store it, and eventually, store enough for a lifetime's use. These days, those who are sorcerers are usually born with the now infinite source of energy inside."

"Wow," Drake said.

"Yes. But that is not all. It is required in Lyzix, and almost always upheld, that sorcerers do not use their energy and sorcery for offensive, direct attacks. This is because the continent has been so peaceful, and that sorcery used incorrectly could be possibly fatal to Lyzix's well-being. This is why many are unsure of who and what sorcerers are. They don't use their power to attack, like most would think. In most battles, sorcerers are used for defense, healing, and after, rebuilding."

Drake nodded. This was very interesting. Now he understood why he'd never heard about any famous sorcerer war veterans. They didn't exist.

"Other than that, there is really only one more thing you should know," Eleanor said. "Sorcery can be enhanced by the metal silver."

"Really?" Drake exclaimed. Silver was so rare these days! But he'd never known it was magical.

"Yes. Though because of its rarity that I am sure you know of, a sorcerer with silver isn't a common sight. I myself am lucky to have a small bracelet." Eleanor extended her right arm, pulled up her cloak's sleeve slight, and among her light skin he could see a band of shiny, clean, and slightly glowing metal—silver.

"That's amazing." Drake whispered. He'd always been focused so much on his swordsmanship training, and the material side of the world he lived in, without really thinking about the magical side that Eleanor was describing—sorcery, sorcerers, and silver.

"I am glad you appreciated that explanation. Now

remember the knowledge I've imparted. It may come in handy soon." Eleanor said.

Drake nodded, turned ahead, and gave a start of surprise. He became excited, spotting the gate of the Western Town! This was it! He had safely returned from the trials.

And he could still hardly believe he had completed them.

Once the two were inside the town, Eleanor immediately led them to the town's main livery stables. "We must see if Noxy and the others have returned yet. But then—" She trailed off. Through the open doors of the stables, Drake caught sight of a glinting crown. Sure enough, straight ahead was Noxy and the rest of the group.

Drake immediately dismounted, sprinted into the stable and sank into a hug with his comrades.

"We're so glad you are all right," King Noxy said.

The moment Drake broke away, a man approached and shook his hand. "Cyrus," he said, a twinkle in his eye. "You must be the famous Drake. A pleasure to finally meet you. I'm an old friend of Noxy from the Seaside Kingdom."

"He helped us convince Nyle to let us borrow some men." Noxy said, beaming.

"Really?" Drake exclaimed. This was fantastic. They had succeeded in both of their missions. He wanted to hear more, but Noxy held up his hand. "Why don't we go the nearest tavern and grab a bite to eat? We can talk about everything there and get out of this dreadful rain."

"So, you're truly a Spectacular Swordsman?" Leo whispered later as they were all gathered around a table eating their fill of the feast Noxy had ordered.

"Yes," Drake said. "I just need to continue specific training and..." He looked uncertainly at Eleanor. They hadn't discussed what his swordsmanship training would look like now that Sahara had disappeared.

"That we will figure out soon," she said. "How did the Seaside Kingdom visit go?"

Drake was happy to hear that the events had gone down well but gasped when Noxy told them of the Titan ambush.

"Was everyone okay?" Drake began to scan his friends for signs of wounds.

"Noxy took a bad slash to his back, but it's almost completely healed now," Amanda said. "Other than that, no other serious injuries."

"Good," Eleanor said, but she looked at Noxy sympathetically. Before she could speak, however, he waved a hand. Drake was sure it was a sign not to worry about him, and he smiled slightly. The two were beginning to connect.

"Did any of the Titans escape?" She asked.

"Yes, multiple," Jerome said grimly. "Including the leader and one of her close guards."

"Well, Chada will definitely know that you were down in the Seaside Kingdom," Eleanor said. "Yet he probably expected us to enlist help. Hopefully, it doesn't provide him with any new information that gives him the upper hand."

"I hope not," Noxy said. "Anyway, the army will be coming in a few days, and…"

As Noxy continued talking, Drake found himself focusing on Chada. He had been so preoccupied with the trials that it had just occurred to him that it was possible Chada knew where his master was. He recalled seeing Sahara in Wendil that last time, attacking one Titan and the next, so powerful and so driven, it was impossible to believe he had perished in battle. If they attacked Wendil now, with the new army, they could not only get the kingdom back, but perhaps discover Sahara's whereabouts.

Chada clearly had reason for holding onto the kingdom. If they could take it back now, in an early attack, they could delay or even ruin his plans. Then this chaotic and confusing sequence of events would be over.

"I've been thinking." Drake glanced around, making sure the innkeeper wasn't eavesdropping. He was nowhere to be seen, but Drake lowered his voice anyway. "I've completed the trials. King Chada's power is growing. We have an army on the way." He took in a deep breath. "We need to attack Chada, now."

There was silence for a moment. The group looked at him. Then Noxy spoke.

"No!" the king hissed. "It's barely been a week since the attack of Wendil. I understand you're happy about the trials, but preparing for such an attack takes time."

"The longer Chada has to settle into Wendil and fortify it, the harder it will be for us to take," Drake said. "We need to strike now."

"What we gain in speed we will lose in unpreparedness," Noxy said.

"I think Chada is holding onto Wendil in the hopes you will come back, so then he can take you captive," Eleanor said. "Wendil is his 'trap' to catch you."

Drake growled to himself. This was exactly why he didn't like to work in teams. Why couldn't they see it the way he did? Why did he have to spend time convincing them about something that was so obvious to him?

"I think Drake has a point. We shouldn't wait too long.

The army is a few days out. We'll have some time to pre-pare," Jerome said.

Drake looked at him gratefully. "Yes, thank you, Jerome."

"Drake, listen," King Noxy said. "I know you're anx-ious to take revenge on King Chada, but I'm sure he will be counting on this. He'll use this early attack to catch us off guard—and you'll be walking right into his hands. You are rushing into—"

"I am not rushing into anything," Drake no longer bothered to conceal his irritation. "King Noxy, how long do you want that wretch of a man in control of your kingdom? He's taken enough from us. We need to take it back. And we need to take something of his: his confidence."

Drake could tell he'd hit a nerve. A flash of anger appeared on the king's face and he glanced down at his lap. Drake knew King Noxy regretted leaving his people and Drake had just reopened the wound.

"Drake." King Noxy sighed. "I—"

"The boy might be right, Noxy." Cyrus said.

King Noxy hesitated for a long moment, looking at them all. Finally, his eyes settled on Eleanor.

"What do you think?"

"I think it may work," Eleanor said. "But we need to make sure we're completely ready. If we rush too much, it will be our downfall."

"I second that," Noxy said. "Very well then. We'll begin the preparations in the morning."

The group cheered, and Drake felt like he was soar-ing. Everything he'd hoped for was happening so fast. He hoped that he would be able to discover where his master was, and that he could be reunited with him, because Drake could not imagine his master dead. He and Sahara could then return to their old life in Wendil—and this is what he'd been hoping for ever since the attack had happened. And though a few things had changed since then, that fact had remained.

*

"I'll be with all of you in a moment," King Noxy said as the group finally left the tavern. "Give me a few minutes."

The door closed behind them and King Noxy rested his head in his hands. You couldn't just make a plan of attack in a couple of days. Those things took time. And training. Patience. Discipline. So, he couldn't believe he had just agreed to Drake's plan. What was he thinking?

He was so preoccupied with his thoughts that he jumped when a waiter asked, "Would you like another drink, sir?"

"Yes," King Noxy said, and then paused. After a moment's consideration, he added, "and could I get a larger mug?"

King Noxy sighed. Drake had made some good points, and he could see where it would give them an advantage, but the timing worried him. Could this be what Chada wanted? If they attacked, were they playing into Chada's hands as Eleanor had suggested? But if they succeeded it was true, they could completely turn the tide in their favor. And so, he had agreed.

But his conflicted feelings weren't worrying him so much as Drake's attitude. He was concerned Drake was becoming a bit too arrogant since he'd completed the trials.

Thinking too highly of his abilities, which never led to any good. King Noxy had had personal experience with that.

As the waiter brought a large mug of ale and set it down, King Noxy remembered when he was young and overconfident. There had been a spate of thefts in the kingdom. Noxy, only recently crowned, had taken a squad of men to investigate. However, he'd been careless. The bandits had struck. His three men had been killed easily, and King Noxy had almost died with them. If the outer guards hadn't found him bleeding to death, he would have never made it.

And so, as King Noxy took a long swig of ale, he knew that it was up to him to make sure this worked. He was the strategizer, the king. He needed to show enthusiasm, inspire them, and carry them on his shoulders if they ended up failing. Because, in the end, wasn't that what all kings were for?

*

Lieutenant Ossenna walked through the castle of the captured Kingdom of Wendil with a sense of dread. Her king would be angry. Very angry.

She remembered the ambush on Noxy and the group. She and Mondoor had sat in the trees, scanning them for the supposed swordsman Chada wanted. And he hadn't been there.

Ossenna had realized her mistake too late. Mondoor thought he knew for sure the swordsman would be there. Yes, she should have verified to make sure he was right, but she was still furious with him. Mondoor limped next to her, using his sword as support. She had bandaged his wound, but it would need a proper cleaning once they were done meeting with the king. Otherwise, the injury wasn't as bad as it could have been.

That was the only good news.

She had sent the other Titans to the barracks and the injured to be healed. Ossenna didn't know if Chada would punish them, and frankly, she wasn't too concerned about it. Right now, she was only concerned for herself, and Mondoor.

There was a very good chance they would be executed, like her predecessor, Kuhar, a few days prior. He hadn't been able to capture the boy during the attack on Wendil. Now, Ossenna had to tell Chada that they had failed to capture his target—for the second time.

Mondoor limped slowly behind her as they turned a corner and made their way down a dimly lit hallway. They stopped at the end of a passage, in front of two enormous doors. As she raised her hand to knock, the doors suddenly unlocked and swung open.

She reluctantly stepped inside, followed by Mondoor. The room, dimly lit by torches on the walls and by two fireplaces, was practically empty. Chada had cleaned out most of King Noxy's things—books, tapestries, crests, and more—once he had taken control of the kingdom.

And there, he was, in the back of the room. King Chada, in all his glory. He sat on a dark oak throne raised up on a three-step platform. He was dressed in a long, red cloak with black fur around the edges. He wore an elegant crown. His face was hidden in shadow, but Lieutenant Ossenna sensed his penetrating glare. She swallowed nervously as she sank to one knee.

He flicked a spider off of his throne and into the nearby

fireplace. Ossenna saw it disappear into the ashes. Would that be what happened to her? She hoped not.

The king turned back towards the Lieutenant and then glared at Mondoor. She saw out of her peripheral vision that Mondoor stuck his ground, his eyes staring at the floor.

Ossenna was drawn from her thoughts by Chada's voice. "I trust you have a good report, Lieutenant."

She grimaced. "Err, not exactly, Your Majesty."

"What do you mean, not exactly?" King Chada snarled.

Ossenna swallowed hard. "He wasn't there."

King Chada froze. "He what?"

"He wasn't there, Your Majesty," Ossenna said. "Just the king and some of his other companions."

"Did you figure out where he was? Where he went?" King Chada's voice was trembling with anger.

Ossenna winced. "No."

"So you let those incompetent mud-heads drive you away?" King Chada bellowed. "What is wrong with you?"

"Well—"

"No! Quiet! I do not want to hear excuses!" King Chada leaped off of his seat, drew his sword, and grabbed Ossenna by the hood. He pulled her close, held the sword up to her throat, and looked her directly in the eye. She heard Mondoor gasp.

"Ossenna," Chada whispered. "This is the second time Drake has slipped through our grasp and my patience has practically been killed along with Kuhar." Ossenna began to tremble. "You're a valuable fighter, and I prefer not to waste my anger on such talent. You have one more chance. You will keep your position, but other Titans will rise in rank above you." King Chada threw Ossenna to the ground. "Understood?"

Ossenna nodded, quickly, getting up and stepping back towards the doors.

Chada then turned his fiery gaze on Mondoor. "And you? You were one of the survivors—but the only remaining member of her personal guard, correct?"

"Yes," Mondoor replied.

"And you are the one who trailed Drake and his companions, but you did not tell Ossenna that Drake had left?"

"No, but I didn't—"

"Save your breath." King Chada held up his hand. "You were under Ossenna's command. I ordered her to target Drake. It is her fault she did not get the information she needed. Your courage, bravery, and willingness trying to track Drake to the Seaside Kingdom was commendable. For that, I'm promoting you to General."

Ossenna's mouth dropped open.

"General?" Mondoor exclaimed.

"Yes, you buffoon," King Chada's gaze hardened, as he looked to Ossenna. "Is there a problem, Lieutenant?"

Ossenna stayed completely silent, yet her emotions were roiling inside her like lava in a volcano.

King Chada turned back to Mondoor. "But listen—just like Ossenna, any more failures, and I will be furious. Not that you will see much of my fury because you'll be dead. Do you understand?"

"Yes," Mondoor squeaked.

"Good. Now leave, both of you, before I change my mind! And Mondoor," he paused for a moment, "get yourself treated. An injured general is of no use to me."

Chapter XII

Drake ducked a lightning slash from King Noxy. He then counterattacked with his own dulled blade. King Noxy parried the strike, and Drake leaped back to avoid a sneaky stab towards his chest.

It had been a few days since they'd arrived back in the town. Eleanor had created makeshift sleep spots for them in the library, though they had hardly slept because they were preparing for the attack. As Drake threw a swift sequence of strikes at Noxy, he thought about Jerome working day and night to get as many weapons as possible made and readied. All the other blacksmiths were extremely impressed with his work ethic and skill. Drake supposed Jerome's dedication in the forge was a tribute to his master.

Meanwhile, Eleanor had been working furiously at the library, writing letters and trying to find more information about the Spectacular Swordsmen. She'd also visited the mayor of the Western Town, requesting men to assist with the attack. He had taken some persuading, but had eventually agreed, while making it very clear he wanted them to return alive and well.

Drake and Noxy's swords clanged against each other. Drake tried the 'spin and slash' but was parried. He had noticed that he'd significantly improved since the trials. So much so that he found his mind drifting as he sparred with no detriment to his abilities.

"You are one skilled swordsman, Drake, but remember, there is always something new to learn," Noxy had told him firmly. "The person who thinks they know everything will meet their downfall at something they refused to learn."

King Noxy threw a hard overhead strike. Drake pushed Noxy's sword to his left, then swung his sword around and up, sending Noxy's sword spinning away from him.

"Not bad," Noxy said with a grin.

"Thanks," Drake replied.

Drake took a sip of water as Noxy retrieved his sword. They were near the gates of the Western Town where people walked in and out, periodically stopping to watch them training before hurrying on their way. As Drake looked at the gate, a hooded figure in a large, brown cloak began walking towards them.

"Umm, King Noxy?" Drake felt his hand tense. He grabbed his sword as the hooded figure drew closer and closer. He was ready to leap into action when he heard an exclamation behind him.

"Xylis! Thank goodness you're here! It's so good to see you!" Drake whirled around to see Eleanor striding towards the man, who pulled down his hood and embraced her. He had pale eyes and wavy brown hair. "How are you?" Eleanor asked. Xylis gave a small grin and gestured to the group. "Ah, yes, right. This is Xylis, a very old and dear friend," Eleanor said. "Actually, he helped me with some of the

Spectacular Swordsmen research long ago but was called off to the south for a mission. He lives down there now, but I wanted just a bit more help. So, I wrote to him. He'll be a great asset. He's a sorcerer."

"A sorcerer?" Jerome exclaimed. Drake was surprised, too. He'd never met two sorcerers in the span of a week. He doubted many people had.

"Yes," Xylis replied. "As is Eleanor."

Eleanor nodded as Leo, Isabella, and Jerome looked at her in awe. Drake smiled as he remembered Eleanor's powerful conjuring of the foes he fought during the trials.

"Well, I think it's time we come up with an exact plan of how we're going to attack Chada," Eleanor said, once the rest of the group had introduced themselves. "I've explained everything that has happened to Xylis already, so he knows what's going on. And because the army will be here soon—"

As if on cue, three guards approached. "The Seaside Kingdom army is approaching and should be here in a few hours. Once they've arrived, they'll be ready to fight."

*

King Chada sat on his throne, looking out the window into the dark sky. He knew General Mondoor was waiting, but he was too busy thinking. Mondoor's report could wait.

"Your Majesty?" General Mondoor said again. Chada twitched with annoyance. It could wait until the general had worked up enough courage to speak.

"Your—"

Chada finally turned around in his throne. "General, what did you find?"

"We received a report from our scouts—Drake and

his friends have gathered an army. They're going to attack. They've prepared the whole thing." Mondoor shifted from foot to foot, rubbing his hands together and twitching constantly.

King Chada stared at the general. Mondoor slunk back under his gaze. Chada, however, was not angry. He was quite the opposite. This was just what he'd been hoping for. He'd had a sixth sense that the group would journey to another location to enlist help. And he had been right.

"Get the Titans ready." He stood up. "Have them get into position inside the kingdom gates. When the enemy comes, they must meet them right outside the walls."

"Yes, your Majesty," General Mondoor said, running off. King Chada was then left alone. He stood for a moment, staring at the throne room doors.

This was perfect. Drake and his friends were falling for the trap. Arrogance was a fatal weakness for those with power. And it was working on Drake, just as he'd planned.

King Chada, inspired by this new intelligence, headed out of his throne room. Minutes later, he was opening the castle doors. His Titans cheered upon seeing him, and he smiled thinly in return. More of them continued to stream in, converging into an enormous sea of black spread out across the city of Wendil, his new city. His new Kingdom.

"Today is a day of justice!" King Chada yelled. They would all be able to hear him. "One of the greatest battles we will ever fight!"

"Hurrah!" the Titans replied.

"King Noxy, Wendil's king, is gathering an army. With him is Drake Philosopher, the boy we've been hunting for the last decade. They will be marching here soon. We need to be ready. We need to show them who we truly are. No mercy!"

"Hurrah!" the Titans yelled again.

"Who is with me?" King Chada yelled. Cheers echoed back.

Chada smiled broadly. Everything was happening according to plan.

And soon, Drake would be his.

*

"So, this is it," Leo said.

The group was sitting in the library. Drake couldn't believe this was finally happening. The big day. The day they would attack.

"So, one more time for the plan?" King Noxy said. The group responded with a groan. This would be the fourth time he'd reviewed it with them. Drake knew the king was nervous and that he wanted to make sure everything was under as much control as possible. But sometimes, there was a limit.

"I'll command the army, leading them into battle. Amanda, I'll need you doing your best to tend to our wounded. We don't have many healers, so there'll be a lot of work for you. I hope you can handle it."

"Of course, Noxy," Amanda said, determinedly.

"Leo and Jerome, I want you to stay close to me. I don't want you two getting into the fray too much."

"Well then, good thing I'm a great shot with a bow, right?" Leo said.

"Oh, shut up," Isabella groaned.

King Noxy gave a small smile. "Eleanor, you'll be staying

here, of course." He then turned to Drake. "As I said, you, Cyrus, Isabella and Xylis will have the most important job. You will sneak inside the castle, using the secret entrance on the north side that leads to the dungeons. After letting out the captured citizens of Wendil, if there are any, you can target Chada." He sighed. "Drake and Isabella, are you sure you don't want me to go in your place?"

Drake looked at him firmly. "I have to do this, King Noxy. He's after me. I want to face him."

"Don't even try to dissuade me," Isabella said. She had volunteered to go with Drake and would not back down, which touched him greatly. He was glad that she would stick with him through this, even though it was dangerous, and they hadn't known each other for very long.

King Noxy looked around at the others. "I think that is all. Gather your belongings. We'll meet in the town square in half an hour."

The group hastily stood up and began embracing one other. It would be the last time they would be together until after the battle. Drake did not let himself think what their reunion might look like. He wouldn't dare dwell on the idea that some of them might not be there. Eleanor looked down at Drake with a friendly smile and he gave her a much stronger hug than he intended.

"Thank you," Drake said.

Eleanor patted him on the back. "Of course, Drake." As he walked away, she put a hand on his shoulder. "Wait a moment."

"What is it?"

"I want you to remember something," she said. "Chada is a very sly and sneaky man. He's a rat, if you will."

"What does that mean?"

"I suspect he will think he can bait you with promises, threats, or taunts. I want you to remember my words. He always has a bigger picture in his head. I don't ever want you to fall for his gimmicks, okay? In the end, they're all simply words. Understand?"

"Yes," Drake said. He was definitely not planning to let Chada get into his head.

"Good," Eleanor replied. "Now, I think there's a battle you need to prepare for."

With one last smile, Drake strode out of the library. He could sense in the distance, his fallen home of Wendil.

Soon, it would be theirs again.

Chapter XIII

The armies of the Seaside kingdom and the reinforcements from the Western Town were readying for battle in the forest on the edge of the plain surrounding the Kingdom of Wendil. Drake could see Wendil from where he stood, and, clenching his fists with anger, spotted a few Titans on the walls.

"Today, we are here to fight evil itself!" King Noxy cried. "In and outside those walls are the evil Titans, and the mastermind behind it all, King Chada. We are here to defeat them. You all know the plan. Fight for your lives, my friends. And I wish you all luck."

"Hurrah!" the soldiers yelled.

"For glory, for the people, and for freedom!" King Noxy shouted, and the soldiers echoed him.

The army then saddled up their horses, drew their blades, and organized their belts. Before King Noxy gave the signal to charge, he rode up to Drake. "Be careful," he said, "and come back as soon as possible. Okay?"

"Yes," Drake replied.

King Noxy smiled. "I have faith in you Drake. Don't think I was reluctant to do this because I doubt you. You are a special and capable young man—but please, stay that way, in one piece."

Drake took a deep breath, drew his sword, and tried not to let his nerves get to him. "Thanks. I will."

As King Noxy turned back to survey the army, Drake's mind drifted back to the battle. He needed to end this, and fast. And he had to watch out for Cyrus, Xylis, and Isabella. Protect them at all costs. His new friends would not meet the same fate of his master, whatever that was.

His mind flashed back to the trials. He remembered moving in slow motion, cutting up the magically conjured foes, and that inspired him.

He was ready for this. This was what he was made for. This was his destiny.

Then, the battle horn sounded.

The horses stormed out of the forest, Drake on one of them. The archers followed, stopping at edge of the forest to launch their arrows.

Another battle horn sounded in answer to their own, and a sea of Titans burst out of Wendil's gates and locked into the phalanx position. Drake felt a pang of concern. They didn't seem to be too surprised by the attack. Perhaps Chada's scouts had notified the king of their preparations. Yet King Noxy barely seemed fazed.

"We need to disrupt their phalanx so the archers can get some hits in there and the main army unit can overrun them," he yelled.

Drake looked out among the Titans, watching the charging army with a mixture of anger and determination in their eyes. Drake felt his weight shifting under the galloping horse as he continued to ride towards the sea of black ahead of him.

And though they were in a battle, a gruesome thing, he could not help feeling free and exhilarated. He'd never felt like this before, let alone been in charge of his own squad.

He was taking back his kingdom.

When they were halfway to the Titans, Drake steered his horse to the left, away from the army. Xylis, Isabella, and Cyrus followed. They went very wide around the phalanx and sped to the wall where King Noxy had said there was a secret entrance. But some Titans spotted their move and rode in front to block their path.

This was it.

The battle was beginning.

And now there was no choice but to fight.

Drake rode at one Titan, then leaped off his horse and onto the ground—it was easier to maneuver that way. After this, he cut down the Titan in three strokes, and turned to the next. They clashed swords, however, the Titan, using a move Drake had never seen before, rotated his sword and disarmed him. Drake knew he had to act fast, so he threw a wild punch.

CRACK!

He broke the Titan's nose and knocked him out. Drake kicked another Titan aside and bounding towards his sword, scooped up his weapon and cut down another three. He was just standing up when—

"Drake!" a voice squealed from the left as something barreled into him. He heard a swish of metal and his vision spun as he tumbled to the ground: He saw the brown dirt, green trees, blue sky, flowing auburn hair...

Drake braced against his fall and recovering his footing realized that the something that had barreled into him was a person. Isabella! He felt an extreme rush of gratitude, realizing he probably would have died if she hadn't done that.

"Well…I, um…thanks…" He trailed off.

"Don't mention it," she replied, breathlessly.

The group then jumped back on their horses and raced towards the sidewall. As they dismounted Cyrus said, "We have to find the Wendil crest. After we get in, we'll free the prisoners and then attack King Chada."

The four began to search frantically, kicking up dirt and grass. Drake tried pressing the walls, looking near plant roots, but had no luck. He was just rising when he heard a victorious shout.

"Hey look! I found it!" Xylis was pointing at the wall. Cyrus, Isabella, and Drake ran over to the sorcerer, who pressed a line of stones engraved with a crown around a shining golden sword, outlined by a shield: the crest of Wendil. Drake assumed some kind of spell made the stones separate revealing a passage and a stairway leading down into the depths of the earth. It was pitch black.

"Ready?" Drake asked the others.

Isabella nodded.

"I'll take the rear," Xylis said.

Cyrus struck a light and lit a torch he'd been carrying in his belt, then he took the lead down the stairs.

The passage was very worn, dusty and grimy. Drake guessed it hadn't been used for years. Soon, the stairs leveled out and a passage led them to a large hallway, lined with bars and cell doors.

"The dungeon." Drake shivered with fright as they walked past the cells, afraid Titans were waiting in ambush. Water dripped from the ceiling, and every time he heard a loud noise he jumped. They needed to find a way out of the dungeon and up to the main part of the castle, so they could then travel to the throne room. The problem was, Drake had rarely been down here. He knew the way, but it would take him a moment to get his bearings.

And that's when he heard the voice.

"Help me."

"What was that?" Drake cautiously walked towards a nearby cell, his sword drawn. Maybe it was a Titan? It was a trap, and they were trying to lure him somewhere? His breath sounded too loud. Everything sounded loud. Blood pounded in his ears. He took one more step and very slowly peered through the bars in the door. He almost fell over with shock. There, in the cell, was a weary and filthy Sahara.

Sahara was alive!

His master!

He was alive!

"Sahara!" Drake wanted to tackle him in a hug, but the cell door was locked, and there was no way in. Sahara's face lit up with a weak smile.

"How do we get him out?" Cyrus asked.

"I can use my sorcery," Xylis said. "It'll only take a second." He whispered some kind of phrase. A wisp of light swirled into the keyhole. The door unlocked, swung open and Sahara walked out in shock.

"He's a—" he said, pointing to Xylis.

"Don't worry. We'll explain everything later," Cyrus said. "Xylis, you should probably free all the other prisoners. There's more here, right…Sahara?"

Drake's master didn't question the identity of his new companions, but simply nodded. "Yes. All along this floor."

"On it," Xylis replied. As he ran down the hallway, he unlocked the doors and directed the prisoners towards the secret stairs ready to join the battle against the Titans.

In the meantime, Drake hugged Sahara, and said the words that he'd wanted to say ever since he had found out about his destiny.

"I'm sorry. About the night before the attack, and—"

"Drake." Sahara patted him on the back. "Don't worry. All I care about is that you're safe. It's all water under the bridge."

Drake nodded, relieved.

"And I'm sorry for my outburst. It was unexpected, and I was exhausted," Sahara said.

"Forgiven." Master and apprentice hugged once more. Drake sank into it, feeling so elated that his master was alive and back with him. He could not even begin to express his gratitude.

He pulled away, however, when he heard the clash of swords, an explosion, and then saw Xylis burst through a cloud of smoke charging towards them. "We have company!"

Suddenly, Titans burst through the remaining smoke. "Get them!"

Drake dashed to the stairs, quickly followed by the others.

"I'll try to hold them off!" Sahara yelled, turning back around.

"No! I've already lost you once. I'm not going to lose you again!" Drake screamed.

"The most important thing is getting you to King Chada so you can confront him. Besides, I have some tricks up my sleeve," Sahara said.

"But—"

"No buts," Sahara said, and Drake let Xylis pull him away. He sneaked one quick glance behind him to see Sahara fighting four guards. Worry tightened its grip on him, but then, he felt someone squeeze his hand.

"He'll be okay," Isabella said, and something in her voice made Drake believe her. They ran on, but the guards were gaining on them. As they exited the dungeon, Cyrus stopped and took a stance at the door. "I'll deal with these! Keep going!"

Drake opened his mouth then closed it again, because he knew there was no arguing. His friends were risking their lives for him and there was nothing he could do about it. Which made him all the more angry. This is why he did not want help, nor did he need it. He had never wanted this to happen.

They raced down the corridor and turned a corner to find Titans blocking the end of it. They continued to run turning up a stairway ahead. When they reached the top, they saw a large archway leading into the throne room. The three ran inside and skidded to a halt. The large doors slammed behind them.

It took a moment to adjust to the light. The room was lit only by two fires burning on either side of the room, the flames making dancing shadows on the walls. Then they heard a voice. A man sat on a throne in the back of the room. He wore a red cloak with a black fur lining, and black boots. A golden crown stopped his black hair from falling into his eyes.

"Hello, Drake. I've been expecting you."

Drake's eyes darted around the room, to find four Titans advancing from the shadows. The swordsman waited until they were only a small distance away before he leaped at the first and struck him down with a quick blow to the neck. He then spun around and sliced the second in the arm and stabbed his sword through her abdomen. Isabella whipped out a dagger and attacked the third Titan, stabbing him in the heart, while Xylis cast a glowing magical shield in front of Drake as a Titan tried to attack him. The Titan rebounded on the shield, smashing into the wall and falling to the ground, crawling weakly into the corner of the room to hide.

The man on the throne glanced at the Titans, a look of disgust passing over his face, and then looked back at Isabella, Xylis and Drake. He raised his eyebrows. "Impressive," King Chada said.

Drake had no words. This man was completely evil. Full of malice and jealousy. And the lives he'd cost, searching for the Spectacular Swordsmen Line…It was horrendous.

His piercing brown eyes stared into Drake's, daring him to make a move.

"What do you want?" Drake asked finally.

"Ha!" King Chada exclaimed. "You think I would tell you?"

"Just stop this nonsense," Drake demanded.

"And if I don't?"

Drake said nothing. Instead, he ran at King Chada his sword drawn to strike, but he realized too late what the king had in mind. Chada sat up with lightning speed, drew his sword, blocked Drake's strike and knocked him straight to the floor.

"Since you are so great, Spectacular Swordsman, why don't we settle this with a duel?"

Chapter XIV

As King Noxy scanned the battlefield, he saw his own forces clashing with the sea of black that was the Titans. He could discern no definite winner or loser, which wasn't a bad thing. It meant that the Seaside Kingdom army was holding its own. King Noxy only hoped it could do so long enough for Drake and the rest of the small squad to enter the castle and ambush Chada.

Then, a dagger flew right by him, and his horse reared up in panic. King Noxy grabbed the reins and yanked them back, as he turned to where the dagger had come from. He growled to himself. He recognized the man he had dueled with in the grove of trees when he was returning from the Seaside Kingdom during the Titan ambush. The man who'd injured him. Except now, the man's leg seemed healed, and the Titan had multiple purple squares upon his uniform, and was wearing an intricate purple helmet, which seemingly marked him as a general.

He'd been promoted.

The king leapt off his horse as the Titan began to run towards him. Noxy knew that the Titan was here for revenge, as he'd given the general a wound to remember. The king readied his sword, and as the Titan came in with an elaborate spinning slash, Noxy parried with lightning speed, and the battle had begun.

Noxy tried a blow to the legs, but the Titan blocked his strike and then stabbed inward. Noxy sucked in his stomach and twisted to his left. Then he tried to catch the Titan off guard with a stab of his own. It was to no avail.

The fight continued. Strike after counter, after parry, after slash and repeat. Noxy felt sweat beading on his forehead as he slammed his sword down onto the general's creating an enormous clang. He then desperately unleashed a series of swings at the Titan, but still could not penetrate the general's powerful defense.

The two continued to match each other skill for skill for what seemed like hours. They both found a few openings. King Noxy had blood on his arm and leg. The general had a cut near his neck and on his shoulder. Blood trickled from a tear in his pant leg. King Noxy was completely exhausted, and knowing he couldn't keep it up much longer, decided to step up his game. He needed to end the battle, now.

The Titan swung right at the king's head, and so Noxy ducked, slicing the general's leg, reopening the Titan's original wound. The general howled in pain. He kicked Noxy to the ground with his boot and five Titans rushed in to converge on the king. Noxy fought them off, swinging his sword, sticking then blocking, striking then parrying, until they were all dead at his feet.

But the general was now nowhere to be seen. And King Noxy was too exhausted to look for him, so he climbed on his horse and rode through the battlefield. As he scanned left and right, he saw his soldiers slowly falling to the Titans. The Titans' great numbers were overwhelming them, and they were losing now. This wasn't good. Especially since Xylis, Cyrus, Drake, and Isabella hadn't returned. Where were they?

He rode his horse all the way back to Jerome and Leo.

"I'm ready to call a retreat. We're losing men. It seems reinforcements have come. The Titans are being constantly replenished. More of our soldiers have begun to fall. They disappeared around the outer wall protecting the castle, and I haven't seen them since," King Noxy said. It was as if his earlier worries were coming true.

No. He couldn't think like that. There was still hope.

"What about Amanda?" Jerome asked.

"She's healing the injured with her herbs," King Noxy said, "but she can't keep up."

"But Cyrus, Drake, Xylis and my sister are still in the castle, aren't they? What about them?"

Noxy didn't answer. He had a plan B. But he would only use it if he had to. He would wait, for now…and for as long as he could.

*

Drake pushed himself to his feet and leapt at Chada once more. He felt himself shake slightly, from fear and fury, as their swords clashed in a burst of strikes. Isabella raced up next to him to help and Sahara knocked King Chada back with a strong punch.

As Chada rose to his feet, Sahara shouted, "Keep your eyes on him. Don't look away for a second."

Drake nodded, and kept his eyes trained on Chada as

he, Isabella, Sahara, and Xylis closed in on the king. Drake pointed his sword and readied himself to end the fight, to end the madness, to end everything.

But his arm was shaking.

And when King Chada saw that, he smiled. "Ah, Drake. My friend. Do you really want to kill me? You're an innocent kid. Do you want a reputation as a murderer?" He pointed at the sword in Drake's hand. Drake's eyes slowly traveled to the weapon. Did he want to kill Chada? No. He didn't want to be known as 'the kid who killed a king,' even if the king was rotten. He wanted to be a hero.

At that precise moment, Eleanor's words popped into Drake's mind: "But most of all, he will twist and manipulate your emotions. Never fall for it."

But it was already too late.

Before Drake knew it, he was on the floor, a dagger lying next to him. Sahara and Chada were brawling, and metal clangs echoed in the throne room. Xylis was steadying himself against the wall with Isabella helping him. A fresh cut ran across his cheek. And it took Drake a moment to realize what had happened. Had Chada just done all that? In the span of a second?

Xylis cast a shield, sizzling with energy, which divided the room in half. "He's too powerful. We're losing this battle. I'll hold him off."

"But—"

"You heard me!" Xylis yelled. "My job was to help you. That is what I am doing, like it or not."

Drake hesitated, but Isabella pulled him to his feet.

"Drake!" Xylis bellowed. "Go!"

Isabella gave one strong tug and dragged him away from

the fight. As they fled the scene, Xylis held Chada back with his shield, allowing Sahara to disengage and join them. But no sooner had they all exited the throne room, there was a large explosion. The doors were blown apart, revealing the collapsing room. Bricks and rocks crashed down from the walls and ceiling. Drake glimpsed Chada running behind his throne for cover, but Xylis was hit by a large piece of rock. He disappeared beneath the rubble.

"Come on, let's go!" Isabella pulled his arm again. As the trio ran from pursuing Titans, trying to find Cyrus, Drake felt like he was going to vomit. He prayed Xylis was still alive.

But even if he was alive, he was still captured by Chada.

*

King Noxy became more worried as each minute passed without any sign of Drake. He saw more and more of his soldiers perish and realized they couldn't win. This was a mistake. He should have known. Why hadn't he listened to himself? Why?

King Noxy looked toward the castle, his stomach becoming queasy. Drake and the strike team needed to be here. Otherwise…

Thank Lyzix! King Noxy silently rejoiced as he saw Drake, Isabella, Sahara, and Cyrus sprinting towards him. His heart swelled with joy. Sahara was alive, and now he was free—but then he realized Xylis wasn't with them. Where could he be? Was he okay? As much as he hated it, there was no time to worry about that now. He had other pressing matters.

"Retreat!" he shouted at the top of his lungs. "To the Western Town!"

Immediately everyone in Noxy's makeshift army stormed away from the battle. A Titan appeared at the edge of the gates on a horse.

"After them! Don't let them escape!" he bellowed.

Five Titans rode in Drake's direction. King Noxy pulled his horse around and waited, glancing back at Drake and the others every few seconds. He needed to make sure they escaped.

King Noxy would do whatever it took to protect the kid. Anything.

He just hoped anything would be enough.

*

Drake glanced behind him and saw five Titans in pursuit. Then he looked ahead to see the forest and King Noxy waiting for them.

"We're going to make it!" he shouted to his friends and sped up. "Come on!"

As Drake rode closer and closer, he was filled with hope. If they made it to the forest, they could lose the Titans in the trees, and though they'd lost the battle, they would be able to escape. But if they didn't make it…

Their mission would be a complete failure.

Suddenly, pain erupted in Drake's back. As he tumbled to the ground, he heard people yelling his name, and the thundering of horses in his ears. He lifted his face from the dirt, to find Isabella and Sahara shaking and dragging him, and Cyrus and King Noxy looking apprehensively behind them.

Drake slowly rose to his knees then doubled over. The pain was too much. He couldn't move. "Go on," he croaked.

"Nonsense! We can't leave you here!" Isabella said.

"Yes, you can, and you will," Drake said.

"Drake, we're not leaving you," Sahara said, "Now get up—"

"Go!" Drake bellowed, clutching his shoulder blade where the pain was exploding. It seemed as if an arrow had pierced him. Blood rushed to his head while the thundering of the hooves was growing louder. "Leave me here. Xylis is as good as captured. We don't need any more." He could see tears welling up in Isabella's eyes, and Sahara's anger bubbling, but he pushed them away. "Just go!"

Drake could see their trepidation, but as the deafening sounds of horses filled his ears, Sahara and Isabella ran off. King Noxy and Cyrus galloped into the forest on their horses, and with an incredible burst of speed, the two others followed on foot.

Drake closed his eyes, trying to fight the pain. Next thing he knew a Titan was crouching down in front of him, grinning evilly. "King Chada will be pleased," the Titan said. "Tie him up."

Drake felt a hard blow to the head. He hit the dirt and breathed in the scent of the earth.

And then he blacked out.

*

"Leave us," King Chada ordered his guards. Both gave a quick salute and positioned themselves in the passageway as the doors banged shut.

Drake sat up groggily and looked around. His sword and extra weapons were gone. His hands were tied with a rope. He was in Wendil's throne room, and on the large throne sat the man that he hated with all his might. And maybe feared with all his might, too.

Then it all came back to him. The skirmish in the throne room. Their escape. Telling the others to run. Being knocked unconscious.

"Why? Why do you want the Spectacular Swordsman? Why do you want me?" Drake asked. His calm nature wasn't going to last long. Drake was practically a ticking time bomb.

"Ah, is that really what you want to know?" King Chada asked. "Perhaps we shall save that for another day. After all, it does involve you. But there is much more taking place here. Let me ask you a question. Do you trust your friends?"

Drake was taken aback. Though he didn't completely expect Chada to answer his question, he hadn't expected such an abrupt change of topic. He felt slightly uneasy. "Of course. Why?"

"Ah, my boy, you do not understand what you're doing. This—" He gestured to Drake and himself. "This is the future."

"You think I'll join you? Have you gone mad?"

King Chada smirked. "I'm not insane. Merely clever. And insightful. You have a big heart. Unfortunately, your friends aren't built the same way as you."

Drake was now completely lost in the conversation.

"They're using you, Drake. Don't you see? The two thieves: Isabella and Leo—they want prestige. Wealth. You've given them that. And that skeleton of an apothecary? She wants to be respected. You've given her that. Xylis wants to please his master and friend, Eleanor. And Cyrus wants to be reunited with King Noxy. Even your best friend Jerome, and King Noxy, they just want their homes back. They're not helping you. It's all about them."

"What do you mean? You're…you're lying!"

"Am I? You and I could make a great team. We could combine our powers. You would obtain wealth and prestige that is unimaginable."

"I'll never join you," Drake snarled.

"I never thought I'd witness you being so utterly wrong, Drake." Chada sighed and shook his head. "Eleanor has been keeping things from you all along."

"What do you mean?" Drake asked.

"Did she ever mention your parents? I mean… you must be curious, no? If you were part of the Spectacular Swordsmen line, they were too, right?"

"You don't know anything about my parents," Drake shouted.

"That's where you are wrong," King Chada said calmly. "I killed them."

"No, that's a lie!" Drake screamed.

"Silence!" King Chada interrupted. "I killed both of them. And Eleanor was there. She saw it happen. But she didn't do anything. She just ran. Want to know why? She was afraid the same thing would happen to her."

Drake could not believe what he was hearing. Why hadn't Eleanor told him? And she was there? He was being left in the dark. Was Chada trying to deceive him? Drake wanted to believe it was all a lie, but there was truth in the kings' words. Drake sensed it.

He couldn't do anything about his mother or father, nor anything about his friends right now. But there was one thing he could do: resist Chada.

"I'll never join you. You can't break me. I will resist," he said. "My friends are with me, no matter what you say."

"With that attitude, you'll perish just like your parents." Chada laughed. "You are a fool!"

Drake felt blood rush to his head. Enough already! He was going to kill this man.

He leapt for the throne, his hands still tied behind his back, only to be stopped by the slash of a sword. His own blood splattered across the ground. King Chada had cut his chest. Drake felt lightheaded, and he fell forward onto the ground.

"Guards! Take him to the dungeon." King Chada stood over him, a triumphant look on his face. Drake heard the throne room doors open. Arms lifted him by the shoulders and began dragging him away.

"You're lucky I still want you, Drake. Anybody else in this situation would be dead right now." The throne room doors slammed shut.

The guards took the familiar passageway, descended the steps to the very bottom floor, opened a cell door, and locked Drake inside. He rolled forward onto his knees, gasped for breath and clutched his chest. The pain was unbearable, but not as unbearable as his mental anguish. Suddenly, the reality of everything that had happened overwhelmed him. He had thought he was great, but he wasn't. The attack had been his idea. He had led the group to disaster.

He had failed.

He had failed everyone who was close to him.

It was entirely his fault.

Chapter XV

Several days had passed since the battle for Wendil. The battle they had lost.

Light rain pattered as a campfire crackled in the shelter of towering trees. King Noxy was seated warming his hands with Jerome, Cyrus, and Leo. During the retreat, he had lost Amanda, Isabella, and Sahara, and didn't have a clue where they were. On top of that, he had no idea where the rest of the army was. He'd ridden for days, in all different directions, looking for his men and allies, but had found none. According to Cyrus, Xylis had been injured and probably captured. Worst of all, Drake had been taken as well. The king had no idea how to save any of them.

This mess was his fault. He should never have let Drake talk him into this idea. Now they were set back even further than when they had begun.

"We need to figure out how to rescue Xylis and Drake, and how to get out of this mess." Jerome's voice cut through King Noxy's thoughts like a sword.

"How?" Leo asked. "It's hopeless."

Noxy sighed. It had been like this for days. Constantly

second guessing what to do, hiding from Chada who was ready to snuff out the very small amount of fight they still had left. They were short on time, being hunted by the Titans and he had no solutions. "We need to rest," he said, as he had done many times now. There was no need to add exhaustion to the list of things against them. "We'll discuss the plan in the morning."

"But—" Leo protested.

"Sleep!" Cyrus ordered.

King Noxy nodded his thanks to Cyrus, swirled the bucket of water they'd filled earlier at the river, took some in his cupped hands, and drank. He looked at his companions once more before he went to sleep, sure that their hope had dissipated.

He had promised himself in the tavern that it was his job to help them regain their footing, making them believe in themselves just as much as they had before. His job to keep their hopes alive. But that was before they lost the battle. It was hard, especially when he didn't have much hope himself.

This dark thought filled his mind as he settled on the damp ground, rain pattering on the leaves above, the campfire slowly dying away.

*

Drake stood on the slanted roof of a castle tower, an enormous abyss below him. Nothing dwelled down there except darkness and evil.

"Hello, Drake." King Chada circled him. "How nice to see you again."

Drake looked away, trying to block Chada's taunts.

"Drake, you know what you want. I know you'll snap. Why not save yourself some time? Come, impale me with your sword. It must be easy for a Spectacular Swordsman like yourself." Chada sneered.

Drake gritted his teeth. He needed to resist.

"This is exactly what your parents did. They waited and waited, until I finally killed them."

Drake snapped. He charged the king, screaming as Chada gave one more smirk and sliced Drake's chest. Drake tripped. Pain exploded in his body and, before he knew it, he was falling from the roof into the darkness below…

He sat up, breathing heavily. He looked around, but his heart slowed as he realized he was still in his cell. It was only a dream. Like all the others.

Drake had sat in his dirty old cell for days, and every night he'd have that dream, or one similar. When awake, he had been searching for ways to escape, but it was impossible to open the cell door and break out. He had scoured the walls for loose bricks but only found an old rusty water pipe. He had whispered through it every day, but no one responded. He had almost lost hope.

Drake was stuck down here because of his own mistake. He'd had the idea to attack Chada too early. Now Chada was progressing onto who knows what. Drake barely knew anything about his destiny, and the Spectacular Swordsmen line, and now because of the failed attack, he was set back even further.

But that wasn't even the worst of it.

The truth that Chada had revealed to him was astonishing. It couldn't possibly be true. Or could it? Deep down in Drake's heart, he knew that it was. King Chada had killed his parents. And Eleanor had lied to him about it. On multiple occasions.

He was so lost and confused. She'd said that he'd been kept safely concealed. That's why he hadn't died like his other relatives and the random victims Chada had hunted down. But she'd never mentioned anything about his parents. The fact that she'd kept something from him made him feel betrayed, alone, and…

Enraged.

And now, because of this, he was stuck in his own head with this recurring, foolish dream.

Drake punched the wall in anger, and his knuckles began to shake and bleed as he screamed. His voice echoed across the dungeon as all the rage that had been building up erupted from him. He made so much noise that one of the Titans opened the door and angled his spear. "If you don't shut your mouth, I'll make sure you get a good beating next time you visit the king."

Drake didn't listen. He lunged at the guard, but the Titan sidestepped him. Drake felt the spear tip slice his forehead as a boot slammed into his stomach. He collapsed to the floor gripping his side. The last thing he saw was the Titan slicing the spear across his chest.

Right where Chada had already cut him.

Blood blurred his vision, and he slumped against the wall, his chest convulsing. Then, everything went black.

*

Noxy led the small caravan across the grassland, the strands swaying in the wind and brushing up against his cloak.

"Are we going anywhere in particular?" Leo asked.

"I want to try and make the most of where we are now," Noxy said. "There is a kingdom near here. Oldor. I am hoping that some of the army fled there."

As they continued, Cyrus walked up next to Noxy, lowering his voice. "Are you sure about this? You told me you haven't done business with Oldor since Brinus passed."

"And?" Noxy prompted.

"And that this new king could be as rotten as Chada," Cyrus said.

"I know. But if there is the smallest chance the army came here, then we need to check."

"And if they didn't?"

"Then we'll ask for help," Noxy replied.

Cyrus assumed a bewildered and amused expression. "Then you'd better hope this new king is good."

It was only when they finally approached the Kingdom of Oldor that Noxy grew anxious. Cyrus was right, this new king definitely needed to be upstanding. Otherwise, they could find themselves in a whole new form of danger and hopelessness.

They arrived at the gates and a guard above yelled down at them. "Freeze in the name of the Kingdom of Oldor! Do not make any sudden movements."

There were no other travelers that Noxy could see and it seemed a bit excessive. He could only assume because of the attack on Wendil, the king had strengthened his safety precautions.

The guard, followed by an entourage, strode to meet them. "Who are you? What is your business here? Do you have travel documents?"

"I am King Noxy, ruler of Wendil. Three weeks ago,

perhaps more, Wendil was attacked. We tried to take it back but failed. King Chada is now in charge. I have a few of my friends and fellow fighters with me."

The guard nodded. "What is your business?"

King Noxy considered for a moment. What they needed was some backup, extra soldiers, and a place to regroup. "We require an audience with your king."

The guard narrowed his eyes. "I see. There will be extra security."

King Noxy nodded. "Of course."

The king, Jerome, Leo, and Cyrus were escorted into the gates by three guards. King Noxy looked at the castle looming ahead of them, and once more silently prayed that this king was good. Brinus had been a great man, but that didn't mean his heir was the same.

As the group made their way through the castle, King Noxy could think of only one word to describe it: huge. After five changes in direction, King Noxy had completely lost all sense of where they were. He started to worry that the guards would throw them in the dungeons or hold them hostage. It was not at all an appealing image.

Finally, the guards brought them to a set of enormous riveted wooden doors, with large, rusty iron hinges and locks. They wrenched the doors open and accompanied Noxy Jerome and Cyrus into a room lit by large, arched windows tipped with a golden outline. In the center sat a man on a throne on a pedestal. A man and woman in armor, with swords and spears, were positioned on either side of him and next to him stood a man in a long orange cloak and hood.

Placed regularly around the walls were statues of men

in armor and ladies with long, flowing dresses. A fireplace crackled in one corner, and yellow carpets covered the floor.

"Greetings," the king said. "Now, please tell me why you've interrupted my meeting."

"King Noxy of Wendil." Noxy gave a quick bow. "We apologize for any inconvenience but have come in humble need of assistance."

"King Solomon." His deep, booming voice echoed through the throne room. "Now, King Noxy of Wendil, what exactly do you need?"

King Noxy summarized King Chada's attack, their journey to recruit an army, and their failed retake of Wendil. He did not mention anything about Drake and the Spectacular Swordsmen. Better to keep that to themselves.

By the end of the story, King Solomon was nodding thoughtfully. "Guards—leave us! Olinic, Hythra, you may stay. Thoro, you as well. Hythra and Olinic are my personal bodyguards," he explained. "And Thoro is my right-hand man. He is gifted in the art of sorcery."

King Noxy nodded. The two guards saluted while Thoro gave a short, curt bow. Noxy briefly caught sight of Jerome and Leo in a vague state of shock, murmuring about Thoro. King Noxy understood. Sorcery wasn't spoken of much in Lyzix.

There was a moment of silence until King Noxy said, "I heard about Brinus, of course." Solomon's face dropped. "I'm very sorry. He was an amazing man and king."

"Thank you, Noxy," Solomon said. "Any friend of Brinus is a friend of mine. You have my attention. How can I help?"

King Noxy silently rejoiced. King Solomon appeared

to be friendly. He didn't want to let his hopes run away with him, only to be squashed, but…they were getting somewhere. "I need to get to the Western Town as quickly as possible."

Solomon nodded. "It is about a two and a half days' journey on horseback. That is, if you travel most of the night as well."

King Noxy cringed. Every day they travelled was an extra day Drake and Xylis had to survive as prisoners of Chada. "Have any of your townsfolk seen soldiers bearing Seaside Kingdom or Sky Kingdom emblems?"

Solomon shook his head. "I've had no reports, I'm sorry. Is this the army that has scattered?"

"Yes," Cyrus chimed in. King Noxy had almost forgotten his friends were with him.

"We shall keep an eye out for them," Solomon said. "Is there anything else?"

"Yes," King Noxy said. "We need more soldiers"

Solomon sighed. "Noxy, if I could I would supply them, but there has been word of scouts spotted on the outskirts of the kingdom. I must keep my men for my own defense."

King Noxy nodded. "I understand."

"Wait," King Solomon said. "You said that your sorcerer is trapped, along with the swordsman apprentice, correct?"

"Yes," King Noxy replied.

"Well, I cannot give you my men, but I assume you're going to conduct a rescue soon? I can send Thoro to help. His sorcery will speed your progress." The sorcerer nodded, stepped down from the pedestal, and shook King Noxy's hand. "Once you're finished with the rescue, send him back," Solomon said.

"We are truly grateful," King Noxy nodded. "Thank you."

Solomon gave a thin smile. "Good luck!" And the group was escorted out of the throne room by Thoro.

The way out of the castle felt shorter. Soon they were walking through the streets, and ahead of them were the gates.

"I believe the guards took your horses to the stables. I'll fetch them. Wait here." Thoro strode off.

"Hey," Cyrus said to King Noxy, "those scouts Solomon is talking about…they could be Titans. I should probably take a look. Just in case."

"Okay," King Noxy said. "But be quick. And careful."

"I will." Cyrus bounded off towards the castle wall.

Meanwhile, King Noxy glanced up at the sun as the clouds slowly parted. He shielded his eyes with his arm and smiled. This was it. They were heading back.

They now had a chance.

Chapter XVI

Drake was a mess. Since his outburst and attack on the Titan, he had been chained to the wall. Now he could barely move around his cell: the chains weren't long enough. His hair was matted and hanging partly over his face. There were scratches and bruises all over him, and his clothes were torn and messy. The cut from the spear jab on his forehead had still not healed and, since the Titan had cut him in the same place as Chada, he was in terrible pain. Dried blood coated the stab wound, and Drake knew that even when it was healed, he would have a long scar across his chest. A reminder of this time. Of his helplessness.

Helplessness. It was the worst feeling he could imagine. Drake leaned against the back wall with a grimace as the door of the cell creaked open, and in walked a Titan. He had a feeling it was the same one who'd given him the scar. Hot anger boiled inside him, but he couldn't fight even if he wanted to. He would collapse in pain in a second.

The Titan dropped a piece of salty meat and some water on the ground, slamming the cold, iron door behind him without a word. Drake picked up the meat and took a bite.

He took a sip of water, soothing his dry mouth, and leaned back against the wall.

He was just drinking the rest of the water when he heard a voice. He was so surprised the water erupted from his mouth and sprayed across the cell. He sat up slowly, to avoid pain, but he was elated. He looked to his left and right. Of course, no one was there. He didn't have a cell-mate. So where was the voice coming from?

"Drake…Drake?"

Drake looked at the rusty water pipe. That was it! There must be someone on the other side. Someone to speak to. Someone to plot with.

"Drake. It's Xylis!" This time the words were clearer.

Drake's heart rushed in excitement. Xylis! He leaned in and whispered, "I'm here."

"Thank goodness," Xylis said. "Everything okay over there?"

"Yes. What about you?" Drake replied. This was amazing.

"Much better now that we have a way to communicate. They moved me into this cell last night after an audience with Chada."

"What happened? Did it go okay?" Drake asked.

"No. He tried to recruit me, and when I refused, he tried to squeeze the location of the group from me. However, he was surprisingly forgiving. Barely interrogated me at all. When I told him I would never reveal the information, he moved me to this cell. I don't know why."

"Hmm," Drake said. That was strange. Did Chada know about the pipes? Was he trying to set Xylis and Drake up so he could steal the information instead?

No. It had only been a few weeks since King Chada

had taken over the castle. He wouldn't know about these insignificant pipes in a dungeon he had barely used.

"Have you any idea how to get out, because I don't?" Drake said.

"No. Sorcery is not allowed to be used offensively, for direct attacks. I can't do a blasted thing," Xylis replied. "We just have to wait and hope for the group to rescue us before it's too late. But we do have that secret entrance that leads out to the north side."

"Yeah, we do," Drake agreed, but then he heard footsteps. He dropped his voice to a whisper. "Xylis, someone's coming. We'll talk later." The sorcerer fell silent.

A Titan entered Drake's cell. "What's going on?" Drake could see his eyes darting around the room. "I thought I heard—"

"Talking to myself." Drake shrugged.

"Well, you'd better watch out. I may request to have you transferred. And you'll have another fun session with the king…"

"Or," said another voice, "we can have that session now."

Drake felt his anger boil as Chada entered the cell behind the Titan. Two other guards followed. He sneered at Drake. "Thank you for telling me about that secret entrance. Now I know how you snuck in during your little failed attack. I shall have it sealed up right away."

Drake cursed himself under his breath. King Chada had set them up! How could he have been so stupid?

The two guards marched Drake to the throne room, poking him in the back with a spear whenever he slowed. By the time they arrived, Drake felt like his back was a piece of honeycomb. Dried blood caked to his shirt and skin, making it itch like crazy. They threw him down on the floor as Chada took his place on the throne with that annoying sneer.

"So, Drake, I think it's time to bring up the subject of your friends again. Where are they? Tell me, and they'll be spared. If you don't tell me, I'll find them anyway and kill them."

Drake shook his head.

"I knew that was coming. And I'm prepared. Bring him in!" King Chada called.

General Mondoor and five Titans walked in, two of the guards dragging an exhausted Xylis behind them. Drake felt bile rise to his throat. Xylis was cut and bruised all over, and his clothes were torn. He was struggling to get out of the Titans' grip, but that only made them more irritated. They threw him on the ground. General Mondoor drew a knife from his pocket, knelt down, and pressed it against Xylis's back.

"If you fail to help me, Drake Philosopher, then your friend Xylis will have a nice carving in his skin," Chada said.

General Mondoor lifted Xylis' shirt and began to trace the knife across his back, making a small trail of blood. "Right here?"

King Chada smiled. Drake took a long, deep breath. The king was making him choose. Drake hadn't known Xylis for long, but he had proved himself a loyal and good companion, and Eleanor was his friend and mentor.

But the others...

They had helped him during his darkest times. They had cared for him and comforted him. He couldn't give them away. It was his friends or Xylis. But Xylis was now his friend as well...

How could he choose?

"Speak, or forever hold your peace," King Chada said as General Mondoor dug the knife a little further into Xylis's back. The sorcerer maintained a brave face and shook his head at Drake.

And then, thinking as fast as he could, Drake, tore himself out of the Titan's grip and kicked his leg back, knocking his guard to the floor. The sensation of pain flooded his mind, but he gritted it out. He needed to do this, for Xylis's sake. And his own.

Everything seemed to slow down as he kicked General Mondoor off Xylis, causing the general to slam into the wall. The remaining five Titans ran at them. Xylis punched one back with his bound hands. Drake dodged another and threw a third a kick. It hit the guard right in the stomach, and the Titan went flying into one of his counterparts, knocking them both down. Drake, right then, felt a burst of confidence. They could win!

His hopes were crushed, however, when he felt arms grab him and throw him to the floor. That was it. His chest exploded in pain once more. Two guards immediately pounced on him, pinning him to the ground, and the remaining ones grabbed ahold of Xylis.

King Chada stood over them and said simply, "Drop them both off in their cells. We'll find another time to talk." Drake caught a glance of King Chada's evil smile as he settled back onto his throne.

Before he knew it, the Titans were tossing him back in his cell like a sack of garbage. The doors closed with a bang, like a tomb being sealed for eternity.

*

Cyrus hadn't given his real reason for searching the forest. He wasn't looking for Titan scouts. He was searching for something far more important, but there was no need to get King Noxy's hopes up until Cyrus knew he was right. But he had a feeling they were there. It was almost a sixth sense. He couldn't explain it, but he'd been able to sense their presence for as long as he could remember. And he was feeling it now. He followed a path through the trees, getting closer and closer until he entered a clearing and spied a flock of the most noble and highly regarded creatures in Lyzix.

With their long, striped, tiger-like bodies, and heads, wings, and claws of an eagle, these wymers were the most magnificent of their species that Cyrus had ever seen. He smiled because these creatures were exactly what they needed. As he stepped forward, all the wymer heads turned towards him. They stared at him with their yellow eyes. One squawked while another clacked its beak. Beads of sweat formed on Cyrus' forehead as he extended his hand. Would they accept him? He hadn't communicated with wymers in a long time.

He moved gradually nearer to the beasts until he could touch the closest lightly on the beak. Immediately the wymers relaxed and crowded around him. Cyrus blew a sigh of relief. He looked up at the sky and smiled. He needed to find King Noxy as soon as possible. He knew exactly how his new beaked friends could help.

*

"Where's Cyrus?" King Noxy, Jerome, Leo, and Thoro were still waiting at the stables by the gates of the Kingdom of Oldor. Cyrus had been gone a while, and the king was worrying. "He should be back by now."

"Maybe we should search for him," Jerome suggested.

"Do you think he's been captured?" Leo lowered his voice. "What if King Solomon is right, and there are scouts and—"

"Young man, the Kingdom of Oldor is very well guarded," Thoro said. "I would be very surprised if any Titans got near here."

"Yes," Noxy agreed. "And I know Cyrus. He wouldn't be that careless. He's a master of stealth and combat." But King Noxy was trying to reassure himself. As more time passed, he felt his heart rate rising. Soon he couldn't take it anymore. "Come on." He mounted his horse. "We need to go look for him."

With a signal from Thoro, the gates opened, and they made for the nearby forest. King Noxy rode in first, slowing his horse to a trot and drawing his sword. He had to be ready for anything.

Leo scanned the trees with narrowed eyes, two daggers held at the ready. Jerome looked worried, constantly checking the tree canopy above them. Thoro seemed fairly calm, though he was glancing around while holding the reins of Cyrus's horse in his hands.

The forest became denser the further they went in. Branches scratched against them and the tree canopy became thicker, hampering their vision. They weren't getting anywhere. The king could tell the sun was getting close to its peak. He felt as if his worry would slowly tear him apart. That was when he heard Cyrus's voice.

"Over here, Noxy!" he called.

The king couldn't see, so he steered his horse in the direction of the sound. The group followed, and soon enough they found a clearing. As they pushed through the last of the shrubs King Noxy gasped to see Cyrus surrounded by wymers. He had thought his friend was looking for Titans. It came as a shock.

Cyrus grinned gesturing them over. He seemed to enjoy the looks of surprise on Thoro's and Noxy's faces, and the confusion and bewilderment on Jerome's and Leo's.

"Are the horses ready?" he asked.

"Yes," King Noxy said. "What are these wymers for?"

"Wait," Leo said before Cyrus could speak, "are they for—"

"Getting to the Western Town, yes," Cyrus said.

King Noxy raised his eyebrows. It was a solid plan.

Leo frowned. "But that's not what I was going to—"

"Is that all they're for, my friend?" King Noxy asked. "Or is there more?"

"I think we can use them for finding the army, too," Cyrus said.

Leo scowled. "But that wasn't what—"

"And there's one more thing they can help us with," Cyrus said. "The most important, in my opinion."

"Is it for rescuing Drake and Xylis?" Leo asked quickly, before anyone could cut him off.

"Yes," Cyrus replied.

"Finally," Jerome smirked at Leo, "the thief has gotten something right."

"Shut up," Leo replied, and as usual, the two proceeded to argue.

Meanwhile, King Noxy embraced Cyrus, while Thoro sat off to the side observing the wymers who were looking at him curiously.

"Well done, my friend," Noxy said. "Now we must take to the skies."

They approached the wymers who, now that they had met Cyrus, appeared completely docile. Before Noxy knew it, he had mounted, wrapped his hands in his wymer's golden fur, just as Cyrus had showed him, and was up in the air. How he'd held on for the takeoff he couldn't even remember—it had all happened so quickly. But now with the wind whipping his face as he sat on his very own wymer, its soft fur brushing against him, Noxy realized riding a wymer was a sensation unlike any other. He'd always wanted to fly on one and he felt guilty for feeling so elated when everything else was so bleak.

As they approached the Western town, however, his worries returned. His stomach tightened, and he felt extremely unsettled.

Would Isabella, Sahara, and Amanda be there? Drake and Xylis were in King Chada's hands and the last thing King Noxy wanted was more of his friends in peril.

King Noxy steered his wymer towards the distant walls of the Western Town. He saw guards milling about, and as they approached, he felt his stomach lurch once more. His friends had to be there. Please let them be there.

As he flew closer, he could see townsfolk walking along the cobblestone paths. He spotted the library and directed his wymer to descend towards the building. He turned to make sure the others were following: Cyrus and Thoro on one wymer, Jerome and Leo on the other. Naturally, the blacksmith and thief were fighting over who would control the creature.

King Noxy sighed. The last thing he needed was those two recklessly crashing into town on a wymer. "You two better watch yourselves back there before you plummet to the ground," he shouted. He immediately heard the bickering quiet. "Thank goodness," he muttered. "My head would've exploded if I had to listen to any more of them."

In addition to the occupied ones, another five rider-less wymers followed behind. At least they'd all stayed together.

As the wymers circled the library, Noxy noticed, with surprise, a garden behind the old building. He didn't know the library even had one. He directed his wymer to land there next to the tall wood and stone walls, and then dismounted. The others followed suit. He walked past several tables, placed on the central lawn with books sprawled over them, and into the library.

"I'll wait out here," Cyrus called. "To watch the wymers."

"Thank you," King Noxy said, not bothering to turn around. Instead, he continued along the passageway lined with shelves to the main room of the library. Past the small librarian's desk and the main door was a smaller door.

Eleanor hurried through it. "Good day. How are—" She froze. "You're back! And alive!"

King Noxy surprised even himself when he embraced Eleanor, and then he beamed as he saw Amanda, Isabella, and Sahara. King Noxy felt as if a wymer that had been standing on his chest had now flown away. All the pressure was lifted. He could breathe again. They were here.

They all exchanged stories and shed a few tears of joy until someone noticed that Cyrus was missing.

"He's out in the garden with the key to our rescue," King Noxy said.

"Rescue?" Sahara asked. And then his eyes widened. "For Xylis and Drake?"

Immediately, the group fell quiet. King Noxy gave a small, curt nod. Everyone stared down at their feet, except Eleanor. He could see sadness on her face, but she also had a determined look—a burning fire in her eye.

"We shall get them back," she said. "Drake and Xylis are both strong. I have a lot of faith in them—and in us."

King Noxy smiled and before anyone could say anything else, he introduced Thoro. "He's here to help break Drake and Xylis out of prison."

"King Solomon is a good man," Eleanor said. "Give him my deepest thanks."

Thoro nodded.

Eleanor then turned to King Noxy. "You said Cyrus is out back with the key to the rescue?"

"Yes."

"Well, let's join him. There is something we must share with you as well." She led them back into the garden, where they all exchanged more hellos with Cyrus. The group looked questioningly at the wymers, but Eleanor so clearly wanted to speak that Noxy said he would explain the rescue later.

"The townsfolk are angry," Eleanor said, quietly.

"What are you talking about? I thought they loved us," Leo said.

"Let her speak," Isabella said, but Leo ignored his sister.

"Have they turned against us now because of that stupid atta—"

"Quiet Leo," Eleanor scolded. "The Western Town's citizens did once admire us, but all the people who volunteered to join the attack on Chada are now missing. The mayor is considering punishing us for getting his town into this mess."

"But these wymers are going to help us get the army back," King Noxy said. He saw looks of amazement from the group, especially Isabella, who seemed fascinated by the creatures. Even Jerome and Leo looked in awe, though they just had ridden upon one. And almost crashed it, in fact. "We'll send four soldiers, one on each wymer, to search for the scattered army in different towns and kingdoms. Meanwhile, the rest of us will fly back to Wendil and sneak into the dungeons to rescue Drake and Xylis."

"Excellent," Eleanor said. "I'll find the right men to search for our missing army. You guys just focus on the rescue. I shall leave you to it, Noxy"

The king nodded, and she then bid them good luck and headed back into the library.

King Noxy looked up. The sun was setting, casting a red glow on the rooftops of the Western Town. If he was correct, it would be the middle of the night by the time they reached Wendil. First, they had to ride through the small forest, but they could do it. At least King Noxy hoped so.

He looked around at his friends' determined faces and said the words that made it official.

"It is time to begin the rescue."

Chapter XVII

King Chada sat on his throne with General Mondoor standing below him. "Mondoor, what have you found?"

"Sir," General Mondoor said, "we found Lieutenant Ossenna."

King Chada remembered the woman who had led the ambush on Noxy in the plains near the Seaside Kingdom and had failed. "You did indeed? Where has she been?"

General Mondoor winced. "Apparently, she was attacked during Drake and King Noxy's attempt to retake this kingdom. She was injured and wasn't able to call for help. She will need a bit of time to get healthy. Our healers are treating as we speak."

"I see," King Chada said. It was a pity. Despite her disappointing performance earlier, Ossenna was a talented woman. The king would make sure she was well rested and then bring her back into service. But never mind that now. He had other things to focus on. "Tell the guards to bring Drake here. Get the execution axe. And remember to bring Xylis."

"Of course, my king." General Mondoor quickly left

the room. King Chada leaned back on his throne, weary. He needed to know where Noxy and the rest of Drake's friends were. And obviously, simply injuring Xylis would not be enough. That was clear from Drake and the sorcerer almost escaping his clutches. King Chada needed to do something worse—the worst thing he could do, to get the information he needed.

He'd request the presences of Xylis or Drake again. But if they weren't cooperative, it was simple what he would do, really.

He would just kill the sorcerer.

*

The group sat on their four wymers, in the forest, talking through the rescue plan one more time. The leaves of the trees rustled in the gentle night breeze and it was almost pitch dark, providing perfect cover.

"Does everyone understand their jobs?" King Noxy whispered. They all responded with nods. "Good." He snapped his fingers. "Fly."

The four wymers lifted off the ground with their riders: Jerome, Amanda, Sahara, and Cyrus. King Noxy watched them circle above the trees and clouds until, in the place of his friends, all he could see was the glowing moon, looming above him.

"Now," King Noxy addressed Thoro, Isabella, and Leo. "To the second part of our plan." He had chosen these three to help him break out Drake and Xylis because Isabella and Leo were skilled at sneaking around, and Thoro was a sorcerer.

"Drake used the secret entrance in the last battle, so

they will most likely have it guarded. We have no choice but to enter there, and we must be prepared to fight. But first we need to get across the plain without being seen."

Leo and Isabella nodded seriously. King Noxy had never seen Leo look so determined. The two siblings could not be more different, but right now they both seemed ready for what was coming.

The king began to creep through the forest. When they reached the edge, he saw something in the distance fly up into the air. Arrows flew after it. Then it dove down and out of sight. It was a wymer. "Good. They're doing their job and distracting the guards. Now we need to do ours," King Noxy said. "Let's move."

They immediately crouched down as low as they could in the grass and made for the first tree. When they reached it, King Noxy felt a burst of relief. He prayed it would continue to be this easy. They moved onto the second tree, then the third. Noxy was impressed with Isabella and Leo's stealthiness, but it was too slow. How long before a Titan crossbow or arrow hit either a wymer or a person? They had to hurry.

They were coming very close to the wall when a guard turned towards them and froze. As King Noxy dove to hide in the grass, the guard took out a horn and pressed it to his mouth. Leo immediately whipped out a slingshot, drew back the string, and released it. The stone sailed through the dark night, and clobbered the guard in the center of his forehead. He dropped the horn and flopped over the wall, falling inside the Kingdom of Wendil. Leo then dove in the grass after his shot.

King Noxy was shocked. "How did you learn to shoot like that?"

"I've used a bow and slingshot since I was six," he said.

"Huh." Isabella started. "Remember when I asked you to help me with some kid who was antagonizing me, and you said you weren't accurate enough?"

"I liked that kid," Leo said. "Besides, you were antagonizing him."

"I was not." Isabella shot back.

"Not the time to argue about this," King Noxy said, while standing up. Maybe Isabella and Leo were more alike than he thought. "We need to keep going before people discover we're sneaking in." He looked at the section of wall in front of him and found the small carving of Wendil's crest, but when he touched his sword to it, the stone spread open to reveal…

More stone.

King Noxy cursed. They'd sealed it off. Could Drake and Xylis have given it away? No. They would never do so… unless they were tortured, a voice in the back of his mind told him said. He growled angrily. If they were tortured, he would make sure to confront Chada when he could. A fist to the face or a sword to the heart would change the king's mindset very quickly.

But right now, they needed to find a different way in. He looked frantically over the walls and up at the towering castle. There was a slightly cracked window that he might fit through. It was worth a shot.

"Over the wall. Now!" he hissed. They quickly scaled the wall, the sounds of battle becoming louder. The wymers were swooping around while Titans in the streets and on the wall fired at them.

At the top, Noxy sprinted to the other side and seeing

no guards near, jumped down. Leo and Isabella followed him, Leo almost falling off the wall. Isabella steadied him with a smirk. Thoro brought up the rear, and the four began to sprint towards the castle. When King Noxy got closer, he realized the window was lower than he thought, and that was perfect. But it was too far up to risk climbing.

"I can levitate you up there," Thoro said, as if reading King Noxy's mind.

"Quickly," King Noxy said as he started to rise.

Thoro kept him in the shadow of the castle, which pleased Noxy. The moment he reached the window, he drew his sword and tumbled in. The others soon joined him. There were no Titans along the vast hallways, which meant they had easy access to the stairway leading to the bottom floor and dungeon.

As King Noxy hurried down the hallway, however, he felt sad. This castle was where he had spent most of his life. Now it had been stolen by one of the worst men he could imagine. Noxy slowed as he passed a painting of himself with a sword strapped to his belt and his crown glinting in the sunlight. There was a ragged slash through it, probably the work of some Titan or Chada himself. He stopped completely.

How could he have let Chada take Wendil? How? Half of this life, in this very castle, now belonged to a wretched and corrupt man.

"King Noxy, we need to go," Leo said.

"We can't waste any time." Isabella pulled on his arm.

They continued down the stairwell to an old worn door. King Noxy yanked it open and inside found two Titan guards who jumped into action. But he was quicker. He jabbed his sword into the first Titan's stomach and kicked the second down the stairs. Noxy then ran to the first level of the dungeons and scanned the corridor.

"How long has it been since you cleaned this place?" Leo whispered.

"I don't use dungeons often," he said. The walls were covered in grime, and water dripped from above. Some cell doors were open, hanging off one hinge, or even missing completely. Puddles covered the floor, and all of the cells appeared to be empty.

Without missing a beat, King Noxy began to look inside each one, swiftly moving from one to another. This was worrying. Drake had to be here. And what about Xylis? It was only when Noxy peeked inside one of the last cells that he saw Drake. Alive! Not in the best condition, but alive.

This was it. The moment of truth. Thoro whispered something. A small light wisp entered the keyhole, and the cell door opened. Just like that. Was it almost too easy?

"Drake!" King Noxy exclaimed.

"You came." Drake said in a raspy voice, looking at Thoro strangely.

"A helper," King Noxy said.

"You didn't think we would just let you rot here, did you?" Isabella smiled.

"Where's Xylis?" King Noxy asked as Thoro freed Drake from his chains. Drake pointed down the hall and in a matter of minutes, Xylis was free as well. But no sooner had they all exited his cell than they heard a clang of metal. Two Titans were storming down the corridor. They needed to escape. Now.

King Noxy ran at the Titans and knocked them aside. He ran up the stairwell, following the path back towards the window, with Isabella, Leo, Thoro, Drake, and Xylis close behind. But when they got there, he realized that they didn't have a way to get down.

But wait.

Thoro and Xylis could use their sorcery. "Levitate us," King Noxy ordered, "and bring us over the wall."

He felt himself being lifted into the air. He floated out the window and began to descend over the wall. He landed on the other side, and the other five soon followed. They began to run along the large stone structure until they were out in the open grassland.

This was it. Now they just had to escape.

Yet at this moment, King Noxy heard panicked shouts of guards, and heard thumps of arrows as they landed in the dirt near him. He turned around and saw Titans rushing outside to give chase. As Noxy felt himself tighten up with fear, he heard a shout behind him.

Suddenly, a wymer soared over him, and Jerome leaned down from the creature and snatched Isabella by the hand, while the wymer itself scooped up Leo. The thief hung from one wymer claw, cursing as they sped off into the night.

Two more wymers swooped down. Amanda grabbed Xylis and the wymer grabbed Thoro. Sahara was able to seize Drake and finally, just as an arrow was headed right towards Noxy's head, Cyrus grasped his wrists and heaved him up onto the last wymer.

Noxy looked down and saw the kingdom—his kingdom—grow smaller and smaller, until they sailed over the forest and it disappeared completely from sight.

They had succeeded. They had rescued Drake and Xylis. They were back in the game.

Chapter XVIII

"Drake, I'm really, really sorry I never told you." Drake glared at Eleanor. She stared nervously back.

They were in a room at the Brass Bee Inn, the forest tavern near the Western Town that they had visited on their way to the trials. The rest of the group was downstairs, celebrating.

"Sorry isn't going to cut it right now," Drake said harshly. "You watched Chada kill my parents, and you didn't stop him."

"Chada is not giving you the whole story."

"Oh yes," he snapped back, sarcastically. "I forgot to mention how you ran away."

Eleanor looked completely shocked. She hid her face in her hands.

"Sorry," he mumbled. He shouldn't have said that.

When she looked at him again, there were tears in her eyes. "Did Chada tell you why I ran?"

"He said you were afraid that the same thing would happen to—"

"I ran," she interrupted, "because I had you with me."

"You…you what?"

"I was a good friend of your father's brother, so I knew your parents. I was with them when Chada came, along with someone he was working with at the time. They attacked and killed your parents before I knew what was happening. And then they turned on me."

"What did you do?"

"I fought them off, of course," Eleanor said. "Hard as I could. But Chada had a sorcerer with him—and do you remember what I said about sorcery? No offensive magic?" Drake nodded. "Well, this sorcerer was a special case, and could use his powers as he wanted. And he could use them well. Paired with his silver shard, and with Chada, I knew I would eventually lose. So, I grabbed you and fled."

"Oh," Drake suddenly felt extremely guilty. Eleanor had saved him?

"That means…I owe you my life?"

"No." Eleanor was firm.

"But—"

"No buts. You don't owe me anything, Drake. You have every right to be upset. I failed your parents…"

Now it was Drake's turn to get Eleanor back on track. "You did not fail them. You didn't know what was happening, and you couldn't have changed anything even if you did."

Eleanor opened her mouth, hesitated, then closed it and smiled. "Thank you. And thank you for not being angry with me."

"How could I?" Drake asked. "You saved my life."

"And don't do anything to try and repay me, okay?"

"Fine…you have a deal," Drake said, but he could see from Eleanor's eyes that she didn't believe him.

*

Cheery music was playing in The Brass Bee Inn as King Noxy took a sip of beer. Drake was now dancing with Jerome and Leo, while Isabella stood watching them with a half amused, half ashamed look. Sahara and Eleanor were at the bar, making extra drinks. Xylis, Amanda, and Cyrus were telling stories of their adventures, while other folks in the tavern listened intently. Thoro had begun his trek back to Solomon only a few hours before, but had promised to convince Solomon to let him help them again if they needed. King Noxy had thanked him many times before finally allowing the sorcerer to leave.

He was just taking another drink when Drake came careering into him and knocked him over. They fell to the ground, spilling Noxy's beer and soaking them both. Laughter broke out around the inn as Drake helped King Noxy up.

"Sorry," he said, sheepishly.

King Noxy patted him on the back. "No harm done, my friend. Keep dancing. You're getting better. Though I must say, you'll have a tough time topping Leo."

Leo was currently doing a dozen fancy moves and flips with more and more people gathering to watch. A few girls Leo's age were taking it upon themselves to watch as well, blushing when Leo winked at them. Isabella looked away from her brother, shaking her head. King Noxy smiled.

"Yeah, I must say, he's doing quite well," Drake said, and with that he was back on the floor, joining Leo and Jerome.

King Noxy ordered another beer from the waiter and took a long swig. He was elated that the rescue had gone so well. At the end, it had been close, but they had managed to escape. On their return, Amanda had immediately fed Drake herbs to help his chest cut heal. To think that boy had gone through the whole escape with not a hint of complaint, yet his chest had been one big mess of blood and raw flesh. It was going to leave a scar, but Noxy would make sure Chada got one twice that size.

Drake and Xylis had both explained what had happened in the dungeon, and that King Chada was trying to snuff out the group before they made any further moves. They hadn't learned anything else, but it didn't matter. He was just happy they were safe.

His mood quickly shifted, however, when the door opened, and three soldiers walked inside. They glanced around, and as King Noxy watched them suspiciously, he saw them speak to someone near the door. A few seconds later, a woman pointed to King Noxy, and the three soldiers started towards him. His hand immediately went to his sword. Were they on his side? He was ready to warn the group when he saw all three had the Seaside Kingdom's insignia on their uniforms. They were his. And even better, they were probably here to report on the search for the army.

King Noxy relaxed, taking his hand off his belt and swigging another large portion of his beer. He set down the mug as the soldiers stopped in front of him, took short bows, and the leader stepped forward.

"Your Majesty, we've found a few squads of the army," he said. "We've sent out more soldiers and horses to ride further, but we haven't had much luck yet."

King Noxy felt himself slouch in disappointment, but he tried not to show too much emotion. They were doing the best they could. "Thank you," he said, halfheartedly. "Hopefully we'll have more luck soon. Is there anything else I should be aware of?"

"Yes," the soldier said. "The Titans are recovering quickly from the rescue and attack. They might be sending out scouts."

"I'll keep an eye out." King Noxy felt himself become even sadder. This was exactly what they didn't need. "You're dismissed."

The soldiers left, and he went back to his ale. He considered what he'd just heard. They were celebrating now, but would they be celebrating in a few days? Likely not, if the soldiers were right. He prayed for some news of the army's whereabouts.

As for King Chada's quick recovery, he knew he needed to send out some scouts himself, to get an idea of what the Titans were planning. It wasn't a job for regular soldiers. He scanned the crowd, and his eyes landed on Drake, Jerome, Isabella, and Leo. The answer was right in front of him. He knew exactly what to do.

Later that day, King Noxy gathered the group outside the inn to discuss their next plans of action. "I've just received a message from our scouts. The majority of our soldiers are still missing, and they've seen the Titans regrouping and preparing. King Chada's sending out his own scouts, while we're here drinking and dancing. We need to make some headway as well."

"What do you have in mind, King Noxy?" Xylis asked.

"Well, the Western Town isn't exactly a big fan of ours

anymore, but we have to negotiate an alliance with them. We need a main base and stronghold as Wendil isn't in our grasp. Meanwhile, you four…" He gestured to Drake, Jerome, Isabella, and Leo, "will scout out the Titans' moves."

"Why us?" Isabella asked.

"You've proven yourselves capable in battle, and your stealthiness could come in handy. Drake will be in charge. I need you to spy on their army, their training methods and weaponry. See what they are doing. Try to figure out what future plans they have. And then report back."

The four teens glanced at each other. Drake felt nervous and excited at the same time. He trusted they could do it, but they needed to be very careful. He was the leader and he had to keep his friends safe. Otherwise, he could never forgive himself.

Leo checked his belt. It had three throwing knives hanging from it and a crossbow. Isabella, who had a collection of daggers, and Jerome, with his signature hammer, did the same. Drake was, of course, carrying a sword. They said farewell to Noxy, and he wished them luck.

Just before they departed, King Noxy yanked Drake aside and whispered in his ear. "Listen to me, very closely. Don't you dare enter the castle. It's risky enough as it is. And I know how you are. Don't even try to get close to King Chada. Do you understand? We can't afford for you to be captured again."

Drake nodded, and with that King Noxy saw the four friends walk off in the direction of the forest.

"Did you tell him?" Sahara asked. "I want to make sure he's safe."

"I did." King Noxy paused, looking towards the distant

Western Town. "But somehow I have a feeling he isn't going to listen."

*

It had been a while since they left King Noxy. Drake, Jerome, Isabella, and Leo were creeping through the forest near Wendil, watching their surroundings. They hadn't found anything yet. Drake was, in fact, surprised there were no Titans about. He'd expected Chada to be a little more alert after the rescue.

As if on cue, Drake suddenly heard leaves rustling. It was light, almost as if the wind was doing it. Then, the rustling became crackling, and the crackling turned into crunching. There were indeed Titans in the woods. Drake frantically waved to his friends. They darted behind some trees and pressed their backs against the trunks to hide.

Drake's palms felt sweaty as he gripped his sword. He looked to his left, but couldn't see Leo, who had been near him only seconds before. Drake felt his stomach drop. Where was the thief? Maybe the Titans had taken him?

He got his answer, however, when he saw Leo bound out on the attack. Drake wanted to shout and tell him to stop. What was he doing? They shouldn't be drawing attention to themselves. They should only fight if they had to, but Leo had already forced their hand. He tackled a Titan to the ground. Immediately the rest converged on him.

Drake had no choice but to fight, so he lunged from behind the tree at the nearest Titan and sliced him across the back. This gave Leo a split second to leap back from the others, retreating away to recover. Drake attacked the next, cutting him across the throat, and then he spun and smacked the third in the head with the flat of his sword. The fourth ran at him, but Drake blocked his strike and kicked him back into a tree. The Titan was knocked out.

"Well," Leo stuttered. He looked wide eyed at the dead Titans and then Drake. "That was…um…"

He was in shock. Jerome and Isabella too. Drake fumbled for the right words. "It's…it's a part of what we're doing. I know it's gruesome, but it's either them or us. We need to get moving."

"How are we going to sneak into Wendil without being spotted? The Titans will be on the alert after the rescue," Jerome asked with a tremble in his voice. Drake felt slightly guilty about how the small skirmish had affected them. But he couldn't worry about it now. They had too much else to think about.

Drake looked at the Titans as he pondered this question and suddenly realized what they could do. "I have an idea."

It wasn't easy to strip the Titans of their uniforms, and Drake and his friends had to clean some of the blood off. The clothes were a little big on the teens and really uncomfortable, but they looked good enough. Drake almost hated himself for wearing the uniform of the enemy, but it was for a good cause. He just kept telling himself that.

They got into a small diamond formation with Drake at the head. He hoped it might make them look like they actually knew what they were doing. Then they marched toward the town.

As they appeared within view of the wall, a Titan spotted them. "Open the gates!" he yelled. Five Titans descended the steps and met them on the plains.

"What's your business?" one asked.

"We've returned from a scouting mission. The general asked us to report back directly," Drake said.

The Titan held up a hand then joined his comrades and began whispering. Drake was breathing faster and faster, almost hyperventilating. Would they let them in? Or would they refuse? Or even worse, would they discover they were imposters and throw Drake into that dreadful dungeon again?

Finally, the Titan turned back and said, "Enter."

Drake sighed with relief. He, Jerome, Isabella, and Leo were just about to clear the gate. when the Titan said, "Wait."

Drake was sure they were caught. The Titan must have recognized them. His heart thumped against his chest. What were they going to do? They would become four porcupines with arrows lodged in them if they tried to run and would be overwhelmed if they tried to fight.

"And aren't you four a bit young?" Drake let out another quiet sigh of relief. The Titan didn't recognize him.

"New recruits," Leo said, deepening his voice. "Chosen for our size to be scouts, so we can sneak around. Agile and nimble, that's us."

The Titan nodded thoughtfully. "I see. Well, move along. General Mondoor won't be happy if you're late."

As they made their way towards the castle and the more populated parts of town, Drake noticed houses that had been transformed into training areas and workshops. Titans were making weapons, and there were squads out on the streets, training and practicing for the battles ahead. He tried to focus on what the Titans were doing, but as they neared where he used to live, he found it harder to concentrate. He saw Jerome's blacksmith shop, the small library where he borrowed books, the tailor's shop where he bought his clothes. Then finally he reached his old house.

His mind flashed to training with Sahara and playing in the streets with Jerome when he was young. He even remembered meeting King Noxy one time. He noticed Jerome looking around sadly, too. The Titans had taken the Kingdom of Wendil because of him. King Chada had wanted Drake because of The Spectacular Swordsmen Line. It was all his fault. But this only made him feel more determined. They would retake Wendil. He would discover more of this Spectacular Swordsman Line. King Chada would be killed, and peace would be restored Lyzix.

He and the others stopped at another blacksmith and weaponry shop. Fires raged inside and someone was hammering metal. To get an idea of what their force and weapon count was, they needed to go in.

The shop was crowded with Titans being equipped with or buying weapons of all sorts; swords, spears, crossbows, bows and arrows, shields, hammers, and axes. There was no shortage. Piles of metal bars and wooden boards were stacked against the wall in readiness for more weapons to be forged.

Out in the back, two Titans sparred on a small grassy area. They seemed to be advanced fighters. When one pushed the other down, the victor kicked the loser in the head, knocking him out. Drake shuddered. Not only were the Titans ruthless, but they were also well equipped, and they didn't mess around.

They exited the forge and continued towards the castle. They slipped around the castle walls astonished to find no

Titans in sight. But as they scouted, Drake heard some voices drifting from a castle window set up high and covered by shutters. He wasn't able to make out the words, but the voice sounded very much like…

"Wait," he whispered.

"What is it?" Jerome asked.

"I think I hear Chada's voice coming from that window."

"We should probably go," Isabella said.

"But it might be important," whispered Leo.

"We must find a way to overhear him. Just for a second," Drake said. Isabella glowered and muttered something about boys and stupidity.

Drake's stomach churned. He was disobeying Noxy, but this could be important.

Besides, where there was risk…there was usually reward.

CHAPTER XIX

Noxy was standing in the mayor's tower in the Western Town's square. "Sir, you don't understand," he said, politely. The meeting was not going well. Noxy needed the town as a base, but Marcemus, the mayor, was having none of it. "We need—"

"I understand what you need," Marcemus said. "But King Chada is fighting against you, not us. If we stay out of your affairs, we'll be fine. I've learned this from previous events, Noxy. It's good leadership."

"We could give you protection," Xylis offered.

Marcemus looked at King Noxy sadly. "I can't help you. We're a small town, and we've already lost too many men for your cause."

King Noxy sighed. They couldn't do much else. The mayor had made up his mind. "I guess we'll leave." He stood up from the table.

"I'm sorry, my friend. I hope we meet again under happier circumstances." Marcemus patted Noxy on the back. Regrets circled through King Noxy's head. He should've known it would take more time to defeat King Chada and the Titans.

He should have never let Drake get ahead of himself. He was grabbing the door handle to exit when it swung open and in stepped an old woman. King Noxy squinted. "Eleanor!"

"Your Majesty." She turned towards Marcemus. "Greetings, Sir Marcemus."

"Hello, Eleanor. I assume you received my note about the meeting."

"Yes, but I'm afraid we must reschedule. There are more important matters."

Marcemus narrowed his eyes. "Such as?"

Eleanor gestured to King Noxy and company. "These people must be allowed to stay."

"Oh no, not you too!" Marcemus groaned.

"King Noxy has been trying as hard as he can to find our scattered army," she said. "We need them. Chada is vicious and ruthless, and he will come after us at some point. If we're loyal to Wendil, Wendil will be loyal to us."

Marcemus frowned and stared out the window. King Noxy knew he was trying to decide. Eleanor's words were strong, but were they enough?

"Marcemus, you can't seriously be debating this?" She went on. "Do you understand what they're doing? By trying to stop Chada now, they're preventing him from attacking here! In addition, King Noxy has sent multiple soldiers out to look for the army, so they can finish the job and return safely. You want that, don't you Marcemus?"

There was silence. Then the mayor sighed. King Noxy knew what he was going to say. They would have to find a new base of operations. The mayor was going to say no.

"Well…" Marcemus hesitated. King's Noxy's heart felt like it was going to burst out of his chest. "Fine.

Fortifications will be made. Defenses will be put up. But do not make me regret this decision."

King Noxy felt a rush of happiness. He beamed at Eleanor. The Western Town was back with them! They had a base. Now, they had to decide what to do next.

*

With Jerome, Leo, and a reluctant Isabella acting as lookouts, Drake quickly scaled the tower to the window where he'd heard the voices. It was possible Chada was discussing something important. And that could give them a big advantage. Clutching the edge of the sill, he brought himself to eye level with the window and peered through a crack in the shutters.

In the middle of the room were two men. One, clearly Chada, leaned over a desk. The other wore a dark blue cloak with a hood over his head so big Drake could only see his long, pointed nose. A thin jagged scar ran across the side of it. He had clearly been injured—maybe by a sword slash?

Drake knew the castle fairly well, so it came as a surprise that he didn't recognize this room. A red carpet covered the floor. A bookshelf full of books and scrolls filled the wall behind Chada. Wooden chairs were scattered in no apparent pattern. Perhaps Chada had added onto the building? But he wouldn't have had enough time. Maybe there were just things about the castle that Drake had never known.

"One more thing I must tell you," the hooded man was saying, clearly wrapping up the conversation. "Listen closely. It's very important." He had a slick, slimy voice, and Drake had a hard time deciphering what he said.

"Of course, my magical friend," Chada said. Magical friend? What could that mean? Perhaps he was a sorcerer?

"He has found one piece of the artifact we need," the man said. "It lies in the northern jungle of Lyzix."

What was he talking about? What artifact?

"Indeed?" King Chada sounded gleeful. "That is fantastic."

"I'm going up there to retrieve it."

"Perfect," King Chada replied. "I'll remain here, keeping an eye on Drake. Once you have it, bring it back to me. We shall decide what to do with it from there. And say nothing to anyone. Take my Titan, general. There will be a couple platoons stationed along the way. Pick them up and use them if you run into trouble."

"Thank you," the man replied, and he exited the tower. Drake climbed back down below the sill to rejoin Jerome, Isabella, and Leo as King Chada began to pace the room.

"We need to tell the others," Jerome said.

Drake nodded in agreement and looked at Isabella. She avoided his gaze, clearly aware that she'd been wrong. Drake didn't press his point. People were wrong all the time. Was he wrong to worry about this conversation? Perhaps. It could be nothing, but Chada seemed so excited. What was this "one piece," and why did Chada need it?

*

Eleanor sat in her back room rereading the entire pile of scrolls she had gathered on her desk while the others had been on the rescue mission. All the writings she had found, concerning the Spectacular Swordsmen, all in one place.

She had practically finished reading through them and hadn't found a thing. Everything in here was information she already knew. The group was coming over to the library soon to discuss the next plan, and she had to be ready to answer their questions. She was beginning to despair of ever understanding a Spectacular Swordsman's full role. It had to be written somewhere, or…had she been fooling herself all along?

As she read through the last scroll, she found herself scanning the information. It was about Atticus, the last Spectacular Swordsman, and how there hadn't been any of them since him.

Yes, yes, she already knew this.

At the very bottom of the page, however, in a crinkle in the parchment she came across a small paragraph. It was only about six lines long, and she didn't think she'd ever noticed it before. It was handwritten so poorly that it looked like chicken scratch. But when she read it, she realized that it was game-changing.

The Spectacular Swordsmen did not only have themselves and their skills to defend the vault of silver in the center of Lyzix. They were also in possession of a special weapon that was made up of two parts—a strong sword made of Obilor bone and a sphere of silver. This weapon was known as the Spectacular Sword. It was passed down along the Spectacular Swordsmen Line and would act as a key to the vault, opening the secure defenses in times of crisis so the silver could be accessed. The sword would also be a strong and powerful weapon against any who dared face the swordsmen.

After Atticus's disappearance the sword and sphere were parted from one another, never to be seen again.

Eleanor's mouth dropped open. She was right! There was something under the center of Lyzix, and it did have to do with sorcery. She had not been expecting a vault of silver. That could be severely detrimental to Lyzix if any sorcerer with ill intentions got their hands on it.

And now there was a sword, too? There was a specific sword the Spectacular Swordsmen had to wield, and it acted as a key to this vault. What could this mean? Was the training that Drake had done completely useless? No, it couldn't be. He had completed the trials. This just must be an add-on, or addition to his power.

And if this sword was a key to the vault of silver that Chada wanted so badly, the sword had to be found.

*

King Noxy sat in the library with Eleanor, Sahara, Xylis, Amanda, and Cyrus, pondering the breakthrough the librarian had just made.

"An ancient sword that was the weapon of the Spectacular Swordsmen?" Xylis asked. "And a vault of silver under Lyzix?"

"Yes," Eleanor said. She seemed to be carving permanent holes in the carpet with her pacing.

"This is much more serious than I could have imagined," Xylis muttered.

"Indeed," Eleanor replied. "But for now the vault of silver is not our major concern. I think we should focus more on the key."

"Yes, I agreed," Sahara said. "But I've never heard of anything like this sword. It must be extremely powerful if it's made of Obilor bone."

"I would say so," King Noxy said. "But what are we going to do?"

"That's the problem," Eleanor said. "I don't have a clue."

"Maybe we can track it down," Amanda suggested. "Do we know where it is?"

"No," Eleanor said. "The paragraph just mentions how the sword and sphere were parted after Atticus's disappearance, and were never seen again. There's not even a hint."

"That's a lot of use," Xylis grumbled.

Eleanor ignored him. "I don't know if we need to combine the sword and sphere so it works once more, or what, but I think our best bet is to retrieve both items and keep them out of King Chada's hand while we figure it out more. I don't know if he's aware of it, but I have no doubt it would be deadly if it fell into his hands."

The library bell rang loudly, and Drake, Jerome, Isabella, and Leo raced inside. The door slammed behind them.

"Are you trying to rip the door off its hinges?" Xylis asked. "Is everything all right? Did you get attacked? Spotted?"

"No, we're okay. But we have something urgent to tell you," Drake said. "Chada is looking for some item in the Northern Jungle. This mysterious man told him about it. The man is going up there to find it with General Mondoor."

The group looked at Drake in astonishment.

"This isn't good." Eleanor said.

"At least we know where part of the weapon is," King Noxy said.

"Wait." Leo looked at Drake. "It's a weapon? King Chada didn't say anything about a weapon, did he?"

"No," Drake said. How could King Noxy know it was a weapon?

"Here." Eleanor handed him a scroll. "Read the bottom."

Drake read it and handed it off to Jerome. He couldn't believe that yet another big component of the Spectacular Swordsmen's heritage had been revealed. He now had his own weapon? And Eleanor had been right about the center of Lyzix—there was sorcery in there.

"But which part is Chada after? The sword? Or the sphere?"

"It doesn't matter," Eleanor said. "We just have to keep them out of Chada's hands until we figure out what happens when they're combined."

"Drake." King Noxy said. "Just pause for a second. I take it you went near King Chada, even though I told you not to?"

Drake cringed. He had to admit that he'd disobeyed. He just hoped King Noxy would take it well. "I heard his voice coming out of a window. I thought it might help."

"Yes, and it was very useful, Drake," King Noxy said. "But next time, please try to exercise some self-control. If you want me to trust you with these missions, you must listen to my instruction."

Drake nodded. "I promise."

Eleanor changed the topic quickly. "Drake, who was with Chada?"

"No idea. But he had a long nose," Drake said. Leo snickered. Isabella shot him glare. "There was a jagged scar across it. He was wearing a really large blue cloak, and Chada referred to him as a magical friend."

Eleanor frowned, seemingly pondering this revelation.

"Probably a sorcerer. But we'll focus on him later. What is of utmost importance right now is the artifact. We must go after it."

"But, Eleanor, are we sure this is wise?" Her eyebrows raised at King Noxy's words. "The last thing we should do is rush into things again."

"This is essential. If Chada gets the sword and the sphere, he will have great power. And we are at a disadvantage because we don't know what the weapon truly does."

"Mondoor and the sorcerer are barely ahead of us," Drake said. "If we leave soon, we can catch them up. Follow them or even overtake them."

King Noxy, surprisingly, gave a nod. "I guess I understand. It is more urgent."

"Then we should leave as soon as possible. Solidify the lead," Cyrus said.

"Gather weapons, horses, and food," King Noxy said. "Chart a safe course, navigating the jungle is treacherous—"

"That's going to take too long," Drake protested.

"And we'll leave at dusk," King Noxy said, sternly. "Are you coming with us, Eleanor?"

She shook her head. "No. I'll stay here and see if I can figure out more about the sword, sphere, and vault. Be extremely careful. I don't trust Chada. He may have wanted you to hear that conversation."

Drake and the rest of the group nodded. She was right. It could be a setup, but Drake was confident Chada had not planned for him to hear that conversation. He hoped so, at least.

"Good," Eleanor replied. "And I'll focus on raising a

new army. By the time you return, I'm sure that King Chada will be ready to attack again."

King Noxy sighed. "We must be on our toes."

At that moment a gust of wind caught the shuttered windows and blew one of them open. As light flooded in, and everyone shielded their eyes, Drake was struck by a terrible irony. Outside it was such a bright and beautiful day, but their future was looking as dark as it had ever been.

He was suddenly overwhelmed by all the questions that had been nagging him ever since he had found out about his tie to the mysterious Spectacular Swordsmen Line. What truly were The Spectacular Swordsmen? What was he expected to do with this sword and sphere? If he opened the vault, he would be doing Chada a favor. Was there something else? Perhaps he should kill Chada with it. But was he up to it? And who was this sorcerer? This whole situation was becoming more and more frustrating by the minute with all these new developments and...

Eleanor put a hand on his shoulder, causing him to startle. "Could you stay back a moment, Drake?"

"Sorry, what?" He'd not been paying attention. The others were already filing out of the library while Xylis looked through a few books on Eleanor's desk. "Is something wrong?"

"I don't know. You tell me," Eleanor said.

"I'm fine," he said. He could deal with this on his own.

Eleanor frowned. "I know that's not true. You're feeling what any sane person would be feeling in this situation. You're worried about what happens next."

Drake gaped at her. "How do you know?"

"I can see it in your face."

He sighed. "Fine. I guess if there's anyone I should talk to about this Spectacular Swordsmen thing, it's you."

"Ha! Drake, you flatter me," Eleanor said. "As for the Spectacular Swordsmen "thing", I'm working on that as we speak. Don't worry."

"But everyone is depending on—"

"No," Eleanor said, simply, "Look at me, okay? Pay attention. I know you think everything is on your shoulders. But it's not. Your friends will help you. I will help you. All the others who are involved will help you. The world is depending on them as well. You're just at the center."

Drake nodded. "But—"

"No buts," she said, sharply. "Answer these three questions honestly. Do you believe in the people of Lyzix?"

"Yes."

"Do you believe in your friends?"

"Yes."

"And most importantly, do you believe in yourself?"

"Yes."

"That is the only future you need. Believe, Drake, and it will come true in some way. Maybe not the way you expect, but it will come true."

Drake smiled. Maybe she was right. "Thank you, Eleanor."

She chuckled as she walked Drake to the door. "Thank you, Drake. And be careful."

Drake left the library feeling exhilarated. As he strolled towards the tavern where his friends were preparing for their journey, he felt for the first time that he could handle it. He didn't feel reckless, but quietly confident.

After all, he believed in the people of Lyzix, his friends and best of all, himself.

*

"Well spoken," Xylis said, as Eleanor closed the door. He glanced at the shelves behind her.

Eleanor narrowed her eyes. He'd been her apprentice in sorcery for a very long time. "Something on your mind?" she asked.

"Yes," Xylis said. "The Northern Jungle is largely uncharted. Surely it's madness to go without a guide or explorer to accompany us?"

Eleanor was planning to soothe his worries, when a slight breeze wafted around the library, picking up dust. She turned around slowly and looked to the windows. She must have forgotten to close the shutters. She fastened the shades, but the wind continued to blow around the library.

She stepped back. Xylis stood ready to cast a quick spell. Dust picked up in front of them, and the wind blew harder as a small whirlwind formed. They took a few more steps back. What could this be? The whirlwind grew higher and higher until it reached Xylis's height. Then it took a human shape, made out of dust. Eleanor's mouth dropped open as a man landed on the ground and smiled. "Maximus," she croaked.

Xylis seemed just as shocked, if not a little angry.

"Didn't you say you needed an explorer?" Maximus said in a scratchy voice with a thoughtful, but slightly guilty look on his dusty face.

Chapter XX

"Lieutenant Ossenna, I'm glad you are healed, and could finally make it."

"Of course, Your Majesty." Lieutenant Ossenna bowed to King Chada.

A fire crackled in the background as he sat on his throne gazing thoughtfully at the large candle on a decorated wooden table next to him. It was time Ossenna received her last chance to prove herself. "I want you to lead a platoon of Titans in a small ambush on The Western Town. I want to keep Drake and his friends occupied. Can you do that?"

"Yes, Your Majesty. Just one platoon?" she asked.

"Yes," King Chada replied. "And be warned." He narrowed his eyes and tightened his lips. "This is your last chance. Don't let me down."

"Of course, Your Majesty. Thank you for this opportunity," she said.

King Chada nodded. "Ready the platoon. I'll let you know when I want you to depart."

Ossenna bowed and left the room. King Chada stared deep into the fire almost as if he were trying to find relief from the craziness of Lyzix. He imagined himself in control. Dominating the continent. He and his Titans ruling over everything. Every town, kingdom, and creature bowing to him. Drake and his wretched friends dead, gone, swept away from Lyzix forever. They deserved it. Especially Drake, after the trouble he'd caused him. And not just since Chada had taken over Wendil...

The king shook the thoughts from his mind and refocused on the image of himself, ruling everything. It was amazingly appealing. And with enough hard work...he would get there.

*

"Maximus?" Eleanor stuttered once more. This was the first time in as long as she could remember that she was completely speechless.

"I know a lot's gone on since...then," the dust spirit said. "But I can explain—"

"Oh, you better explain," Xylis snarled from behind Eleanor. "You're going to tell us everything."

"Xylis," Eleanor snapped. "We need to stay calm and—"

"No!" Xylis shouted. "We haven't seen him since he left thirteen years ago. And now he just shows up out of the blue...looking how he is... with a smile?"

"Xylis." Eleanor put her hand on his shoulder. She didn't know what Maximus was: a ghost, a spirit, or something else, but she knew they needed to listen to him. "Maximus has always been our friend. I'm sure he would've revealed himself sooner if he could. Now, let's hear him out."

Xylis snorted and then looked at Maximus. "You'd better have a good explanation for this."

Eleanor and Xylis both sat down, while Maximus floated over to them with a sad smile.

"You bet I do." He took a deep breath. "Except, there will be parts missing—I can't help that."

"Excuse me?"

"Xylis!" Eleanor said. "Let him speak."

Maximus paused for a moment. "First, I want to apologize."

Eleanor heard Xylis mutter, "You'd better."

"I didn't abandon you. I was captured."

"Yeah right," Xylis said. "By whom?"

Eleanor smacked her apprentice on the wrist, quieting him, and then nodded for Maximus to continue.

"By King Chada."

Eleanor's mouth dropped open once more. What? Did King Chada know that Maximus was related to…no! That was impossible.

"Chada?" Xylis looked concerned now. "We have our own business with him." It was Maximus's turn to look surprised.

"We'll tell you everything, old friend. Just explain why you've been gone," Eleanor said.

Maximus nodded. "Chada interrogated me. Tortured me." Eleanor gasped, while Xylis' eyes widened, and his hands tightened into fists. Clearly her apprentice was now even more angry at Chada.

"Why?" Eleanor asked.

"That's when things get hazy," Maximus grimaced. "I said parts would be missing. And that is due to this," he gestured to himself, the dusty particles floating around his ghostly form. "I don't remember certain things. Memories of old have completely disappeared, and it's taken a long time to regain the ones I have gotten back."

"But then how did you become this…thing?" Eleanor asked.

"All I remember is a sorcerer of Chada, entered my cell, and cast an enchantment on me." Maximus pointed to himself. Eleanor's stomach clenched. Sorcerer? Could this be the sorcerer that had attacked her with Chada? She wasn't sure—she'd have to look into it more.

"After that, my memory almost completely disappeared. I remember being as light as the air, just barely holding on, half present in this and half present somewhere else." Eleanor thought she could make out a tear on Maximus's face. "For thirteen years!"

"I don't know what to say." Eleanor was shocked. How could Maximus have gone through this, and she had not known? Guilt racked her insides. "I can't believe this Maximus. I feel so terrible—"

"As do I," Xylis said. "I have no words either." The two had been childhood friends and were still very close, even after Xylis had believed Maximus had abandoned them.

"Listen, the past is the past. I was able to release myself from the daze that sorcerer put me in, but I am stuck like this, with my memory half faded. There's no use dwelling on it," Maximus said. "Now we're reunited, there are better, more important things to talk about. For instance, I heard you need some assistance with geographical navigation." He smiled widely. "I believe I can help."

*

General Mondoor stood in the forest, twiddling his thumbs nervously. He glanced around, waiting in the shade of the trees for his companion. He wasn't exactly excited for the adventure.

It was something about his companion. The man seemed…different.

The general didn't actually know much about him. King Chada had introduced them only a day ago. He'd told Mondoor the man was a sorcerer called Zebetar. Apparently, he and the king were friends, if you could call any relationship with Chada friendship. Chada had given him scant information on the purpose of the journey. The sorcerer and he were to travel north to uncover the first of two pieces of a mysterious weapon belonging to the ancient Spectacular Swordsmen Line. It seemed Chada needed it for some purpose in order to beat Drake.

Suddenly, General Mondoor heard dry leaves crackle behind him. He whirled around to see a man with a long blue cloak and raised eyebrows. A long, pointed nose with a scar running across it sat above his smirking lips. His short-cropped brown hair was slicked back.

"We're leaving, aren't we?" Zebetar asked. "Wouldn't want to get behind."

"Yes." General Mondoor nodded. "Let's get a move on. Try to get to that first platoon."

The two men slowly made their way through the dense forest, trudging among the foliage and bushes. General Mondoor tried to forget his suspicions about Zebetar as they walked, but for some reason they stuck with him. And that made him worry even more.

*

"So, you need to go after a sword made of bone?" Maximus asked. "And it's in the northern Lyzix jungle?"

"Yes," Eleanor said.

"That means we'll have to go through the Giant's Forest, and a few other unfriendly places," Maximus replied. "We'd need to watch out for Comas Disease in the Giants' Forest, too. That infection is extremely deadly."

The three sat in the library for long time, discussing the past decade. Eleanor was elated that Maximus had returned. After all, he had been one of her closest friends. They'd had many good times together. She couldn't believe he was back after thirteen years, having disappeared without a trace. They all thought he had abandoned them.

She watched Xylis and Maximus share a loud and hearty laugh and was reminded of a time when they had done so often, so long ago. She felt her mind time travel, and she remembered when she first met Xylis and Maximus, two best friends, almost thirty years ago. They were twenty-year-old hotheads needing a place to settle down. Because she had known Maximus for so long, she took them in. And when she had found that Xylis had a gift for sorcery, she immediately began training him in her ways.

Maximus had been pushed to the side a little. She regretted that now. But when she first found out about The Spectacular Swordsmen Line, Maximus immediately wanted to help her find out more along with Xylis. So, she continued training Xylis while the three of them worked together on her research. Until thirteen years ago.

She had just discovered that the source of the attacks was

King Chada and the Titans, from a letter she'd received from Mayor Kornus, after his town, Marlton, had been attacked. A few weeks later, Maximus said he needed to travel somewhere. He hadn't told Eleanor or Xylis where he was going, just said he'd be back soon. Except he never returned.

She remembered becoming more worried as the days, weeks and months passed by. And Xylis? He became increasingly infuriated and bitter, making it hard for Eleanor to continue her research.

About two years after Maximus left, Eleanor remembered a conversation—one she and Xylis had both tried to avoid. They confessed that they each suspected Maximus had abandoned them, because it was better than believing he had perished. Ever since then, Maximus had been a sore subject for them both. But now she needn't worry. He was back. Maybe not as a complete human, but at least he was with them.

"Eleanor, you've done so much work these past years," Maximus said, and then his face fell. "I'm just sorry I wasn't here to—"

"My friend," Xylis said, "you have no reason to be sorry. It wasn't your fault. It was King Chada."

Xylis extended his hand. Maximus did the same. The dust spirit's hand passed cleanly through Xylis' palm leaving a small trace of dust on the sorcerer's skin.

Eleanor and Xylis looked at each other as he stepped back, and then both fell into a long and impassioned explanation of the fall of Wendil, the failed attack, the experience in the dungeon, and the rescue. They also told Maximus that Chada's Titan general and a "magical friend" of Chada's were going to the northern jungle, gathering platoons along the way, to retrieve a mysterious artifact.

"Does this man have a long scar across his nose?" Maximus asked.

"How did you know?" Eleanor asked.

"Because he turned me into a Dust Spirit."

Xylis and Eleanor gasped. It must be him, Eleanor realized. The same sorcerer who attacked her, Drake and his parents all those years ago.

Maximus looked grim, "He's a very powerful sorcerer. He can use offensive sorcery. The power his silver shard gives him is deadly. We need to watch out for him."

"Indeed," Eleanor said. "I know who you are talking about."

"You do?" Xylis and Maximus asked.

"Yes, but we'll talk about him later," Eleanor said. "Our main priority is the artifact in the north. And Maximus, I know you'd like to help, but—"

"Stop right there." Maximus held his dusty hand up. "I know you don't want me to help. But I am going to, whether you like it or not."

Xylis looked at Eleanor, a smirk on his face. "He'll do a great job, Eleanor."

"Fine, but I can't have you captured again."

"Don't worry, I'll take care of him," Xylis said.

Maximus snorted. "I don't need taking care of. I'm just dust."

Eleanor smiled. It was getting closer to the old days. The triangle was once again complete.

She looked to Xylis. "You should head out at once, but there's one more thing.

Drake Philosopher will be traveling with you."

"He will?" The cloud of dust around Maximus swirled a little faster. "I want to meet him. I want to tell him myself."

Eleanor froze. Drake wasn't ready. He needed time to take in each revelation and process it in turn. "Don't you think it's too early? We need to let more time pass."

"I'm sorry, Eleanor," Maximus interrupted. "But enough time has already passed, and if I'm to travel with him…"

Eleanor looked thoughtful. "You're sure?"

"Yes," Maximus replied.

"I'll get him," Xylis said, but Eleanor had a sinking feeling in her gut as the sorcerer left the library.

Chapter XXI

Drake, Jerome, Isabella, and Leo were cleaning weapons, picking new ones, and getting ready for the adventure ahead. They had to leave very soon.

"What do you think of this hammer?" Jerome asked Leo. The new, shiny weapon glinted in the sunlight.

"Anything's better than your old, beat up one," Leo said, pointing to Jerome's belt.

Jerome frowned. "Never mind." He tossed the new hammer back onto the weapon pile.

"Your old one's fine, Jerome." Isabella shot a look of disgust at her brother. He shrugged. Then she said, "It's definitely better that that wimpy knife you always use, Leo."

"It is not wimpy!" he retorted.

Isabella raised her eyebrows. "And why don't we talk about your strange desire to have five or more daggers on you at once. I mean, come on. I doubt there'll be any assassination attempts against you, let alone five."

As the siblings proceeded to argue, Drake took the chance to speak to Jerome privately. He sensed something was bothering his best friend. "Why don't you want to give up your old hammer?" he asked. Jerome hesitated and Drake guessed what he was struggling with. He'd struggled with it himself on many occasions. "It's alright to tell me," he said gently. "I can help."

"All right, fine. It's all I have left from when my master was alive," Jerome said. "And I don't want to sell it."

"I understand," Drake said, but he knew he sounded awkward. He felt guilty that Jerome's master had perished while his own had survived. Sahara was amazing, and Drake still remembered the rush of relief when he discovered that Sahara was alive. And then the rush of guilt when Jerome hadn't found his master among the prisoners. It wasn't right. It wasn't fair. But it couldn't be changed.

Drake picked up a new, shiny sword, as well as a backup, along with a dagger and attached them to his belt. He was about to walk over to King Noxy and ask if they were ready to leave when Xylis came up. "Could I speak to you for a second, Drake?"

"Uh, sure," Drake replied as he was pulled aside.

"There's someone Eleanor would like you to meet. He is going to help us navigate northern Lyzix."

"Why does she want me to meet him first? Why not the whole group?"

"It's complicated," Xylis replied, a look of sympathy in his eyes. Drake felt his gut tightening.

As Drake followed Xylis toward the library, Jerome gave him a questioning look. Drake shrugged. He had no idea why the sorcerer was being so unexplanatory.

The moment he walked in the library, Drake had to fight back a scream. A large whirlwind sat in front of him.

The top half looked like a human ghost, but the bottom half was gone, replaced by swirling dust particles.

"I'm Maximus," the dusty man said.

"H-hi," Drake stuttered. Who and what was this? "I'd shake your hand, but..."

"Don't worry. I understand. An enchantment was cast upon me when I was captured thirteen years ago by King Chada."

"Chada?" Drake said. "Wow, he doesn't like you very much, I guess."

Maximus gave a thin smile. "Well, he doesn't like anyone in our family. Or our lineage, for that matter."

Drake took a moment to realize what Maximus had just said. "Our...lineage?" He felt very, very confused. Maximus took a deep breath and glanced away uncomfortably.

"Are you...related to me?" Drake asked.

"Yes," Maximus replied with care. "I'm your uncle."

Drake froze. How was that possible? This was too much. Why had Eleanor kept this from him? Why hadn't Maximus sought him out before?

"Drake?" There was worry in Eleanor's voice.

Drake didn't even know what to say. Eleanor had told him that he had no more living relatives, and now he was hearing about this. And what about his uncle's...state? The dusty whirlwind tornado shape? What was that about? Drake could almost see the sneer on Chada's face. Just by being the Swordsman Drake had messed up another of his relative's lives.

"Drake, I'm sorry." Eleanor repeated with a guilty look on her face. "I should have told you sooner."

"Yes, you should have." Drake felt anger building up

inside of him, bubbling fit to burst. Eleanor had kept this from him. How could she? Of all things, this was so important. "Why did you lie to me?" he asked.

"I didn't. I've only just found out he was alive," she replied.

Drake didn't know whether to believe her or not, but it occurred to him that if Maximus knew he had a nephew… where had he been all this time? He took a slow, steady breath. He needed to stay calm. If he had another relative, that meant that there was something bigger here. It meant that Maximus was a part of the Spectacular Swordsmen Line, too.

"I apologize for the sudden revelation. I'll answer any questions you have," Maximus said. "But first, I believe Eleanor wants the group to be introduced, and then we need to head out in order—"

The dust spirit was interrupted by a battle horn coming from outside the Western Town wall, and all thoughts of the coming journey and these revelations disappeared from Drake's mind. He rushed to the doorway to see what was going on. It was devastating.

Through the bars of the distant gate, he could see a platoon of Titans, weapons drawn and ready. A large boulder was heaved over the wall, and it crashed into the street, causing an uproar in the Western Town. Arrows began to rain down and as the battle horn sounded again, the truth settled in. It was an attack.

*

Zebetar was extremely tired of waiting for the general's men. Discipline was obviously not consistent in the Titan army. "Where are they?" he growled.

"They should be coming soon," General Mondoor said.

"Aren't you the darn general? Call them or something!" he exclaimed.

"I will have you know, sorcerer, that your skills are no match for a sword in my hand," General Mondoor snarled.

Who did this guy think he was? Zebetar wasn't going to take any of it. "Really? No respect for superior warriors, I see," Zebetar shot back. The general opened his mouth to speak, but Zebetar silenced him. "Enough of this foolishness. Where's the platoon?"

"I have no idea where they are. They said they'd meet us here."

"Wait." Zebetar heard the sound of leaves crackling and looked up at the trees towering above.

"Do you think that's them?" Mondoor asked.

"Don't know." Zebetar readied a spell incantation on his lips. It could be anyone.

Mondoor drew his sword, and the two were ready to fight.

A few seconds later, two Titans walked through the foliage with many others following.

"Platoon One, reporting for duty," the lead Titan said.

"Good to see you, Platoon One. Get ready. We're heading out soon." General Mondoor glanced at Zebetar. Zebetar smiled. The first step was complete. If they continued like this, they would have the artifact in no time.

CHAPTER XXII

THERE HAD BEEN a time when Drake believed Lyzix would remain peaceful for as long as he lived. He couldn't have been more wrong. As chaos erupted on the streets of the Western Town, he drew his sword.

Eleanor took a dagger from the folds of her cloak. She and Maximus—his uncle, apparently—ran toward the other side of town in case any Titans attacked there, too.

People were shouting for their children and dragging them inside. Others were arming themselves with any weapons they could: wooden sticks, metal pipes, food knives, even rocks from the ground. The guards along the wall and in the street immediately charged the Titans who were flooding the town. Arrows rained down on King Chada's evil henchmen. Small squads of guards tried to stop them, but they weren't having much luck. Xylis muttered to himself, conjuring his signature defensive shields. The incoming Titan arrows bounced and deflected off his magical conjurings.

As the battle exploded into action, Drake had a flashback to when Wendil was attacked. The screaming. The cries of battle. The devastation. This time was going to be different. He wasn't going to let the Titans take the Western Town. This time he was going to fight.

He leaped at the nearest Titan, who had been chasing a man with no weapons, and cut the Titan down. The man stared, shellshocked at Drake's skill, then nodded his thanks and ran off.

Drake felt someone pull him back, and he saw King Noxy, Sahara, and Jerome. "You need to get out of here! This is not safe for—"

"No!" Drake shouted. "This will not be a repeat of Wendil. This is my battle, my fight!"

Sahara opened his mouth to protest, but King Noxy elbowed him. "He can take care of himself. We have bigger problems right now."

With a reluctant look toward the invading Titans, Sahara and Noxy sprinted to the gates. A few of the attackers were trying to make their way deeper into town via the roofs, but Isabella and Leo were holding them back, working efficiently as a team. Drake had never seen them like this. Amanda was also in the midst of the fight with a dagger, along with Cyrus, wielding a spear.

"Look out!" Jerome yelled as a Titan rammed into Drake. He was knocked to the ground. The Titan pinned him down and grabbed him in an iron grip. Before he could wriggle from the man's grasp, Jerome had smashed the Titan with a hammer. The Titan fell to one side, unconscious.

"Thanks." Drake stood up and smiled at Jerome. "See, that old hammer still works as great as any new one."

The blacksmith grinned. He looked at it in mild pleasure. "I guess you're right." Looking back up, Jerome pointed to an alleyway behind Drake. "Look, I think that may be the leader. We should go after her."

Jerome was right. Turning around, Drake saw roughly ten Titans surrounding a woman in a black helmet. She had a large purple square sewn into her black outfit.

"Good idea. Let's go!" They followed her down the alleyway keeping close to the buildings until they turned the last corner.

"No!" Drake shouted, but it was too late.

The Titan leader and six of her soldiers threw lit torches into a nearby pile of lumber then ran off back towards the battle. Drake stumbled as the wood erupted into flames, which shot high into the air. Smoke filled his eyes and lungs. He let out a cough as the cloud of smoke rose to the sky, and the fire began to spread to a nearby building.

"We must stop this!" Jerome called.

"But we don't have any water!" Drake shouted. He turned to where the Titan leader had disappeared. "We have to go after her."

"And just leave a giant fire?" Jerome exclaimed.

"Someone else will deal with it. If we kill their leader, they may retreat."

Jerome sighed. "The town's going to hate us for this."

"Not if we stop the leader." Drake took a last glance at the fire which was now raging through three buildings. The first one to catch fire was already charred black with wooden beams collapsing inside. A section of the wall crashed to the ground, spreading rubble everywhere.

"Let's go," Drake said. They raced around the corner and caught sight of the Titans sprinting down another alley. Drake turned down that lane, Jerome on his tail, only to find six Titans blocking the way, waiting for him with their weapons drawn.

He slowly crept towards them, Jerome skidding to a stop by his side. As Drake leaped at the two nearest, Jerome smashed one of the Titans with his hammer. Drake, meanwhile, swiped at one of the Titans' legs, drawing blood. Another Titan took advantage of Drake's distraction to swing at him, but Drake parried and slammed the Titan against the wall with the flat of his sword. He then spun around, and while drawing another swipe of blood on the first Titan, he kicked him onto the rough cobblestones. Jerome slammed another powerfully with his hammer. Drake smacked his Titan in the cheek with the flat of his sword and finished the last off with a clean head-chop.

Drake and Jerome faced the lieutenant with her one remaining injured guard. Drake expected her to run, but instead, her eyes narrowed. She charged with lightning speed at Jerome and with two blows, a left and right swing, she had knocked him to the floor, and raised her sword to kill him.

Drake almost had a heart attack, but his instincts kicked in. He took two long strides towards his friend and slid his sword under his enemy's downward thrust, blocking the strike. The leader reeled back, spun, and swung at Drake again, but he deflected this strike too. Then with a well-aimed kick he knocked the sword out of her hand.

The leader's eyes widened. Without a second thought, she blew her battle horn and ran off. As she disappeared, she dropped another lit torch in her tracks, abandoning her guard, Drake and Jerome to their fate.

Drake helped his best friend up. "We need to get out

of here," he said over Jerome's grateful thanks, but the fire was already licking the nearby buildings, slowly spreading across the ground and enclosing them.

"Drake!" Jerome sprinted to a small patch of land that still wasn't burning. "Over here!"

Drake followed, already dripping in sweat, the fire roaring in his ears. Before he could reach the opening, however, an arrow punctured his shoulder. He was airborne for a moment, before falling to the ground and tumbling back into one of the burning buildings.

Drake tried to move, but he was paralyzed temporarily from the arrow. He began squirming in place. Tears burned in his eyes from the smoke, and he thought the fire was going to take him, but he managed to roll away. He was going to be all right. But then Jerome screamed his name. Something heavy hit his head. And Drake blacked out.

*

Drake opened his eyes slowly to see blurry shapes circling him. He gradually sat up, until a rush of nausea hit him. He collapsed back onto what seemed to be a bed.

When his vision finally cleared, he saw Amanda, standing over him, holding a clump molo weed. Next to her stood King Noxy, Jerome, and Sahara.

"What happened?" he asked. All he remembered was a lot of orange flame and smoke.

"You were hit by an arrow," Jerome said. "After the skirmish with that leader. We were lucky to get out of there."

Drake nodded. He was exhausted, and his mind was numb from the frightening events of the ambush. "What happened to the Titans?" he asked.

"They retreated," King Noxy said. "After a battle horn blew. They began escaping towards the gate, though most had been picked off by then."

Drake looked at his shoulder. "You pulled the arrow out?"

"Yes." Amanda gestured to the others to leave. "Let me give him some molo weed. He needs to rest. You can talk later." King Noxy hesitated, but then nodded and they went quietly out of the room.

"Open up." Amanda waved a spoon of molo weed in his face.

"But—"

"No buts," Amanda said.

Drake sighed. "Why does everyone say that to me?"

"Probably because you're too stubborn to listen to them," Amanda said, as she pushed his head back and stuck the molo weed in his mouth. He had only tried it a few times, and it had tasted sticky and…odd, but it had helped him feel better immediately. He gulped it down and sure enough, the throbbing in his head began to diminish, as did the aches in his shoulder and back.

"So, what's going on?" Drake asked. "Where is everyone?"

"Xylis, Leo, Isabella, and Cyrus are patrolling the Western Town, investigating the damage."

"Oh," Drake said. "And how are the mayor and townsfolk?"

"Not too happy," Amanda said. Drake knew it. He should have put out the fires. He should have listened to Jerome and not gone after the leader. "But they're not mad at us," she added. "They're furious with King Chada.

Mayor Marcemus is actually proud of us. The whole town knows you and Jerome pursued the leader and frightened her enough to call a retreat."

Drake beamed. The attack had done a lot of damage, but at least some good had come out of it. "That's great!" he said. "Anything else I should be aware of?"

"We're gathering in the library to meet Maximus."

Drake nodded, remembering the surprise visit he had received before the battle. He still couldn't believe what he'd discovered. "Okay. And how long until we depart?"

Amanda checked his arms and legs for injuries. "You should be fully healed by this afternoon. We were supposed to leave yesterday."

"It's been almost two days?"

Amanda patted the bedcovers. "Yes, but don't trouble yourself. We couldn't leave without you, could we? You're the reason we're going north in the first place: to find your weapon." Drake nodded. He was still too weak to argue. "I'm going to check on the wymer scouts, and see if they've found any more of our lost armies. I'll return soon."

As Amanda walked out, Drake sighed. No wymers had returned since the first party. That could mean three things: the scouts had found the army and were trying to get them back home; the scouts were becoming desperate and flying further and further afield with no luck; or the scouts were lost.

Drake hoped it was the first scenario. Or if it had to be, the second. But not the third. Definitely not the third.

The store's bell rang. "Amanda?" Drake called, thinking she was back already. When no response came, he grabbed a small knife that lay on the bedside table.

"Hardly," a voice replied, and a dust whirlwind appeared. Maximus sprouted out of it, his top half appearing while the dust slowly circled around his unseen bottom half.

"You know, you're probably going to scare the wits out of half of the group when Eleanor introduces you," Drake said.

"What's life without a little fun, huh?" His smile slowly morphed into a frown when he glanced at the knife in Drake's hand. "Uptight, are we? You're holding that knife like it's your lifeline."

"I'm nervous." Drake hurriedly put it down. "For the upcoming journey."

"I understand," Maximus said. "But remember, your friends will have your back. So will I. You might not believe that but let me explain why I haven't taken care of you before now. I promised you a story, didn't I?"

Drake leaned back as Maximus recounted his whole experience. He was almost speechless once his uncle had finished. "I'm so sorry, Maximus. I didn't know—"

"No problem, my boy," Maximus replied. "We're reunited. That's all that matters. I wanted to address something else, too. I heard from Xylis that you were very brave during the battle last night."

Drake blushed. "It was nothing."

"But it was," Maximus replied. "You did a great deed, running after that leader and causing the retreat, even though some would call it foolish."

"Thank you!" Drake exclaimed. "I mean, Jerome and I handled it perfectly, and we didn't need any—"

"But your master is right, Drake. More can be accomplished with other people. Sometimes stopping and thinking is the best thing to do. I say this as your uncle, and I want you to remember. It takes a man of great courage to ask for help," Maximus said. "I hope you will be that man someday."

Drake considered his uncle's words. He was perhaps starting to understand what Sahara had always told him—be willing to collaborate. But it didn't come naturally. "Can I come with you when you meet the group?" he asked, finally.

"I don't think you should be moving about yet."

"I want to come," Drake said.

"Your apothecary and herbalist friend wants you to rest, and I hear she can be pretty fierce."

"I'm fine—" Drake argued.

"But—"

"No buts," Drake said to his uncle, and he felt his lips curve into a smile.

"Fine," Maximus sighed. "I see there's no stopping you."

Drake slowly got out of bed, but when he put weight on his leg, his knee wouldn't bend. He toppled forward and landed on the floor. He slowly pushed himself up and climbed back onto bed, sinking down into the thin mattress.

"Okay, it's decided." Maximus said. "You need to stay here."

"But—"

"No buts!" Maximus chuckled.

There it was again! Drake groaned. What was with these people and those two words?

Maximus disappeared leaving Drake alone. Drake leaned back and laid his head on the pillow. Rest? Why was everyone saying he needed rest? He didn't. Now he was going to be stuck here all day, not tired, with nothing but worries on his mind…

*

"Well, it looks like someone was tired after all." King Noxy beamed at Drake.

"I guess." Drake rubbed his eyes and sat up quickly, remembering he was holding up the group. "I'm ready to leave."

"You're sure?" King Noxy asked. "This is no tea party we're going to."

"I'm ready."

"In that case," King Noxy said, "there is one more person you must meet."

A woman walked up to Drake and extended her hand. Drake swung himself out of bed to greet her, and he was pleased to feel no pain from his knee. It was stiff, but much better.

"I'm Reya. Xylis and I used to work together when we were younger. I think we'll make a good team against this sorcerer accompanying the Titans."

"Good," King Noxy said. "Now I believe the rest of the group is assembled at the gate with the horses, ready to go."

"Horses? Why not wymers?" Drake asked.

"Maximus warned us against it," King Noxy said. "Finding a wild pack with enough for all of us to ride down here will be difficult, as they usually only hang around in large numbers up in the north and far west," King Noxy said, as Drake's eyes widened. "It would take too much time. We have horses readily on hand. We'll just have to travel on them for now."

Drake followed Xylis, King Noxy and Reya, a tad disappointed that he wouldn't be able to fly. As the gate came into view, Jerome, Isabella, and Leo ran to greet him, patting him on the back, smiling and hugging him. Then they did their final checks: materials, food, water, weapons, and more.

Drake was too caught up in his head to notice much of what was going on. They were going to find this artifact, whether it be the sword or jewel. He was getting closer to figuring out what his Spectacular Swordsman title truly meant, and he wasn't sure he was ready to find out.

As the group saddled their horses, the only thing that Drake truly processed before they departed was Eleanor coming up to him and saying, "I know you're nervous, Drake."

"Dazed is more like it."

"Whatever your feelings," she said, "remember what I told you earlier. Believe in the people of Lyzix, in your friends, and yourself. You will make it. There's nothing to worry about. Meanwhile, I'll find as much information as I can about these artifacts. And hey," she said, becoming serious once more. "Please be careful."

"You too," Drake said, and with that the group was off. He looked to the horizon where the sun was slowly setting. They were going to make it, just like Eleanor had said.

*

Jerome was still trying to tighten his saddle one last time. As he pulled the straps, he still couldn't believe they were here, at this point, ready to go north to stop King Chada from getting a step ahead in his attempt to seize Lyzix. Jerome was so proud of Drake, and how much he'd gone through, and he was ready to help him in any way he could.

"It's time to head out, my friends!" King Noxy's commanding voice cut through his thoughts. "We need to get moving."

There was a sudden clutter of movement as the group's horses began moving by Jerome, and he was pushed aside slightly by the commotion. The king was right, they had to get moving. General Mondoor and Chada's sorcerer were continuing to get closer to the sword.

Once the horses had passed, Jerome went and mounted his horse. It stood next to two remaining ones; Xylis and Reya were still with Eleanor. They should be coming in a second.

However, when Jerome hopped on, his leg rested against the saddlebags, and he felt a hard object lying inside. Confused, he opened them, and looking inside, on top of the journey's supplies was a glinting bar of tin.

"Jerome! You heard Noxy! He wants us to hurry! We'll wait for Xylis and Reya outside." Drake, Isabella, and Leo were gesturing for him to catch up. He looked back down at the saddlebags, hesitating for a moment. He hadn't seen this before. But it seemed valuable to the group. Perhaps they could sell it? He would hold onto it, just in case.

So, despite the unknowns, and his slight uncertainty, he jumped on his horse, and pocketed the tin.

CHAPTER XXIII

By the time the Western Town was a mere dot on the horizon, Drake, Jerome, Isabella, and Leo were deep in conversation about the artifact in the jungle. Ever since Drake had heard Eleanor mention the weapon, he had been curious how exactly it interacted with the vault, and what else the sword could do. He could not fathom it out, so he asked the others what they thought.

"We'll just have to see." Leo said. "But if we have it, Chada doesn't. He wants it so badly it must be important, so just us getting it first must mean we've practically won. That is worth a trip north any day."

"Maybe the sword does something really special. It's made of…what did Eleanor say?"

"Obilor bone," Drake replied.

"Wasn't that the creature you fought in the trials?" Isabella asked.

Drake nodded. "It was powerful. Shot water, breathed fire. I don't ever want to see it again, and trust me, you don't either." They changed topics.

"Where do you think it'll be in the jungle?" Leo asked.

"Who knows? Atticus probably hid the pieces. There may even been something guarding it," Drake said.

"Unless, of course, Chada set us up," Jerome said, slyly.

Leo let out a short laugh. "Trust me, I think there's a very slim chance that Chada got someone to pretend to head north to get this artifact. I'm sure we are pursuing something very real."

Jerome, Leo, and Isabella began talking about other things, but Drake was no longer listening. He was thinking back to another conversation in the library, briefly after Eleanor had discovered the information about the Spectacular Sword. "Be extremely careful," she had said. "I don't trust Chada. He may have wanted you to hear that conversation."

Drake thought back to the open window. They had found out about this weapon through the enemy and a small piece of information from the library that Eleanor hadn't found in the last thirteen years she'd been looking. Both Chada and the information had made it seem like this artifact was extremely powerful. But nothing entirely proved it existed. And if it didn't…

Then they were on a fool's errand.

*

"Is camp almost broken down?" Zebetar asked. "Because we need to get a move on and get to the jungle."

"Will you relax?" General Mondoor said. "King Chada will not be pleased if someone discovers our plan and route. It'll be a few more minutes."

"Ha!" Zebetar smirked. "Some powerful sorcery must be at work, because now I am starting to believe you."

General Mondoor shot his companion a glare as the

sorcerer chuckled. One of the Titans walked up to Mondoor and saluted him. "We are ready to march, Sir," he said.

Zebetar looked at the sunset and smiled. They were getting closer to the jungle, closer to the prize. Closer to victory. Once they were there, they just had to grab the artifact and bring it back to Chada.

He was jerked out of his thoughts by a lurch of his hand. He felt it weighed down, as if something very heavy had materialized out of thin air and landed in his palm. His eyes darted down, but there was nothing to look at. Nothing was there. Nothing was wrong. It was only his trusty silver shard in his hand, the one that he relied on to make his sorcery more powerful. Nothing else.

It was strange, because he'd never had his sorcery get out of control before.

But that didn't mean it was abnormal, or a cause of concern.

No, certainly not. Zebetar's sorcery had never failed him. It was…it must be the environment, yes. Just the environment. Or some other odd factor. Definitely nothing to worry about. Absolutely nothing to worry about.

*

Eleanor had been searching through documents and scrolls for a half a day now, trying to ignore the sinking feeling in her chest. Still nothing. No thoughts. No ideas. No revealing moments that could tell her what she wanted to know. The last thing she wanted was to send the group into danger, particularly Drake. So she needed to figure out what was wrong, and quickly.

"There's something missing," she muttered as she stood

in the library unfurling a dusty and delicate scroll. "There has to be. It doesn't add up. This artifact. Chada's attacks. Atticus's disappearance. This new sorcerer…"

She paused abruptly. The sorcerer. Her mouth opened with horror. She forgot to tell the group her suspicions; and more importantly, Drake! He would be caught so off guard if he encountered the sorcerer that it could be his downfall. She had to hope Maximus may tell him, or that he would be strong and resilient. She had faith in him. Because, right now, she had other things to worry about.

She set the scroll she had been holding back down on her desk and slumped down into her chair. Where else should she look for more Spectacular Swordsman information? Where were the answers?

Eleanor sat up so suddenly that she knocked a pile of papers from her desk, and she didn't even care. Her head whirled to the top shelves where a small pile of scrolls sat. Her memory flashed back thirteen years. Maximus had been searching through those very same scrolls before he disappeared. Eleanor had put them aside because it had been too painful to think about him. And she'd totally forgotten about them. So she practically tripped over herself as she raced to the shelves and yanked the scrolls down. She cleared her other papers and documents to one side, set the scrolls down and began reading. Her excited heartbeat started to slow, however, as each scroll failed to reveal anything new. Her doubt-filled thoughts increased. The next one, it would be in the next one. Come on, come on! It has to be here. Maximus had to have found something. Please, please, please!

Finally, as she scanned one of the last scrolls, she saw

something at the bottom of the parchment that caused her to screech to a halt. The scroll was talking about someone named Reuben Fox. Who was he? She'd never heard of him before. So, naturally, she began to read.

> Reuben Fox was a man of great honor, born after the Ancient Kingdom and Zar's rule. He agreed with his good friends Loron and Quendal that Lyzix needed a better way to keep itself at peace. So, Fox created The Spectacular Sword, a special sword that would be passed down a line of apprentices and masters, who would wield it to protect the continent. It would eventually become the key to a hidden vault of silver in the center of Lyzix. This vault would be opened in an emergency to power the sorcerers should Lyzix need to fight against a universal threat. And this was the beginning of the Spectacular Swordsmen Line. Reuben Fox was the first.

Eleanor could not contain her excitement. This was the breakthrough she needed. She had to look for references to this Rueben Fox character elsewhere.

But where to start?

She glanced back at the scroll and noticed one tiny scrawled word at the bottom: *Torches*. It was as if the scroll had read her mind. Her heart almost exploded out of her chest. This was in Maximus' handwriting. But torches, out of all words? What in Lyzix's name did he mean?

*

The group had been on the road for almost twelve hours, with barely a break to eat and to rest the horses. "When's our next stop?" Drake asked.

"What?" Maximus had been drifting next to Drake for a while now, apparently caught up in his own thoughts. "There's an inn, Bull Horns Inn, up ahead. Then, we'll have to travel for a while before reaching the Giants' Forest. That's close to our halfway point." He looked down at Drake and smiled. "Not already hungry again, are we?"

"No," Drake replied quickly, feeling his spirits lift a little at the sight of his uncle smiling.

He was just about to ask Maximus more about the Giants' Forest, when he heard a rustle in the bushes. He glanced to the left to see a blur of black race in the opposite direction. It was there and gone in a moment.

What had he seen? He had absolutely no idea. King Noxy and Sahara were too far ahead, and the rest of the group was further behind. Maximus was lost in his own world. Did he see it? Drake didn't know. Maybe it has been his imagination.

"Maximus?" He had to repeat himself three times before his uncle heard.

"Yes, Drake? Do you have something on your mind? You seem distracted."

Drake nodded slowly, "I am. I, uh…" He stopped for a moment. There were a few things circling around in his head. Eleanor's words, his worries, his friends' whispers. In the end, he decided to go with what he had just seen a few minutes ago.

"I just saw something…a bit off."

Maximus frowned. "Go on."

"It was a blur of black." Drake twisted in his saddle to point at the bush. "It was there and then disappeared extremely fast."

Maximus's frown was now etched deeper in his face. "I didn't see anything, but thank you for telling me. King Noxy will want to know."

"Wait, before you go," Drake called. "You seem off as well. Distant. You didn't respond to me for a few moments. You seemed to be thinking of something else. Is everything all right?"

"It's one of the many disadvantages of being a dust spirit." Maximus sighed. "My mind can be as distant as my body, floating off into the unknown. I can't control it." He frowned for a moment. "And I always feel like I am forgetting something, like it's at the forefront of my mind…but I don't know what it is." He sighed. "Well, such is the price that comes with my state, and with my dormancy these the past thirteen years. Now, stay here, my boy. I'll tell Noxy what you saw." Maximus increased his speed and floated to where the king and Sahara were talking adamantly. It was only a few moments before the dust spirit returned.

"King Noxy thanked me for telling him. He said he'd keep an eye out," Maximus said, and then he fell silent. Drake was glad he was able to raise the warning, but now he felt an impulse to ask something that was completely different from what they were talking about, something that he should have asked long ago. "Can you tell me more about my parents?"

Maximus slowly turned towards him. Drake was worried he had said something wrong, until a cheery grin broke out on his uncle's face.

"My boy, of course." Maximus exclaimed. "I had a feeling you would want to know details. And details I have. They were extraordinary people. I had two brothers, and one was your father, of course. Now, I shall begin my account when your father and I were young, and shall I say, not very smart..."

*

Zebetar walked along the broken and worn cobblestone path, watching the stones pass beneath his feet, but he was registering none of it. His mind was consumed with what had happened with his hand. He had attributed it to a weird spasm of sorcery, or the environment, but what if he was wrong? He smacked himself on his arm. He was being silly. Nothing was wrong with him. He was more powerful than most sorcerers that had walked the earth. How could he be worrying about this when he had other, more important things, to think about? The last thing he needed was to be a paranoid fool.

He abruptly looked up, realizing that the landscape was changing. Sure enough, in the distance, towering trees stood almost five hundred feet high. This was the Giants' Forest.

"Amazing," he said.

General Mondoor was at a loss for words. "Definitely. Absolutely stunning."

Zebetar forgot his worries for a moment. "You finally agree with me on something. What a pleasant surprise."

General Mondoor scowled. He gestured to the army to move closer.

"It looks farther than it is. We still have to traverse these hills before reaching it." Zebetar pointed ahead. "The

Giants' Forest marks a little less than the halfway point." And the worst was yet to come.

"It's getting late," General Mondoor said. "What's our plan?"

"We'll make camp on the edge of the forest. I tell you, it's no place to be at night," Zebetar said. "We'll journey through the forest in the morning."

Zebetar took the lead, his boots shuffling in the tall grass. As he moved forward, however, his whole body grew hot. His face was illuminated for a moment with flickering orange light. He jumped back, almost tripping over his long blue cloak. His mind went immediately to the strange magical happening earlier and he felt a sinking feeling in his stomach. Could this be related?

Then he remembered he was nearing the Giants' Forest and dismissed the thought, sighing with relief. It was one of the most magical places in Lyzix. The trees were as old as the continent itself, so they had absorbed all the sorcery that sorcerers had used as long as it had been around. There was almost too much magical energy in the trees. They had to let it out sometimes. It was true strange things happened inside the forest, normally, not outside. But there couldn't be any other explanation.

Zebetar would deal with these strange happenings later. For now, he needed to focus on the journey ahead. That was the most important thing, right now. They would arrive at the Giants' Forest at sunset. They would be halfway through the journey then. Halfway to this artifact that they so desperately needed. Halfway, in fact, to victory.

Chapter XXIV

At the very back of the caravan. Jerome felt himself slowly drooping to the side of his horse, falling asleep. He caught himself and shook his head to keep himself awake. Only a little more time until they reached the inn. Then he could rest his eyes. He didn't know why he was feeling so groggy. He was falling asleep mid-thought. Something was wrong with his body cycle. He was usually up fairly late at night doing blacksmith work. At least, he had been. Stranger still, the others didn't seem to be suffering anywhere near as much as him.

Isabella and Leo were up ahead. Leo was muttering to himself and then smirked, while Isabella was craning her neck to see the rest of the caravan riding ahead. King Noxy and Sahara were in the lead. Drake and Maximus were after them, deep in conversation. Good. Hopefully, Drake was confiding in Maximus. When Jerome was talking to him earlier in the day, with Isabella and Leo, he had seemed distant. It was very strange.

Jerome felt himself falling asleep again and, as he shook himself awake for a second time, he felt a small and subtle tingling in his arm. It sizzled and spread throughout his whole body until he felt calm and relaxed. He tried to stay awake, focusing on the surrounding terrain, but he was not successful. Within seconds, he had fallen asleep once more.

*

"Really?" Drake exclaimed.

Maximus laughed. "Yes, your father was one of the most well-behaved people I know. I turned out quite the opposite. Biggest misfit you'll probably ever meet. It was hard to believe we were brothers. We were so different, but very close. Anyway, back to the story. As we grew older, Lloyd and I weren't able to see each other much, because of my expeditions across Lyzix, as well as my work with Xylis and Eleanor. But when we did, it was so joyful. He was also an exceptional swordsman. Something that, with some more help from Sahara, you will inherit too."

Drake felt himself flush. His father was a great swordsman? He was a member of the Spectacular Swordsmen Line, so maybe that was part of it. But still, something about that connection made Drake feel even happier.

"Time moved on. As I continued to lead journeys across Lyzix, your father became part of the personal entourage for many kings. He was regarded as a very skilled swordsman. I can't tell you more because I was away so much. But eventually I stopped my adventures and stayed with Xylis and Eleanor. That was around the time when I met your mother. Yes, I knew her first. She was a stunning woman, Mirella. She had flowing blonde hair, light blue eyes, and a wonderful smile. Was a fantastic artist too, had an amazing gift with a paintbrush. She did not paint for a living though—instead she was a tailor, yet her skill in art definitely showed itself in her designs and patterns on certain articles and clothing. Anyway, I met her on one of my last journeys in a town north of Wendil. I invited her to dine with my parents and Lloyd.

"I could tell my brother liked her. He was a courteous and great man, but love made him act funny sometimes. I can't remember the amount of times I howled with laughter at something he did or said.

"Luckily, Mirella didn't think he was a raving lunatic. And things just blossomed from there. They began dating, and soon, they announced their engagement. The wedding was beautiful: flowers, candles, a great turnout, and amazing music. I was the best man. Everyone loved it, especially my parents and Mirella's parents."

Drake felt his heart racing. This was a wonderful tale: his parents' love story. He felt eager for more. "And? What happened after that?"

He immediately regretted his question. Maximus scowled, and it almost seemed like bags appeared under his transparent eyes. The dust whirlwind at his legs and feet slowed almost to a stop, and he spoke darkly. "A while later, Eleanor discovered some important information about the Spectacular Swordsmen Line, and right after, I left for my journey. I can't tell you what happened then because… well…I was gone. And, then you know what came next."

Indeed, Drake did. That was when everything went haywire. Maximus was captured and turned into a dust spirit, disappearing until now, Drake's parents had been killed, and Eleanor and Xylis had completely lost their minds.

"What about that other brother of yours and my father's

you mentioned in the beginning?" Drake hoped that he may have another living relative, someone who could tell him even more about his parents. And because Drake's father's side was where the Spectacular Swordsmen Line came from, he also knew that this third Philosopher brother would be a part of the line as well.

Maximus's lips tightened and his eyes hardened. "He… it was a…complicated situation."

Drake frowned. "What do you mean?"

"There is only one thing you need to know about him, Drake. He made bad decisions. Got himself into trouble."

"What kind of decisions?" Drake needed to know.

Maximus hesitated. "I want you to pretend I never mentioned him. He's bad news, Drake, bad news. That's enough talk for tonight. I need to guide Noxy to the inn."

Maximus floated to the front of the group, leaving Drake with some pretty rotten thoughts. This other uncle obviously wasn't respected by the rest of the Philosophers. Why? Why was Maximus so keen on forgetting him?

*

"What?" Saliva flew from King Chada's mouth. "They found out?"

"I'm sorry, sir, but I had no idea." The Titan scout shifted to his other foot. King Chada glared, and then glanced around the throne room. The only sound was the crackling fire, like a time bomb waiting to explode.

King Chada had just finished meeting with Ossenna about the Western Town ambush. But his victory had been short-lived. This scout was just reporting that Drake and the caravan had left the Western Town discussing an artifact and a weapon. How could Drake and his friends have discovered what he was doing, what he was looking for? Everything had been a secret.

King Chada thought back to his meeting in that hidden tower in the castle. He vaguely remembered seeing the window open. Voices carry. Was it possible that someone had heard?

He threw his sword at the wall, making the Titan and the two guards jump back. The clang of metal echoed as King Chada pondered what to do next. How could he be so stupid? How could he have left the window open? This would be his downfall: a careless mistake.

Now Drake and his friends were on their way, he had to retaliate. He must notify Zebetar and General Mondoor. Tell them to go as fast as they could or slow down Drake down. Or better yet, do both. "Guard, bring me the best messenger you've got. Now."

"Right away, Your Highness. He is a newbie, but seems pretty dedicated and—"

"I said now!" King Chada bellowed. The guard scampered from the room.

"Now, you two," Chada looked to the scout and the other guard, "notify Titan platoons twenty through twenty-three that they will be leaving shortly." He slid off his throne. "They must head towards the northern jungle, following in the steps of General Mondoor. They will intercept Drake and his little group and slow them down."

"Yes, my Lord." As the Titans exited the room, King Chada leaned wearily against his throne, wiping sweat from his brow. He had made a terrible mistake. And now he might pay for it. He waited impatiently for the guard to return.

The guard bowed. "Here he is, Your Highness. Ready—"

"Just shut up and get out of my sight before I execute you!" King Chada howled. The guard bolted from the room. King Chada then glared at the Titan in front of him, but surprisingly, the Titan didn't back down. Chada paused. Courage. He could respect that.

"What is your name, Titan?" He leaned forward on his throne towards the black-clothed man with slight curiosity.

"Qualdor, sir," the Titan replied.

"Well, Qualdor, I have a very important job for you. I need you to take this message to General Mondoor." Chada handed him a scroll, and then narrowed his eyes. "Whatever you do, don't let this fall in enemy hands. If you have no way out but capture, rip it up, or burn it."

Qualdor took the scroll, bowed, and left the room. Meanwhile, the king leaned back in his throne, relaxing his mind and trying to calm his earlier burst of anger. He didn't have faith in a lot of people, except his general and the sorcerer. He trusted that they were far ahead. And if they weren't…well, he just had to hope Qualdor would come through.

*

Eleanor set down the five scrolls she had just looked through. She was exhausted, exasperated, and irritated.

After reading Maximus's completely unhelpful word "torches", she had searched everywhere for what he could mean and had found absolutely nothing. She couldn't send him a message to ask him what he'd meant. It would take too long to reach him, and this was urgent. She'd read through all the scrolls he'd set aside again, hoping to find some reference and once again, she'd had no luck.

She slowly lifted herself out of her chair, and stretched her legs, barely aware of what she was doing. She walked around the back room, scanning the shelves, wracking her brains for what Maximus might have meant. Torches. Torches. Eleanor used oil lamps in the library, not torches. Torches were too dangerous: an open flame with so many books in the vicinity. Not a good idea. But if Maximus had written *torches,* then what in the name of Lyzix did it mean?

She walked into the main room of the library, scanned the shelves and walked up the stairs to the second floor. She perused the aisles, checking for some sign of a torch. By the time she reached the end of the last section, she was ready to give up when suddenly she saw a small symbol inscribed on the wall, very close to the bookshelf. If not looking purposefully, she would have never noticed it was there. When she glanced closer at it, her breath caught.

It was in the shape of a torch.

Eleanor placed her finger on the symbol and pressed down. She then stepped back, her heart swelling with joy, as she heard a rumble. The brick on the left side of the miniscule torch symbol began to slowly slide away, revealing a dark, slightly damp-smelling cupboard. And inside was a loose piece of paper, old and crumbling around the edges. Eleanor thought it would barely hold together if she lifted it up. When she saw the title, her mouth dropped open: Reuben Fox Family Tree.

This is what she needed. Maybe she could find out more about Atticus's disappearance through this. She began to skim the names, not recognizing any of them: *Carus, Ignitus, Philib…*

She continued down as fast as she could go: *Marcus, Warren, Io…*

A few names after that, the page ended abruptly. There was no sign of Atticus, Maximus, or Drake.

What could that mean? Was she wrong? Had she lied to Drake without knowing it? If Drake wasn't part of the Spectacular Swordsmen Line, then all her research was a waste. And what would she tell Drake? He would be devastated and angry.

She leaned against the nearest shelf, ignoring its creak of protest, and put her face in her hands. How could she have been so stupid? Drake and his friends were now on a quest for nothing. A journey that could kill them for sure.

She stole herself to look at the Family Tree again and noticed a name on the bottom of the page. In writing that she could barely decipher—she held the scroll carefully up to the light tilting it one way and then the other—was the name *Zeldrin.* The only name on the whole scroll with an *X* over it. It had been crossed out.

Eleanor looked to the bottom of the page, searching for a clue. Why would the name have been crossed out? She tried to think, but she her mind was becoming groggy. She closed her eyes, then opened them abruptly, blinking a few times. She couldn't fall asleep now. But she was so tired!

Eleanor tried to leave the room to get some fresh air, but her legs felt like jelly. Her eyes drooped closed. She leaned against a nearby shelf, and tried to resist the exhaustion, but it wasn't enough. She fell into a deep sleep.

Chapter XXV

"There's the Inn," Maximus said.

Drake looked up and saw a large building at the side of the road, light flooding through the windows and out into the dark night. He wanted to collapse into bed immediately. They were to get only a few hours of rest. Not the whole night, but it was something.

"We need to be on the lookout when we go inside," King Noxy said, as Sahara hurried ahead to secure rooms and food. "King Chada may know that we are following him. He will try to stop us at all costs."

"I'll keep watch outside the inn while you all rest, just in case Titans come this way," Maximus said.

"Don't you need to rest?" Drake didn't want his uncle to exhaust himself.

"My boy, I appreciate your concern, but a dust spirit does not need sleep." Maximus cracked a smile. "The only time I'm exhausted is when the wind blows harder."

Drake returned his uncle's joke with a grin.

A stable boy exited a side door and approached King Noxy as they dismounted.

"What can I do for you, folks?" he asked in a high-pitched voice.

"Our friend just went in to secure some rooms," King Noxy said. "Could you stable our horses with his?"

The stable boy nodded. King Noxy tossed him a few silver coins.

Inside, cheery music was playing, and a group of people sat in the center of the inn, drinking and laughing. The tables were all made of rough, worn wood. Shields and cloth coats of arms hung on the walls. They all displayed the symbol of a bull's head with very prominent, curled horns. One man in the corner swayed to the music. He was holding a mug in each hand and slopping the contents down himself. Another hooded figure sat in the corner. Drake couldn't see his face.

"Stay close." King Noxy was eyeing the hooded figure suspiciously. "No need to draw attention."

Drake nodded, and they walked up to the counter. He felt like he was back in the Brass Bee Inn, and he imaged himself dancing to cheery music, celebrating the rescue, along with the rest of the group. Oh, what'd he'd give to be there.

"A friend of ours just came in." King Noxy said to the innkeeper, a plump, dark-skinned man, with glasses and a small, black goatee.

"Upstairs," the innkeeper replied. "My wife's just shown him the rooms."

King Noxy thanked him and they made their way upstairs. There was a long hallway lined with landscape paintings. In between, the Bull Horns Inn crest was painted on the plaster walls.

Drake was fascinated by the elaborate decor, so he was interested to find out what the rooms looked like. Sahara was waiting for them down the next red-carpeted hall.

"There you are," he said. "Are the others coming?"

"Yes, they'll be here soon. Why don't you two get some rest," King Noxy said.

Drake didn't need telling twice. He and Sahara entered the nearest room. It was simple, with a desk, a wooden chair and two beds. A cloth coat of arms hung above the door, with another picture of the curly-horned bull.

As Drake yanked back his sheets, his master sat at the nearby desk. "Drake," he said, "I want to tell you something. Eleanor believes we should continue training. Even though she doesn't completely understand the role of the Spectacular Swordsman, she wants you to be as prepared as possible."

Drake nodded. Yes! He was going to continue training! It would be just like old times, back when things were simpler, before the life he had known was ripped away.

"We'll sneak in lessons when we can. Starting tomorrow." Sahara paused. He opened his mouth as if he wanted to say something, hesitated and then continued. "And I'll try ease up on you. I just wanted you to be prepared for life, and I may have pushed a little too hard the weeks before Wendil was attacked."

"Like you said in the dungeon," Drake said, "all water under the bridge."

Sahara smiled. "I miss our old lessons."

"So do I." Drake replied, and the two shared a look of mutual respect.

As soon as Drake's head hit the pillow, he immediately fell asleep.

*

Jerome settled into bed while Leo disappeared to find some food. The strange fatigue was hitting him hard. He tried to think back through everything that had happened since the rescue and work out when it had started. Everything had been great until they had begun looking for this piece of the Spectacular Sword. But he couldn't begin to work out how that made him tired. That was just silly.

His mind began to wander, thinking about his master, the group, this artifact in the north, the tin he'd found in the saddlebags. Then, his arm sizzled again.

CRASH!

He whipped upright to face hundreds of small wooden flecks that had once been a table fluttering to the ground. And, as if that wasn't shocking enough, he then watched as all the pieces vanished in front of his very eyes. There was no trace of them, or the table.

It was all gone.

Jerome thought back to the sizzle in his arm. Could this be related?

The more he thought about it, the more he believed it was true. But there was one question nagging him as he stared at the place where the table had once sat.

What was the cause?

*

Drake was looking down at a large drop below him, standing on the slanted roof of a castle tower. There was nothing waiting below. Just darkness. And evil. And suddenly, Drake realized he'd had this dream before.

"Drake." King Chada was circling him. "Welcome back. How nice to see you again. It's been so long."

Drake looked away, trying to block Chada's voice. Why was he here? This dream, it was all too familiar. And it scared him, because he knew what would happen if he attacked the king. He needed to ignore him. He'd wake up eventually. He just needed to hold out.

"Drake, you know what to do. There's no other way," Chada said.

Perhaps Drake could try to overpower him this time. He knew Chada would attempt to bait him. But instead, Drake could slowly approach and then strike. Perhaps that would work.

"I think there is," Drake replied.

Chada seemed surprised for a moment, but he masked it. "What do you mean, there's another way?"

Drake stepped towards Chada, putting a hand on his sword. "There is always another way. Your tricks are getting old. I know what you are going to do."

Chada frowned. "Do you now?" He paused. "Well, I guess I'll just take care of you the easy way."

And taking Drake by complete surprise, Chada leapt at him, and whacked him in the ribs with the flat of his sword. Drake felt nothing but air as blackness slowly solidified around him. He'd fallen into the abyss. He hadn't been reckless, foolish, or hotheaded this time, but he'd still ended up in the exact same place.

Drake woke in a cold sweat, his hands still flailing as if he was falling, when he realized that he was in the tavern bed, safe. He noticed a flickering light ahead of him and the silhouette of Sahara in the shadow of a small candle.

He was still sitting on the wooden chair that faced the desk. Meditating, no doubt. The curtains were slightly drawn open. It was the middle of the night. Drake could see the distant white glow of the moon.

He hadn't had that dream since he was in the dungeon. Why had it happened now, of all times? He was worried that it might be a sign. That it meant something big was going to happen—a final confrontation with King Chada. He knew that he wasn't going to get an answer, so he turned his attention to his master instead.

"Sahara?" he asked. "Is everything all right?"

His master looked surprised. "Drake, my boy. Having trouble sleeping?"

"Yes." Drake didn't know whether to tell Sahara about the dream. He'd had it before, but with the events of the rescue he had completely forgotten about it. Until now. "I had a dream…a dream I've had before."

Sahara stood and leaned against the desk, fully facing his pupil now. He frowned slightly. "What was it about?"

"I was with King Chada, and we were fighting with swords. He was taunting me about my parents. It's always like that." Drake felt slightly childish. "I attacked him, and he threw me into an abyss. That's always part of the dream. I've no idea what it means."

"Don't dwell on it, Drake," Sahara said, though he looked worried. "Who knows why we dream what we dream. I wouldn't worry about it, but tell me if you have more."

"Okay. But what about you?" He recalled other times when he'd seen his master meditating. "Something on your mind?"

"Given everything that's going on, meditating helps

clear the mind. And I was deciding which lesson on swordsmanship I'll teach you next. Speaking of which, since we're both awake, perhaps we should start now?"

Drake's thoughts brightened at this. "Sure. It'll take my mind off things."

It didn't take them long to get outside. Sahara grabbed one of the torches from the side of the path, and held it up, lighting the area around them. Just along the path a field next to the inn appeared to be the perfect place to train.

Maximus was drifting a bit away from the inn, staring at the moon. He wasn't doing a particularly good job of being on guard, seeing as he didn't appear to notice them, but now that Sahara and Drake were outside, they could keep an eye out for any threats and warn the group too, if need be.

"First off," Sahara said, "let me see your tuck and slash. We never finished it." He picked up a broken branch and stuck it in the earth. "Aim for that."

Drake drew his sword, readying himself as Sahara held the torch up and stepped back. He remembered what Sahara had taught him. It was just a stick. He could do this.

He ran forward and jumped, tucking his legs into a crouch as he landed right in front of the stick. He whipped his sword across the wood, sliced it in two and got back into his base fighting position in one fluid move.

Drake saw the glow of the torch flickering on Sahara's face as his master smiled. "That was very good, Drake. I'm impressed! You're obviously ready for the next lesson."

"Thanks." Drake felt proud. It had been a long time since he and Sahara had shared a good, solid lesson together. It was already starting to feel more like the old times: just him and his master explaining the lesson, Drake copying his moves, his worries being sucked away.

"So, your next lesson will be the spin, slash, and stab." Sahara handed Drake the torch. "You begin in this position, facing your target."

Drake paid close attention, watching as Sahara went through the spin, quickly slashing his sword across his imaginary target and then following it with a powerful stab.

"I don't expect you to get this on your first attempt. It took me a few times to understand it, and longer to master it," Sahara said as Drake handed the torch back.

His words were reassuring. Drake readied himself for his first attempt as Sahara grabbed another branch off the ground and stuck it in the dirt. Drake breathed deeply a few times, and then tried the spin. It didn't exactly go as planned. He tripped over his own feet and fell, feeling the dried grass tickle his skin. He slowly stood up and looked sheepishly at Sahara.

"Don't worry," Sahara said. "Swordsmanship's not just about running around and throwing blows at each other. You must be graceful and light on your feet. Let's try again, shall we?"

The second time, Drake nailed the spin, but his slash completely missed. The weight of the sword pulled him past the branch, and he fell to the ground once more.

"Well, you got the spin." Sahara switched the torch from his left hand to his right. "Now just the slash, and the stab should be fairly easy. Then, you're good to go."

As Drake stood up, he began to feel annoyed. Why couldn't he get this right? Maybe it was Sahara. He knew his master meant well, but his words of encouragement made him feel insignificant, almost childish. Drake suppressed his irritation and decided he would think more before he acted. He did not want any more fights with his master.

He tried the move a third time. It was better, but still not complete. Once again, he nailed the spin, and his slash worked, but when he went for the stab, the sword slipped out of his hand.

"Every attempt is getting better. Let's try again," Sahara encouraged. And so it went.

Drake continued to attempt the move, but not once could he get it to the standard Sahara expected. He was frustrated for not being able to perform the move, and at Sahara for pushing him this hard, and his irritation grew with every failed attempt. He tried to keep it in as long as he could, but on what seemed like his fiftieth attempt, his anger broke loose.

"You are so close," Sahara said after Drake had slammed into the branch, breaking it in half. "Just—"

"No!" Drake shouted. "No more "justs" or "buts!" We're done here!"

Sahara looked shocked, and it took him a few moments to actually speak a fully formed word. "But…why?" Sahara asked. "Why do you want to stop the lesson? I thought you wanted to do it tonight."

"I'm done," Drake said. "I'm done with this move. We need to try again some other time."

"I didn't teach you to be a quitter." Sahara was angry. "Continue this lesson, Drake. You're so close."

"No!" Drake raised his voice. "We need to do something else. I can't—"

"Enough of this hogwash!" Sahara yelled. "You'll stay here until you perfect this move!"

"Why do you expect so much of me?" Drake asked.

"Why do you doubt yourself, Drake Philosopher?" Sahara hissed. Drake took a small step back. He had never seen his master so angry, not even on the night before the attack on Wendil. "You have so much potential. Believe in yourself, Drake. Believe!"

"But I have tried, and tried, and tried, and none of those times I have succeeded! I've just failed!" Drake shouted, anger boiling inside him. He felt blood rush to his head, and his knuckles were pure white from gripping his sword.

"That's it!" Sahara threw his own sword on the ground. "I'm finished! Why did I ever agree to this?" He seemed to be talking to himself. "I was right the night before Wendil was attacked. I shouldn't have trained you."

"Then who forced you?" Drake screamed back. "Who?"

"Eleanor!" Sahara yelled.

Drake's mind stopped. Perhaps he had misheard.

"What?" Drake snarled. Anger boiled inside him ten times worse than before.

"Eleanor," Sahara didn't seem angry anymore. Drake could hardly comprehend as the name echoed in his mind. Eleanor. But when Eleanor had told Drake, she said that Sahara had been happy to do it, had been thrilled to train him. She hadn't said he'd been forced. By her, no less.

For a moment, the torch flame was the only thing moving. It swayed, casting a glow on Sahara's face. The light flickered on Drake's limbs, casting his shadow onto the dry field behind him. The wind had stopped, as if it was holding its breath. Sahara stood frozen along with Drake.

Maximus, still drifting in the distance, appeared not to have noticed the argument at all.

Drake almost didn't believe it was true, but then he remembered Sahara's journal. Obviously, Eleanor wanted his thoughts in writing, away from Drake, because she didn't want him to know that Sahara had been forced to train him.

"Drake," Sahara said, seeming to read his mind. "You don't understand. It was different."

"What do you mean?" Drake's anger erupted like lava from a volcano. "You had to accept me because of your reputation. Eleanor forced you, didn't she? Because she knew I was a helpless little—"

"No," Sahara said. "Quite the opposite. What she wanted was—"

"She wanted to prepare me for this destiny," Drake interrupted. "This destiny that she hardly knows anything about."

Drake could barely remember what happened next. He charged at Sahara, screaming about betrayal. Sahara stumbled back as Drake barreled into him, sending them both tumbling to the ground. They rolled over and over, and Drake felt the dry weeds brushing up against his legs, scratching and tearing his skin.

He threw wild blows at his master, most of them missing. Sahara tried to kick Drake off without hurting him, but it wasn't working. Drake felt like his chest was going to explode as Sahara kicked him in the stomach, knocking the wind out of him. His sword flew off his belt, banging to the floor. Meanwhile, Drake landed on his back and rolled to a stop. He stood up. He wasn't done.

As he ran towards Sahara once more time, he saw orange light flickering around him in the dry field. Drake had never been this angry. Maybe this was what happened when you gave into pure rage. Your vision produced violent colors around you. Seeing red, they called it.

Suddenly, he was yanked backwards. He tumbled to the ground and it was only then, he realized that the orange glow wasn't in his mind at all. It was real.

The field was on fire.

Strong arms dragged him away from the dry grass onto the cobblestone path. His head spun and his vision went blurry as he realized what he had just done. He had started the fire with the torch in Sahara's hand. Even worse, he had attacked his master.

The arms lifted him up and whirled him around. Drake felt himself stumble, but when he regained his vision, he looked up to see Noxy. The king was red-faced, his crown lopsided on his head and tangled in his hair. Ash darkened his cheeks. Drake wouldn't have been surprised if he saw steam shooting out of Noxy's ears.

"I don't know what load of horse crap just happened," he screamed, "but you'd better have an explanation once this fire is put out!"

Drake didn't have time to answer. Noxy threw him aside so hard that he stumbled into the wall of the inn. Guilt slowly seeped into him like an infection. He felt like he was going to vomit as he looked around.

The fire roared, the flames shooting high and rapidly eating up the dry grass. Men and women ran from the inn, throwing buckets of water onto the fire and racing back.

King Noxy was among them, but Drake could see no one else he recognized. Sahara was nowhere to be seen.

Drake put his face into his hands, the heat searing his skin and the smoke causing his eyes to tear up. It was Wendil all over again. A terrible disaster. His master, gone. And it was all his fault.

Just like Wendil.

CHAPTER XXVI

QUALDOR PUSHED HIS horse harder and harder as each second passed. He had been on the road for a while now, going as fast as he could to reach Mondoor and Zebetar. He had to warn them about Drake. The king was depending on him.

The landscape was a blur as his horse galloped, hooves pounding the ground. Stars shone down as he rode, scanning the landscape ahead of him, dodging small patches of trees. When he finally saw a stream trickling down a hillside he slowed and dismounted. The horse stuck its head into the water and gulped it up.

Qualdor glanced up at the bright moon looming over him and smiled. He was making extremely good time. He should be getting to Zebetar and Mondoor soon, possibly in the next day. Everything was going perfectly. The transition was the best decision that he could have ever made.

It had been a long time since he'd thought about that—about leaving the Harobi Desert.

And the whole fight with his brothers…

No.

He couldn't think about this, now. King Chada and the Titan army were the future. Qualdor was going to help the king achieve his goal of embodying the Spectacular Swordsman. He was finally somewhere where he had chosen to be and was serving in an army that he had chosen to join. King Chada was a great leader. And Qualdor might finally be in a position to dig himself out of the hole he had dug all those years ago.

He pulled out a small map of northern Lyzix that Chada had given him and studied it. He was only a half day into his journey but had covered about a day's worth of distance.

Qualdor stowed the map away, realizing his horse was looking at him expectantly. With a grunt, he heaved himself onto the beast, snapped the reins and was off once more.

Another day at this pace, and he would probably reach the sorcerer and the general. He just needed to push as hard as he could. Then it would all fall into place. He just needed to be patient.

*

From a large rock, on the outskirts of the Giant's Forest, Zebetar watched the sun slowly peek above the horizon. He had barely slept all night, as his mind wasn't on rest. It was in the large forest in front of him, with its gargantuan trunks and towering trees. They were going in today. Zebetar had traveled through the Giants' Forest once before, when he was much younger, and less experienced with sorcery. It had not ended well.

He'd been with friends, trying to journey to the Seaside Kingdom for business. They had been making good time and enjoying the journey, when suddenly the giants found them. The memory of his friends being stabbed and slashed still haunted him to this day. Only he survived. And he would probably have died too, if he hadn't been dragged out on the verge of death.

Now he needed to be extremely careful. There was no room for mistakes.

"Sir!" General Mondoor was standing behind him. "The Titans are ready to enter the forest if you are."

Zebetar nodded. "Let your Titans know they must obey these rules: they must to listen to everything I say; they need to watch out for giants, and perhaps Drake and his caravan; and there will be ancient enchantments lingering in the forest from long ago, so they must watch out for those, too."

General Mondoor nodded. "How are you going to get us past the giants?"

"You'll see," Zebetar replied. He could tell General Mondoor wasn't completely satisfied with his answer by the way he stalked off, but that was none of Zebetar's concern. He needed to work on his enchantment.

He trekked to the forest edge and leaned against an enormous tree trunk. He remembered his time here all those years ago, the coarse bark and the dried wood of the trees, the sudden unsettling, echoing roars and shrieks.

"Sir?" Mondoor shouted. Zebetar almost whirled around and punched the General. For such a clumsy man, he sure was sneaky.

"Yes, Mondoor?"

"I've explained everything to the Titans."

"Good. Now, let's go. We need to get moving." Zebetar raised his hand, and, silently, signaled the Titans forward.

The Giants' Forest floor was just as Zebetar remembered

it, eerily bare. No moss, weeds, or any plants grew there. The sorcerer spotted gargantuan bones lodged inside trees, leaning up against them or just lying on the ground. The canopy above blocked out most of the sunlight, so only a slight glow remained, making it hard to decipher the many carvings on the tree trunks. Zebetar couldn't tell what they were. Giants were a mysterious kind.

A few moments later, a large roar echoed across the forest, and the leaves rustled in the wind. General Mondoor began nervously fidgeting, reaching for his sword, fingering his dagger. His eyes darted around at the slightest noise. Zebetar heard the Titan's murmuring nervously behind him.

He then grabbed his silver shard from his cloak, muttered something under his breath and brought it across his body like a sword slash. He felt a small tingle in his arm. A blue glow formed in front of him. It expanded all the way back to the last Titans in the formation. It was a concealing spell. Not only were they invisible, but any noise they made was silenced thanks to the sorcery. Now, Zebetar just had to hold it together until they were out of the forest. Then, they would be golden.

*

Eleanor sat up groggily, hearing a steady *pat-pat-pat* of rain on the roof high above her. Light flickered from the nearby oil lamps. She looked to her left and saw the hidden cupboard in the walls. Right then she remembered what had happened.

She'd stayed up late in the library. Reuben Fox was the first Spectacular Swordsmen.

And Zeldrin…

Her head was throbbing. She had been passed out for a good amount of time. She stood up and leaned against a nearby shelf. Her eyes moved to the cupboard. The Reuben Fox Family Tree page was still lying there. She stumbled over, still very tired, and picked up the page.

Then, she froze. In the back corner of the cupboard, there was a small divot. She moved her head so she could see straight down. It was a couple feet deep and blended perfectly into the dark stone. When she looked inside, she saw a flash of white: a scroll.

Anticipation suddenly growing, the stupefying effects of her sleep were gone. She reached inside and pulled out the document. It had a blue and orange ribbon wrapped around it. Looking closer, Eleanor noticed a strange symbol: a circle with two swords crossed over each other. With a double take, she realized that the same symbol was on the Reuben Fox family tree.

Her heart pounded as she opened the scroll. She wasn't completely sure, but she was willing to bet the whole library that this was Reuben Fox's insignia—the Spectacular Swordsmen Insignia.

Inside the scroll was a letter written in loopy and majestic writing. Eleanor did not think twice before reading it.

Brother,

There is not much time. Zeldrin Fox has disappeared since his failure at the trials.

I hate to give up on him, but we must or Lyzix will lose its balance—and the vault will be in jeopardy. We must find a replacement swordsman for me to train, so he or she can begin their work as soon as possible. Once everything is settled, I shall look for Zeldrin. I hope he is all right. But, sadly, he is no longer a part of the Spectacular Swordsmen Line. He has failed the trials, and therefore he does not belong. He must be removed.

Let me know if you find a replacement. See you soon.

-Timus

*

Drake sat on his horse, mindlessly staring off toward the distant sun, now high in the sky. Jerome, Isabella and Leo rode next to him. He glanced at them once in a while, and got the sense that when he did, they avoided his gaze. He could feel them staring at him when he wasn't looking.

His mind kept returning to the scenes of a few hours ago: his master and himself, brawling like animals; the travelers, desperately trying to put out the fire; King Noxy, screaming at him; the fire, towering above all else, roaring in his ears.

And Eleanor. Almost his whole life was a lie. He wasn't just a swordsman's apprentice like any other normal kid. He was being trained to live up to some noble line that had disappeared centuries ago, all their prestige with it. He was being used and his master didn't even want to train him.

Drake nudged his horse forward, annoyed at Jerome, Isabella, and Leo's silence. He looked ahead, only to feel his heart sink to his stomach. Sahara was riding next to King Noxy, and on the back of his arm was something that would remind Drake of the terrible events of the past night forever. He pulled back on the reins, ignoring the snort of irritation from his horse, so that he didn't have to see the burned area on Sahara's right forearm. Maximus had tried to convince Drake that it could have happened to anybody, that it wasn't his fault. Drake wanted to believe his uncle, but if he hadn't attacked Sahara, then the fire wouldn't have started, and his master wouldn't have been injured.

"Drake?" said a slightly weary voice. "There's no need to be so sullen."

Drake turned to see Maximus. "Why?"

"Because it isn't as bad as you think."

Despite being in the presence of his only living relative, his mood worsened. "I just attacked my master, set fire to a field, caused a complete scene, and you say everything's going to be all right."

"You must listen to me," Maximus said.

"Don't tell me it's not my fault," Drake snapped. He didn't need help. He just needed a quiet place to lie down and fall asleep forever.

"But it isn't—"

"It is my fault!" As Drake raised his voice, some of the group glanced in his direction. He stared down at his horse to avoid their questioning looks.

"Don't you remember what I told you earlier?" Maximus said. Drake was too weary to interrupt. "It takes a man of great courage to ask for help. This is not your fault. Let me talk through it with you. You're hurting inside and avoiding that hurt could drive you insane. You need to face it and be strong. It also takes a man of great courage to admit he's wrong and to share his feelings."

Drake sighed. Maximus was right, but he didn't want to believe it. He knew once again his independent streak was getting the better of him, but he also knew he could figure it out himself. The problem was he didn't know where to start. Maybe he did need his uncle's guidance. Maximus was a great source of wisdom.

"Fine," Drake said. A smile spread across his uncle's face. "And I'm sorry for—"

"Don't think twice about it," Maximus said. "We're all human. Well…" He glanced down at his dusty form. "We're human in our mistakes, maybe not our appearance. But I can't tell you the number of times I've lost my temper."

Drake looked up, suddenly interested, envisioning a young Maximus yelling at random people on the streets. "Really?"

"We'll save that for another day, eh?" Maximus replied. "For now, I am telling you, speak to your master. He was trying to explain something earlier. Let him. And then, and only then, will your mind be clear." Drake really didn't want to face Sahara right now. His master had withheld the truth all these years. "Trust me." Maximus winked. "You don't want to fight with him."

It was true. Drake didn't want to. He had to talk to Sahara. He sped up his horse, as his uncle slowly drifted back to Jerome, Isabella and Leo. They broke into a hearty conversation with him, avoiding Drake's gaze once more. It was at that point he decided to get back on the same page with everyone, united again. And in order to do that, he needed to clear the air with Sahara.

Xylis and Reya were riding with Sahara now. King Noxy was just behind them. Drake began to feel queasy as he remembered Noxy bellowing at him in the midst of the fire.

He'd never lost his temper like that—at least, Drake hadn't seen it. He'd even said horse crap!

To reach Sahara he'd have to ride past the king. Before Drake could avoid him, Noxy dropped back. The clopping of his horse began to match Drake's.

"Drake—"

Without a moment's hesitation, Drake decided to save King Noxy's breath. "What I did was completely irresponsible, very stupid, and I shall never do it again."

"Actually, what I was going to say is that your uncle is very wise."

Drake gaped. "You heard our conversation?"

"I hear a lot of things," King Noxy said with a twinkle in his eye. "But that's beside the point. I know you think you've disappointed your master."

"And you," Drake added.

"Yes, and maybe me, but you must talk to him as Maximus advised," the king said. "You act rashly sometimes, but I've always admired your courage and determination. Now, go talk to your master."

Drake pulled ahead, flushing with embarrassment as his horse trotted to Sahara. When his master turned around, Drake couldn't read the look on his face. Disappointment? Surprise? A flash of anger? There wasn't a way to describe it.

Xylis and Reya pulled back leaving Drake and Sahara alone. "I want to speak to you about last night." He didn't know what to say so he just let the words pour out. "I'm really sorry about what I did. There's no excuse and…" He trailed off as he caught sight of the pinkish burn on the back of Sahara's arm. Forever a reminder of that night.

"I see," Sahara said, calmly. "I won't lie. I was extremely

surprised you acted the way you did, and frankly, disappointed." Drake felt his heart fall. "But I take some of blame."

"It was all my fault." Drake wasn't going to deny it. "I attacked you and—"

Sahara held up his hand for quiet. "I said Eleanor forced me to take you on. Forced is perhaps the wrong word." Drake felt his heart rise. He longed to hear that Sahara had truly cared for him, that it wasn't just a job to train him. "I should have told you long ago about Eleanor asking me to train you. But I couldn't find a way to say it without revealing the Spectacular Swordsmen Line, and you being a part of it. I, as well as Eleanor, wanted to wait until you were ready," Sahara explained.

"Were you planning to tell me yourself?" Drake asked, "or..."

"To be honest, I had no plan and neither did Eleanor. We were unprepared. And I suppose this is what created our fight." Sahara looked calmly into Drake's eyes. "But I have never believed you to be a burden. I was very happy when I began to train you, and you've been like the son I never had."

Drake felt his heart swell. "You've been like my father, since you started training me."

"We may fight sometimes, Drake, but we always come around. Remember that," Sahara said. "And remember that I will always care for you. No matter what."

Drake beamed. He would definitely remember that, cling to it if need be. His master looked down at his forearm, "And don't worry about that. It was more my fault than anything."

Drake smiled. "Thanks."

Sahara then leaned in closer and lowered his voice. "I heard King Noxy's yells about horse crap."

Drake nodded. "They were indeed thunderous."

"Yes, and if it hadn't been such a serious situation, I may have crapped myself."

Drake burst out laughing, along with his master, feeling freer than he'd been since they started on the journey. And it was then he realized that the burn wouldn't just remind him of the crazy events a few hours ago. There were other things that he would remember more. Like his uncle's wise words, and King Noxy's explanation.

And Sahara's praise.

Chapter XXVII

ZEBETAR GLARED AT the surrounding forest, hating every single bit of it, as he moved his legs automatically and felt his cloak becoming unbearably hot. Sweat poured down his back. He felt paralyzed, not daring to move anything except his lower body, in case he broke the concentration required for his enchantment. He could feel the general's eyes on him and hear the unmistakable noise of a weapon being drawn at every small sound. It was madness. He desperately hoped it would all be over soon.

The canopy of trees hid the sky above, but the forest had darkened significantly indicating that the moon had risen, and the sun had set. The journey through the Giants' Forest usually took a day, so they must be near the end. And that was a good thing. The concealing spell was exhausting because of the size of Titan force he had to cover. He was really feeling the effects. He needed a break, but they had to march on.

Zebetar stumbled over a small root in the ground but managed to regain his footing. He still had that vertigo feeling.

"Are you okay?" Mondoor asked.

"I do not need your kindness, general," Zebetar snarled. "Yes, I'm fine. We're nearly there."

"All right," General Mondoor replied, letting the subject drop.

The next few minutes were agony for Zebetar. His limbs ached and shook, and his eyes felt as if they had locked into place. But he pushed on knowing they would be in a far more dangerous situation if one of the giants spotted them without a concealing spell. He felt like his whole body was going to implode when he saw a break in the trees. It led to a plain that was dotted with rolling hills. They were out of the Giants' Forest.

Zebetar's spell broke abruptly, and he plunged to the ground just outside the forest. General Mondoor checked on him, but Zebetar held up a hand before the general could speak. "I'm fine," he said, already feeling the vertigo disappear.

A few moments later, he stood up. They had made it through the Giants' Forest. They were halfway there. And he hadn't been maimed or killed by a giant. Zebetar felt joy and energy flowing back into him. "I'm better than fine, actually."

"What's the next move, then?" General Mondoor didn't seem to notice the sorcerer's abnormal change in mood.

"We're still at least a day away," Zebetar said. "So we should probably get—"

A loud thumping noise interrupted him. He whipped around, an incantation forming on his lips, energy readying in his palms. He was on verge of letting it fly when something exited the forest. It wasn't a giant, but another Titan.

The man's horse skidded to a stop. He leapt off and ran to meet them. Zebetar felt a pang of worry. Why had King Chada sent him?

The Titan bowed and handed him a scroll. "Drake and his friends have discovered your quest to travel north," he said. "King Chada asked me to give you this."

"What's your name, Titan?" General Mondoor asked as Zebetar took the scroll.

"Qualdor."

"Well, Qualdor, your actions are greatly appreciated. I shall make sure you're rewarded," General Mondoor said, and the two continued to talk as Zebetar read.

Zebetar and General Mondoor,

There is not much time. Drake and his wretched friends have found out about the artifact. They're headed in your direction as you read this.

Be on the lookout for them. Titan platoons have been sent to intercept them. I am counting on the platoons slowing the enemy.

You MUST focus on getting to the northern jungle. Bring the artifact to me. Then the plan shall begin. If the group finds you with the artifact, send your Titan platoons after them and flee. The artifact is the most important thing. And remember...

Failure is UNACCEPTABLE.

-King Chada

Zebetar passed the scroll to Mondoor in silence. Drake and his friends had found out. That wasn't good. Zebetar wasn't expecting to be in a race for the artifact. He was tempted to leave the two platoons and continue with the general, alone. The extra soldiers were slowing them down, but they would be useful if they found themselves in battle. They just needed to travel as fast as they could to beat Drake and his friends to the jungle. They needed to get that artifact first.

"Qualdor, you may join our ranks," Zebetar said. "But if there's a message to be sent, you will be the man to do it."

After they were left in private, the sorcerer turned to Mondoor. "We have to pick up the pace if we want to get the weapon."

Mondoor nodded. "We'll do our best. I'll promise the platoons a reward when we return."

"Good." Zebetar said, and so he continued with the Titans, but his mind was still consumed with getting to the jungle on time. They had to get that artifact before Drake did.

At all costs.

*

Jerome watched his best friend speaking with Sahara, glad that the two appeared to be making up. He'd been shocked to hear the chaos coming from the field the previous night. The screams had come next, and he'd run out with Leo to find the field ablaze, flames roaring high into the sky. Isabella had joined them as they watched in horror while the fire engulfed the field. They found Drake leaning against the inn, practically frozen with shock. They had helped him inside and tried to get the story from him, but he wouldn't speak. They'd heard later from Sahara. No one had really spoken to Drake since.

As Jerome continued to watch Drake and Sahara, he remembered the long nights he'd spent with his own master, learning to make weapons, keeping the forge ablaze, even using a hammer as a weapon if need be.

His master had taught him the tricks of the trade: better ways to mold and fold metal, and how to decorate a sword to make it something to cherish. He'd even watched Jerome make his first hammer and had been so proud. That was Jerome's fondest memory. He'd loved it when his master taught him new, more complicated things. It showed his master believed he was one step closer to becoming a fully-fledged blacksmith.

And then his master had been killed, his home taken, and he'd been thrown into this whirlpool of unbelievable events, alongside his best friend. Jerome couldn't shake the feeling that something else had changed, too. Not just in his life, but in himself.

The tingle in his arm. The table disappearing. Was it real or had he been seeing things? Everything had looked and felt so real. And if they were, then what was happening?

"Jerome!" Leo sounded panicked. "Jerome, where are you?"

"What do you mean, where am I?" Jerome asked. "Are you blind? I'm right here!"

The group had turned around at the commotion, and now both Isabella and Leo were calling him, as if they couldn't see or hear him.

"He's gone!"

"Gone?" Reya called from the front of the caravan.

"There's his horse, but he's not on it. Jerome, where are you?"

Had the group lost their minds? Suddenly, his horse reared back, and Jerome toppled to the ground.

"Oh, there he is!" Leo cried.

Jerome was pulled to his feet. Xylis and Leo were looking at him with concern.

"You gave us a real fright there," Xylis said.

"You just disappeared for a few seconds," Leo said.

"What do you mean, disappeared?" Jerome felt bile rising in his throat.

"One second, you were there, and the next, gone," Isabella said. "Like sorcery."

Jerome felt queasy as he looked down at his horse. The group seemed to be recovering from the shock. Drake shot him a questioning look, mixed with worry and…was that fear?

Jerome didn't know how to reply. These strange events were happening too often, and he didn't know what was causing them. Was that sorcerer of Chada's making these accidents happen? But why would he do that?

Jerome set his hand down on his lap and inadvertently touched the small pouch hanging from his belt. He saw himself a few days before looking inside the saddlebags and finding that shiny, clean piece of tin. And in that moment, he was almost one hundred percent sure he had found the cause of these bizarre events.

"You know, we should probably let Noxy about these… happenings," Leo said.

Isabella called to the king and Jerome was just starting

to say that he already knew what they were when they were both interrupted by a large boom. It echoed across the hills. Jerome stood up in his saddle but couldn't see anything. Maximus and King Noxy looked around nervously and then shrugged it off as if it were nothing. By that time, they had all reached the top of a hill. Ahead Jerome saw trees towering at what looked to be five hundred feet high. The moon slowly rose above them. They had made it to the Giants' Forest.

In their excitement, Leo and Isabella seemed to have forgotten that they were going to talk to Noxy. Jerome did not remind them, and he never mentioned anything about the tin.

Chapter XXVIII

At the edge of the Giant's Forest, Noxy called a halt. Drake could tell, by the way he sat more upright in his saddle and cleared his throat, that he was going to break into one of his pep talks. Drake sometimes let his mind drift when Noxy did this, but the forest looked perilous, so he stayed alert as the king spoke.

"The Giants' Forest is dangerous, so I'll repeat what I've said many times on this journey. We must be cautious and vigilant. I don't know what that noise was earlier." Nervous mutterings broke out among the caravan. "But we can't worry about that. We must focus on the task at hand. Comas Disease, as Maximus warned us before we left, is something to watch out for. Xylis and Reya will conjure a concealing spell to protect us. We'll take occasional breaks. Otherwise, we'll go through as fast as possible to ensure our arrival at the artifact before Mondoor and his sorcerer."

Drake felt bile coating the insides of his throat. He noticed that most of the group seemed equally worried as they readied to enter the forest. Leo was grinding his teeth, which did not help Drake's confidence.

Drake glanced over to Xylis and Reya, who were muttering incantations under their breath. He e he He saw a thin red capsule expand around the group, wavering in the darkness of the forest's canopy. It was the concealing spell. The sorcerers were at work, and Drake allowed himself to smile. Surely with such an enchantment, they would have no problem getting through. But then he sighed. The stay at the inn was supposed to be an uneventful few hours of rest and look what had actually happened. He had to be cautious and vigilant, just like King Noxy said.

As their horses walked into the forest, Drake ducked under a large fossil sticking out of a nearby tree. Other fossils were embedded in the eerily bare forest floor. The trunks of the trees were enormous. You could have made a decent-sized home out of them. Some of the trunks bore carvings but Drake couldn't see what they were. As for the canopy of the trees, the leaves were a sickly dark green, letting in little light. It was strange and slightly worrisome.

The time passed quickly. The group took breaks every so often, usually hiding in a hollowed-out tree trunk or in a particularly dark patch of shadows. They heard an occasional roar from the Giants, but they sounded far away.

"We should be out of the forest in a few hours," King Noxy said. "Before the sun rises."

As they rode and nothing happened, Drake could see the group becoming more relaxed. He couldn't help feeling the same way. King Noxy had made the forest sound so menacing, but the strangest thing so far were the large fossils poking out from the trees.

"Hey," Isabella said. "What do you think you'll do after all this is over?"

Drake paused for a moment, considering Isabella's sudden question. What was he going to do? Continue training with Sahara? He'd been too focused on everything that had been revealed to him by Eleanor and King Chada's attacks to think about a normal life. What would a normal life even look like?

"Not sure," he said, honestly. "I suppose I'll have to discover more about this Spectacular Swordsmen business. What about you?"

Isabella shrugged. "King Noxy said we'd be able to live in the castle. I've always wanted to be a writer or healer, so I may focus on that."

"That's really cool." Drake felt himself relax even more. There was nothing wrong here in the Giants' Forest. They didn't need to be so tense. "What was King Noxy talking about, making it out this place was so dangerous?" he whispered.

Isabella giggled. "I don't know. It seems fine."

"I know, right?" Drake agreed. "There's no way we're going to run into any trouble here."

He'd no sooner spoken than the earth gave a mighty rumble. He grabbed his horse to prevent himself from falling off. He saw the magical shield flicker and shot Isabella a worried look.

"What's going on?" she asked in an unusually high voice.

"Don't know, but I think we'll be fine."

The quaking then became louder. There was a high-pitched shriek and then a loud crack. A tree, shorter than the rest, crashed towards them. The shield flickered again then disappeared. Drake let out a gasp, because behind it, a giant appeared, almost sixty feet tall. She wore a small skirt made out of big leaves and had twigs and thick branches tangled in her long hair. She was brandishing an enormous, pointed spear, taller than her, that seemed to be made from one of the trees of the forest.

She gave another shriek making the horses scatter. Drake's horse neighed, bucked and galloped away from her. Drake grabbed onto its mane and turned around to see Xylis and Reya holding off the giant with their defensive sorcery.

Maximus floated up in the air and, waving his arms, sent small whirlwinds of dust at the giant. She was pushed back and struggled to swing her spear. King Noxy drew his sword. Cyrus followed suit but was immediately struck from his horse by the butt end of the giant's spear. He plowed into the ground. King Noxy steered his horse over to check on him. Drake looked around for Amanda. Maybe she could heal him quickly. But, Amanda, Sahara, Jerome, Isabella, and Leo were nowhere to be seen.

Drake's horse was still cantering away from the battle. He pulled back on the reins, struggling to spin the stubborn creature around. "Come on," he muttered, "come on!" He hated not being able to help his friends. With a mighty tug he was able to get the horse turned around. He urged it back to the battle, but his horse stumbled on something, got spooked again and bolted to the left. Drake was left helpless, his horse running without listening to him. He clung on but could not take control. As they hurtled through the forest he was getting completely turned around. He heard noises to the left, and tried to urge his horse that way, then more noises to his right. Where was everyone? Finally, he heard a giant scream straight ahead and, with a roar of impatience and frustration, he changed course once more.

That was when he was knocked cleanly off his horse. As he tumbled to the ground, his horse shrieked and he heard the crack of bone on something.

Drake rolled to a stop and found he was tangled in the limbs of someone else. He kicked away, sprang up, and saw a Titan. He was so shocked that the Titan lunged forward and sliced Drake's leg with his dagger before Drake could draw his sword and return the strike. More Titans rushed at him. He cut them all down, the reality of the situation dawning as he fought. The Titans had found them. It was an ambush.

A Titan charged and Drake kicked him back. He sliced his sword across another's abdomen. The Titan collapsed against a nearby tree, blood spurting through his hands as he clutched his belly. Drake looked around. That was the last of them for now, at least. He hurried to his horse and ran his hands up and down its legs. It was okay and gave an amused snort, as if to say *you're welcome*. Drake felt the corners of his mouth twitching as he leaped on, but his smile quickly disappeared as Reya and Leo appeared around a nearby tree trunk, urging their horses on while looking wildly behind them.

"They're coming!" Leo screamed.

Drake swung his horse around to follow. Behind him Titans stampeded from around the tree, followed by two giants, who were smashing their fists into trees and uprooting smaller ones from the ground as if they were mere spears. Drake weaved between tree trunks, trying to catch up with Reya and Leo as they galloped ahead.

The roars of the giants faded, but when Drake turned around to check if he'd outrun them, an arrow sank into his arm. It made him buckle, and he slid down the side of his horse. He grabbed onto the saddle, lifting his feet as the ground raced beneath him and his horse continued to gallop. He glanced back, feeling his arms burn. Several Titans on horses were after them. All around them Titans yelled, and giants roared: more enemies than he could ever have guessed.

His arms gave out right then, and he collapsed to the ground in a small clearing, hitting his head and limbs on the compacted dirt. His sword flew from his grasp as he rolled, only stopping when he hit a tree trunk.

He fumbled for his fallen weapon as Reya and Leo leaped off their horses to help. He wanted to tell them to continue and not to worry about him, but he was so out of breath, he could only focus on the immediate threat: the Titans. As they charged, some on horses and some not, he lunged at them as best as he could.

The first he targeted was shot with an arrow from Leo. The second he swung at with his sword, cutting the Titan in the hip then impaling him through the abdomen. Drake felt sick to his stomach but remembered King Noxy's coping mechanism. He could not dwell on the Titan's death. He immediately went after another. Right blow, left blow, another right blow, and suddenly the number of Titans he had defeated was increasing. He felt like Sahara, when his master looked like a whirlwind of man and sword.

He turned to another Titan, but his first blow was immediately blocked. Taken by surprise, he stumbled back barely dodging a wild swing from the Titan. He threw a punch, giving her a large nosebleed, and swung left. But then someone shoved him to the side, his sword flew out of his hands, and his body hit the floor. As Drake crawled to his sword, grasped it, and stood up, he found himself facing seven more Titans.

He spun, striking down one…two…three. He ran at the fourth, trying to execute the tuck and slash, but the Titan anticipated his move and knocked him to the floor once more.

Drake leapt to his feet and backed away. A thin magical shield formed in from of him, courtesy of Reya, and the Titans turned their attention to her. This gave Drake a few moments to breathe. But no sooner had he stopped to rest than he saw a Titan aiming a long javelin at Leo's back.

"Leo!" he bellowed.

Leo turned around, but Drake had reached the Titan in time. He tackled the man down, knocked the spear from his hand and stabbed him through the heart.

Leo gave a weak smile. "Thanks."

"Anytime." The Titan's death was gruesome, but it could have been Leo that had been killed, or Jerome, perhaps even Sahara.

"Come on, you two!" Reya yelled. "We're near the edge of the forest! We must get out!" Drake and Leo jumped on their horses, following Reya as she wove in and out through the trees.

Ahead, Xylis, King Noxy, and Sahara were fighting a giant wielding a huge flaming log, while Titans ran around them, attacking the giant one moment and them the next. The others were nowhere in sight.

The giant threw the log. They all scattered as it broke into pieces causing the fire to roar higher. It licked at the leaves and branches of the colossal trees, yet stayed contained. The thick wood was hard to burn.

The giant lashed out towards Reya, who deflected his strike with a magical shield. He stopped momentarily. They all raced on, dodging tree trunks, Titans, horses, flying arrows, rocks, crossbow bolts, and twigs. As Drake steered his horse around a particularly large tree, he caught sight of Leo suddenly hit by an enormous club. Drake heard a crack as his friend fell to the forest floor, his leg bent at an oddly shaped angle. A large wound opened along his leg.

"Leo!" Isabella screamed as she rode by, but she could not stop because the giant had now focused his attention on her. She had a blazing, determined look on her face as she raced to the edge of the forest.

Drake stopped his horse and leapt off. He slung Leo's limp body over his shoulder and sprinted towards the light shaft cutting through the trees. The edge of the forest was near.

Come on. Come on. Come on! He could make it. Just a little more.

"Drake!" Isabella was in front of him, still on her horse. He saw her blazing look morph into horror. Then, he glanced behind him. Three Titans grasped him and pulled him back. Leo rolled to the floor with a thud, but the Titans ignored him. All they wanted was Drake.

He fought them as best he could, but a fist hit his stomach and he felt woozy. Someone pulled him from the fray. There was lots of screaming. A giant roared. He heard the sound of a quarrel leaving its crossbow bolt, a sharp pain in his shoulder, and then he smelled the earthy scent of the forest rushing to meet him.

His head hit the floor, and his eyes shut hard.

*

Eleanor walked through the Western Town, her cloak flowing behind her in the light breeze. It was late at night. She saw the occasional light flickering in the nearby houses and heard the sound of music and laughter before a tavern door slammed shut.

She had spent practically the whole day studying the letter. She was curious about the Zeldrin character who'd obviously failed the trials and been kicked out of The Spectacular Swordsmen Line, but the other swordsman, Atticus, he worried her.

He had disappeared and was nowhere to be seen on the Fox family tree. And this concerned Eleanor. How could she have not found his history yet. Could she be certain he was a Spectacular Swordsman? Her research had not been simple, easy, or been dismissed. She had put so much time into it. And now, if Atticus was proven to be someone else, someone other than Eleanor had thought, this changed everything she had been fighting for.

Eleanor made for the tower in the center of the town square. The mayor's tower. She needed information on the Fox family. They all seemed to be involved with the Spectacular Swordsmen Line. Eleanor needed to see if she could find something that proved Atticus was a part of the Fox lineage. She was also determined to find out more about Zeldrin.

As the Foxes seemed to be a fairly prestigious and wealthy family, she had a feeling Marcemus might have some information. Most towns had documents regarding wealthy families. She was reluctant to expose her interest in the Spectacular Swordsmen Lineage or Drake's involvement with it, but she was desperate.

Two guards stood at the entrance to the tower. She pulled down her hood and said,

"I request an urgent meeting with the mayor." The guards simply nodded and escorted her inside.

Before she knew it, she found herself sitting in the mayor's office on a velvety dark blue chair next to a small table. The mayor sat across from her. She held a cup of tea in her hand, and Marcemus was looking at her expectantly. "What brings you here this late at night, Eleanor?"

"I'm hoping you have information on the Foxes and their lineage," she said, stiffly. The first test: would Marcemus guess why she was searching for this? She hoped not.

Marcemus gave a jolly smile. "The Foxes? Why yes, of course. One of the most prestigious families in Lyzix throughout the ages." He stood up. "I assume this is for the library?"

"Yes," Eleanor said without hesitation. "We're…lacking information on them at present." At least that part of her response was true.

Marcemus bustled to a nearby desk, opened a drawer, and shuffled through some documents. "By the way, I've not seen King Noxy or his companions recently."

"They've left on an important journey," Eleanor said.

Marcemus moved to a bookshelf, looking through the books as he held other documents in his hand. "Their heroic actions against the Titan ambush on our town was greatly appreciated." He looked at her awkwardly and added, "I apologize for my fiery behavior when you vouched for them. You were right. I wasn't seeing the whole picture."

"Do not worry, Marcemus. The fault was mine. I caught you off guard."

A moment later, he had grabbed a few books from the shelf and sat back down. As Eleanor sipped her tea, he pushed the books and documents towards her across the table.

"Thank you," Eleanor said. Here it was hopefully, the information she'd been looking for all this time, right in front of her.

"My pleasure," Marcemus said. "You know, speaking of the Titans, I believe King Chada is a part of the Fox lineage, if that interests you."

The cup tumbled from Eleanor's hands, spilling tea all over the carpet. "What?" She pulled a handkerchief from her sleeve and tried to clean up the mess.

Marcemus frowned. "Don't worry about the carpet. It's old. And yes, Chada is a part of the lineage. Some of the Fox descendants even lived here: Timus and Xemus, both brothers. Xemus was the librarian and mayor at one point."

Eleanor was frozen with surprise. "Seriously?"

"They're buried at the local cemetery."

She couldn't believe her ears. King Chada was a descendant of the Foxes? And members of the Fox lineage had lived here? She gave the carpet a final wipe and, as she picked up the cup and put it back on the table, something stirred in her memory. Timus? That was the man who had written the letter about Zeldrin. And if he had been sending it to his brother…he must have been sending it to Xemus.

Eleanor thanked the mayor and apologized again for the tea spill. She carried the book and documents home, in a sort of a daze, trying to digest this astonishing news.

King Chada was part of the Fox line, related to the Spectacular Swordsmen line. Related perhaps to Drake. How would she tell him?

But wait. Perhaps she could still be missing something, another important piece of information. She knew exactly where she needed to go next to find out if all of this was true.

If Timus and Xemus were a part of the Fox lineage, and were buried here, she needed to visit their graves. She needed to go to the cemetery.

Chapter XXIX

When Drake opened his eyes, his vision was blurry. All he could see was bright blue. As he rubbed them to improve his sight, he felt something moving and shifting beneath him. He was lying on a horse with ropes binding him down. He struggled to untie them and sat up. He could hear low murmurs coming from behind him. Turning around, he saw three dark shapes moving at the same pace he was. As his vision improved, the shapes turned into Jerome, Isabella, and Leo.

"What happened?" he asked.

"It's been a bit since…" Jerome trailed off, but Drake knew that he meant the events in the Giants' Forest.

He tried to remember everything: the Titan's attack, the giants, Leo's injury, and then someone pulling him from the Titans before he blacked out. Then he noticed Leo, ropes binding him to his horse, just as Drake had been, a grimace painted on his face. Drake winced and fought the impulse to cover his eyes. Leo's leg was bloodied and swollen, though a wooden splint now kept it fairly stabilized. Drake felt a pang in his stomach thinking of how much pain his friend was in.

"Are you okay?" Jerome asked.

"Yeah, thanks. You?"

"Yes. Except that," Jerome cringed, looking at Leo's leg. "It's terrible, isn't it?"

Drake nodded, having no words to reply. He turned around to see Isabella riding behind them, gazing downward with a shocked expression on her face. Sensing Drake's stare she jumped, clutching her heart. "Drake!" she squealed. "You're awake!"

"I'm sorry about Leo," he said.

"Don't worry," Isabella said, quickly. Drake could see her trying not to look at Leo's limp body.

"And that's not the worst of it," Jerome said. Drake's stomach clenched. He couldn't bear to think someone else had been injured or even that one of them had died. No. He would have known. They couldn't have died. He'd had seen them all during the battle. But what if something had happened after he blacked out?

"It's Amanda. She's alive," Jerome said, quickly, "but we're not completely sure what happened to her."

"What do you mean?" Drake asked. Jerome seemed to shrink back.

"You should just come and see," Isabella said.

Drake was bothered by the fact they wouldn't give him a straight explanation, but when he saw her, he understood their reticence. It was worse than he could ever have imagined.

Amanda was lying down on her horse, a peaceful look on her face, but with a deep cut starting at her neck and extending about halfway to her elbow. Most of the blood seemed to have been cleaned up, but it looked horrific. The edges were raw and pink, and there was a black and yellow substance oozing out of the wound. It smelled awful. Small wisps of what looked like smoke slowly curled up from her skin as if it were burning away.

"She's been infected." Drake whirled around to see Xylis. "And it's progressing fast."

"How?"

"We're not sure," Xylis said, his voice flat. "It comes from a plant that's only found in the forest. I know it's Comas Disease. Maximus agreed too. He even warned us about it right before we departed, but how she got it, I don't know."

"Can you heal it with sorcery?" Drake asked, desperately. He remembered Maximus mentioning it, but he had no idea it would be this bad.

"It would be very risky," Xylis said. "There's a good chance we'd push the infection even deeper and kill her outright."

"Then what can we do? There has to be something."

"No, Drake. Like I said, its Comas Disease," Xylis said, sadly. "She has five days …tops."

Drake's head begin to spin. Five days? Why? Why were so many people having to suffer? First Sahara, imprisoned in the dungeons with the others from Wendil. Then those in the army, lost and scattered. Then Xylis, imprisoned in the dungeon. Now Leo and his leg. And Amanda…their only healer.

And only five days.

*

"I've been flying for a day and a half straight, Your Majesty." Qualdor was so exhausted and sweaty he felt as if his Titan suit would be glued to him for the rest of his life. His mind flashed to finding his wymer up in the north, sucking up crisp, clean water from a stream, and then to his ride, how he sped through the air, the majestic eagle wings and striped tiger body warm beneath him.

Qualdor gave Chada a scroll. It was an update from Zebetar and Mondoor. They'd decided to have him travel back to Chada after all.

"Your willingness and persistence will be rewarded." Chada read the scroll and handed it back to Qualdor. "They're making better time than expected. This is good. This is very good."

"What would you like me to do now, Your Majesty?"

"Stay here for the time being," King Chada said. "We must prepare for their return. And I must think, in silence, about my next plan of action."

Qualdor bowed. "Of course." He left the room, but as the doors closed, he glanced back at his king and did a double take. The king was moving his mouth as if he were speaking to someone. Then the door shut.

Qualdor shook the thought off. How silly was that? There was no one else in the throne room. Or maybe Zebetar had contacted Chada through sorcery, and he was talking to him. Yes. That had to be it. There was nothing else that could make sense.

*

Zebetar breathed deeply, taking in the earthy, wonderful smell of the swamp. Next to him, the general gagged.

"All okay there, general?" he asked.

"I don't understand. How does the smell of this place appeal to you?"

They were in a vast swamp. Moss, weeds, grass and other plants covered the ground. There was not a single patch of land that wasn't wet or half submerged in murky water. The trees were bent and warped like hunchbacks. Vines covered the trees, winding down like hair plastered to skin.

"There's nothing wrong with the smell," Zebetar retorted.

"Were you born here or something?" Mondoor asked. "Because I can't imagine how you could ever stand a stench like this."

"I've been through here a few times. You get used to it. And I'd prefer that you go back to calling me "Sir." You know, with some respect."

"I was only doing that in front of the Titans. There's no point when they can't hear us."

Zebetar sloshed through a small pool of murky swamp water. Once he was back on land, he muttered something, and the water that had soaked into his cloak immediately dried. Heating enchantments were quite useful, that was for sure.

It had been a day and a half since Qualdor had left, and they hadn't heard back. He wasn't worried. They had a small head start on Drake. Chada should be pleased, though he never sounded it. Zebetar wished the king would stop writing, "Failure is Unacceptable" at the end of his messages. And there was still the problem of how they were going to find the artifact. It could be anywhere in the jungle.

And then there was the swamp. He needed to focus on that right now. They were extremely lucky to be traveling through it by day when the biggest dangers were quick-sand or hazardous water holes. At night, things were quite different. From bog-inhabiting monsters to traversing the hazardous terrain, the swamp was a dangerous place to travel in the dark.

And then there were the Swamp Spirits. They were the worst: the way they entered and possessed things. They only came out at night but could wreak havoc. Zebetar had never personally encountered one, but he'd heard stories and spotted their ghost-like bodies floating during the day multiple times. He had no desire to meet one at night.

Feeling slightly frazzled, Zebetar looked ahead and saw the swampy terrain slowly flattening out. Less water and the trees began to straighten. And suddenly, in the distance, the sorcerer spotted large trees clumped together in a rich shade of green. They were at the end of the swamp and were entering the jungle.

*

It was a day and a half since the Giants' Forest dilemma, and as they made their way through a very murky, wet, and smelly swamp everyone was lost in their own thoughts.

The sun was high in the sky as Drake felt a sickening feeling rise inside of him. Amanda had only three and a half days left, and she was beginning to look really ill. Her skin was much paler than usual. The black and yellow substance caused by the Comas Disease was covering half her wound. And the raw pinkness was spreading out to healthier parts of her skin.

His worry about Amanda tainted his excitement at getting to the jungle. Yes, they were closer to the weapon, but they didn't have a clue where to find it. They didn't even know which piece of the Spectacular Sword it may be. The group had talked about it on and off for days now, but it hadn't gotten them very far. All they had decided was they would go into the jungle together and then branch out to go on the search. It wasn't much of a plan.

King Noxy had suggested the sword or sphere would probably be treasured in a shrine or temple of some sort, guarded by a monastic order, perhaps. Leo had suggested whomever stole it probably just threw it in a lake or buried it. If they wanted to keep it from other people, surely that was the best way. Isabella had wondered whether someone had hidden away with it, much like Amanda had hidden in her cottage outside Wendil. She thought they should be looking for a hermit of some sort. In truth, nobody knew, and the more they talked the more ridiculous their attempt to find the artifact appeared.

Drake looked down thoughtfully into a nearby pool of water only to see a very, very faint outline of a figure in the reflection. It appeared to be wearing a mossy cloak. Drake rubbed his eyes and looked again, but it had gone.

"Interesting beings, Swamp Spirits." Maximus floated next to Drake. "One of the only magical creatures you'll find in this dump."

"Does it just float around all day?" Drake asked, thinking how this didn't sound strange at all now that he was used to his uncle's appearance.

"All day, yes," Maximus said. "Generally, the sun makes them invisible and prevents their magical powers from working. They're completely dormant. What you saw there was rare. But at night, things are different." Drake hadn't realized how much he didn't know about Lyzix until this adventure. Sahara hadn't taken him outside Wendil at all, really. Swamp Spirits were definitely new to him. "At night Swamp Spirits are able to possess any natural thing in the swamp: trees, water, anything. They're very defensive and territorial creatures. So, if people walk through here at night, a swamp spirit might possess a vine, for example, and make sure any trespassers get tangled up until they can never escape. Or the swamp spirits will make large pools of water explode and drown people."

Drake pondered this for a moment, imagining walking through the swamp at night and suddenly having a vine wrapped around him, slowly choking him.

CRACK!

Drake's horse whirled around and bucked wildly. Drake gripped onto the reins. He caught sight of a tree trunk splitting at the bottom. It crashed into the nearest pool of murky water. The water almost engulfed King Noxy, Sahara, and Cyrus.

"Dear Lyzix!" Maximus exclaimed. "Maybe the swamp spirits are getting stronger during the day. We should get out of here as fast as possible." He pointed ahead where they could all make out the shape of trees on the horizon with a cloud of mist hanging over them: the jungle. After so much persistence and so many obstacles along the journey, they had made it.

Everyone urged their horses on, all except Jerome who was still looking at his hands and then back at the tree as if shell-shocked. Drake paused and sighed. He had a very strong feeling that he knew what had caused the tree to fall, and it wasn't any kind of swamp spirit.

*

It was late afternoon when the group entered the jungle. Drake could barely see what was in front of him. There was so much vegetation that the trees seemed at one with the undergrowth. Everything was a luscious green. Plants and bushes covered the ground. Heavy vines hung from the trees, and Drake could've sworn he heard very faint noises, as if there were a chorus of creatures waiting to greet them.

But he wasn't taking in his surroundings as he should have been. Wasn't as alert as King Noxy wanted. No. He'd just talked with Jerome and was in a state of shock.

Whatever was in Jerome's saddlebag, it did not look like tin. And these weird occurrences with Jerome that were happening had to be explained somehow. The only thing he could think was trying to get Jerome to talk to one of the adults, and he'd done just that. Yet Jerome had said once the group stopped, and he found a good time, he would do it. Drake just hoped that wouldn't be too late. If he had to go tell someone before his friend, then he would. But for now, he would wait.

As he mulled over his dilemma, he began to notice fruits and berries among the foliage surrounding them: delicious looking figs, bananas, mangoes, berries that were red, black, blue, purple, even yellow and orange. Drake definitely wasn't anxious to try them, but the jungle seemed much friendlier than the Giants' Forest.

He looked up at a particularly juicy fig and his mouth began to water. In fact, within seconds the fig looked so incredibly delicious that he could think of nothing else but eating it. He stood up in the saddle, wobbling, as the horse snorted and neighed, stamping its hoof, and Drake reached towards the luscious fig.

"Drake, no! Don't touch that!" Cyrus screamed, but it was too late. The moment Drake's fingers clasped the fruit, it sprouted a small hole like a mouth and tried to bite him. Drake pulled back, shocked and toppled off his horse. His fall was cushioned by jungle brush.

"Drake!" Hooves pounded behind him, as Sahara and Cyrus rode to see if he was all right.

His master spoke first. "What happened?"

"I don't know." Even as he spoke, his mind cleared. "It was like it entranced me into grabbing it."

"It did," Cyrus said, grimly. "Most fruit here is enchanted. They have poisonous bites. Sometimes, they've been known to work together. They carry you into the tree canopy and hold you there.

"What happens then?"

"You die of the poison and the fruits slowly digest you. If you're lucky an animal will find you first," Sahara said. "Lots of deadly creatures around here, too."

"Like what?"

Sahara sighed, "I'm starting to regret not teaching you more about Lyzix's geography and habitats."

"Magical creatures and such," Cyrus answered, ignoring Sahara's laments. "The further north you go, the worse they get. Not that the South is a party. But, there's one creature I hope you never have to run into."

"What's that?" Drake rubbed his wrist.

"The Giant Poison Snake," Cyrus said. "Fifty feet long and extremely thick. They aren't found anywhere else but here. There's only four or five left in Lyzix. But that's four or five too many." Cyrus shuddered. "They have a large barb on the end of their tails, and if it hits you, you're poisoned. Its bite is also deadly, but its ability to spit webs of poison is worse. They also have the unique attribute of collecting treasure."

"Wow," Drake said, "that's crazy."

"Hey! Hey! Guys, come up here!" Jerome's voice cut through all the other sounds of the jungle. They hadn't even noticed him riding ahead.

Drake, Sahara, and Cyrus all glanced at each other, and then galloped to meet him. They burst into a clearing with the rest of the group and in the center saw a large pile of treasures of all kinds: golden goblets, silver and gold bars, rings, crowns, and much, much more.

Surrounding the treasure pile, almost as if in an arena, stood statues of knights, maybe twenty-five feet tall, holding empty torch holders in one hand and spears in the other. They all faced the treasure pile, looking up at it in awe.

And lying on top of the pile of treasure was a gilded sword. Drake looked at it curiously. It was reflecting the light, so the blade looked pure white. How was that possible? No sword looked like that.

He sucked in a large breath. Upon the hilt, he caught sight of a small circle, with two crossed swords engraved inside it. Above that was a large hole in the sword. He let out something between a gasp and a cry of victory. He didn't know for sure, but the two crossed swords had to stand for something related to swordsmen. And the hole had to be for the sphere. The whiteness…that was the Obilor Bone.

He was willing to bet the entire Kingdom of Wendil

that this was the Spectacular Sword—without the silver sphere, of course.

There was a hiss, and the group looked down to see the ground they were standing on slowly melt away to reveal greenish-blue water. The horses reared back, bucking, and Drake was almost thrown off as the horses ran skittishly around the clearing which was now surrounded by a murky moat.

The group calmed their horses and drew their weapons, sensing a battle. Drake noticed that King Noxy looking worried. Jerome looked scared. Sahara looked uncertain.

Suddenly there was a tremendous roaring sound as something burst from the water. The trees around them were soaked and immediately began to disintegrate with a low hissing noise. The air filled with smoke. At the same time, the torches in the knight's hands flared up with green flame. Everyone yelped in surprise except Drake. He could sense something towering above him, but the air was too full of smoke and fog for him to see what it was.

Suddenly, something thrashed through clearing. It was a snake speeding towards them, flicking its tail. Drake could see something oozing from it and then, with a start, he saw a bright, green barb, and felt his stomach drop. There was only one snake that had that kind of barb.

It was a Giant Poisonous Snake.

Chapter XXX

"Any sign, general?"

"No, for the last time, I don't know where the blasted sword is," General Mondoor shouted. "Nothing's changed since the last time you asked."

Zebetar didn't answer. He had other things to worry about than Mondoor's snarky mood and comments.

They had been in the jungle for several hours scanning the surroundings for any sign of the sword. But the ground cover was so luscious that Zebetar was barely able to see past all the green foliage, the trees bursting with fruit, the hedges with their berries. It was just too lush. It was ridiculous to think they would just come upon it by chance, but what else could they do?

He collected his thoughts and tried to scan the jungle again when he heard a sharp cry. He whirled left and through the dense jungle caught sight of something green, hissing and spitting. Cautiously, he crept closer and poked a hole through the vines that were obscuring his view.

People were standing on horses, surrounded by statues of knights and a moat of greenish-blue water. Inside the moat, an enormous pile of treasure towered near an equally enormous snake.

What shocked Zebetar most of all was recognizing who was standing below the snake.

It was Drake.

*

The Snake hissed. Drake barely had a second to react. He rolled off his horse and dropped to the ground as his steed thundered away. Just then the snake's poisonous tail whipped right above him making a breeze, which whistled and ruffled his hair as it soared by. The snake's tail smashed into a nearby tree. Drake leaped to his feet as his friends shook themselves out of their shock and attacked.

King Noxy waved his arms at the hissing snake while Sahara tried to sneak in from behind and stab it. But Drake's master couldn't get many good strikes in. Even when he did, his sword bounced off the snake's scales. The tail flew in from all sides and the king and Sahara barely dodged it.

"Drake!" Xylis yanked him back. "I saw the sword. We need to get it and get out of here. That's what we came for!"

Drake nodded. Reya joined them and the three sprinted towards the towering treasure pile, picking up speed as they went. The snake launched a large web of green poison at Drake. He ducked his head, almost falling into the green murky water. The web hit a nearby knight statue, which began hissing as the venom ate through the stone.

Then Drake heard a shout.

"No!" Cyrus rode towards him from out of nowhere, but he was too late. Drake felt something very hard thrash into his back, causing him to career forward and almost fall into one of the snake's poisonous webs. He collapsed at the foot of the treasure pile, the wind knocked out of him. Holding his sword at the ready, he struggled to his feet. And as he turned, he gave a cry of fear. One of the knight statues was stomping towards him, holding the torch at its side and its spear pointed ahead.

Drake stumbled back, slipping on a small pile of gold coins and sprinted away from the statue. But the statue was faster. Drake just managed to duck the spear blow aimed at him. Then he spun, ran under the statue and took a wild swing at its legs. All he did was put a small chip in the stone.

"Don't worry about them!" Reya shouted. "We'll deal with them. You focus on getting the sword."

Drake gave a determined nod, and, changing course, headed for the giant mound of treasure instead of the snake. He felt a sizzle of energy and turned to see a stone knight dissolving from one of Reya's defensive enchantments. It had been just about to attack him, but Reya had defended him just in time. He would have to thank her for that later.

Drake reached the treasure and began to sprint up the pile, sword in hand. The first three steps he took filled him with triumph, but the fourth step send him toppling over, banging his head on a goblet and slamming his face against a golden bar. As his face burst into pain and began to throb, he slid down the pile, losing his footing until he grabbed onto what seemed like a large golden throne. Drake didn't know how the snake could have found something like that out here, but he was too preoccupied to care.

This was going to be a lot harder than he thought. He looked up at the towering mound. It was probably the same height as the knight statues, possibly taller. How in the name of Lyzix was he going to get up there?

Suddenly, something careened into the pile. He was knocked over by a large wave of gold and silver. Goblets, weapons, coins and bars crashed into him as he rolled down.

Rearing above him was the giant snake. Its mouth open and he ducked just as its jaws came down right above his head. He stood up once more, only to see the snake spit venom at him. Drake dove to the left and grabbed onto a sturdy golden statue to stop himself sliding down the treasure pile. There was a hiss from the snake behind him as the venom hit the treasure where he had just been standing. The swordsman stood back up and continued to climb. He was getting closer and closer to the top when, out of nowhere, a giant stone spear struck his stomach, knocking the wind out of him. He looked up to see one of the knight statues. He grabbed the spear, which the knight was still holding, to push it away and realized that he was being lifted higher and higher until he was nearly level with the top of the pile.

The knight didn't seem to notice Drake holding on to his spear. Drake was now right above its head still hanging onto the weapon. The snake spotted him though. Its red eyes glittered as its tail crushed one of the knight's legs. Before Drake knew it, he, the knight, and the spear were slowly tipping towards the pile of treasure.

And it was then that Drake was struck with the most daring, and probably the most moronic idea he'd ever had.

The knight and spear tilted further and further towards the pile of treasure. The snake reared back and tried to bite down on Drake, but at the last second Drake leaped up and landed on the snake's head. He sprang off it with lightning speed and landed on the top of the treasure pile.

He scooped up the special sword and turned to face the hissing, spitting snake. And in that moment, he felt as if time slowed down. He felt his hair and clothes rustle in the wind. The sword grew warm in his hand as high above him the sun gave a brilliant flash of gold. And right then, the truth sank in. He had the sword.

He faced the snake with new confidence, holding the sword in front of him. As it opened its jaws wide and darted at him, he sidestepped. The treasure pile shuffled beneath his feet, but he maintained his balance, wound back his sword and swung it forward as hard as he could. He plunged it into a weak spot in the snake's neck. The sharp, Obilor bone blade sank easily through the scales, and the snake's red eyes immediately went hazy. Drake felt triumph fill him as he pulled the sword out of the snake's flesh. The lifeless body crashed down into the treasure pile.

Drake shouted in triumph, but it was short-lived. With a rattle and the sound of metal on metal, the treasure pile began to collapse, taking Drake with it.

He fell from the top of the pile, hitting the ground hard. The sword flew from his grasp, landing a few feet away. Drake rolled to a stop at the opposite end of the clearing, near a knight statue. He heard the group thundering behind him, shouting, but then their voices stopped, and the galloping ended abruptly. He looked for the sword to see that it was gone, replaced by a large, unmistakable sea of black: The Titans.

"What a fantastic feat." A man in a blue cloaked loomed over Drake. He twisted and spun the Spectacular Sword around in his hands. He had narrow eyes, slicked-back hair and a long, scarred nose. "Now, if you don't mind, I'll take this."

*

Eleanor spent a day and a half after the mayor's visit pouring through all the books and documents he had given her. By the time she set off for the cemetery she felt that she knew enough about the Foxes to make the visit worthwhile.

The cemetery in the Western Town wasn't very large, but it was nicely planted with a fountain in the middle cascading sparkling water. Eleanor strolled through at a brisk pace, looking at the faded names on the stones. She was the only other person there apart from a young man, kneeling at a small gravestone and a middle-aged woman who tossed a bronze coin into the fountain then strolled away.

Eleanor was looking for the name Fox and felt herself getting more anxious the more she looked. Had the mayor been lying? Of course not. What reason would he have for lying? He now considered Drake, King Noxy, and their entourage, as friends and allies.

Her heart sank with every tombstone she approached that didn't say Fox.

Cicor Males, lived thirty-two years, blacksmith of the Western Town.

Regena Liles, lived eighty-seven years, mayor of the Western Town.

She was beginning to think she would never find it. Perhaps she'd missed it and would have to start again. But then a gravestone caught her eye. She read the name Fox, and her heart near exploded with joy. And Fox again on the gravestone next to it. The very people she was looking for.

Xemus Fox, lived sixty-nine years, librarian and mayor of the Western Town.

Timus Fox, lived fifty-four years, brother of Mayor Xemus and his honor guard for three years.

Eleanor crouched next to the gravestones. They were fairly plain like most of the graves, but both had small, gold-colored medals lying next to them. They were too rusted for her to tell if they said anything. She looked closer and in smaller writing the gravestones showed the men's dates of birth and death. Nothing else. Nothing she could use. She was once again at a roadblock.

She stood up with a sigh and stared for a few moments at Timus's grave. It was then she noticed a small chip in the stone at the very bottom. Looking closer, she felt her breath catch. There, so miniscule barely anyone would be able to see it, was the circle with two swords insignia.

Eleanor immediately pressed her hand to it and closed her eyes to think. Almost immediately she heard the quiet sound of stone grinding on stone. She opened her eyes and there in front of her sat a secret compartment. Inside she saw a very old scroll.

She pulled it out recognizing the familiar blue and orange ribbon, and the circle with the two swords insignia. She unraveled it as fast as she could, aware that any jerky movements might damage the delicate ancient paper and read it eagerly. She had been waiting for this for over thirteen years: real information about the Foxes and the Spectacular Swordsmen Line.

Timus,

I think I've found someone. His name is Atticus, and he's young, but he seems to have a good heart. He isn't a part of the Spectacular Swordsmen Line at all, but these times call for desperate measures. I shall send him as quickly as I can.

Let me know any news about Zeldrin. We must find out where he has gone—he knows everything about The Spectacular Swordsmen, and we don't want that information to get out.

We must talk in person. I will come to you too as soon as I can. Lyzix's vault must remain guarded and safe. I hope Atticus will be the one, but we must be wary.

I will see you soon.

-Xemus

Eleanor massaged her temples. This was extraordinary news. She could hardly take it in. There were two lineages in the Spectacular Swordsmen's history. One that started with Reuben Fox and ended with Zeldrin. Another that started with Atticus.

That meant Atticus was not related to Rueben Fox. He was not related to Chada either and Drake wasn't related to Chada. That was definitely not what she was expecting, yet it was a huge relief. She had to put the scroll aside for a moment just to process the news. Then she reread it.

Timus and Xemus had been so desperate to find

Zeldrin's replacement that they looked outside of Rueben Fox's descendants.

But it also meant that if Zeldrin hadn't failed, and the Spectacular Swordsmen lineage had continued from him, then…

Then King Chada, indeed, would have been The Spectacular Swordsman.

*

Drake glared with utmost hate at the sneering sorcerer. He stood up and slowly backed away towards the rest of the group.

"Don't even think of putting up a fight." The sorcerer stopped twirling the sword and strapped it to the outside of his cloak. "You are completely outnumbered."

"That doesn't matter," Drake said. He didn't know this man, but Maximus had told him that he had cast the spell that had changed Maximus into a dust spirit. On top of this, he was working with King Chada. Anyone who was a friend of Chada's wasn't a friend of Drake's.

"Trust me, Drake, one day you'll meet the same end as your parents, probably at Chada's hand just like them. Bravery can also be stupidity, you know."

"And you have all of the latter and none of the former, Zebetar," Maximus said, floating forward next to his nephew.

"Ah, Maximus." Zebetar smirked. "I see you've adjusted to your new…state."

Drake's anger hit boiling point. He charged at Zebetar, wanting to remove the man from the face of the earth for hurting his uncle. But he'd only taken a few steps when he heard a scream.

Everyone turned to see Jerome's face bright as the setting sun. He was drenched in sweat and clasping his hands together as if he were fighting to stop them from moving. Drake felt himself seize up with fear. Jerome was clasping the piece of tin that he'd shown Drake. From it burst the classic shield Xylis used, and then, suddenly, it exploded around them and propelled into a nearby tree.

The tree collapsed, and Drake felt himself almost vomit as he saw it fall towards Cyrus. Cyrus took a dive to one side, but the tree still landed on him. He disappeared from view under the tree's shaking branches.

Jerome glanced from the tree to his hands with a look of pure horror and self-loathing.

Drake charged toward the tree, anxious to help Cyrus, but the Titan general blocked his way and threw a wild swing with his sword. Drake parried with lightning speed and swung for the general's legs. The general blocked his move with similar ease, and so it went, back and forth. Drake tried to tuck and slash once, but the general parried his strikes. Drake then attempted the spin, slash, and stab. He nailed every step and stabbed towards his enemy's abdomen. The general only just blocked the strike in time. The sword still cut into his hip, leaving Drake with an opening. He lunged forward to strike again but saw a flash of blue out the corner of his eye. Drake turned to see Zebetar swing a silver triangle downward while yelling an incantation. A second later, Drake was blasted back by an invisible force, his normal sword colliding against a rock.

Drake watched the general grab his hip and stumble away, leaving Drake with Zebetar. Drake wanted nothing more than to take out Zebetar. He leaped to his feet and recovered his sword. Zebetar immediately shot a blast of energy from his silver shard. Drake dove out of the way, sliding on his stomach and straight away leaping back up again.

"Come on, you can do better than that," Zebetar mocked, as another ball of light flew Drake's way. "Do what your parents could never do. Resist me."

The silver slashed again, and more energy permeated out towards Drake. It barreled into him, sending him reeling back. Drake recovered his footing and focused on the sorcerer. What had he just said about his parents? "It was Chada who killed them!" Drake yelled.

"Ah, did he take all the credit?" Zebetar asked. "That's so like him. And you didn't know, Drake that I was there as well? I did just as much as him to make sure they died."

Drake felt shock and horror rising in him. How could he have been so blind-sided, so ignorant! The sorcerer whom Eleanor had mentioned, who she had fought, who had been with Chada, was the very same person who was standing in front of him.

"And so," Zebetar continued with a sneer, "if you want to live, along with your friends, I suggest you stand still, and let me do my work!"

Drake was done. Done with these sociopathic maniacs. He sprinted as fast as he could towards Zebetar, drew a spare dagger and when Zebetar tried to react, Drake slid as low as he could and plunged the dagger into the sorcerer's calf. Blood sprayed everywhere. Drake caught hold of the sword still in Zebetar's belt, leapt up, and spun around. Zebetar could hardly stand upright. Blood flowed from his calf wound, but that did not stop him from glaring at Drake, his face contorted with hate. Drake's confidence rose as he held his sword at the ready.

"You've had your moment, Drake," Zebetar hissed, "and now it's over." He swung the silver in a circle this time. A purple ball of light flew out so fast that Drake couldn't move before it struck him. It threw him backward and knocked the Spectacular Sword from his grasp. The weapon landed in Zebetar's hand. The sorcerer laughed.

The sword was back in his grasp.

"Your skills are no match for mine, Philosopher. Say goodbye to your weapon."

But as Zebetar prepared to swing his silver shard again, someone stepped in front of Drake, and a wavering purple shield expanded in front of him. Zebetar's spell deflected off it and the nearby plants burst into flames and fizzled to nothing. Sparks flew from the shield as Zebetar shot another blast of energy at it. This time, the light from the shield became brighter and brighter. So bright that Drake shielded his eyes and stepped away. When he reopened them, he expected to see Xylis or Reya in front of him, but when he focused again, saw Zebetar fighting not Xylis…or Reya…

But Jerome.

Zebetar's surprise morphed into anger. The sorcerer threw a flurry of spells at Jerome. Drake's friend dodged them all. Zebetar started to retreat. Jerome ran after him and then everything seemed to slow.

If Zebetar escaped, Drake would lose everything. The sorcerer still had the Spectacular Sword. Blood pounded in Drake's ears as he joined Jerome sprinting after the escaping sorcerer and general. The sorcerer was limping, the dagger still lodged in his calf. He was slowing down. Drake sped up, his every muscle aching, getting closer and closer to Zebetar. They were going to get the sword! He was going to have it!

But then Zebetar whirled around and let a spell fly. The grey ball of light soared through the air. Jerome's eyes widened, and Drake realized his friend wasn't going to move out of the way in time. It was going to hit him! He looked at Jerome and made up his mind. He needed the sword, but he needed his best friend more.

Drake leaped in front of Jerome. The grey ball of light crashed into him. Drake felt his suddenly limp body fly through the air, and before he was rendered unconscious, he knew that the sorcerer had escaped.

The enemies had the Spectacular Sword.

Chapter XXXI

"How are we going to return to the town?" Sahara asked, fear and panic in his voice. "A quarter of the group is out cold and severely injured, and we've lost the Spectacular Sword. Our horses have gone. And by the time we get back, Amanda will already be—" Sahara stopped. Jerome heard him swallow. There were no responses from the others.

Jerome sat motionless on the jungle floor, staring at Drake's body. Next to Drake, Cyrus was laid out, his leg hideously injured.

Truthfully…Jerome felt like utter crap.

The image of the tree collapsing on Cyrus replayed in his head. He couldn't see anything else, not even his shocking sorcerer's abilities or the brief duel with Zebetar. Jerome had no idea what this meant, but he didn't care right now. What he did care about was Cyrus's maimed leg. It didn't even remotely look like a leg anymore. Jerome wasn't a healer, but he highly suspected that it would have to be amputated.

And then there was Drake. When he finally came around and was conscious, Jerome didn't know whether his best friend would strangle him or hug him. Guilt racked his insides. He should have been faster. If he'd been one second quicker, he could have dodged the attack and Drake wouldn't have had to jump in front of him. But his best friend had, and now he was unconscious with no sign of when he would come back.

Jerome had never wished for his master more than now. His master would have said that accidents happened, and that there was no use dwelling on the past, what you could and could not have done. Jerome couldn't have controlled Drake's impulse, much as he wanted to. That was not in his power. So, he needed to focus on what he could do. Which, at the moment, wasn't much, unfortunately.

"We'd best be off." King Noxy's voice cut through Jerome's thoughts.

"Amanda's time is ticking. So is Cyrus's and Drake's. We need to get them all to a healer. We'll have to risk moving them. It's our only choice." He sounded slightly panicked and he was nervously twiddling his thumbs as he glanced around the clearing.

Jerome sank back into his stupor, only to feel strong arms hoist him up by the armpits.

"Come on, Jerome. Let's go." Xylis, pale, tired, and sullen, still forced a smile as he helped Jerome to his feet. Behind him Isabella and Leo were talking in hushed tones. King Noxy, Sahara, and Maximus stood together, no doubt discussing their next move. Reya was examining the giant body of the dead snake, as well as some of the treasure in its stash, but she showed no sign of excitement or even pleasure. Instead, it was grief she displayed, and Jerome knew exactly how she felt. They had won, but the cost was too high to enjoy it.

Xylis shook Jerome's arm. "Jerome, please. I know what you are feeling, and why you're feeling it." His eyes darted to the sack at Jerome's belt. "And I believe you have something that Reya and I have been looking for."

"What do you mean?" Jerome looked up at him in surprise. "It's yours?"

"Show me."

Jerome grabbed the metal from the saddle and handed it to Eleanor. Jerome saw Xylis's face fall once he took it. The sorcerer looked at him firmly. "How did you obtain this?"

"It was in there, the whole journey."

"Why didn't you say something?"

"It's a piece of tin, why would I need to say something?" Jerome was getting annoyed. Xylis was now worked up over the stupid piece of tin when they had so much else to worry about!

"That's not tin," Xylis said. "That's silver."

Jerome froze. Silver. He looked at the bar. Silver…Tin, they looked similar, yet were so different. Drake had been right! How could he have been so ignorant not to listen to him? It was silver, it did have magical properties, and Jerome would bet anything this was what caused him to maim Cyrus.

"Look, Jerome," Xylis said. "I'm not mad. You obviously didn't know it was silver."

"Drake had suspected it was something other than tin. I was going to talk to you about it, but—"

"We ran into the sword, and then Zebetar came. I understand—it's fine. Just next time, maybe show it to me, or someone else, a little earlier, so we can catch it, before something like this happens."

"Okay." Jerome mumbled.

Xylis sighed. "Jerome, you also have to understand, this is not just you. Silver has caused sorcerers, especially untrained ones, to react very badly to sorcery. I've seen it with my own eyes. It could have been worse. Cyrus is alive and he's okay. I am sure he will not only forgive you, but be proud of your new abilities."

"This has happened to sorcerer's before?" Jerome could barely hear himself speak. Despite some lingering guilt, he felt relief pouring into him. So, he wasn't completely abnormal and strange. He was normal—well, at least for a sorcerer.

"Yes," Xylis replied. "Drake and Cyrus will both be okay. They'll just need some time to recover."

Jerome was feeling better than he had before. "What about Amanda?"

A flicker of worry crossed Xylis's face. "She'll…she'll be okay too. Anyway, I need to discuss a few things with everyone else before we head out. But, Jerome," the sorcerer looked at him seriously, "remember what I've just said. It's one hundred percent true."

As Xylis walked off Jerome sank down to the ground. He was shaking with a strange mixture of—how would he describe it—relief, fear, happiness even? The strange events that had been occurring along the journey were suddenly explained. The tin, which was really silver, had been helping his sorcery develop. He was a sorcerer. He'd always fantasized of doing more than just working as a blacksmith. He loved creating weapons, but he'd always longed for something more: excitement or adventure maybe. But he'd never imagined being a sorcerer.

The more he thought about it, the more it exhilarated him. Was he going to start training? What was going to happen?

"Hey, Jerome, everything all right?" He turned around to see Leo using a long sword as a cane. Isabella was a few yards behind her brother, seemingly reluctant to join the conversation.

"Oh…uh, yep, all good." Jerome's eyes wandered to Leo's broken leg. "Feeling a little better?"

"Sort of." Leo hesitated. The thief had risen after Zebetar and Mondoor had escaped with the sword, and was still a little physically sensitive. "It'll definitely be better when it's finally healed." He seemed on the verge of saying something else but stopped, which was unlike him. Jerome studied the thief's body language. He actually seemed to be pretty relaxed considering the situation they were in. Did he possibly feel more protected when with Jerome? Perhaps. Though even if it was true, it didn't make Jerome feel any better.

"I heard about your manifestation."

"What? Oh." Jerome went quiet. At Leo's words, the tree incident appeared in his mind for the umpteenth time. He tried to focus on the good part, but it was no use, the image kept replaying.

"That's good news, right?" Leo said, caution in his voice.

"Yeah," Jerome replied. Was it? Yes, and no. He guessed the manifestation itself was a good thing. But the way it had happened would haunt him for some time. And his decision to keep the silver would torment him.

"Well, you'll make a great sorcerer. I'm absolutely sure of it," Leo blurted.

"You think so?" Jerome stared at Leo, surprised at his

empathy and compassion. He didn't usually express himself like that.

Leo stared back for a long moment. "Oh, shut up." He smacked Jerome on the arm, and the two grinned.

Isabella shook her head. She wiped her face, pushed her hair out of her eyes, sucked in a deep breath and turned to look at Drake's unconscious body. Jerome could see a small tear on her cheek, and he felt a surge of guilt. How could he be so insensitive, laughing with Leo when Isabella was so very upset about Drake and the others. He blamed himself for Cyrus's and Drake's injuries—and that already felt as bad as it could get.

"All right everyone." This time it was Maximus explaining the plan. "I've charted the route. We need to go back the same way, out of the jungle and through the swamp. But do not despair, because I have good news." The group perked up at this. "There are most likely wymers in the plains after the swamp. Since they are available, we will use them to get back to the Western Town." The group cheered this. "However, once we get back, we'll have to confer with Eleanor, and…" He sighed. "I'm not sure what we'll do."

"We should go now," King Noxy said. "Amanda's succumbing. Not a second should be wasted."

Xylis and Reya abruptly heaved up Amanda, and Cyrus, while Sahara lifted up Drake. Jerome stared at Drake's limp body then looked away, knowing his best friend was in that state because of him.

They set out on foot, back through the entrance to the clearing. Time passed as the group trekked on in silence. Jerome's mind continued to replay the falls of Drake and Cyrus, his heart thudding. He was going to go insane.

"Jerome." Xylis and Reya had drawn up next to him. "Cheer up, my friend," Xylis said. "I know it's hard to be happy in this situation, believe me, I do, but you must push through these mental barriers to find hope. What are your hopes, Jerome?"

"That we return safely, that Drake, Cyrus, and Amanda heal, and that we can stop Chada," Jerome said.

Reya gave a sad smile. "Hope and it will come true. Just do your best to believe. You have a bright future ahead of you with your sorcery. Why don't we talk about that?" Jerome looked up. It would take his mind off things. "You will need to be trained in the art of defensive sorcery. Usually pupils find a master or a small group to train with," she continued. "We could find you one when you return. It's really up to you."

Jerome was struck by a sudden thought. "Could you be my teachers?" He liked Xylis and Reya, and they were skilled in their craft. They were part of this amazing group of friends, so he could train whenever he was with them. But then his thoughts froze. He probably wasn't going to be with them much longer. Once they'd figured out a plan, who knew? Maybe once they returned, they would all go their separate ways. And if the group did split up, he had nowhere to go back to. Nowhere to call home.

"Jerome?" Xylis said.

"Sorry, you were saying?"

"I was saying that I've never considered myself as a teacher, but if that's what you really want, then I would be delighted."

Jerome felt his heart swell.

"Yes," Reya said, "I would be happy to as well."

He beamed at them both and they returned his smile. How quickly moods changed.

"We should wait a bit to start though," Jerome said, looking at Cyrus, Drake's, and Amanda's bodies. "Wait for things to…return to normalcy. At least, somewhat."

"Yes," Xylis said.

"But we'll try to begin your training as soon as possible, to help control your sorcery." Reya shot a sidelong glance at Xylis. Jerome felt another rush of guilt. "We can start explaining some spells right now and the history of sorcery, perhaps along with the silver aspect, it's important in the long run."

And so it was that Jerome's mind slipped free from all troubles and worries as Xylis and Reya plunged into their explanation of Lyzix's sorcery. The memory of the tree and Cyrus would surface occasionally, but then Jerome would remember what Noxy had told him: *Accidents have happened before when sorcerers manifest their powers.*

Jerome would have to talk to his new teachers about it. But the best thing about being trained as a sorcerer was that he would ensure something like the accident with Cyrus would never, ever happen again.

*

Zebetar saw the end of the swamp come into view and quickened his pace tenfold.

"Come on, we need to move!" he yelled to General Mondoor.

His hood had fallen off and his blue cloak billowed behind him, but Zebetar wasn't deterred. He sloshed through the wet swamp. The bottom of his cloak was wet, his boots were soaked, but he was getting closer and closer to the plain, where he knew things would take off.

Literally.

"What's the plan?" the general huffed behind him. "Because walking back to Chada isn't going to work."

"Of course it isn't you fool!" Zebetar hissed without turning around. "We're going to fly back."

"Fly? How in the world—"

"Quiet!" Zebetar exclaimed. "You'll see. We need to get the Spectacular Sword back to Chada and to safety as quickly as possible."

When they reached the plains, Zebetar racked his brains for all the information on wymers he'd heard over the years. They liked places with a lot of vegetation.

He glanced around, spotted a grove of trees, and sprinted over to it. When he found nothing, he walked slightly further to another, and this time, he was lucky. There sat one lone wymer, drinking from a small stream. General Mondoor caught up to him, panting. Zebetar briskly walked to the wymer and without giving it a chance to react, leapt on its back.

"Get on," Zebetar ordered. With a look of surprise and admiration, Mondoor swung his leg over the wymer and pulled himself on. Meanwhile, Zebetar muttered an incantation under his breath. There was a whoosh, and a green ball of light sank into the ground.

If Drake and his friends came this way, they would have a difficult time finding any wymers at all. His "ward-off" enchantment would chase away wymers for at least a few hours so Drake and his friends were delayed in pursuing them. That was all he needed to make sure he returned to Chada first.

He was actually looking forward to reporting to the king. They had the Spectacular Sword, and they knew that the blacksmith from Wendil, Drake's good friend, was now a sorcerer. No hidden surprises. Their next goal was to look for the sphere, and then fuse the weapon back together in order to open the vault. Things were progressing quite well.

Zebetar smacked the wymer's sides, and with a yell of fright from Mondoor, they took off.

*

Eleanor was deeply troubled. Now she knew that King Chada was a part of the original lineage, it added a third motive to his undying quest to destroy the Spectacular Swordsmen legacy and use the Spectacular Sword. No wonder he wanted the Swordsmen gone and the sword for himself. She needed to tell the others as soon as she could.

The library bell jingled, and she heard heavy footsteps and metal clinking. Not a sound she associated with her normal customers. Four soldiers stood in the doorway. Immediately, she pulled a dagger from her cloak and had an incantation ready on her lips. The four soldiers raised their hands immediately.

"Stop, miss, we come in peace, we're on your side," one said, looking frightened.

Eleanor stopped mid-incantation and lowered her dagger. "You are?"

"Yes. We couldn't find King Noxy, so we came straight here," another said.

Eleanor still felt suspicious and though she lowered

her dagger, she kept it firmly in her hand. She didn't think Chada would send Titans after her, not right now. "Why are you here?"

"We have news of the army." And immediately, after those words, her remaining suspicions were soothed. She set her dagger down as she remembered the four scouts, flying off into the night. It felt like ages ago.

"Is it good news?" she asked.

"Yes," the third scout replied. "We've located the army. They had dispersed to the east of Lyzix, in the plains below the Moai Mountains, but we have them marching back here as we speak. No more than two days away."

The librarian momentarily forgot what she had just found out about King Chada and Zeldrin. "That's fantastic!"

"If it is all right, we'll fly back to keep an eye on them as they make their way back."

"Whatever you need to do," Eleanor said.

"Where's King Noxy?" the scout leader asked.

"He and others are up north," Eleanor said, quietly. She expected that the group had reached the jungle by now, but she had no idea how long it would take them to get the artifact. "I'm hoping they'll be back soon."

"I know King Noxy," the scout leader said. "He's a fighter. They'll return soon enough."

As the soldiers left the library, the bell ringing behind them, a thought crossed her mind. She didn't know if it would work, or if it was too late, but it all she needed was a quill, a scroll and a very convincing argument.

Chapter XXXII

It was dark as Jerome sloshed through the murky swamp, his boots and pants soaking up water. He looked at his reflection in the moonlight and saw a depressed, anxious face staring back. How had everything been so good and then turned so terrible? He looked up as a tree's shadow loomed over him and felt the shivers. Something rustled, and he jumped, before realizing it was only Leo. He'd thought it was a swamp spirit.

As Jerome kept a watchful eye on the terrain, he thought back to what Maximus had said about swamp spirits: how dangerous there were. They were only travelling through the swamp at night to get Amanda help as soon as possible. She was only getting worse. She had at most two days left, but they weren't completely sure. Her skin had become paler, and she was constantly covered in sweat. Almost all the wound was covered in the black and yellow substance now, the Comas Disease. The veins bulged out of her neck and arms, as the disease took over her body.

Jerome hoped the plain was up ahead. He was panting from the effort of dragging his boots through the bog water.

He went back to watching for swamp spirits, knowing to call Xylis or Reya immediately if one showed itself. There was only one incantation to eject it from the object it possessed. And Jerome was definitely not going to try to fight one off, not after what happened when he'd used sorcery last. He was saved another painful replay of Cyrus's injury when the plain came into view. He sighed with relief. They were almost there. Then they would look for wymers and would hurry back to the Western Town.

SMACK!

A wooden branch hit Jerome, causing him to stumble backwards.

"A swamp spirit!" Xylis cried. "Come over here!"

Jerome didn't listen. Suddenly, all his anger about losing the kingdom, his master, and hurting his friends poured out of him. He grabbed his hammer and, without realizing it, used a little sorcery as he brought it down hard on the tree's trunk. The trunk split. Jerome swung his hammer back, readying for another strike, when another tree branch plunged into his ribs, causing him to land in the murky grass. Xylis and Sahara closed in on the tree. A green ball of light flew from Reya's hands as Sahara weaved, and dove around the tree trying to slice it with his sword while the tree swung its branches like arms. The green light was sucked into the tree. There was a loud wail and a ghost-like creature exited the bark. The tree then fell to the ground, completely still.

"I understand you're angry," Reya pulled Jerome up. "But you mustn't let it get ahold of you. Stay calm."

Jerome didn't respond, feeling ashamed of his reckless decision. He looked down at his feet as Sahara and Xylis approached.

"Come on," Sahara said, "we'd better get moving."

They barely had any trouble with swamp spirits after that except for one that possessed a puddle and dumped a wave over them. Jerome was able to contain himself from attacking it. They'd only got soaked, that's all.

Night became day as they entered the plain, and more hours passed as they continued on foot, searching for wymers everywhere.

"Why aren't they here?" Leo asked.

"I've no idea," King Noxy replied. "Everyone knows this is one of their favorite watering spots."

"Wait." Xylis stuck out a hand. The whole group stopped. Jerome saw Xylis and Reya share a look.

Sahara voiced what Jerome was thinking. "What is it? Is there something wrong?"

Xylis just held up a hand. The two sorcerers walked slowly ahead, Reya muttering something while Xylis looked at the ground.

"Aha!" Reya exclaimed. "I think sorcery was used here. I wouldn't be surprised if it was a spell to ward something off—in this case, wymers."

"It must have been Zebetar," Leo said.

"We need to find another way home, then?" King Noxy asked.

The group suddenly seemed to deflate. Their postures sagged, and their faces turned sad. Jerome sensed that they were feeling the same thing: defeat. Amanda was on the brink of death, Cyrus was in immense pain, Leo was injured, and Drake was unconscious. Their enemies had escaped with sword, the whole reason they had come up north. And now, they were stranded here with no way home.

Then he remembered Reya's words. *Just do your best to believe.* The group didn't seem to be believing right now. Jerome thought long and hard about their options and it was as if a bright fire had suddenly lit inside of him. "An enchantment!" he exclaimed.

"An enchantment?" Sahara frowned. "What are you talking about?"

"Is there an incantation that can undo Zebetar's sorcery? Like a counter enchantment of some sort?" Jerome asked.

Reya and Xylis glanced at each other. "Not that we know of," Reya said. "But I suppose we could try."

Jerome saw some of the group's faces brighten, and he felt a new confidence. Perhaps they were not completely helpless. "Yes, I think it's a good idea if you try."

The two sorcerers closed their eyes and began muttering under their breaths. In their hands colored balls of light formed, but they reached a certain size then halted. Jerome waited for the balls to be released, but they just continued to glow in the sorcerers' hands. He saw beads of sweat begin to trickle down their foreheads. Eventually, the sorcerers gasped for breath, and the lights disappeared. Reya collapsed to her knees. Xylis bent over, panting like a dog.

"We can't do it," he said, "Zebetar's sorcery is too powerful. We need one more sorcerer in order to break it."

It took a moment for Jerome to register what Xylis had said. But when he did, he felt a nervous grin break out onto his face. "You have one right here."

Xylis and Reya both looked at him, and to Jerome's dismay they shook their heads. "It's too dangerous," Reya said. "You're untrained, and we can't afford any more accidents."

He almost agreed with them, but the way Reya had spoken made him feel angry. "This is our only hope to get out of this hole we've dug ourselves into, and you refuse it?" He raised his voice. "Sometimes, we need to take risks."

Even though he was terrified, Jerome closed his eyes and imagined first, the silver in Xylis's pocket rushing to him. He felt the cold metal in his hand and then, believing in himself, imagined wymers flocking over these fields. He imagined Zebetar's enchantment as tangible and then pictured himself cutting through it. Light and energy formed on his hands. He felt triumph filling him as it grew bigger and then he felt himself growing hot. Sweat formed on his forehead and soaked his hair. It stung his eyes. And he realized he couldn't do it. He didn't have enough power, just like Xylis and Reya. He felt as if the counter enchantment was going to overtake him, as if he was going to vanish into thin air. And then, just as suddenly he felt stable again. The ball of light left his hands. He opened his eyes and saw it sink into the ground and disappear.

"You're lucky I decided not to strangle you, right then and there," Xylis said. The rest of the group looked from Xylis to Jerome in shock.

Jerome grinned sheepishly. "Someone had to do something."

"Yes," Reya said. "And though it was stupid, you did a good thing. That was some impressive sorcery. Xylis and I did not have to do too much."

"You helped?"

"We became worried when we saw you struggling. So yes, we helped. It seems with the three of us combined, we were able to break Zebetar's spell," Xylis said.

Jerome smiled. Though the way his sorcery had revealed itself would still haunt him…this moment would be a great counter to the other.

"Guys! Look!" Leo shouted. Jerome whirled around and whooped with joy.

The enchantment had indeed been broken. In the distance a small pack of wymers was making its way towards the group. They went to meet them, Cyrus in the lead.

They were heading home.

*

Eleanor was exhausted from her days of research. She just needed a break in the fresh air, but she couldn't stop rehearsing her speech to the group. How was she going to explain what she'd found out? She was supposed to be in a good mood, headed to the tavern to grab something to eat, but she couldn't stop her mind from spinning.

"Everyone! Look! Incoming wymers!" a guard shouted from the top of the wall.

She whirled around to see multiple specks flying into view. Some townsfolk ran, afraid of another attack. Others drew weapons. The guards on the walls seemed to be getting ready to fight. But when the wymers skimmed the tops of the houses, Eleanor saw King Noxy, his crown glinting in the sunlight. She didn't have time to even mentally celebrate before one wymer almost barreled into the shop behind her. She sprinted to meet it and heard the riders shouting in panic. "Help! Get a healer! Quick!"

That wasn't good.

Townsfolk, horses, and carts were now stopping in the street, or swerving around the wymers. A crowd was gathered to watch. Reya and Sahara leaped off the first wymer, carrying someone. Eleanor's stomach gave a lurch. Had someone died?

"Out of the way! This woman needs treatment, now!" Sahara cried out. Three soldiers ran to meet him. They took the body and raced to the nearest apothecary.

Meanwhile, King Noxy and Isabella were dragging two other bodies from the wymers, helped by two more soldiers. They sped after Sahara and Reya. Eleanor felt faint when she saw who they were. One was Cyrus, and the other was Drake.

She ran up to Xylis. "Are they okay? What happened?" Maximus was floating next to Jerome, who seemed to be helping Leo stabilize himself.

"Drake was knocked out cold, and he has a few broken ribs. Cyrus—" Xylis paused. "Cyrus has a maimed leg. It may need to be amputated."

Eleanor gasped. She was glad that Drake wasn't too badly injured. Broken ribs weren't terrible. But Cyrus? Losing a leg?

Xylis then pointed to Leo. "Leo broke his leg, but he's still his usual flippant self."

The thief shot a reassuring grin at Eleanor but then grimaced. "Amanda is the one we really have to worry about."

"Amanda? What happened?"

"Comas disease," Xylis said. "The wound looks horrible. She's getting treatment right now, I hope, along with Drake and Cyrus."

Eleanor felt sick. She was extremely glad no one had perished, but four serious injuries? She looked at Xylis for a moment, feeling a rush of gratitude that her apprentice was okay, and gave him a hug. Xylis sank into her embrace. The strong camaraderie between them never wavered.

A moment later, Jerome and Leo reached her and, without even thinking, she embraced them as well. "I'm really sorry about your leg, Leo."

"It's fine." He winced. "As long as I have my crutch, I'll be okay." He shot a wink at Jerome, and the blacksmith cracked a smile.

Eleanor then looked to Maximus. "Good to see you, my friend." They shared a look of deep compassion, since they couldn't hug, but Eleanor felt it was good enough. She then gestured for them to walk with her to the apothecary. "You need food and water. And we need to talk."

"Yes," Xylis replied. "We do." He lowered his voice so only Eleanor could hear as they bustled down the street. "We discovered something very interesting, and it has to do with Cyrus's leg."

"Oh really?" Eleanor wondered whether Zebetar had used an unknown spell that Xylis wanted to ask about.

"Jerome is a sorcerer."

Eleanor continued walking, but she felt tingles of surprise all over her body. She placed a hand on Jerome's shoulder. "That's wonderful." Jerome looked at her blankly for a moment, then smiled.

"His powers revealed themselves during a battle," Xylis said. Jerome immediately looked away. "That was how Cyrus's leg was maimed. But it was an accident. I'm planning to train him along with Reya."

"Oh dear." She looked at Jerome. "How did that come about?"

"He had a little help." Jerome hung his head as Xylis

continued. "A piece of silver he discovered. It was actually the one you gave us. Our saddlebags and horses got mixed up."

"Indeed? We'll need to be more careful next time, then," Eleanor took a moment to compose herself. She couldn't blame Jerome. He hadn't known what he was getting into. But it was so unfortunate that Cyrus had been caught up in the sorcery. "I'm so sorry, Jerome, that your powers had to come in this way. It's happened to sorcerers before, though. Don't worry," she said. "But please know being a sorcerer, though a challenge, is ultimately very rewarding. If you'd like, I'd be willing to help with your training."

"You would?"

"Of course," Eleanor said. "And now I have news. The scouts found the army. They have returned."

"That's fantastic!" Xylis exclaimed.

"Yes," Eleanor said, as they reached the apothecary shop. "Now, let's check in with the rest of the group. We need to catch up and then take action. We have a long road ahead of us."

*

"Can you sit up?" Drake felt a gentle hand pulling him up, but he immediately slumped back again. He felt like lead, and there was a throbbing pain in his ribs. His head ached. His vision was blurry.

A woman stood over him. "Amanda?" Drake guessed rubbing his eyes.

"No," the woman said, simply. "But she's is getting better. She'll live."

Drake smiled and leaned back in his bed, feeling relief and satisfaction seep into him. Amanda would survive.

"Now, take this bowl of ointment and rub some on your ribs. It will ease the soreness."

There was a loud bang. The woman jumped in surprise, and Drake heard the shuffling of footsteps. In the doorway he could just make out Jerome, Leo, Xylis, Eleanor, and Maximus.

"Miss Eleanor," the woman said, "this is an apothecary, and I must insist that—"

"I apologize, Carla, but I need to speak to Drake and the others. Alone." Jerome, Leo, and Xylis all beamed at Drake while Maximus shot him a wink. "It's urgent."

As Carla disappeared into another room, Jerome and Xylis dashed to Drake's side. Maximus floated over, and Leo had help from Eleanor.

"Shouldn't you get your leg treated?" Drake asked.

Leo grinned. "Nah, it can wait. Besides, it's been healing okay without treatment."

"How are you feeling?" Maximus was floating next to Drake's bed. "That was a rough spell. We were so worried."

"Better, thanks." Drake glanced around to make sure no one was there and lowered his voice just in case. "Eleanor, did you find anything else out?"

"Yes, but more importantly did you—"

At that moment, Amanda and Cyrus were brought into the room on beds pushed by Carla, Sahara, King Noxy, Isabella, and Reya. There were yells of delight and even a few tears. Isabella beamed at Drake, her bright blue eyes glowing. He felt himself flush slightly. All this attention was embarrassing him.

Once everyone was settled, the shutters were closed and

they were in private, Eleanor said, "At last I can ask. Did we get the sword?"

Drake saw the groups' faces fall. "Didn't we get it back?" he asked.

"No, pal," Jerome said, sadly. "Zebetar and General Mondoor disappeared on us. They still had it with them."

Drake had seen them escape, but had held out hope that the group had chased after them and reclaimed the sword. His disappointment must have showed in his face, because Xylis tried to cheer him up. "You were wonderful against that snake. That was an extreme move if I ever saw one." Drake felt a burst of pride.

"Snake?" Eleanor asked, sharply.

"Drake's timing was perfect," Maximus said, and right then the story exchange began.

Eleanor's discoveries, however, topped all of the group's adventures. "And Zeldrin is an ancestor of Chada," she said, finally. "That means Chada is a part of the original Spectacular Swordsmen Line!"

Drake dropped the bowl of ointment he'd been holding. It clattered onto the ground.

"You're joking!" Leo said, "But what about Drake? Isn't he—"

Drake didn't hear what Eleanor said afterwards. He felt like he was going to pass out. Chada was a part of the original Spectacular Swordsmen Line? He couldn't believe this was possible. Could Chada, in addition to wanting the sword, sphere, and silver vault, also be jealous of Drake? If Zeldrin hadn't failed, then Drake wouldn't have been a Spectacular Swordsman. Chada would have. King Chada didn't only want Drake's title, he believed he deserved it, that he was entitled to it.

The epiphany barely had time to settle in before Reya asked, "So, what are we going to do about the sword?"

"Do we have a choice?" Drake was shocked to see it was King Noxy who had spoken.

"What do you mean?" Sahara asked.

"I trust Eleanor completely when she says that this sword is a big deal. Don't you?"

Drake's friends nodded, and there were many determined and firm confirmations that they did. "We knew the sword was a big deal when we went on that journey," Noxy said. "And now, with everything else that Eleanor has discovered, especially this new information about Chada's motives, then we don't have much of a choice but to act."

Eleanor nodded. "The Seaside Kingdom's army has just returned, and so have the Western Town reinforcements. I've even managed to convince Solomon to send some men to help. Unfortunately, he's had to keep Thoro with him, but we will have some help from Oldor." A few faces brightened at that statement. "It's all worked out well, except for the sword, of course. Now it's in Chada's hands and his next move could be devastating. I know it seems reckless, and unwise, especially since what happened the previous time we did this. Yet this time, it's necessary. The future of Lyzix depends on us."

"So no pressure," Leo muttered.

Eleanor ignored him. "We need to come through."

The group came to a consensus. They would gather the necessary materials and people and launch an assault upon Chada.

Drake, though happy to see that the group was agreeing, felt unsettled. If they were agreeing to do something this risky, then they were desperate. And he winced at the thought of what desperation could lead to in situations like these.

CHAPTER XXXIII

Drake and Sahara were outside, behind the library training near a well-manicured garden Eleanor kept. As Drake swung his sword at full speed, his master easily deflected the strike and smoothly transitioned into a complicated flurry of offensive moves. Drake ducked and leaped, dodging them all. The two swordsmen swung direct strokes at each other, their blades clashing and locking in the middle.

"Impressive," Sahara said. "You've really grown in your abilities ever since Wendil was attacked."

"I've felt it, too. Ever since Eleanor told me about the Spectacular Swordsmen and then the trials. Everything feels more natural to me. I've also had the opportunity for much live practice."

"Isn't that the truth!" Sahara exclaimed. He then gave a thoughtful look to Drake. "I'm very proud of you, you know?"

Drake beamed. "Thanks." He looked to the back door of the library, leading into Eleanor's room. He knew Maximus and Eleanor were in there, discussing the coming battle. Everything had been moving so quickly since they'd agreed on their plan.

Across the Western Town, Drake could hear the sound of metal clanging and people shouting. New weapons were being constructed on a constant basis. People were bustling around town, delivering messages, purchasing weapons, going to training sessions, preparing food, packing wagons. Drake had never seen the Western Town so alive.

"Are you ready to spar one more time?" Sahara asked.

Drake looked up. "Yes." He felt a slight hesitance but had no idea what it meant.

Sahara frowned but said nothing. The two readied their weapons. When Sahara gave the signal, Drake immediately leapt into action. He knew if he wanted to best Chada, he would have to work as hard as possible.

Drake swung a very smooth right slash then a left slash, but Sahara blocked his strikes with more ease than usual. Drake felt himself losing ground as Sahara drove him back towards the plants. He ducked a strike and tried to slither away but felt the flat of Sahara's sword hit his back. As he turned around, he was knocked over by another sword strike. His own weapon disappeared into the nearby flowers.

"Are you okay, Drake?" Sahara pulled him up. "I thought you were prepared to block that."

"So did I," Drake grumbled. He wasn't angry at his master. Something else was bothering him. He couldn't stop thinking about it.

"You don't seem very energetic," Sahara said as he retrieved Drake's sword. "Are you nervous?"

"No," Drake said. "Well, yes, but that's not it."

Sahara set the weapons down and folded his arms. "Then what is it?"

"Eleanor said something earlier during the meeting." Drake really didn't want to repeat it.

"She said a lot of things during that meeting, Drake," Sahara said.

Drake sighed. "It was about Chada. How he was a part of the original line. About how…how he could've been a swordsman. How am I supposed to think about that? And how can you act as if it doesn't mean anything? It changes so much!"

"Like what?" Sahara asked.

Drake suddenly felt frustrated. "It changes what could have been. I'm a false Spectacular Swordsman, just a substitute for the rightful ones."

"Exactly. It changes what could have been," Sahara said. "But it doesn't change the present in the least."

"But—"

"No buts, Drake," Sahara said. Drake rolled his eyes. "You have always been the rightful Spectacular Swordsman of this generation. Zeldrin failed the trails. They started a new line, a line that had more talent than Zeldrin. That should tell you right there that you deserve it."

Drake wasn't convinced. "But Chada—"

"Is a ruthless, heartless, pitiless shell of a man who has no morals, and no place on Lyzix," Sahara said. "The Spectacular Swordsmen were all about honor, Drake. They never had any ill intentions. Chada would never have deserved to be one of them. You, on the other hand, do, and you are the rightful swordsman."

Drake leaned in and gave Sahara a strong embrace. His

master was such an amazing man. He felt terrible for all the times they had disagreed and fought. And now, silently, with only himself as his witness, he vowed he would never fight with his master again.

"Better?" Sahara asked.

"Yes. Thank you."

They were interrupted by Eleanor calling from the library door. "Drake, it's time. The army is gathering outside." Maximus and Eleanor were going to stay behind, and they wanted a final word with him before he left. Sahara urged him inside.

"Such a charming young man," Eleanor said as she and Maximus beamed at him.

"He's my nephew, all right," Maximus replied. Drake flushed with embarrassment and pride.

"How are you feeling?" Eleanor asked.

"Nervous," Drake said, honestly.

"You'll be fine." Maximus reached out his dusty, transparent hands and placed them above Drake's shoulders. As they fell through Drake's solid body, he felt a strangely cold sensation run through him. "You have wonderful friends to support you, the army to fight on your side, and best of all your own fantastic courage, skill, and determination. You will succeed."

"But we have something that will help you." Eleanor reached into the folds of her cloak and pulled out a beautiful long sword.

Drake gasped. The blade was made of bright, shiny steel, outlined with a sharp diamond, and the hilt of hard oak.

"This was mine," Maximus explained. "I left it with Eleanor for safekeeping before I went on my last adventure."

"But it's outlined with diamond," Drake said.

"Yes. With the steel interior, and the sharp diamond edge, it is actually extremely strong and powerful. A very fine sword," Eleanor said.

"I excavated the diamond shards myself out of the Moai Mountains in the northwest." Maximums added.

Drake was at a loss for words. How could his uncle give him something this priceless? "But why give it to me? Why don't you use it yourself?"

"Me?" Maximus laughed. "I can't use a weapon. I'm dust, remember? It's better you have it." He turned serious. "With the coming battle, you'll need it more than I do. Until, of course, we get the Spectacular Sword back. Consider it a gift for all the times I should have been with you and wasn't."

There was an uncomfortable silence, but then Sahara peered into the library. "I think we should get moving."

"Of course!" Eleanor hugged Drake. "Good luck."

Drake smiled back and then looked into his uncle's kind, worn, dusty eyes.

"You'll be fine," Maximus eyes had a determined kindness in them.

"I know it."

*

"Take a seat." The request was simple, yet somehow the three Titans before him did quite the opposite.

"Sit down!" Chada bellowed.

General Mondoor, Ossenna, and Qualdor nervously sank into the chairs in front of Chada's desk. Zebetar, who was leaning against the wall, turned his long, scarred nose towards the king. The five of them were in one of the high towers of the castle: the one he and Zebetar had used to plan the sorcerer's journey north.

Chada unclipped a bone-white sword from his belt. It had an insignia of gold engraved on it: the circle and two swords. "So, we have the Spectacular Sword. Well done, Zebetar. Mondoor, I applaud your bravery. And your willingness to be my messenger, Qualdor."

Mondoor and Qualdor bowed while Zebetar nodded. "So, what are we doing now? We search for the sphere, I assume?" the sorcerer asked.

"Not yet. First, we must eliminate Drake and his friends." He saw Zebetar frown but did not address it. "It's time we attack. Mondoor, Qualdor, Ossenna, I want you to ready the Titans, as we'll be departing soon. Return when you've finished," Chada said.

As the three Titans left the room, Zebetar slowly walked from his spot against the wall and leaned over the desk, still frowning.

"Is there something wrong, Zebetar?" Chada snapped.

"Attack? Why are we attacking?" the sorcerer asked.

"Because we need to destroy our opposition now."

The sorcerer looked taken aback. "Why?"

"It will create a much easier path for us to get the sphere," King Chada said. "And then, we can use the sword—"

"I think you are losing sight of the goal, Chada. Our goal. His goal—"

"No longer," King Chada snapped. "He is mistaken."

"Mistaken?" Zebetar roared. "He knows more about this than you and I combined, Chada!"

"Stop!" King Chada bellowed. "Enough of this! I will not

listen to this foolishness. Zebetar, we are going to do it my way. If we do not attack them, there will be consequences!"

"That's not the plan." Zebetar snarled.

"But that is what we will do!" King Chada yelled back. "There will be no argument!"

The king and the sorcerer were nose to nose. A ball of light danced on the tips of Zebetar's fingers. King Chada could tell an incantation was ready on his lips. Meanwhile, the king had the Spectacular Sword in one hand, and his own sword in the other. He was so angry that he and Zebetar continued to stare at each other for a good while after Mondoor, Ossenna, and Qualdor had arrived in the doorway. The king finally stepped away from the sorcerer, faced the Titans and began to calm down.

"All five of us will target the group, while our Titans seize the Western Town. This decision is final." He paused, and looking out the window, saw the Titans assembling in the town. This was it. Time to put his plan into action.

"And one more thing. When we attack, we kill every, single, one of them."

*

Drake, Jerome, Leo, Isabella, and King Noxy stood outside the Western Town gates later that day, as the sun began to set, taking in all the preparations for the attack on Wendil. Perhaps a quarter of the entire army was now assembled. Meanwhile, soldiers and civilians bustled in and out of the gates carrying weapons and supplies. Soldiers were being given last-minute food. Weapons were being distributed. Xylis stood on the town walls supervising it all as King Noxy did the same from below.

"Well, guys, we're here." Leo said, awkwardly.

Isabella rolled her eyes. "Is that really all you can say?"

"I don't know what else to say."

"Well, then—"

"Guys, please," Drake didn't want the siblings arguing. "Let's not do this again. I know you're nervous, and I am too." He looked at his three friends. He hadn't known the thieves long, but they'd already been through so much together. And Jerome had been his best friend for as long as he could remember. "We can do this. We just need to believe in our abilities and remember why we're fighting: to save Lyzix from Chada's tyranny."

Drake felt a hand on his shoulder and found himself facing King Noxy. "I have faith in you, Drake, but I want you to remember one thing." He leaned in closer. "I know Chada hurt you and your family. But our main priority is the Spectacular Sword. Do not let your anger cloud your judgment. Don't go running off." Drake nodded. "Stay calm. We'll make sure we punish Chada for what he's done. Just use us. We're here to help you."

"Hey! What's that?" Xylis shouted from the top of the town walls. He was pointing to the plain. Drake and the group squinted out into the distance. Behind them, the hustle and bustle stopped, and there were murmurings in the assembled troops. And then, Isabella gasped, King Noxy cursed, and Drake felt all his hope and confidence sucked out of him. Out on the plain small, black dots were beginning to form, arranged in platoons.

He knew, right away, that this was no coincidence. It was the Titans. And he had no doubt that Chada was with them, leading an attack.

Chapter XXXIV

Drake stood a moment longer, looking out at the sea of black uniforms. He was stupefied. He could not believe that King Chada and his army were facing them, right now. They didn't have their army completely assembled outside the gates. Those inside were not armed and ready. They were completely unprepared.

He saw King Noxy's mouth opening to say something, but no sound came out. Jerome was rigidly staring out onto the open plain, his hand hovering an inch from his hammer. Leo's face was pale, and Drake found he was squeezing Isabella's hand. She, too, looked petrified.

Drake felt his hands go numb and, for a moment, he was lost in visions of the past. He was back in Wendil, during the attack that had started this fantastical chain of events. He saw himself watching as Wendil was invaded by Titans. He remembered the people he knew falling to the ground left and right, dead and injured. He remembered looking frantically in the house, searching for his master, gathering the supplies he would need to survive. He saw himself looking up onto the roof, where he glimpsed that evil figure a crown glinting on his head. And he saw the Titans disarming him, getting ready for the killing blow before Sahara rushed in to save him.

And then, as he ran away with Jerome, he remembered looking back at Wendil, flames consuming the buildings, the castle crumbling, and Titans flooding the street.

The attack on Wendil. He felt sick to his stomach. This attack would be just like that. Except this time, he knew his enemy, Chada. And what Chada wanted. There was so much more at risk.

A distant snap of a multitude of bowstrings and the whistling of the wind brought Drake back to the present. A soldier a few paces away collapsed on the ground. Another soldier farther away went down with a thump as well. Then, two more were struck down. As a fifth fell behind him, Drake heard a slight squishing noise. The man had an arrow lodged in his throat.

And then, Drake heard a scream. And a crackling of flame. This time the arrows had flames lit on the end. And that sent everything into chaos. Some men ran in every direction, seemingly trying to escape. Others howled in rage and stood their ground, looking furiously at the distant Titans who had struck down their comrades. Most everyone else turned and stampeded towards the town gates.

Drake felt his vision blur as a man's hand smashed into his forehead, right near his eyebrow. He stumbled, coughing as the dust and dirt was kicked up. He felt more arrows whistling by him, thumping into the ground. More soldiers cried in pain as the Titan archers hit their mark.

King Noxy appeared out of the chaos and grabbed onto his arm. "We need to get inside the town, now!" As

Drake was carried along by the crowd, he looked in vain for Jerome, Leo, and Isabella. As more people fell around him, pierced by the sharp, flaming arrows plummeting from the sky, Drake ran through the Western Town gates. He made a sharp right and followed King Noxy to a secluded corner in the cover of the wall. It was hidden away, and the sounds of battle were muffled slightly.

With surprise and relief, he saw the whole group gathered, including Xylis, Eleanor, and Maximus. The only two missing were Cyrus and Amanda, still in the apothecary healing from their injuries. Hopefully they would stay safe; for now, they had other things to focus on.

All of them were breathing heavily while flaming arrows rained down on the buildings of the Western town and crackling fires burned all around. They could hear yells and screams as the Titans charged the walls. Drake couldn't take it anymore. His earlier shock and fear faded away.

"This can't be another Wendil," he said, fiercely. The group looked defeated. Downcast. Hopeless. Finished.

"Our army is unprepared and being scattered once more," Noxy said. "There's no way we can recover."

"So, what are we going to do?" Drake raised his voice.

"Run," Leo said simply.

"Run?" Drake snarled. Leo recoiled. "Run?"

"You need to stay safe," Eleanor insisted. "This battle was lost from the moment Chada showed up." The crackling of flames was getting louder. Smoke curled into the air above the rooftops.

"We need that sword!" Drake bellowed, the smoke stinging his eyes. "We busted our backs all around northern

Lyzix to get it and figure out my destiny and stop Chada, and now we give up?"

"Drake, you know what happened in Wendil—"

"Yes, I was there! I saw what happened in Wendil!" Drake screamed.

The smoke was beginning to thicken. The yells and cries of pain had now been lost to the sound of the fire. "That is one of the most regrettable events of my life—" He broke off, coughing, feeling finished himself. If the group was hopeless, and they were this close to defeat, how could he inspire them? And then, his gaze rested on Maximus. He was hard to see through the smoke, but Drake was sure he gave him a small head incline, as if to say keep speaking. As if to say he supported Drake. To say he believed in him.

Drake closed his eyes and sucked in a deep breath. He inhaled again. And again. His visions of the battle of Wendil dissipated, and he imagined fighting Chada himself and winning.

When he opened his eyes, he felt a new sense of calm. "I know it's hard to believe we'll win," he said. "But too much depends on us. We must have faith. If we support one another and believe, we can succeed. I guarantee you, Chada is hiding behind that giant force of Titans and he has the sword. He's brought it right to us. We need to go out there, get what we can of the army in order, and go take Chada. He cannot step a foot in this town. There will, never, ever be any more attacks like Wendil's."

And as Drake shouted this, he realized that he would keep that vow as long as he lived.

The group stared at him for a moment, and then their

eyes slowly brightened as they filled with hope. They began to draw their weapons.

"Drake's right. We got this!" Leo exclaimed.

They were now firm-faced, ready for battle, their weapons drawn. They sprinted out of the alleyway into the smoke-filled streets. But as Drake ran towards the gates, he heard Reya yelling behind him. She turned, and she quickly shoved molo weed in his hand. "From Amanda's stash—just in case," she said, and then she raced off.

Grateful for Reya's clever thinking, he ran towards the gates once more, as King Noxy barked orders to the soldiers who remained in the area. Then, the group was banging on doors of the main tower shouting for anybody inside to exit.

Drake burst into the tower, and surprisingly, found a large number of soldiers crowded inside. "All of you," he shouted, "outside, into the street! King Noxy has orders for you!"

He then raced into the tower. "You all, come with me," he cried to a small squad of archers with longbows slung over their backs. He didn't wait to see if they followed. Instead, he leapt up the ladder, his adrenaline fueling him as he burst out of the trapdoor onto the wall. The air was better here. Yet pillars of smoke rose up all around, and Drake could see flames spreading across the town.

He turned his attention to the Titans advancing towards them, the front lines now very close to the gates. At the back of the army, he made out the glint of the golden crown on Chada's head. They locked eyes for a moment, though Chada was still far away. Drake vowed he would seek the king out, once they had a better hold on the Titans attacking below.

Behind him, one of the archers asked, sardonically. "Are you going to be leading us?"

Drake turned around. "The Western Town is, as you see, under attack. If you don't want to help your town, that's fine. But I do, and I need your help to do it."

The archers looked among each other, surprised at his abruptness. But Drake had spoken sharply on purpose to shock them into listening. He couldn't have them doubting him. And thankfully, it worked.

"What are the orders, then?" the archer asked.

Without blinking, Drake replied. "Ready your bows. Prepare your arrows. Let's get up on the wall." He pointed to a spot directly above the gates. "We're going to fire like crazy."

CHAPTER XXXV

King Chada watched his army as it neared the Western Town walls and began to slow down.

He could see that wretched boy Drake on the wall above the gate. He was up to something. He only had a few archers with him, but the boy was determined. "We need to lure the group, especially Drake, to us. Kill them immediately and their army will be nothing more than a bunch of leaderless men. The Western Town will be easy to take after that."

"We should use the sword," Zebetar pointed to the majestic weapon slung over Chada's back.

"My thoughts exactly." Chada turned to the sorcerer, Mondoor, Qualdor, and Ossenna. "The five of us will bring the sword to the wall and attack. I guarantee they will attempt to get it."

"What then?" Mondoor asked.

"We fight back, hard." Chada voice became very cold. "Eventually, we eliminate them, everyone, especially Drake." Qualdor began to speak, but Chada cut him off. He knew what the man was suggesting "Yes, Qualdor. Best to get

Drake off his game. Tell him what you need to tell him, get him weaker. Then, you can leave him to me."

Qualdor nodded, a smirk on his face, and the three Titans began talking amongst themselves about the plan. Meanwhile, Chada and Zebetar exchanged glances. The sorcerer put a horn to his lips and blew.

"It's time, Titans. Advance!" Chada bellowed.

*

Drake watched the Titan army from the wall. They were very close now, and there was no one except him and his archers defending the gates. It was time to act.

"Ready your arrows!" he shouted. He'd never done this before. Was that the right order?

"Do you mean nock?" one of the archers muttered.

"Yes, yes," Drake said, slightly embarrassed. "Nock your arrows!"

He heard the simultaneous nocking of arrows on bow-strings. He waited a moment. "Raise your bows! Aim," he shouted, and then a moment later, "fire!"

The whistling of the arrows slowly faded as they flew upward and then began their descent. Drake, feeling satisfied as the arrows thumped into the Titans below, encouraged the archers. "Nice shot, men. Again. Nock your arrows!" This time, there was more confidence in his voice.

Apparently, the archers heard it too. They readied them-selves quickly. "Aim. And fire!" Another volley of arrows rained upon the Titans, disrupting their formation. One squad had now completely halted. Drake didn't know what was taking Noxy and the group so long to pull the rest of the army together, but he had to hold off the Titans for as long as possible.

"Focus on the front platoons, closest to the gates!" he shouted. It was essential to stop the Titans putting up defenses, such as shields and other mechanisms, and attempting to breach or scale the wall. Some of the Titans were already running at the walls with ladders and grapples.

"Nock! Aim at the scalers! And fire!" Drake yelled. He heard the whoosh of arrows directed towards the Titans attempting to get to the wall. There were cries of pain, but Drake didn't have time to assess the results. He was already shouting the next orders.

"Nock! Aim, the front-line platoon! And fire!"

"Nock! Aim, the frontlines again! Fire!"

"Nock! Aim, at the scalers! Yes, good! Fire!"

The front-line Titans were beginning to hold up their shields, but Drake's archer force had completely demolished the scalers, as well as a few front platoons. Now others trying to advance were slowed by the pile of bodies.

"Nice job, men!" Drake shouted.

One of the archers slapped him on the back. "Well done yourself, commander."

The trapdoor then burst open, and Leo appeared. "Drake! The walls have been breached by a few squads of Titans! We've gotten some of the army in place, but it's not enough. We need help!"

Drake cursed. He'd thought he knocked them all down. He needed to get to the breach, but the archers would need a commander. The decision was made for him. He saw the back line of Titans getting ready to send a volley of their own. They had to get off the wall, immediately.

"Everyone, down the trapdoor, now!" he screamed. Drake watched as the Titan bowmen drew back their strings and released. The arrows flew in an arch above their heads as his men hurried down the ladder. Drake grabbed Leo pushed him down the trapdoor and then bent to climb in himself. But he was too late. An arrow tore the unprotected skin of his calf. He collapsed on the tower's floor, shuffling as fast as he could to the cover of the wall, crying out in pain. Leo ran to him. "Are you all right, Drake?"

Drake breathed in deeply. He looked at the wound. Though there was a lot of blood, he could see that the arrow had not cut too deeply. He'd been lucky. Remembering Reya's gift from before, he grabbed some of the molo weed, and, eating it, turned his attention back to the battle. He heard another volley of arrows thump down on the exposed wall above them.

"We need to get out and help them," Drake said. "Archers! Get near the doors. Fire at any enemies you see. We're going to clean the inside of the town of Titans, now."

Then, with Leo at his side, Drake ran outside, to see the streets full of men in black. They were being held off by a small group of soldiers, King Noxy at the center, but it wasn't enough.

"Fire, now!" Drake screamed.

He and Leo ducked out of the way as arrows went whizzing over their heads. The small group of Titans that had breached the walls began falling one by one. Drake rushed in, slashing one Titan across the knee and stabbing another through the shoulder when suddenly a group of heavily armed soldiers came through, led by Sahara. They plowed the rest of the Titans down.

Drake had an idea. "Sahara! I need these shield bearers!" he exclaimed. "Can you spare them?

"Yes, there's more coming. But why?"

"No time to explain!"

Sahara nodded. Drake called the shield bearers to him while Leo followed, confused.

"We left the wall open. We need close-combat fighters that can clear it quickly. And they have archers. We need people who can protect the archers, while someone who can see the battlefield calls out commands. Then, hopefully, we can pick off the Titan bowmen. After that, we'll be open for a charge."

Once they were inside the tower, he quickly explained this plan to the archers and shield bearers. "Shield bearers, you go first. There may be Titans up above. We need to clear them out first. Line up along the edge of the wall and plant your shields. Once they are all lined up, archers, you follow. Leo, you're in command."

Leo nodded. "Of course."

As Drake watched the last archer disappear up the ladders, Leo shot him a nervous wink and climbed up after them. Drake looked at Sahara. "I'm going to check on how they do. Then, we'll need to assemble all the close-handed combat soldiers we can."

The moment he poked his head out of the trapdoor he saw Leo crouching against the raised lip of the wall closest to him. The shield bearers were holding their shields up, placed against the wall. The archers stood, in their cover, arrows at the ready.

"Nock! Drop shields!" Leo ordered. There was a clang of metal. "Aim! Fire! Shields, back up!"

"Again!" Leo yelled as Drake crawled towards the cover where his friend sat. "Nock! Drop shields! Aim and fire! Shields, back up!"

Drake felt his satisfaction growing. The tactic worked beautifully. They were taking down Titan bowmen while their own archers stayed safe.

"Keep those points coming, boys! It's time we take these Titans down, once and for all!" Leo yelled.

The archers gave a cheer. As a volley of arrows from the Titans soared over onto the wall, the shield bearers brought their shields close together. The arrows were deflected, and the ones that pierced the wood had almost no effect. Metal guards implemented further inside the shields prevented the arrows from falling through. Even then, Drake and Leo stayed hidden behind the lip of the wall and were unscathed.

"Keep firing until you've taken out their bowmen," Drake told Leo. "Then, target the front lines. Once you do, we'll lead a charge against them and give them everything we have, all right?"

"Yes, General Drake!" Leo exclaimed. Drake allowed himself smile. Everything was going fairly well, especially considering how the battle had begun. "And if I need reinforcements in a certain area, or if there's danger, I'll wave my sword as high as I can, okay? The diamonds should glint and give it away immediately."

Leo nodded. And so, Drake was off. But as he leaped back to the trapdoor, he caught sight of the Titan front lines. They had now advanced past the fallen platoons and were coming up to the gates. The Western Town wasn't out of the woods yet. Drake dropped through the trapdoor, down the ladder of the tower and sprinted into the town again.

He immediately heard Sahara shouting, "And here he is. Everyone, ready yourselves!"

A whole crowd of soldiers clapped and hammered their weapons on their shields. The noise was tremendous, and King Noxy, Xylis, Reya, Jerome, and Isabella pushed their way towards Drake.

"Is the rest of the town all right?" Drake asked.

"Yes." Xylis nodded. "We've stationed some guards. They should be okay for now."

Then Leo shouted from the tower door. "The archers have started firing on the front lines. The Titan bowmen are dead," he said. "You're all clear."

Drake nodded appreciatively. He couldn't have gotten to this point in the battle without Leo. "Keep firing."

Leo saluted and as he disappeared back up the tower. Drake faced the army. "We'll be mounting our charge now." There were loud cheers from the army as Drake ran to the gates. He was no longer feeling nervous as he and Jerome yanked the rope and pulley system, and then flicked the lever that activated the gate raising mechanism.

Drake settled himself in front of the amassed men, with the other members of the group lining up beside him. The gate clanked and rumbled, then rose.

"Now!" Drake screamed as he sprinted onto the open plain, where the front lines of the Titans raced towards him.

Leo's arrows thumped into the Titans, throwing the ones in front into chaos. But the next volley was directed into the middle and back of the pack to avoid any friendly fire.

Drake was the first to reach the Titan line. He immediately cut down three Titans in front of him. As he raced to the next nearest enemy, he saw Sahara and Noxy's swords whirling, Isabella's deadly flashing dagger and Jerome's hammer. Xylis and Reya had created a magical shield in front of some of the cavalry as they cut through the Titan lines. It wasn't much, but it did give a little boost to their remaining mounted force.

Drake felt as if he were back at the trials. His mind went almost blank. It automatically focused on the enemy ahead of him. He parried a few powerful strikes from a Titan and then lopped off his head with a spin stroke. It was a direct imitation of his trial against the knight, and he did it without even thinking. Then, he moved on, making his way deeper into the Titan army, feeling like he was in a sea of black. He cut down more Titans then felt a fist to his ribs. Stumbling back, he quickly countered a sneaky swing to his opponent's legs, and then pushed through more Titans.

He could see the army constantly beating on the unrelenting Titan front-line, while arrows rained down piercing the back half of the Titan's army. He spun around, performing another spin stroke and slicing his sword across a Titan's abdomen, then he froze.

There, scaling the wall was King Chada with his golden crown glinting in the sunlight. With him were Zebetar, General Mondoor and two other Titans. But what drew Drake's eye was the sword slung at Chada's belt. There it was: The Spectacular Sword. And Chada was going to climb over the wall right where Leo was standing. His friend was in danger. Drake barely had any time.

"Leo!" he screamed, but over the sounds of battle, he knew it was fruitless. He waved his sword above the Titans as he shoved them aside, hoping the diamonds would indeed give away his position. But he couldn't afford to just wait and hope. He began to weave his way back towards the wall. If he could get through the gates and up the tower, perhaps he could hold them off.

Chada was climbing higher and higher. Leo continued to direct the archers to fire upon the Titans, not noticing Drake's frantic movements below. Drake looked around desperately for any of the group. King Noxy, Sahara, and Isabella were near the gates, defending the entrance from the Titans. He waved his arms frantically as he burst through the Titan line. His friends ran towards him while leaving others to defend the entrance.

"What's going on?" Sahara shouted.

Drake didn't stop, so they chased after him as he ran to the tower. "Chada…men…going up to the wall…Leo… archers…are…danger," he gasped. "Warn…others."

He flung open the door to the tower as Isabella raced to get the rest of the group. Sahara, King Noxy and Drake sailed up the ladder. Drake punched his hand at the trap-door and, ignoring the flaring of pain in his knuckles, burst out onto the wall.

Leo looked at him in surprise. "Drake, what—"

They were only just in time. Drake tackled Leo to the ground and the two rolled out of the way as a sword slashed right where the thief had once been. General Mondoor appeared over the wall, and he and King Noxy began to fight. Then the two unknown Titans appeared over the walls. Drake recognized one as the lieutenant who had attacked the Western Town before.

The archers had momentarily frozen, but as the lieutenant sliced one down, they retreated while the shield bearers stepped forward. But before they could attack the lieutenant, Zebetar rocketed over the wall. As he landed, Drake saw the dreaded silver shard come spinning down. Zebetar yelled something, and a giant force of energy exploded towards the shield bearers. They were all knocked back, falling into each other and yelling in pain. A few archers toppled over the walls.

Chada himself then came over the wall as Drake was engaged with the other unknown Titan. As they clashed, he felt himself shiver slightly. Swinging downward, the Titan easily deflected his stroke and pushed Drake back. Leo flew in from the side, but the Titan elbowed him in the stomach sending him careering away. The Titan turned back towards him, and Drake froze. This was just like the third trial.

He felt himself seize with fear as the Titan began to push him back. He deflected the strikes, but each time, they came closer to hitting their mark. And, they came in lightning fast. He was backing up twice as fast now. Drake took one more step and realized he'd backed up too far. He was now up against the tower wall. There was nowhere else to go. He saw victory in the Titan's eyes.

There was a shout from below. "They've breached the gates! They're coming!" Drake glanced around in a panic. King Noxy and Sahara were ambushed by Chada, Mondoor, and Zebetar. The lieutenant was advancing upon Leo. Most of the archers and shield bearers were scattered or dead. He looked down to see his soldiers running, and Titans flooding the streets. And then, he felt something ram into his stomach. He lost his breath and fell from the wall to the ground.

Chapter XXXVI

Drake flailed his arms yet landed sooner than he had anticipated. He felt wood chips fly around him, and realize he was lying inside the bed of a wagon. It had broken his fall, where he would have otherwise landed hard onto the cobblestones below. Drake slowly stood up, angry and slightly sore, but wasn't out of the fight yet.

As he struggled to his feet, a squad of Titans immediately spotted him and raced over. He had no time to glance up to see if King Noxy, Sahara, and Leo were okay. Instead he focused on the foes ahead of him.

Throwing a quick parry, Drake twisted and impaled one of the Titans at the kneecap. Then, he followed it with a quick slash upward. He tried a thrust, but one of the Titans deflected his strike. He was able to catch the blade of another man and, twisting his arm in a circle, flung the Titan's blade aside and kicked him back. He sliced the fourth across the thigh. The fifth he threw three furious cuts at his chest, but the Titan was able to block Drake's strikes, and sent one stab of his own. Drake deflected this quickly and recoiled. He was getting too reckless. And a little tired.

The Titan didn't allow him any rest. He lunged forward, swinging downward at Drake. Drake slashed upward, catching the blade. He then forced the man over. The Titan was knocked out as his head met with the ground.

Drake had a moment to survey his surroundings. More and more Titans continued to flood into the town swallowing the Western town's forces in a sea of black. He looked up at the wall and saw only King Noxy and the lieutenant Titan dueling up there. Chada, Zebetar, Sahara, Leo, Mondoor, and the unknown Titan were gone.

Drake looked back towards the gates and groaned as he readied his sword. More Titans were filing towards him.

Then, an arrow flashed by Drake and impaled a Titan right in the chest. Another lodged itself in a Titan's leg. And then all the Titans running towards Drake slowly went down, pierced with arrows. Drake made short work of the three who did get to him. When he finally turned around, he found Leo with his bow behind him.

"Are you okay?" Drake asked. "What about everyone else on the wall? Did you see them leave?"

"No idea. I came down to help you after I saw that jerk knock you off the wall," Leo said. "They can't be far."

It was then Drake saw a group of Titans being pushed back by a familiar sizzling shield. They charged at it again only to find their weapons and armor suddenly disintegrating against the shield. Xylis and Reya appeared behind it, along with Isabella and Jerome, who were now attacking the Titans. And, to Drake's relief, he could just make out the dusty form of Maximus, and the solid form of Eleanor making their way towards them.

"Isabella got the group." Drake tried to catch her attention, but the chaos of the battle was too much.

"Drake!" He dove as Leo screamed his name and heard a sword whistle over his head. He rolled to safety, and then sprung up to face the unknown Titan once more. Drake charged in, swinging right, left and right again. The Titan blocked them easily.

Drake recognized this fight. It was similar to the third trial, and he couldn't help wondering why. Was it the fighting style? It was so familiar, much like the way Drake himself fought.

And he then got his answer. As he deflected the Titan's strike, stabbed and parried, he heard a voice behind him. "Step away from my nephew, Qualdor. Now."

Drake glanced around to see Maximus floating above him. Yet he looked different. There was no kind smile on his face, but a look of anger mixed with resentment. The dust around his uncle's body was rotating faster than he'd ever seen.

Drake looked back at the Titan—Qualdor, he guessed—and wondered how Maximus knew his name? The Titan's eyes widened as he looked at Maximus's dusty form.

"Maximus. I thought I'd never see you again," he laughed. Everything seemed to slow down. Though the battle was still happening, Drake's mind was completely focused on the two men before him. In his peripheral vision, he could see Leo, staring openmouthed, at the scene in front of him.

"Don't give me any of that!" Maximus snapped. "I can't believe you joined Chada, after everything you've done.

You're still supposed to be in the Harobi Desert. You deserve to stay there for the rest of your life!"

Harobi Desert? That was where criminals were sent to live under constant supervision. If this Qualdor belonged in the Harobi Desert, then he must be a criminal. But how did Maximus know him?

"Maximus, what's going on?" Drake asked. Qualdor turned towards him. He was laughing as he pulled off his face covering. Now that his features were visible, Drake could see he bore a resemblance to Maximus and an even more unsettling likeness to Drake himself.

"Your uncle never told you, did he?" Qualdor smiled. "Well, now we can't have that, Maximus, can we?"

"Qualdor, no! Don't—"

"Maximus is not your only uncle, boy. I am, too. Brother to your father, and this dusty disgrace in front of me. Yes. I am a Philosopher."

Drake looked at him, openmouthed. How many revelations could he take? He felt like his muscles had seized up. He was related to the man in front of him, in a Titan uniform, fighting against his own family.

There is only one thing you need to know about him, Drake. He made bad decisions. Got himself into trouble. Maximus's words repeated in his head, back from the journey in the north. This was him. The third Philosopher brother. The one who was bad news.

Maximus had a sad and defeated look on his dusty face. Leo simply looked on in shock. Drake felt himself becoming angrier and angrier. He felt he was being tossed around, like a spear reused too many times. The moment he seemed to have figured himself out, some new weapon would lodge itself into him and throw him off course.

Qualdor smirked, obviously enjoying the shock he'd caused. "Well, Drake. What do you think?"

Drake looked at him, stone-faced. The sounds of battle came back to him: the Titans flooding through the gates, the yells of pain and triumph, and most prominently his own pounding heart.

"This is what I think." Drake lunged forward. Qualdor blocked his strike, but Drake knew exactly what to do. He thought of his own weaknesses that he'd discovered in the trials, the extremely quick strikes that could best him if done correctly. And, the first moment that Qualdor swung, Drake blocked it. Then he threw five strikes in the span of a couple seconds. And sure enough, the fifth found an opening. His sword raked across Qualdor's chest.

Overcome with shock, Qualdor collapsed on the ground. Drake had not killed him. But Qualdor had been severely injured. Drake tried to calm himself. He turned away from Qualdor, and locked eyes with Maximus. The two stared at each other. Maximus had an apologetic look. Drake was not sure what to feel or do. He was angry, but he also pitied Maximus—his uncle had suffered so much. What could Drake even say?

He didn't get a chance to decide. There was a shout, a thud and Sahara burst out of the tower door. He sprinted past Drake, Leo, and Maximus. It took Drake a moment to realize he was holding two swords. And one of them was the Spectacular Sword.

Drake's jaw dropped. Sahara had the sword. Drake began to follow his master, not caring that it would lead him directly into the attacking Titans because victory was so close. There was another slam behind him. Mondoor ran out of the tower door, his face burning with anger. Drake knew right then that he was looking for the sword. He must have seen Sahara, because he began to sprint towards the massive crowd of soldiers and Titans. Right towards Drake.

The general barely slowed as he raised his sword in a smooth arc over his head and struck. Drake parried the blow, but no sooner had he done so than he felt a fist pound into his stomach. He gasped for air as he dodged a slice that would have separated his head from his neck. Then felt a kick in his side, and Mondoor's fist slammed into his face, knocking him to the ground.

As Mondoor sprinted away, Drake felt a rush of adrenaline. The general was chasing his master, one of the best people in his life, and along with it, the sword that could affect the entire future of Lyzix. He had to go after him.

He leapt up and, seeing Mondoor disappear into the crowd, sprinted after him right into the Titans. Ignoring the fearful and angry shouts of the group for him to stop, he held out his sword, impaling, slashing, and stabbing the Titans out of the way. He could see Mondoor moving much quicker ahead of him and felt himself get angry. How could the man be moving so fast? And then, the crowd suddenly thinned, the Titans seem to draw back giving him a straight shot at Mondoor.

Drake raced past the other fighters, his sword out in front of him and for the first time realized he was gaining on the general! They were in the town square, now. It was barely recognizable. Bodies were sprawled across the ground. Fires were everywhere. Smoke clouded his vision, but not enough to prevent him seeing Mondoor disappear into a building down at the far end of the square. This would be the final stand, he thought. This is where they could get the sword, and win.

Drake sprinted after Mondoor and threw the door open. He found himself in a small hallway. A table was overturned, and there were drops of blood leading up a spiral staircase. He heard yells echoing above.

Drake took the stairs three at a time. His footsteps pounded on the stone as he raced up. It felt like it took him forever, yet he finally reached a door at the top of the stairs and flung it open.

Sahara and General Mondoor were facing each other, blades locked in the shape of a cross. They both glanced towards him. Then taking advantage of the distraction, Sahara pushed Mondoor hard into a nearby bookshelf. The general slid to the floor and lay still, unconscious.

Drake and Sahara stumbled towards each other. "Are you okay?" Sahara asked.

"Yes. You?"

"Surviving," Sahara grinned. He then pulled out the Spectacular Sword and handed it to Drake. "Here it is. You deserve it. It's yours, after all."

"I don't think so," a voice said. Drake tensed. Standing, with his sword at the ready, was King Chada. "Give back the sword, and we'll have no problems here."

"What?" Sahara snapped.

"I've had enough of this foolishness; this running, hiding, taunting. It's time the sword was mine and you disappear." Chada took a deep breath. "Give it to me."

Sahara snorted. "Over my dead body."

"Suit yourself," Chada said. And then, in a blur, the king was running at them, spinning in the air and bringing his sword down upon Sahara.

Sahara stopped it, but only just. Chada then attacked Drake, who blocked the strike and tried a stab inward. Chada easily topped the thrust and sent Drake reeling backwards with a kick. Then, to Drake's horror, Chada bore down on his master, striking him with his sword and backing him up to the window. And then, drawing a scream from Drake's throat, King Chada nailed Sahara in the head with the hilt of his sword and sent him through the window. He landed on a nearby rooftop. Glass crashed down around him, cutting Drake's master everywhere. Sahara, lifted his head, looking for Drake. They tried to make eye contact, but his head immediately flopped back down, and Drake knew he'd lost consciousness.

Chada seemed to have forgotten Drake was there for a second, and Drake ran furiously at him to catch him off guard. Chada turned around just in time, but his parry was off, and Drake snuck in a low blow to his leg. The king recoiled in pain, scowling, and the two circled each other in the tower.

They didn't speak, didn't taunt, didn't yell. They simply stepped towards each other and fought.

Drake attacked the king with a determination he'd never felt before. He focused all his willpower upon Chada, slash after slash, stroke after stroke. He tried everything he could, sweat pouring down his forehead. He remembered the trials in which he defeated the knight, the Obilor, and the swordsman. He remembered the ambush of the Western Town when he'd been injured yet managed to force the lieutenant to call a retreat. He remembered the Giants' Forest, where he'd battled giants and the Titans, putting all his focus into keeping the group safe. He remembered the battle with the poisonous snake, Zebetar, and Mondoor in the jungle, and how he had managed to defeat the general there.

And he remembered the way he'd cleaved through the Titans, trying to get to Mondoor, only a short time ago. He had all the skills he needed to defeat Chada. Drake was the Spectacular Swordsman, wasn't he? He was the chosen one. And yet with every blow his strength and confidence diminished.

Drake had never fully felt the might of Chada's swordsmanship until now. Even with the Spectacular Sword in his hands he felt himself losing ground. As he dodged to the side, trying to avoid a blow, he felt his vision disappear for a moment and then reappear slightly blurry. The Spectacular Sword was pinned underneath Chada's own sword. The king smiled evilly down at him and forced Drake to his knees.

"The time has come, Drake. It's unfortunate you won't be able to see the demise of Lyzix. But apparently, when you're alive everyone holds out hope. So that hope must be extinguished, along with you."

King Chada slid his sword down upon Drake's, and Drake knew the king was getting ready to kill him. But he was not going to let himself die this way. None of the group was near. Sahara was unconscious. It was up to him.

As Chada pushed Drake's sword close to Drake, he felt his grip trembling. Yet at the last moment, Drake gave one final push, and sending Chada back, Drake plunged his sword straight into Chada's wrist. The king wailed with pain as the white blade dug in. The Spectacular Sword dropped to the ground, but Drake caught it quickly. And then, as he looked down on his enemy, he heard the sounds of battle amplify from below—the screams, cries of victory, the crackling of the fires. Drake brought back his sword and prepared to strike Chada down. He took a deep breath. This was it—the end. He'd done it. He'd protected his right as the Spectacular Swordsman.

Yet right before Drake's sword connected with Chada, his vision went black, as if the sun had been blotted out in an instant.

Drake stumbled back; his vision was completely gone. He didn't know what was happening. He'd gone spontaneously blind. He flailed the Spectacular Sword wildly and heard a scream. Something crashed into him. Drake fell to the ground, and his vision cleared.

He was on the floor of the tower. And right near him King Chada was sprawled on the floor with a large cut across his chest. His lifeless eyes stared up into the sky. Drake must have hit him when he flailed the sword. The deed was done. King Chada was dead.

Drake felt a mix of guilt and exhilaration. The fight was over! They had won! But he didn't know what to think about murdering Chada. He had killed many Titans in battle, and that felt awful, but this was different somehow.

Drake slowly stood up, and then felt like he could throw up. Sahara was gone. Mondoor's body was gone. And in the doorway, glaring, with his silver shard and long, scarred nose, stood Zebetar. His face was full of more hate and malice than Drake had ever seen.

"You may have won now," Zebetar snapped, "but this

war is far from over." He muttered something, waved his silver shard, and a translucent ball formed around him. It became bright, brighter, and brighter.

"What are you doing?" Drake cried.

Zebetar didn't respond. Instead, he sliced his silver shard down. As the tower exploded around him, Drake was thrown into oblivion.

Chapter XXXVII

Dust flew everywhere. Jerome coughed and spluttered, struggling to get a clean breath of air. When he opened his eyes, he saw nothing but black. He tried to move his arms, but they felt as if they were glued to his side. He had no idea where he was. All he remembered was running after Zebetar as the sorcerer ran to the square and into the mayor's tower. Then, everything was jumbled together into an indecipherable memory.

Jerome moved his left leg, and felt pain burst in his side. At the same time, he heard a crumbling sound. He breathed in deeply, feeling the material around him. It was hard, hard as rock. Jerome tried to move again, feeling more pain as a stone slid off him. He slowly sat up, pushing the pieces aside. When he could finally see his surroundings, he almost threw up.

Thousands of chunks of stone were scattered around him. What used to be the square, now look like a destroyed mine. The buildings in the distance were still half standing, while the ones closer to Jerome were nonexistent.

He had no idea what had happened. He tried to stand

up and move around but sank back down as he felt the pain in his side flare up again. Drake, Isabella, Leo and the rest of the group, where were they? And where were Zebetar, Chada, and the Titans?

It took him a few moments to realize he could hear people shouting in the distance. Trying his best to bear the pain in his side, he slowly stood up. He took two steps through the rubble and then fell, cracking a rib against a block of stone. The pain in his hip was almost unbearable. He saw a white light coming towards him. It was growing brighter and brighter. It was going to burn him up. He was going to die. He was going to die.

The light took on the shape of a crown floating in front of him. And then, as it approached, he realized it was sitting on King Noxy's head. The king was scrambling over the mass of rubble to get to him.

Jerome tried to lift himself up to greet the king, but all the energy had been sucked out of him. He collapsed again and was caught by two soldiers.

"Jerome! Can you hear me?" King Noxy yelled. "We have to get him to the remaining apothecary, on the other side of town! Quickly!"

Xylis and Isabella now appeared.

"I'm alive, I can hear you!" Jerome rasped. "But where are the others?" Surely one of them knew where the remaining group was. Drake, Sahara, Reya, Leo? Maximus could probably survive because of his dusty form, but what about the others? He needed to try and find them, especially Drake. Drake was his best friend. If he was in need, Jerome would find him and help him.

He was deaf to the calls of King Noxy, Xylis, and

Isabella. He shook them off as they tried to pull him back. He ignored his hip and stepped through the rubble. He needed to find his best friend. He pushed Xylis's hand away, but the second he began to move quickly, a rush of vertigo sent his head spinning. Yellow spots danced before his eyes and sank back to the ground.

"Jerome?" Xylis was standing over him.

"Where are they?" His voice sounded like it hadn't been used for a day.

Xylis's face fell. "We don't know. We can't find them. They may be…gone."

"Gone?" Jerome echoed. "You mean like they left for a haven of some kind? Like they're waiting for us somewhere? Like they're not here, but safe?"

Xylis shook his head in anguish. "No Jerome! They're gone, as in we don't know where they are!"

Jerome looked out at the ruined square and felt a tear fall down his cheek. He suddenly remembered every bad thing that had ever happened to him: his master's saddened face when Jerome disappointed him, the attack on Wendil, his master's death, Drake's and Xylis's capture, the whole journey north, and now this.

He screamed in anger. He felt detached from the world, like he was floating in a middle ground. How could half of the group just be killed in the battle, especially his best friend? He never imagined something like this, never, even after Wendil had been attacked. He wanted to believe they were alive, that they were safe, but how could they be? Whatever had completely devastated the Western Town had torn the group apart. He had always assumed everything would turn out okay. That they would win, with no losses or deaths. He couldn't have been more wrong. Jerome felt like life itself had lost all meaning. "What do we do?"

Isabella took his hand. "We need to look around. See if they're here. They could be alive."

Jerome nodded. He felt his mind clearing slightly. There were no bodies. There was no evidence they had been killed. Perhaps there was still hope. He struggled up and began to move through the rubble. As he concentrated on scanning the piles of debris, the pain in his side reduced to an obnoxious throb, no longer as terrible as it had been. He and the others moved slowly across the square, looking for some sign of life, sometimes shouting names, sometimes listening for any sign of life. And then, suddenly, he heard the sound of stones hitting the ground and there were shouts of joy.

He snapped his head in the direction of the noise and saw a huge pile of stone and wood. From behind it, Eleanor and Reya emerged carrying two bodies. Maximus and Leo followed them. Jerome hardly heard their calls for help. He only had eyes for the two bodies, limp and lifeless: Sahara and Drake.

He fell to his knees. How could this happen? He had been about to celebrate on seeing the women, thief and dust spirit, only to be greeted with this.

Then, he felt Eleanor shaking him. He looked up to see a bright, big grin on her face. "Jerome, it's okay! They're alive. And Chada is dead!"

Jerome looked back at the bodies. Drake's and Sahara's eyes fluttered open. Within a few seconds they were sitting up slowly and looking at their friends. It was only when Jerome was sure that he was not dreaming, that a familiar white blade caught his attention.

"And they got the sword," he said.

The group then all sank into one enormous hug, and as they embraced each other, Jerome felt tears of joy and gratitude streaming down his cheeks.

They had won.

*

Later that evening, they all gathered in the apothecary shop. Cyrus would still have to have his leg removed. It was too damaged to heal. Amanda still needed more time to fully recover, but considering how she'd looked when they'd brought her, she was doing well.

Drake was recounting the story of his epic battle with Chada, walking his friends through the account blow by blow. He'd already told them the story many times, but when he reached the part with Zebetar they all still gasped.

"But I don't understand why Zebetar blew up the tower and himself in the process," King Noxy said, frowning. "Why would he kill himself?"

"I don't know," Xylis said. "Do you think he could still be alive?"

"Don't be silly, that was such a big explosion I wouldn't be surprised if all of Lyzix heard it," Leo said. "Zebetar was at the center. There's no way he could have survived."

"I guess." Drake looked at the thief. "Did the Titans just retreat after the explosion?"

Now the group focused on Leo. "They stopped in shock and looked over to where it happened. Then they continued to fight. Not many got away, though."

Drake grinned. "You couldn't have been more helpful during that battle."

"Oh, it was nothing."

"It was very impressive, Leo," Noxy said. "You're more than worthy to live in Wendil's castle. You commanded the archers superbly." He then looked at Drake. "And you, my boy. We wouldn't be here without you. Thank you for showing us the right way to handle the situation." Drake smiled.

As the group continued to talk, Maximus floated over to him. "Drake?" he whispered. "Can I speak with you outside for one minute?"

Drake was too happy to refuse. He was angry that Maximus had not told him about Qualdor, but he decided to give his uncle a chance to explain. They walked out into the street. Celebrations were taking place everywhere. Banners hung from buildings and trees. They displayed the crests of Wendil, the Seaside Kingdom, Oldor, and the Western Town united. People cheerfully strolled the streets, and groups of soldiers sat outside enjoying mugs of ale.

"I want to apologize," Maximus said. "I know you're angry about Qualdor, but his memory is painful for me. He was sent to the Harobi Desert." Drake looked up in surprise. He'd thought that had been a lie, a bluff, from Qualdor to raise tensions. Apparently not. "His crimes were great. He stayed there for many decades. That was what I meant when he made bad choices. And I didn't want you to know that you were related to such a criminal." He sighed. "Or maybe I just didn't want to admit it, making it true for myself."

Drake looked at Maximus. "It's okay. I understand." And he did. Though he was upset, he knew Maximus always had good reasons. It was what made their relationship work.

Maximus smiled. "Thank you, Drake. I could not be prouder of your behavior in the battle. You are one fantastic young man. Keep growing and being open to learning, and you'll be multitudes greater than you are now."

Before Drake could thank him, King Noxy exited the apothecary. Drake noticed some of the group peering through the window, watching him. "We have a proposal," King Noxy said.

Drake frowned. "Now what?"

"We defeated Chada and the Titans. I think it's time to take back the place that we've all been pining for." Drake felt his eyes widen and his body tremble with excitement. "I'm going to send part of the army to make sure it's safe," Noxy said, "and then, we can return to Wendil."

*

As Drake stood next to Sahara on the balcony of their new training room in the castle, looking at the city below, he could not help tears of joy pouring down his cheeks.

He couldn't believe he had finally returned to his home, after all this time.

It was three days after the battle. The army had taken care of the small force of Titans that had remained at Wendil and reclaimed the city. The group, and all Wendil's refugees, had settled themselves back in their homes. The armies had been sent back to Nyle and Solomon. King Noxy had wanted to go himself, but there was much to do to get the castle in order. He was planning to visit Nyle and Solomon sometime in the future, to thank them for their help.

Eleanor had come to search Wendil's libraries to see if there was any information remotely related to the Spectacular Swordsmen. Just because the war was over didn't mean Drake's job was. He was going to continue training with his master to become the ultimate defender and guardian of Lyzix.

But Drake was still stewing over how he'd killed Chada. He was surprised and troubled that he did not feel much remorse, but the king had gotten what he deserved. The man had done the same to countless others without hesitation, so he didn't deserve pity. But Drake worried about Zebetar, too. He knew there was no way the sorcerer had survived the explosion. Yet the man's final words still troubled him. "Just remember, this war is far from over," he'd said. His body had not been found.

And how could this war not be over yet? Chada was dead and they'd won. Perhaps Zebetar knew something he didn't about the Spectacular Swordsmen and their legacy. He'd have to deal with that later. But right now, he wasn't going to worry about it. He was alive, thanks to the Spectacular Sword. In fact, it was his only explanation for how he had come out of the explosion alive. It must have done something to save him. He was planning to ask Eleanor next time he had the chance.

"What an amazing view," Sahara said.

Drake shook himself out of his stupor and remembered where he was. The sun was setting, streaking the sky with pink and blue as the stonemasons finished their work for the night. They were restoring Wendil to its former glory, without any of Chada's additions, with a little help from some sorcery from Xylis and Reya.

"Yeah, it is," Drake looked back into the room. It was much nicer than the rooms they used to train in. The inside was gilded with complex patterns and there were expensive weapons and majestic war paintings hanging on the walls.

But the swordsman still missed his old house and his old life with his master. He was struck by a sudden idea. Maybe the old days weren't so far away after all. "Can we spar one more time before the night ends?" he asked.

Sahara looked surprised. "You've worked hard today, Drake. Surely you want to be with your friends, not spend time with an old man like me?"

"I don't think so," Drake said. "You're just worried you're too old to beat me in a sparring match."

Sahara raised his eyebrows. "Now, that sounds like a challenge. Don't get cocky, kid. Remember, I've taught you everything you know."

"So, it's a yes then?"

"You know it."

Drake grinned as they walked back inside. They grabbed their sparring swords and faced each other across the room. "Usual scoring?"

"Since you seem to be feeling overconfident, why don't we make the point system higher?" Sahara said. "Give you a better chance to best me."

"Ha!" Drake barked. "Don't fool yourself!"

"Well then, let's see what you got." Sahara said.

Drake couldn't help smiling as they circled each other. It felt just like old times, even better.

"Are you going to strike?" Sahara asked. "Or are you afraid I'll take you down in one move?"

"Now who's overconfident?" Drake shot back. He leaped at his master, spinning, swinging, slashing, stabbing and he knew right away he was back home.

Right at home.

IT WAS A week after the battle with King Chada, and Wendil already felt like a new place. Everyone was settling back into their routines. Everyone felt grateful to be alive. The restorations were ongoing, and King Noxy did not remember a time when he was more optimistic about the future of his Kingdom. This little incident, that he and Sahara were now investigating, was nothing. King Noxy was sure of it. He wasn't going to let it spoil their victory over Chada. He smiled as he and Sahara took the path into the nearby forest.

"Some week it's been, huh?" he said.

"Yeah," Sahara said. "Amanda, too, that's great news!"

"I was able to allow her back as a citizen, because of her help with the campaign against Chada. We would have lost many times over if it wasn't for her," King Noxy said. She and Cyrus had just returned from the Western Town, both fairly healthy and on their way to recovery, though Cyrus had lost his leg. Eleanor had also journeyed over to Wendil to stay with the group and conduct a search in the Wendil library for more Spectacular Swordsmen information.

"I'm just glad everything's worked out so well," Sahara

said, but then his good mood faded. "Well, maybe not everything." He hesitated. "Do you think we'll find anything, Noxy?"

"I hope not," the king replied. "You gave me quite a scare yesterday, running into town shouting about a man being attacked."

Sahara shivered. "It's just…I've never seen injuries like that before. They were strange. Almost out of a dream."

And it had been lucky Amanda had the right herb, King Noxy thought, otherwise things could have gone south really quickly. The strange thing was, the victim couldn't remember anything. That was why they were out here looking for clues to find out what had happened to him.

King Noxy ducked under a large tree branch. The air immediately became colder, the sunlight blocked by the thick canopy of trees, but King Noxy was determined to be cheerful.

"How's Drake's training coming along?" he asked.

"Pretty good," Sahara replied, trudging through the weeds. "I need to talk to Eleanor soon, though, and ask her what other ideas she has for Drake's training."

"I'm sure she'll have something up her sleeve."

"We should be getting close to the last lesson soon," Sahara said. "The last few weeks he's proven himself to be quite skilled."

Noxy poked his head around a trunk. Still, nothing suspicious. "What is this last lesson, may I ask?" No answer. "Sahara?" Silence.

The king turned around. There was no one behind him. "Sahara!" he called, frantically. Where was he? King Noxy began to hear the forest whispering to him, the leaves rustling in the wind. Something wasn't right.

"Hello, Noxy."

The king whirled around, his heart pounding, blood rushing into his ears. He saw something flicker into view ahead of him: a shimmering, wavy, image not completely solid. But there was no mistaking the blue cloak and scarred nose. No, it couldn't be. That was impossible.

"You think you've won," the image rasped, "but you could not be more wrong. There's much more to this than you understand. And that will be your downfall."

The image disappeared a second later. Noxy heard a noise above him. He looked up to see a blur of black that quickly disappeared. The forest went silent, and Sahara appeared right in front of Noxy's eyes, completely unharmed.

"We need to get back to the Kingdom. Right away," Noxy said.

"Why?" Sahara looked confused.

"I hope I was hallucinating, but I don't think so."

"Just say it!" Sahara urged.

King Noxy took a deep breath. "I believe I just saw Zebetar."

*

Maximus urgently floated up the spiral staircase of Wendil's castle, looking for Eleanor. He'd been shocked to discover King Noxy's and Sahara's report of seeing Zebetar in the area. Having warned the rest of the group, they were going back to the forest with soldiers to search for any signs of Titans, or sorcery cast by Zebetar.

Maximus floated slightly above the floor as he came to

the end of the staircase and began moving down the long hallway. Eleanor had her room up here, along with some of the others in the group. But he didn't expect to see anyone else. Drake and Sahara were at the Western Town searching for more information about the Spectacular Swordsmen, and Cyrus was overseeing the reconstruction.

Maximus reached the door to Eleanor's room, and used a small wind gust to attempt a knock. Except the door simply swung open. The whistle of the wind he had summoned unsettled him slightly. Maximus poked his head inside.

The room was a mess. The bed had been overturned, the carpet almost shredded, and the small desk was split into three pieces, one part lying upside down against the wall. The bookshelf had fallen over, and books, scrolls, and papers were sprawled across the floor.

What had happened here? Maximus slowly floated over the destroyed desk, and then realized that the large window overlooking Wendil was shattered. An almost human-shaped hole looked back at him. Maximus was stunned. Eleanor was nowhere to be seen. Something terrible had happened.

He glanced around trying to take it all in and caught sight of something glinting on the floor. It was a small bracelet: Eleanor's silver sorcery enhancer. She never went anywhere without it.

It was then that he recognized the true horror of the situation. She had been taken against her will.

Eleanor had been abducted.

First I want to thank you, the reader! I truly appreciate you taking the time to read my book, and I hope you enjoy it as much as I loved writing it.

An enormous thanks to my editor, Amanda Conran. An author herself, she has provided invaluable counsel and encouragement since we began working together. This book would not be where it is without her keen eye for detail and significant input. I have tremendous gratitude for her as a person and as a role model.

To my many peers and mentors who have encouraged me throughout this endeavor, with special mention to:

My incredible friends Alyssa Spagnuolo, Rohan Kakita and Tejvir Samra. They have expressed ongoing interest in my book developments and milestones over the years, and I deeply value their friendships.

My amazing drum teacher Alan Schechner, who has taught me that patience and repetition are key to success. I hope to acquire Alan's mad drumming skills one day.

Thank you to my beautiful extended family who has supported me on this journey and provided so much encouragement along the way. A special thanks to my Zia Shari, who provided perspective and ideas for the cover design.

To my Mom and Dad, to whom I also dedicated this book. Their support and encouragement over the years has

been incredible. I am so grateful for their love and guidance, for imparting moral values to live by, and for teaching
me through example. I could not have been blessed with
better parents.

And finally, to my Almighty God, an ever-constant
source of wisdom and truth…with Your faith in me, I soar.

Nicolò Mazza, a sophomore at St. Ignatius College Preparatory in San Francisco, discovered his passion for writing in fifth grade, and has delighted in reading for as long as he can remember. The Forgotten Sword is his first published work and a true labor of love. In addition to writing, Nicolò competes in both water polo and swimming. He is a member of his high school Jazz Band, and has been playing the drums since the age of four. He is involved in multiple clubs and community service work, and resides in a small town in Northern California.

9 798985 985504